I0772366

WINTERS' WAR

Copyright © 2024 by Life Cunningham

All rights reserved.

Book Cover by Helena Nikulina

ISBN: 979-8-9892790-7-4 (ebook)/ ISBN: 979-8-9892790-6-7 (paperback)

ISBN: 979-8-9892790-8-1 (hard cover)

ASTRAPÍ
THE KÍTR
PHOENIX ISLAND

THE BLACK CONTINENT
S DESERT
EBONY
LIVÁDIA
KARDIA
NOTIO PAGO

PART ONE
BLOOD-STAINED
SNOW

CHAPTER ONE
CRYSTAL

The frozen snow crystals hit my face like tiny shards of glass, making it hard to see much of anything in my path. I could tell the wolves pulling my sleigh were tired and overwhelmed by the snowstorm. Finding food had never been so difficult.

Beneath the screech of the harsh wind, I could hear the faint sound of cracking. I looked over my sleigh and saw dozens of cracks protruding from under us. That made me realize we were no longer touching any solid ground, but we were sliding over ice. I tried to turn us around, but it was too late. The sleigh went down under, dragging me and my wolves along with it.

My body was in shock after hitting the water. It felt like I was being pierced with daggers all over my skin, and the pain was only getting worse. I desperately tried to swim back to the surface but could barely tell up from down as I lost strength. All I could see were the meaningless struggles of my dying wolves until they gave up and became completely motionless, one after the other.

Am I going to die here?

If I died here, what would my family do? My mother and younger sister couldn't hunt. My father was too sick to even hunt enough food for himself if he wanted to. If I died here, would their fate soon align with mine? I couldn't let that happen.

I struggled until my body was numb. My insides felt like they had turned to solid ice. I gulped the cold water down. It made me feel so weak. To just force it into my lungs, almost completely filling them ... It was like swallowing death itself. I couldn't even think anymore. My mind drifted until there was nothing but darkness, silence, and the cold embrace of my failure.

***

"Crystal."

I awoke to the sound of fire crackling away. Quickly, I sat up and saw that I was laying right in front of a fireplace in a room that was foreign to me. My body was wrapped in layers upon layers of thick blankets. It didn't make any sense to me. I should've been dead.

To my right was another girl lying asleep, also wrapped in a heavy number of blankets. Her long brown locked up hair was wet, and she was shaking from the cold.

To my left was Lumi, curled up, shivering in the corner with a towel over her. I wondered if she was the only one to survive, and that thought only forced grief into my mind.

I pushed aside the thick blankets and saw that I was completely naked. Looking back at the fireplace, I realized that my wet clothes were hanging above it; right next to them was a white fur robe. I quickly grabbed it, wrapping it around myself. It felt like I was being hugged by a warm cloud.

I walked over to Lumi and crouched down to pet her soft, damp fur. My hands trembled with every touch. I couldn't take her whimpers.

"I'm sorry I dragged you into this," I whispered to her under my breath. Her whimpers stopped, and I heard someone else.

"Crystal," the voice called.

I jumped up and turned around to see no one but the girl, still asleep.

"Hello?" I said, waiting for someone to answer. There was only silence. I guessed that it must've been my imagination.

"Crystal," the voice called out again, making me jump. It sounded like it was coming from beyond the room, so I went over to the door, slowly opened it, and peeked my head through. On the other side stretched a long empty corridor going from right to left and was lit only by torches.

"Crystal," I heard the voice coming from the left. It startled me not only because it was sudden, but because there was still no one in sight. I looked back at the girl still fast asleep and went through the door quietly, shutting it behind me so as not to wake her.

When I followed the voice down the hall, it led me to a descending spiral staircase. I could hear the voice coming from down below. My feet were bare, so when I walked down the staircase, I felt the shocking cold shoot through my body. I walked on the tips of my toes. It was as if it took an eternity before I finally reached the bottom. At the bottom of the stairs was a hallway with only one door at the end.

"Crystal," the voice said louder this time, yet it was still calm. Whoever was calling out to me had to be behind that door. I made my way to the door, which had a giant symbol of a snowflake engraved into it. This was my first time seeing one like this, but oddly enough, it felt familiar. I placed my hand right in the middle of the engraving to feel its smooth and satisfying texture, but after a couple of seconds, the symbol on the door began to glow.

I took a step back, not knowing what else to expect. I had never seen anything like it. The door slid open all on its own. As if it were responding to my touch.

As it opened, a frigid wind that made me shiver came from within. I peeked my head inside and saw that the room had rocky walls carved with unfamiliar ruins of what I could only assume to be a dead language. The space itself was filled with nothing but a stone, circular pedestal and a wand sitting atop it.

Was this it? The thing that's been calling out to me? It was just some random relic. A glorified stick! Even so, I felt drawn to it.

I slowly inched myself closer to it until I was within arm's reach. Before I could grab it, I heard someone behind me ask, "What are you doing in here?"

I froze in place out of fear and slowly turned to face them. She was old and had gray hair. Her brown skin was slightly wrinkled, like a young grandmother. She tilted her head and squinted her eyes, waiting for an answer.

"I ... I don't know," I told her.

"Well then, let's start off with something you *do* know. What's your name?"

It took me a moment to answer. I didn't know where I was taken or who this woman was. And I wasn't sure how much I could trust her.

"Don't tell me that head injury of yours made you forget your own name? Surely you must have one?"

I gently touched my head, feeling a bandage wrapped around it. I had completely forgotten about the injury. She must have been the one to stop the bleeding.

"Crystal Winters," I finally answered.

"Well hello Crystal, my name is Aza," she told me while putting her hand out for me to shake.

As I grabbed it to accept the greeting, I said, "I don't know how I got here. Did you save me from drowning?"

"Well, no, I can't take the credit for that. All I did was tend to that head injury of yours. My daughter, Ana, was the one who dove into the water to save you."

"I imagine she's the same woman who was in the room I woke up in?"

"Yes, and I'm surprised that she just let you wander around by yourself."

"She was asleep when I woke up. I didn't want to wake her."

"Well then, you should be joining her. You're still not fully healed yet. Come, let me change your bandages." She turned to make her way out.

"Wait." I turned and pointed to the wand and asked, "What is this?"

"It's nothing," she answered, not even looking back at the relic.

"Why is it here? It looks important."

"It belonged to an old friend of mine. I swore to her that I would keep it safe. Now, let's go," she rushed. "This room is off limits."

I took one last glimpse at the wand and decided that I should mind my own business. It didn't belong to me. It didn't matter how strong a bond I felt towards it. I listened to Aza and followed her out of the room regardless.

She led me back to the room, changed my bandages and gave me a nice hot bowl of soup.

"So," Aza started to say, "how did you get trapped under that ice in the first place?"

"I was out hunting," I told her. "Got attacked by a lynx." I touched my head as I spoke, saying, "I fell and hit my head hard. I don't know how long I was out. Everything gets a little hazy after that. I tried to find my way back home, but I got lost. Found myself right over a frozen lake. You can probably guess what happened next."

"It was foolish of you to go out alone. A young girl like yourself. How old are you? Sixteen?"

"Seventeen," I corrected.

"Still too young to go alone. Do you have a father? Or perhaps a brother?"

I wasn't sure if that information should've been shared. Our family was currently in a difficult situation, and sharing that seemed detrimental to our wellbeing and safety. Especially to a stranger I knew nothing about. I sat there for a while, deciding how I should answer.

Aza seemed to understand my hesitation and said, "I myself don't have much family left. Most of them died in a war that you probably wouldn't know much about. And my husband passed away when Ana was just a child. We aren't the only ones who reside in this temple, but when it comes to family, we're all we have left. And because of my age, she thinks that it's up to her, and her alone to provide for us."

I looked over at Ana who was still sleeping on the other side of the room. We weren't too different from one another. That independence and desire to protect ran deep in our veins. I looked back at Aza and decided that since she shared a piece of her life, then it was only fair for me to share a piece of mine.

"My father's been sick these past few weeks. He's completely bedridden. And I have no brother. Just a younger sister. And my mother has to take care of her while I'm gone. She's too young to join me. Or at least *I'm* too young to watch over her in such a dangerous environment. I can't be responsible for what happens to her if I can't protect her."

"Ahh, so you're the firstborn. That's a heavy weight you must carry. Having to be the one to provide for the family especially."

"It is, but I don't mind it."

"Is that so?"

"My mother taught me how to survive. And my father taught me how to defend and protect. They're both so good at it. It's inspiring. I want to be like them. And if providing for them is the way to do it, then I'll do it without hesitation."

"If you mean that, then you'll turn out to be a promising young woman."

"Yeah, I do mean that. That's why I can't stay here any longer."

Aza tilted her head and squinted her eyes in search of clarification.

"The only reason I went out hunting was because we were running low on food. I need to go back out as soon as possible to hunt, or they'll starve."

"How long do you think it will be until they completely run out of food?" Aza asked.

"I'm not sure. Most likely two days."

"Well if you're here, then that means it will last even longer. You're in no condition to leave."

"But if I wait to hunt now, then I won't have time later. We'll run out of food before I catch anything."

"Then I'll just have to give you some food to take with you."

"No. I can't take your rations."

"They're not rations. There's more than enough."

"Why are you helping me? I'm a complete stranger."

"Because, you remind me of someone."

"Is that so? And who might that be?"

"An old friend of mine. They passed a long time ago, so I doubt a young girl like yourself would even know their face, much less their name."

"I'm sorry to hear that they passed."

"It's nothing to be sorry about. Death is simply the next stage of a spirit's existence. I'm just glad that we could keep *your* spirit in this world with us."

"Thank you for that by the way. I don't know how I can possibly repay you."

"You can repay me by getting some rest." She walked to the door and said, "I'll see you in the morning," then left, closing the door behind her. I laid down on my blankets with a sigh of relief. I didn't need to worry about my family for now. And once that weight was lifted off my shoulders, rest found me easily.

CHAPTER TWO
KIRA

I awoke in my room with Ranne at my bedside, strapping on her iron boots in an attempt to get ready for the day.

"What the hell are you still doing in my room?" I groaned. "You should've left before dawn."

"Cut me some slack, Kira. I overslept," Ranne explained.

"You're being careless. Hurry up and get out. My servants will be here any minute to—"

Knock knock.

It was too late. They had already arrived.

"Don't worry," Ranne reassured me. "As long as you don't act weird about it then no one will think anything of it."

I hated her naïveté. She hasn't changed at all since we were kids. Or maybe I changed too much. Either way, the situation irked me. She walked over to the door, opening, it and greeted the maids with the same energy as before.

"Good morning, ladies. Don't mind me, I was just going over a newly assigned mission with the princess. I'll get out of your way."

Ranne passed by them with her brief excuse, leaving my maids looking more confused than satisfied with the answer. They looked back at me, and I returned a glare at them. Their eyes told me that they wanted to know more about my situation, but *my* eyes told them to forget they saw anything. They seemed to understand that much at least.

One maid went to my restroom to warm my bath while the other came to me with a warm cup of tea. "So, I'm guessing I don't need to pass on the message from The King?" she assumed.

"What message?" I asked while leaning up, making sure to cover my bare body.

"Oh, I thought your guard would have told you ..." her face went from confusion to clarity. If she wasn't sure before, then she knew now without a doubt what Ranne was *really* doing in my room. "Well," she continued while handing me my cup of tea. "The King wants you to meet with him at noon. He says he wants to talk to you about a new mission."

Her words came as a surprise. It had been a year since my last assignment. And I had only been on it because the fate of our kingdom had been at stake. Whatever the task, it was probably *Shēna* related. Why else would my father want to get someone as powerful as myself to do a task for him?

Once I was given the information, and the maid was done preparing my bath, they both swiftly exited the room, leaving me alone to start my day. With just a single sip from my teacup, the grogginess that weighed me down was banished from my body and replaced with a newfound vigor.

I always hated gray tea. It was disgusting. But I can't deny the effects it has on my body. On any Shēna's body for that matter. The boost it gives to the Rēa flowing through my veins makes me feel like I've been reborn every time I drink it.

I jumped out of bed and went straight to the washroom to enjoy my bath and didn't waste any time as I dipped my body into the warm water. Forcing myself deeper until my head was fully submerged, I closed my eyes to block out the light; water went into my ears to block out the sound. My morning and nightly baths were the best parts of my day. Being submerged in complete darkness and nothingness was comforting. It left me alone. I didn't have to worry about the maids gossiping about my affairs. My father looking down at me. And when I meditated ... when I truly let go of all thoughts and feelings, I didn't have to listen to the chaos that constantly goes through my mind on a daily basis. Unfortunately, I still had to breathe so the feeling of oblivion would only last for so long. It made me wonder if I'd be happier taking my own life than to live the rest of my existence within these castle walls.

After continuously repeating the process of diving in and out of the water for thirty minutes, I finally decided to drag my damp body out of the tub. I walked back into the room and passed by a mirror. If there was any quality of my being that I was actually fond of, it would have to be my face.

I've been told by many about my face being the most beautiful out of every woman in the royal bloodline. But that was only because I took after my mother; an outsider peasant who married into the family.

Every time I looked in the mirror, I saw her. A kind and loving woman who left this world too soon. I lost her when I was just fourteen.

Now the only thing I was left with was my father. The man who gave me his pale, almost porcelain skin and his blood slender red eyes which stained my face. Ruining my mother's legacy.

I left the mirror, wishing that I could leave behind all my insecurities along with it and went straight for a towel to dry off with, then to one of my Royal garments. A black laced corset. An outfit that made everyone stare in a weird way, but I actually liked the attention. It was more than my father had ever given me.

Once I was done with getting into my dress, I immediately went over to my nightstand, where I kept a small black chest with a golden keyhole hidden within its drawer. After taking it out, I placed the palm of my hand right on it, pouring my Rēa into it—my own life force—and in that same moment the box popped open.

Inside of the box was a black wand. *My* wand. My *Spirit Caster*. I placed my hand onto it, picking it up as its dark spirit intruded into my own. It made me think back to the first time I wrapped my fingers around the Dark Spirit Caster. I was thirteen years old when my father passed it down to me.

The shock that ran through my soul was immense. *No*, shock was the wrong word. What I truly felt was fear, and I didn't know why. The moment right before, all I could feel was pride. Seeing my father finally acknowledging my worth filled me with so much joy. But for some reason as soon as I touched the damn thing, I was scared by the weight it carried along with it.

I didn't *just* feel fear whenever I picked it up. I felt the anxiousness of its past that traveled with it, and it filled me with dread.

CHAPTER THREE
CRYSTAL

I woke up to what felt like a damp rag dragging over my face until I opened my eyes, realizing it was actually loving kisses from Lumi's tongue. I embraced her, cheerful over her recovery and, per her request, I finally got up to enjoy the morning with her.

Lumi and I sat alone in the room. The woman who slept in here before, Ana, the one who risked her life for mine, was gone. Just like Lumi, I imagined that Ana fully recovered, too.

The cold started to get to me after only wearing a fur robe. My eyes darted back to my clothes that hovered over the fire and I immediately went to check on them. They were dry so I changed into my old attire.

I looked into a mirror to see my reflection and got a glimpse of my snow-white hair, pale skin, and blue eyes. All traits that came from my mother's side which only I inherited. Wren's a spitting image of our father with her chestnut hair and brown eyes.

Knock knock. My thoughts were interrupted by the door.

"Come in," I said aloud, preparing myself to see Aza. But it wasn't her. Instead, it was her daughter, Ana, standing in the doorway. Her skin was brown like the darkest mahogany wood you could ever find, and her locked hair was the shade of burnt umber.

"Hey," she said with a smooth voice and an open hand, "my name's—"

"Ana, right?" I answered before she could. "Your mother told me."

"Yeah, that's right," she said with a calm smile. "My mother told me about you too. It's nice to finally meet you, Crystal."

"Well, I'm glad that I'm finally meeting the woman who saved my life."

"It was nothing."

"You went below the ice in the middle of the night during a snowstorm to save some random person you've never even met. That isn't *'nothing'*. You could've died."

"I think the potential life being saved greatly outweighs the risk."

"Well, thank you."

"Don't mention it." She eyed me up and down before changing the topic. "How are you feeling?"

I paused for a moment to think. "Lightheaded," I said.

"You're probably just hungry. Come with me," she told me as she turned to exit the room. I hastily followed as we went through the halls and down to the lower levels of the temple until we were in underground tunnels. After a few minutes, we finally made it to a dining hall with a few people scattered around at some of the tables.

She led me to one of the tables and said, "Have a seat right here. I'll be right back with some food."

I nodded my head before she walked off, leaving me alone with my own thoughts. I took a seat and tried to get comfortable, but before I could relax the voice violently tore into my head once again.

"Crystal."

I didn't understand what it wanted.

"Crystal."

I didn't understand why it called my name.

"Crystal!"

It had to be the wand. I *needed* that wand. It kept calling out to me and I needed to know why. No matter what, I had to make the voices stop.

"Crystal, are you alright?"

I looked up and saw Ana standing at the other side of the table, while waving a bowl of hot food in front of my face for who knows *how* long.

"Y-yeah. I'm fine," I lied while grabbing the bowl from her. "Thank you."

The mouthwatering smell of salmon hit my face immediately, putting a smile on it. It was smoked and mixed in with chowder. After the first bite I started to feel a bit better. Perhaps she was right. Maybe all I really needed was food.

"Wow you're really tearing into it," Ana laughed. "You really *were* hungry."

"Sorry," I laughed back. "Salmon's my favorite. My father taught me how to catch them. And my mother taught me how to smoke them. It's just been a while since I had any."

I looked up at her and caught her warm smile. Something that I wasn't too familiar with. Something friendly. I'd never really had friends. Someone close to my age that I could just talk to. I liked this feeling.

As soon as I opened my mouth to speak again, the voice in my head decided to do the same. *"Crystal!"* the voice shouted, forcing me to shudder.

Her smile melted away as she asked, "What's wrong?"

"It's nothing."

"Are you sure?"

"Yeah, I ... I just need a breath of fresh air," I told her while getting up.

"Do you need me to come with you?"

"No, I'm ok. I think I can find my own way. I'll be back." I said while already walking away. The voices hadn't stopped. I needed to go to the source to end them.

Once I was out of sight I retraced my steps, running back up the stairs and through the corridor until I finally made it to my original path. My mind started to rush as it called out to me. The voice got louder and louder after every step I took, which only meant that I was getting closer.

I made it to the snowflake engraved door and opened it with just the touch of my hand, just like before. This time I wasn't going to hesitate. I walked right into the room and saw the wand sitting there just as it did before. I reached my hand out but before I could grab it, someone pulled my arm back.

It was Ana, and she no longer had that cool and collected look about her. Nor did she have a warm smile. This time, there was a look of rage in her eyes like a wolf before it bared its fangs.

In a deep and intimidating voice, she asked, "What are you doing in here? My mother told you that this place was off limits, didn't she?"

Her grip became tight around my wrist causing my throat to run dry before I could answer.

"This thing ..." I said while directing my view back onto the wand. "It keeps calling out to me. What is it?"

A beautiful aura rose from the wand and put me in a trance. I didn't know if Ana could see it, but *I* certainly could. My other hand moved to grab it but before I knew it, she forced me to the ground, pinning me down with the force of a wild animal.

"Now listen here," she said into my ear, slowly. "The people in this temple have one simple job. It's to *protect*. And the thing you were about to lay your fingers on is one of those things we've sworn to **protect**. I'd die before letting that Spirit Caster fall into the wrong hands."

Spirit Caster? It had been the first time I had ever heard that name. But I desired it. The relic that was a catalyst for the voices.

"Let me guess," she continued. "You're working under the orders of King Cole. Are you a member of his Five Armaments?"

Although he was our king, his title was still foreign to me. I had never laid eyes on The King, and I'd never even stepped foot in his capital city, Ebony. For anyone to think that I had any connection to him just sounded foolish.

"Ana, listen." I tried to speak as calmly as possible. "I don't work for The King, and I don't even know what these *Five Armaments* are. I just—"

"You're lying!" She shouted over me while raising her fist, ready to strike.

I shut my eyes, readying myself for the blow. But nothing came. I opened my eyes back up to see Aza standing over us while holding Ana's fist back.

"What are you two doing in here?" she asked in a stern tone like a mother stopping a squabble between two of her children.

"She was trying to steal the wand!" Ana answered quickly.

"I wasn't going to steal it!" I argued.

"Then what *were* you going to do with it? Borrow it? Because you certainly didn't get *our* permission!"

"I don't know ... I'm sorry, I just ... it keeps calling my name. The voices won't stop. I think it wants me to take it."

I imagined in their minds I must've sounded insane. They couldn't hear the voices like I could. I was the only one ... so maybe I *was* insane.

Aza let out a hard sigh and said, "Let her go."

The command came as a shock to me, just as it did for Ana.

"What?" She asked in disbelief. "You're not actually falling for this are you? It's an act!"

"This isn't an act," Aza said as she pulled her daughter up onto her feet, finally giving me room to breathe. "When a Shēna wields a Spirit Caster, they gain the ability to hear the voices of those who held the weapon before them."

I used the pedestal for support to get back to my feet while asking, "What is a Shēna? I don't understand any of this."

"Wait, don't touch—"

I glanced at where I placed my hand and immediately understood why she wanted me to stop. But it was too late. I had already touched the Spirit Caster, and within that same second, a flash of blue light nearly blinded me.

Once my eyes adjusted, I saw snowflakes falling all around me. A thin layer of ice covered my hand, freezing it with the wand. I forced my hand to break out of the ice by yanking the wand off with my other hand, causing small pieces of my skin to tear off with it. The wand fell to the floor which made me realize that not only did my hand freeze, but the floor too. In fact, the entire room was covered in ice and snow. Aza looked at me with an amazed expression while Ana looked fearful.

"W-what just happened?" I asked them, hoping they would have an answer.

"Crystal," Aza said slowly and carefully. "I think we need to talk."

CHAPTER FOUR
KIRA

I walked through the large hallways of the castle until I finally reached the doors to the golden throne room. As soon as the guards noticed me, they wasted no time on opening the set. Ranne was already in the throne room, standing tall in front of my father as she waited. Once I made it to Ranne's side I immediately bowed before The King and simply greeted him with a single word.

"Father."

"Kira," he greeted back with indifferent eyes.

I looked up at him and asked, "What's the assignment?"

"Well, at first I was going to have you two investigate a Shēna sighting down in Livádia. Apparently, there were more than a few onlookers who witnessed a young girl *flying* through the sky."

"Do you think they got ahold of a *Wind Spirit Caster*?" I guessed.

"I'm almost positive that's the case. But there was an anomaly that forced that investigation to change hands. So, I gave the job to Adam. The new job that I'm giving you requires you to go to Nótio Págo."

Those words alone made me shiver. Nótio Págo was a desolate tundra with unbearably low temperatures. It's the last place I wanted to go. Adam was lucky to be assigned to such a lush and beautiful land like Livádia.

"What's in Nótio Págo?" I asked.

"I felt something. No. Rather, *someone*. Either way, it's a threat."

"Wait, you felt a Shēna from all the way out there?" I asked, shocked that such a thing could even be possible. "Their power must be tremendous! Shouldn't we mobilize the entirety of The Five Armaments if we're going to face someone like that?"

"Unfortunately, they all have their hands full. You're the only one who's available and suited for the task."

To think that my father would put so much trust in me. The task sounded immense. I wasn't sure if I alone could handle it.

The lack of confidence must've been written on my face because the next words that came out of my father's mouth were, "Do not fret, Kira. The Rēa that I felt lasted for only a moment. I doubt that their power is consistent. If I had to make a guess, then I'd say that whoever let out such power is most likely just coming into it. That means that all I felt was their *potential*. As long as you can snuff them out before they can reach *said* potential, then they won't be a threat to you."

"Do we have any leads on where this new Shēna might be?"

"No. Everything I just told you is simply a gut feeling. There are no other leads. When you get to Nótio Págo, you'll have to figure out the rest yourself."

A *gut feeling*? It all started to make sense to me after he said those words. This wasn't an actual threat, nor did it take high enough priority for anyone else on the team to take care of it. He was sending *me* because the task wasn't worth anyone else's time.

"I understand," I told him.

"Good. Now if there are no other questions, then go. I don't want any more time wasted with unnecessary chit chat."

"Of course," I told him as I turned to exit the throne room. "Let's go Ranne."

Once Ranne and I were at the door my father called, saying, "Oh, and one more thing. When you find them, I want you to *kill* them, and everyone they're associated with."

I stayed silent for the command while the guards escorted us out. The silence continued for a while as we walked through the royal halls until Ranne finally decided to break it once we were alone.

"I hate when he gives that order."

"And why is that?" I questioned, already knowing the answer.

"Because sometimes the people he makes me drive my blade through are completely innocent."

"Does it matter?" I chuckled. "You're a Zubarian aren't you? You were born and raised by this kingdom to kill Shēna. It's your duty to slay any who don't side with us."

"But is it truly justice? To lay waste to people who don't deserve it?"

In all reality, no. It probably wasn't justice. What I was going to do was most likely going to be a sinful act. But I'd rather have innocent blood on my hands than have my father be completely disappointed in me for not having the stomach to handle my royal duties.

After a long pause, I finally answered her. "It doesn't matter if they're a loving mother, an elderly citizen, or even an innocent child. Anyone who possesses the strength to overthrow us is an immediate threat that *must* be eradicated."

CHAPTER FIVE
CRYSTAL

"Tell me Crystal," Aza asked, "do you know what a Spirit Caster is? Do you know anything about your heritage?"

Aza made Ana leave the room so that it was just the two of us. That was a good idea on her part. The situation was stressful enough without Ana trying to bash my face in.

I didn't know anything about the Spirit Caster. This was my first-time hearing of it. And my knowledge of my family tree was almost nonexistent. I only knew the names of a few grandparents.

"I'll take your silence as a no," she continued. "What about Eve Winters? Does that name ring a bell?"

"That was my grandmother's name," I answered, shocked that this stranger would bring it up. "I don't know much about her though. My mother never really talks about her."

"Grandmother, you say? So, you're Eira's daughter. That makes sense. You're the spitting image of both of them."

"You know my mother?" I asked, completely caught off guard by the statement. "And you *knew* my grandmother?"

"I knew your mother back when she was just a young child. Your grandmother was a good friend of mine." Aza walked over to the pedestal and picked up the wand before saying, "This belonged to her." When she spoke, it sounded like she was reminiscing memories too personal to speak on. "Before Eve died, she gave it to me and told me to protect it."

"And that thing …" I said slowly, still fearful of its power. "That thing is a Spirit Caster? That's what froze this room?"

"Correct," she smiled.

"But how? How can an item like that exist? It's like—"

"Magic?" she finished. "Yes, I suppose that is the correct term for it. It's said that Spirit Casters were made as a gift from the gods for people like you."

"Like me?" I asked while tilting my head, unaware of what she was getting at.

"A *Shēna*," she said bluntly.

"You've said that word before, but I still don't know what it means."

"That's to be expected. Although the existence of Shēna is common knowledge, some believe them to be completely extinct while others wonder if they ever truly existed to begin with. And I'm guessing a young girl like you who lives in the middle of nowhere would have almost no way of finding out about said heritage without being told. The reason their existence is so up in the air is because years ago, before you were even born, King Kieran decided to start a purge on your people since he believed you all to be a threat. His son and our current king decided to keep that legacy going. Thus, all Shēna have gone into hiding."

"But I don't understand. How are the Shēna," I swallowed hard, "how am *I* a threat?"

"Because Shēna are the only people in the world who can activate Spirit Casters. For me, this wand is just a useless stick, but for you it's a powerful weapon."

She stretched her arm out to hand me the wand, but I was left frozen in its sights as if it were a living creature that was more dangerous than any predator I'd come across.

"Don't be shy. Take it."

I finally reached out to grab it, half expecting the room to freeze once again, but instead the change came from inside me. A jolt of energy vibrated from my hand to the rest of my body, giving me goosebumps.

It was light in my hands and had a smooth texture with multiple snowflakes engraved into it. The designs glowed a light blue when my fingers brushed across its wooden finish.

"The wand you're holding in your hands right now is the Ice Spirit Caster, and it's one of many. Like the name suggests, it allows the Shēna who uses it to gain control over ice magic. It will be a great asset to you."

"Wait, *asset*?" I interrupted, finally realizing that she was actually *giving* this thing to me. "I don't *want* this."

"But it called out to you," she argued. "If you actually did hear it, then that means Eve *wants* you to have it. Her spirit sees you as a part of her legacy."

"And I get that. But if what you're saying is true; if I'm really a Shēna, then that means having this not only puts me, but my entire family, in danger. They're the only thing in the world that I care about and I'm not losing them over some wand."

I put the wand in her face and, after a long pause, she finally took it back. Once it left my hand, it felt like something was ripped from me. Like a piece of my soul was gone. As if I just gave up a limb. But no matter what attachment I thought I had to it; it didn't change the fact that it would only be a liability in my life.

"I understand," Aza sighed. "Well then, I guess it's time to get you back to that family of yours."

***

"You don't have to do this," I said to Aza as men from the temple passed by, putting barrels of fish along with two recently hunted bucks onto the sleigh. "You've already done so much for me."

"Oh, it's nothing," she waved me off.

"This is enough food to last my family most of the year. I'd hardly call that nothing."

"Don't worry, we've got extra. We can afford to give a few away to someone in need. Especially since your Eve's granddaughter. You're basically family."

Her smile was the same as Ana's. It seemed like the Apple didn't fall too far from the tree. Both of them showed kindness without a second thought, even if it came to their own detriment. And for that I was truly grateful to them.

"Thank you," I said to her, "for everything."

I reached in to embrace her and she wrapped her arms around me.

"You ready to go?" I heard Ana say. I looked behind me to see that her eyes were avoiding mine.

"Y-yeah," I stuttered.

"Then let's go," she said plainly before walking over to the sled.

Only an hour had passed since Ana attacked me. I could still feel the heat from her boiling blood. She was still holding all that rage for me on the inside. Stopping herself from trying to finish what she started.

"Don't worry, she won't bite." Aza reassured me, answering the question I was asking on the inside. "I already cleared everything up with her. She no longer sees you as a threat."

"Yeah ... I know," I sighed, unable to convince myself that there was truly nothing to worry about. "Well, I should get going. Again, thank you for everything."

"The pleasure was mine," Aza beamed. "Until we meet again."

I smiled back and turned around, making my way to the sled. Once I hit my outer thigh twice, Lumi came running behind and we walked until we saw the wolf that was connected to it.

It was many times larger than Lumi. Practically the size of an entire horse. This was only my second time laying my eyes on a wolf this big. The first was with my father when I was younger. He told me to never attack them for two reasons. The first reason was because they were peaceful creatures. Only threatening if they themselves felt threatened. The second reason was because the average person couldn't possibly make it out alive after an attack from them.

Lumi started to growl at it. A worthless attempt to intimidate. This thing could tear Lumi to shreds if it really wanted to, so I quickly knelt down to pet her and said, "It's ok."

Ana climbed onto its back while saying, "His name's Silver. You don't have to be scared. He wouldn't hurt a fly, unless he was given a reason to." Lumi and I hopped into the back of the sled before Ana asked, "You ready?"

"Yeah," I answered. "Aza and I charted a path to my home. Just go northeast from here."

"Northeast?" She said as she hovered her hand over her forehead, shielding her eyes from the sun. "Got it." She leaned in closer to Silver's ear and reached her arm out in front of him towards the direction we had to go. Then, she finally whispered, "Run," causing Silver to take off.

It was like magic. I had never traveled at such speeds before. The wind blew through my face as if there was a blizzard, but the skies were clear. I felt free.

Lumi felt the same. I could tell from the way she stuck her head over the sled with her tongue flapping out with the wind. I'd never seen her so excited.

I decided to take the chance to just sit back, relax, and enjoy the ride.

***

We came to a stop once we reached a large frozen lake surrounded by tall trees.

"Why are we stopping?" I asked.

Ana jumped off of Silver's back and said, "Silver needs a break. He's been running for too long without pause."

After disconnecting him from the sled, she went to the back of it, took out a large spear and walked over to the lake. I followed and crouched down, knocking on the ice to test its durability. It was solid. Seemed like it would take a while to break through, but with a deep breath, Ana took aim and chucked the spear right into the ice, instantly breaking through to the water.

Breaking the ice wasn't an impossible task but to do it in just one strike was more than impressive. It's the kind of strength that I would expect from a starving animal.

She called Silver over and once he came, he drank from the lake without hesitation. I ogled his spotless white fur and rubbed my hands through it. He stopped and glared at me, forcing me to take my hands off him. But to my surprise, he simply started licking my face before going back to the water. At least *he* didn't hate me. Unlike someone else.

"Why didn't you take the wand?"

The question caught me off guard. I looked over at Ana and asked, "What?"

"Why didn't you take the wand?" She repeated herself in an annoyed tone.

"You sound disappointed," I said while cocking my head to the side. "Isn't your job to protect it? You should be happy that I left it behind."

Ana sighed and explained, "I protect the wand because I believe in its potential. Not only in its potential to destroy, but also its potential to create. It all depends on who's holding it. If it were to fall into the wrong hands, then it could destroy lives. But if it were to fall into the *right* hands, then it could change the world for the better."

"And what side of that coin do I land on?"

"That's what I'm trying to figure out. If you aren't on the side of justice, then I think it's better off out of your hands."

"I'm not on anyone's *side*," I snapped. "I didn't even know what a Shēna was until today. And their history is the least of my worries. The only thing I care about in this world is my family. If it doesn't involve them, then I couldn't care less. *That's* why I didn't care to take the stupid wand."

Ana clenched her fist and pointed at me, saying, "I hate that dispassionate mindset. I believe that if you're not doing your part to fix the problem then you're *a part* of the problem. You have so much potential but you're wasting it. If you wait until it's too late to start caring, then you'll live to regret it."

Ana waited for me to respond but all she got was silence. The truth was, I didn't know what to say. She might've been right, but I still didn't want to get wrapped up in any of this.

Tired of waiting for an answer, she turned away from me in anger and called for Silver, taking him back to the sled so we could get back to our journey.

***

Although Silver was fast, because of the silence, it felt like it had taken an eternity for us to finally pull up to the old wooden A-frame cabin.

"Is this it?" Ana asked while looking up at it.

"Yeah," I said while trying to hide my grin. "It is."

Ana jumped off Silver as Lumi and I hopped out the back of the sled. I turned back to try and lift the barrel of fish, but Ana shoved me aside and grabbed both of them by herself. Back at the temple it seemed like the men struggled just to hold one, but Ana didn't break a sweat.

"Do you need help?" I asked.

"No, I got it. This might be too heavy for you," she told me while walking onto my front porch and carefully putting the barrels down before going back to the sled to repeat the process with the deer. Once she was done with that, she went straight back to Silver and hopped onto his back to leave.

"Wait," I stopped her, "I know that you hate me right now, but I wanted to thank you again. You've done so much for me in such a short amount of time. You saved my life and I'm still incredibly grateful for that."

She looked down at me with dejected eyes and simply responded, "Just think about what I said, Crystal," before taking off and riding out of sight.

She gave me a lot to think about. On the one hand I truly believed that the legacy of a Shēna had nothing to do with me. But on the other hand, I wondered how many suffered because of my absence from the role. I'd never met another Shēna, so I didn't truly grasp their situation. I only knew my family. And we'd been happy with our secluded lives. Did I really want to risk that happiness for a group of people I'd never even laid eyes on?

My thoughts were broken once I heard someone shouting my name. This time, not a voice in my head but something more tangible. More familiar. I turned back towards the house and saw my sister running towards me with only her nightgown on. She jumped to me and I grabbed her, preventing her bare feet from touching the snow again.

"Crystal! You're home!" She sobbed.

"I've only been gone for one night," I laughed.

"I thought you'd never come back."

"Wren, I already told you. I'll always come back to you."

"Wren!" My mother called as she peeked her head out of the door. "What are you doing out—" she stopped as soon as she caught sight of me. "Crystal?" She shuddered and dropped a set of folded clothes before quickly sprinting over to me just as Wren did, embracing me in a tight hug. "You were supposed to come home before sunset yesterday! What happened to you?" she asked while inspecting the bandages on my head.

"Don't worry mom, I'm fine," I assured her.

"'I'm fine' won't cut it. You're going to tell me exactly what happened while you were gone."

I let out a weak laugh before saying, "That's good. Because there's a lot I have to say."

***

After bringing the food into the house and getting settled in, I sat my mother down at the table and explained everything to her. All the way from my hunt to finally coming home.

"Did you know?" I asked.

"Did I know what?" She feigned ignorance.

"Did you know that I was a Shēna? Did you know that *we* are Shēna?"

There was a long pause as my mother carefully thought about her answer. "Yes," she finally said.

"Why didn't you tell me?"

"To keep you safe. If you know about the Shēna then you also know about the burden that comes with being one."

"Did that burden weigh heavy on you?" I asked after a brief pause.

"It weighed on my mother. She was always on the run. And she dragged me along with her. No child should live the way I did. Especially not you and Wren. So, I put it all behind me."

"I can *and* would have understood that," I stood out of my chair and leaned in closer, "but I still feel like I had the right to at *least* be aware of our situation."

She looked up at me and said, "Crystal, believe me when I tell you that ignorance is bliss. If you truly believe you have nothing to hide, then no one will suspect anything from you." She stood up along with me to bring her eyes to the same level as mine and continued saying, "Promise me that you'll never get yourself wrapped up in any of this. It will only lead to despair for us all."

"Mom, I don't think—"

"Promise me, Crystal!" My mother yelled, leaving only silence behind the shout.

"Ok, mom. I promise."

"Good," she finally said before looking around the room and changing the topic. "And would you look at all this food? With this much I should be able to make a nice hot bowl of soup for your father. That should make him feel better. Wren!"

Her door swung open as she ran to us like a dog. "Yes, mommy?"

"Help me unpack this stuff and cook. We're gonna have a big dinner tonight so let's start early."

Wren immediately jumped for joy. She enjoyed cooking with our mother just as I did when I was her age. It looked like things were finally settling down again, but I couldn't shake what my mother made me promise. It was something I had already planned on. I didn't want anything to do with my heritage or the wand. But Ana's words were still burned into my mind and completely conflicted with what my mother told me. Was this really a lifestyle I'd come to regret?

CHAPTER SIX
KIRA

I despise Nótio Págo. It's the farthest land south of The Black Continent. Not to mention the coldest. The way that the light reflects off the ice hurts my eyes and the wet feeling of snow in my boots is unbearable.

"I can't wait until we can find this stupid wand and get out of this godforsaken place!" I complained.

"Hey, lighten up Kira! It rarely ever snows in Ebony!" Ranne said obnoxiously. She got closer and wrapped her arm around my shoulders, saying, "You should just sit back and take it all—"

Before she could finish her sentence, I swiftly kicked her in the back of her leg and pushed against her chest to force her down into the snow.

"You shouldn't act so casual around your future queen," I smirked.

She picked herself up while smiling and brushed off the snow from her long, straight black hair. The sunlight reflected off her jet-black armor slightly less obnoxiously than the white snow. There was a charm to her dark face that on certain days had me captivated. Unfortunately for Ranne, my irritation for the snowy tundra blinded me from that charm.

"Come on," Ranne smirked back. "Can't I act a little casual with a friend?"

"You're not my friend," I argued. "You're more like my plaything."

"That's cold," she laughed.

"Well, considering where we are, I believe it's fitting."

I looked over and saw a guard walking right towards us. He bowed before me and said, "Princess, we've interrogated everyone in the nearby town just as you asked."

"And?"

"We now know the location of the temple we're searching for. It's southwest of here. Should be just a few hours away."

"That's good news," I smiled. The closer we were to the Spirit Caster, the sooner we could go home.

Right at that moment, the other guards who came with us pulled up in a few wolf sleds that I had requested along with the interrogation of the town.

I turned to Ranne and said, "We're ditching the horses. The wolves will be faster out here."

"Aww," Ranne gave a heavy sigh.

"What's the problem?" I asked.

"It's just," she started to say, "the horses started to grow on me. I was gonna name mine *'Kira, Jr.'* because she was so moody."

I glared at her, completely unamused by her jokes and said "Ranne, you're an idiot. It's a good thing you have your looks going for you. Just remember that they won't last for long. When that time comes, there will be nothing stopping me from wiping you out of existence with my magic."

"I'll keep that in mind," she smirked.

I turned the opposite direction and shouted, "Let's go!" to everyone in the area. Everyone jumped on a sled, including Ranne. I jumped on the same one as her and held onto her shoulder as she cracked the reins, forcing the wolves to speed off.

After some time, we were still far away from our destination. Even though that was the case, I felt a strange feeling. I looked over in the distance and saw a lone A-frame cabin sitting in the middle of the icy tundra.

"Ranne, stop!" I yelled.

Ranne pulled the reins, stopping the wolves from going any further. The other guards followed our lead and stopped beside us. I glared at the old house for a few moments before anyone said anything to me.

"Kira, what's wrong?" Ranne asked.

"There's someone over there," I answered. "Someone with a potent amount of Rēa."

"Are you sure?"

"Yeah, there's no doubt about it. It's a Shēna. We're going to investigate. Everyone, prepare for battle."

***

I knocked on the door, waiting for someone to answer; it took a few seconds before I could actually hear something on the other side of the door. The sound of someone rustling around inside with footsteps heading towards us could be heard by all of us. I moved my hand into my cloak, grabbing onto my Spirit Caster, ready to pull it out to defend myself just in case they decided to struggle. My men did the same with their swords.

Once the door finally opened, I looked down to see a young child. It was a small girl with short brown hair and big brown eyes. "Hello there," the little girl said politely.

"Um ... Hi," I awkwardly greeted back. I took my hand off my Spirit Caster, lowering my guard. This obviously wasn't the person we were looking for. I didn't feel a spec of Rēa coming from her, not to mention she was too young. I crouched down until I was eye level with her and asked, "What's your name?"

"Wren," she answered.

"Ok, Wren, tell me, are your parents home?"

She nodded her head, turned around, and walked deeper into the house, leaving the door open behind her. I looked back at my men to give them an order.

"Ranne, you head in with me. The rest of you stay out here and stand watch. Make sure no one escapes."

The guards performed a quick bow and carried out the order while Ranne and I walked into the house. There was a lot more space inside than I anticipated. I looked across the room and spotted Wren walking back to us.

"My mommy's coming now," she said.

A few moments later, her mother came out. She had silver hair with pale skin and was wearing a light blue gown.

"How can I help you?" she asked.

"My name is Kira Black and I'm looking for an ancient relic of sorts."

Her expression went from welcoming to frightened in an instant. At that very moment, she fell to her knees and bowed her head. A reaction I got often, but I could sense much more fear from her. As if there was a much larger reason for her to fear me than the average person.

"Your Highness!" she yelled out.

I walked up to her as she was still on her knees and asked, "Have you ever heard of an item called the Spirit Caster?"

She looked up for a moment and then right back down. "No, I haven't."

I could tell she was lying. I reached inside my cloak and pulled out the Darkness Spirit Caster. My body started to glow with a pitch-black aura.

The pressure of it shook the house and shrouded the room in shadows. This time, I pointed my wand in her face to give her an example of what I was looking for.

"So, you're telling me you've never seen an item that looks just like this?"

A look of terror struck her face.

"I-I've seen it ... But I don't know where it could be."

I didn't believe her for a second. It seemed like she needed an incentive to cooperate with us. I turned to look at Ranne and nodded my head towards the little girl. She sighed, obviously not wanting to have any part in this, but she knew that an order was an order. Ranne grabbed the hilt of her sword, pulling it out and swinging it to Wren's neck but stopped it once it touched her skin. It just barely cut her. She was so fast that Wren didn't even notice that the blade was at her own neck until a few seconds passed. She showed a look of panic on her face.

"Stay completely still," Ranne said to Wren. "It wasn't on my agenda to kill a child today, but I will if I have to."

Her eyes darted to her mother and tears quickly poured down her face.

"Just stay still Wren!" Her mother cried.

"Now, I'm going to ask you one last time," I said with a smile. "Where is the Spirit Caster?"

Suddenly a door swung open and slammed against the wall. The noise stole everyone's attention, and in the doorway was a girl, probably still a teenager, with long white hair and blue eyes. I wondered if she had been in the room eavesdropping on us the entire time.

"Who are you?" I asked, pointing my wand in her direction.

She put her hands up and yelled, "Stop! I know where the Spirit Caster is!"

I could feel the magic coming from her. She was the one we'd been looking for. I lowered my wand and let the black Aura in the room disperse.

"What's your name?" I asked.

"Crystal Winters," she answered.

I walked over to the nearby table and sat myself down, gesturing to the empty seat beside me.

"Well then, *Crystal Winters*. Let's talk."

CHAPTER SEVEN
CRYSTAL

This woman was dangerous. I could feel it. She could have killed us all in that moment if she wanted to, and she wouldn't bat an eye while doing so. I had no other choice but to do as she said.

I carefully walked over to the empty seat next to her and sat down before taking a moment to look her over. Her hair was so black that it was sucking in the light around us, making it look as if a black mist surrounded her. I couldn't tell if it was my imagination or if it was her magic, but regardless, it gave me shivers. What was even more intimidating were her eyes. They were crimson like blood under moonlight. It felt like they were piercing through my very soul.

"Do you have the Spirit Caster with you?" she asked.

"No," I answered. "It's in a temple not too far from here."

"Alright, you'll retrieve it for us then."

"What? Why me?"

She laid her head on the table, closed her eyes, and pulled the hood from her cloak over her head.

"Because I'm tired."

This woman seemed extremely childish. My mother referred to her as *'Her Highness,'* which meant she was of royal blood. She was probably raised with a silver spoon in her mouth and always got her way. But I could imagine why it would be hard for anyone to say no to her.

"I also don't wanna be sent on some wild goose chase in the cold," she continued. "It's better to send someone who actually knows its *exact* location. Oh, and just to make sure you don't pull any crazy tricks, I'm giving you a time limit. You have until sundown. If you don't make it back by that time, then I'm killing everyone in this house."

"What?" I cried.

"Don't worry. I won't hurt them if you come back before then. It's just an incentive to make sure you don't waste any of my time. I wanna leave as soon as possible. But I'm serious. Their lives mean nothing to me. I *will* kill them if you keep me waiting."

"That's not enough time!" I shouted. "If I go on foot then it will take me too long to get back!"

"Then you should get moving," she said plainly.

The knight who threatened my sister removed the blade from her throat and sheathed it while walking to the front door, opening it, and yelling, "We're letting this girl through."

She looked back at me while gesturing towards the door. I got up, grabbed my hunting knife from off the table and hurried to the door. When I got outside, I saw Lumi barking at the knights and quickly called her to my side so I wouldn't be alone on this trip.

As I sped off, I noticed small snowflakes coming down while the wind started to push me back. Another storm was coming. This was bad. I needed to make it back safely this time. I couldn't waste the day on getting lost or nearly dying again. This time, I was racing for our lives.

***

I trudged through the snow for hours with my body desperately needing a break, but there wasn't any time for that. I kept on going until something finally stopped me. A voice. It called out my name.

"Crystal."

The same voice I'd heard from before. The voice that originally led me to the Spirit Caster. It was captivating. It made my body move on its own and pulled me along my path even when it felt like I was too tired to go on. It was like going into a trance. Once I snapped out of it, I realized that I'd finally reached my destination. The Ice Temple. I told Lumi to stay and sit before I went inside to avoid any unnecessary attention.

Once I made it inside, there was no one in sight, but the sound of cheering could be heard from afar. I followed the sound until I was right in front of a doorway leading into a large room filled with what seemed to be every person who stayed in the temple. I quickly hid before I could be discovered and observed the commotion from afar.

Everyone in the room was sitting in a circle. Everyone except Ana, who stood in the center, and Aza, who walked on the outskirts. One person laid on the ground unconscious right at Ana's feet.

"Who wants to go next?" Aza asked the group, causing three men to eagerly raise their hands. "Let's see, which one should I choose."

"Why not all of them?" Ana suggested.

"Are you sure?"

"Yeah. I need a challenge."

"So be it," Aza chuckled.

Although the men seemed surprised by the results, they still didn't hesitate to get up and surround her on all sides.

"We'll definitely get you this time," one of the men said to her.

"There's no way you can take us *all* on," another one said.

Ana ignored them and put her fists up while closing her eyes and taking a deep breath.

After a long pause, Aza shouted, "Begin!" and all three of them went to attack.

One man aimed right for the back of her head, but Ana spun around blocking the punch and, using the rest of her momentum, knocked the man back with a punch of her own. Another man went to kick her, but she blocked it with her own leg and simply pushed him away with one hand, knocking him right to the floor. The last man came from behind her and swept his leg against hers. Since she only had one leg grounded, she fell right to the floor. For anyone unprepared, this would have been their final moments in battle, but Ana was prepared. She pushed herself from the floor, almost doing a handstand, just to kick the man right in the face before he could make another move.

This battle was astonishing, but it wasn't my focus. All it told me was that this was my chance. If everyone was in here for what seemed to be some kind of group training session, then that meant there was no one standing in between me and the Spirit Caster.

I retraced my steps back to the corridor running down the spiraling steps, reaching the hall and arrived at the snowflake engraved door. Once again, I placed my hand against the door so it could glow and open before me. The Spirit Caster was in the same spot I left it in. I grabbed it and started to make my way back up the steps. As soon as I was back in the corridor it looked like I was home free until I heard a voice from behind me say, "Crystal, what are you doing back here?"

I was spotted. I turned around and saw Aza and Ana looking at me with a concerned look on their faces.

"We just finished up group training. I didn't expect you to come back so soon."

Ana looked down at my hands and asked, "What are you doing with that Spirit Caster?"

I had to think of an excuse fast. Telling them the truth could've put every single person in this temple in danger. I didn't want them to get mixed up in my problems. So, I told her what she wanted to hear.

"I thought about what you both said before. About my grandmother wanting me to have this. I think I'm ready to take on the responsibility."

"Really?" Ana asked, seemingly unconvinced of my little lie.

"Yes, really."

"This is an interesting turn of events," Aza said. "Another Shēna finally living up to their potential. Maybe you can even be as great as the *hero of Phoenix Island*."

"Who's that?" I asked, actually curious about the title.

"Another Shēna, supposedly," Ana answered. "But most people believe him to be a myth."

Most people also believe Shēna in general to be a myth, so it wouldn't surprise me to find out that he truly did exist. For a second her words intrigued me. Hearing that Phoenix Island had its own Shēna was interesting to say the least. But at that moment, like so many other things, it didn't matter.

"So now that you're finally taking the wand," Ana continued, "what exactly do you plan to do with it?"

"Try to understand it."

"We can help with that," Aza started to speak but I cut her off.

"I want to do that on my own. It's my burden. I should be the one to deal with it."

"I understand."

"Can I take it with me?"

"You're its rightful owner," she nodded. "I can't stop you."

"Thank you," I told them before turning to leave. I thought I might've fooled Aza, but Ana still had probing eyes that I could feel staring right through my lie. I didn't think it mattered. As long as Aza believed me, then there was nothing Ana could do about it.

"Oh, and Crystal," Aza said, forcing me to turn back around. "I trust that whatever you do with that wand will lead to the betterment of the world."

Those words stung. She was putting her trust in me, and I was lying right to her face. But ... It was for the lives of my family. So, it had to be done. This was the only way that everyone would stay safe.

I nodded my head and hurried out of the temple. Getting the wand wasn't the only hard part of all this. I still had to make it home before the storm became too heavy.

***

The sun was getting low after an hour of running through the thick storm. I could barely see a thing and had no idea where I was or what direction I should've been going in. I was completely lost.

I dropped down to my knees and screamed in frustration, not knowing how I was going to make it back in time. I failed. I was supposed to take care of everyone. I was supposed to protect them. They all relied on me to save them, but there I was, stuck in the middle of a blizzard. Once again, *I* was the one that needed saving.

Suddenly, the snowflakes stopped falling. They just sat there in midair as if they had frozen in place. The wind stopped howling and everything was silent. Even Lumi stopped. It seemed as if time itself had come to a standstill, and I was the only one still in motion.

"Crystal," I heard the voice call me again. This time it sounded clear. More tangible. I turned around and saw a woman standing behind me wearing a long white fur coat. Her hair was the same color as mine but much longer, almost reaching the snow on the ground. "What are you going to do with that Spirit Caster?" she questioned.

I hesitated to answer. "Who are you?" I asked.

"My name is Eve Winters," she answered.

"'Eve Winters'? That's the name of my grandmother."

"Precisely," she smiled.

Could she really be implying that she was my grandmother? I was told she died a long time ago. I couldn't deny that this woman had a striking resemblance to me.

"How are you still alive?" I asked.

"I'm only alive in spirit," she laughed. "I'm no longer a part of the world of the living. We're only able to communicate because of that wand you're holding in your hand right now."

I looked her up and down, barely able to believe it. Just a week ago I didn't know that magic even existed and now today I was talking to a ghost.

"What do you want?" I asked.

"I already told you. I want to know what you're doing with that Spirit Caster."

"I'm going to hand it over to the princess."

"You shouldn't do that. The members of the royal family are too power hungry. Nothing good will come of the world if they gain the power of all the Spirit Casters. They'll just make new Shēna follow them to kill the rest."

"Well, what do you suggest I do? If I don't give this to her my family—*our family* will die!"

"Not if you fight."

"But the Princess, she's too powerful. I've never seen anything like what she can do. "

"But I have. I've beaten it once before. And I know that you can too if you use the power of the Spirit Caster."

"I'm sorry, but I can't do that. I need to put my family first. We'll be spared if I do this."

My grandmother let out a disappointed sigh.

"Do as you wish," she said, raising her hand as if sending me off and vanishing out of sight. The snow started to fall again, and the wind roared. But the area around me looked different somehow. I looked around and, in the distance, I saw it. My home. The sun was vanishing just beyond the horizon. It looked like I made it just in time.

I sprinted the rest of the way and when I got closer, I saw my sister and mother sitting outside on their knees in front of the Princess and her guards. My father was being forced outside with them. They grabbed him and threw him into the snow. All he could do was lay there, coughing and wincing in pain.

"Wait! I'm here!" I shouted as I ran to my father to help him up. "Are you ok?" I asked.

"Yes, I'm fine Crystal. Don't worry about me."

"Wow, you actually made it back on time," the princess laughed. "I was just about to put them on the chopping block." Her laughs died down and a humorless expression formed on her face. "Where's the wand?" she asked.

I pulled the wand from my belt with the intent of tossing it over to her, but something stopped me. The words that my grandmother had said repeated in my head. It made me wonder if I was truly making the right choice.

"Give it to me," she ordered.

"Wait," I said. "Why do you want this wand so badly?"

"Does it matter?"

"Yes, it does. I don't want to just hand you the keys to my own self destruction. How do I know you won't just use it to hurt us in the end? How do I know that you'll even keep up your end of the deal?"

"Well, you'll just have to trust me."

"And why's that?"

"Because if you don't give me that Spirit Caster within the next five seconds then you'll all die regardless."

Before I could even think of a response, she started her countdown. "Four."

It looked like I didn't have a choice.

"Three ... two ..."

"Wait!" I shouted. "I'll give it to you."

"That's a good girl. Now hand it over."

I tossed it over to her and she caught it, examining it closely.

"Good," she smiled as she turned around to walk the other way, but then stopped as if she was in deep thought. Almost like she was debating something in her head. The princess raised her hand in the air and snapped her fingers. Suddenly, I heard my mother scream before I looked over to witness her being impaled by a guard's sword from behind.

"Eira!" My father cried.

He tried to run to her but fell in his attempt. I just sat there completely frozen. I couldn't comprehend what had happened. I didn't understand.

Another knight came behind my father, raising his sword up and swinging it down. Blood splattered everywhere, staining the snow and Wren's dress. She was in the same position as me. She had a blank expression, unable to process anything. I didn't know what to do. I wanted to move my body, but it felt impossible.

Suddenly, I heard a loud bark. I looked down and saw Lumi running towards the guards, ready to pounce. I wanted to tell her to stop but I choked on my own words. She ran to Wren and stood by her side growling at all of them. She was protecting her. Putting her life on the line to save her family. That's what I should have done. Why didn't I do anything?

When I was younger, my father told me that since I was his first born, it was up to me to protect everyone when he's gone. Aza told me I was supposed to be great, Ana told me that I had the potential to change the world, and my grandmother's spirit told me to fight back. So far, I had disappointed everyone by not only lying, but by being a complete coward.

"Fight!"

I heard her voice again. I should have listened. Mom and Dad were gone. But Wren ... I wasn't going to let them take her too. My job hadn't changed. It had always been the same and as long as there was still at least one living family member breathing then it would never change!

"Why are you just standing there?" I heard my grandmother whisper in my ear. *"If you don't move they'll kill her."*

I finally made a sound. It was a scream, but not one of terror. It was a scream of strength and dedication. It was a scream that would let the entire world know what my intentions were. It was one that was meant to put an end to this madness. I broke out of my trance and finally screamed.

*"I **will** protect her!"*

I unsheathed my hunting knife from my belt and sprinted towards a guard who had his back turned towards me, grabbed him from behind and sank my knife deep into his neck. As soon as I pushed the blade into him, blood squirted out into the air as if it was gushing out from a fountain. It covered the blade and my arm in a thick and sticky red warmth.

I now had the attention of every guard in the area and prepared myself for anything as they came charging at me while swinging their blades in my direction. I jumped out of the paths of their swords, attempting to evade every attack but got numerous cuts across my body. I was heavily outnumbered, and my knife didn't have the range to reach any of them. At this pace, I wasn't going to survive this battle, much less win it.

"Wren! Get out of here!" I shouted. At that moment, it didn't matter to me whether or not I'd survive, just as long as Wren had a chance to do so herself. But she didn't move. There was too much fear and shock holding her back. I needed to reach her and get out of here. As soon as the thought came to mind, I heard a shout.

"Skoteiní Volí!"

Suddenly something hit me right in my side with so much force that I was sent hurtling a few meters through the air and into the snow. I was shot by something. I didn't know what hit me. But it felt explosive.

The guards all backed away from me to make way for the princess. She had a terrifying dark aura over her entire body as she pointed her wand towards me.

"You're a feisty one, aren't you?" The princess laughed. "I'm impressed that you were able to kill one of my men. I like your spirit. Unfortunately, that spirit makes you and your family a threat, just like all the other Shēna who could pose a threat to us." The tip of her Spirit Caster formed a small black ball of pure energy. "Goodbye, Crystal Winters. ***Skoteiní—***"

Before she could finish the incantation, Lumi jumped up and bit the princess's wrist, forcing her to shout in pain and drop her wand into the snow. The same knight who threatened Wren earlier instantly drew her sword and slashed at Lumi, drawing blood and forcing her down to the ground. She lifted her sword to finish Lumi off but before she could, a spear flew right past her face, forcing the knight to jump back.

We all looked at where it came from. Everyone around me looked puzzled by the new face, but it was one I knew all too well. She sat atop her giant wolf, surveying the area and taking everything in as if trying to figure out how this all started.

"Ana?" I found myself whispering in shock.

"Who the hell is that?" Kira asked before snapping her fingers and saying aloud, "Guards, take her down."

Their sights were off of me and went straight to Ana. Without hesitation they all charged at her.

"Ana!" I shouted. "This has nothing to do with you! Just run!"

Ana didn't listen. Instead of running she decided to jump off of Silver and fight. She reached for her side and pulled out a hunting knife. The guards tried cutting her down with their swords, but she dodged every single one of their attacks; all the while she made counter attacks against all of them with her knife, wounding some and killing others.

"She's turning our men into mincemeat, Ranne," Kira turned to her knight but seemed unamused when she saw that Ranne was smirking. "What's that stupid grin for?"

"My apologies, Princess," she said while pulling out her sword and walking towards the battle. "It's just been a while since I've laid eyes on an enemy with such skill." Ranne then sprinted towards Ana while her back was turned.

"Ana, watch out!" I warned her.

She finished off her current enemy and turned to see Ranne running right for her at an incredible pace. Ranne swung her sword at Ana leaving her almost no time to dodge.

"Damnit," Ranne said, "I missed."

Blood poured from Ana's face as she covered it. Once Ana moved her hand away from her face, I could see a large gash cutting from her right brow, through her eye and down her cheek.

"No, you got me," Ana confessed.

"I was aiming for your *neck*."

Ranne wasted no time going back on the attack. Ana tried to dodge but every swing nicked her body. I couldn't tell if she was slower from her eye injury or if this knight was just inhumanly fast.

While everyone's attention was on their battle, Wren had made her way to the other side of the princess, snatched the blue Spirit Caster out of her hand, and started running towards me.

Kira quickly reacted, yelling, "You brat!" while pointing her wand straight at Wren. ***"Désmi Thanátou,"*** her voice echoed, causing a thin black beam of light to shoot from the tip of her wand and right through Wren's leg. The Spirit Caster flew right out of her hands and next to my side as she fell into the snow. Without hesitation and despite the pain in my side, I reached for the wand to pick it up.

Kira stomped her foot on Wren's back to pin her down, forcing a scream out of her. It seemed like she was going to perform that same spell again. At the same time Ana was dangerously close to losing her battle with the knight. I prayed to the *sister gods* and hoped that this wand would get all of us out of this.

As soon as my fingers wrapped around it, my head started racing. Overflowing with words I had never spoken. They flooded my mind, and I subconsciously repeated those words.

"Let the ice rain down

Freeze my enemies to death

Lead them all to oblivion

Cheimoniátiki Kataigída."

The princess looked up at me and once she realized what I was doing, she shouted "Stop!" but it was in vain. Heavy winds burst from around me, swirling in every direction. Snow and ice flew through the air, making it hard for anyone to see. It was an instant blizzard that forced everyone down.

I did it. Without ever having any prior knowledge of magic, I was able to completely manipulate the weather. It felt unnatural yet empowering. Almost *godly* even.

The voices in my head died down and I was able to think clearly again. I looked down at my hands and saw that they were covered in ice making it hard for me to let go of the wand. I forced it off and once again ended up tearing small parts of my skin, leaving my hands cold and bloody. I guess that was the cost of using a magical power that I had no experience with.

I looked at my sister who was still in the snow trying to get herself up but struggled with her wound. I got to her and picked her up, but I couldn't leave without Ana. Luckily, she had the same thought about me.

"Crystal!" I heard her shout behind me. She was back on Silver and stretched her arm out to me. Once I grabbed it, she pulled Wren and I up before shouting "Run!" Triggering Silver to go full speed away from our attackers.

"Lumi!" I called to get her attention. She struggled to get herself up but in the end was able to follow deeper into the blizzard and out of sight.

CHAPTER EIGHT
KIRA

hards of ice flew everywhere. I blocked my face, saving it, but at the cost of both my arms getting sliced all over despite the. The fierce wind blew me back into the cold snow. I looked up but could barely make out anything from the flurry.

I couldn't believe it. How could I have been so careless? I didn't think she'd be able to cast such a powerful spell. She didn't seem experienced. Could she have communed with her Shēna ancestors? That was something I hadn't done in years.

I shuffled through the snow, finding my Spirit Caster and picked it up before hearing the crunching sound of snow behind me. I instinctively pointed my wand towards its source.

"Désmi Thanátou!"

The Spirit Caster shot off a thin beam of dark energy in that direction.

"It's me!" Ranne yelled.

"Ranne?" I cried out.

She got closer in sight. A bloody cut was on her cheek. My attack must have hit her.

"Ranne, are you ok? Are you hurt? I'm sorry!" I said in a panic.

"Don't apologize to a lowly knight like myself Kira. It's unbecoming of a princess," she said with a smile. She crouched down, wrapped her arms around me and picked me up, carrying me to the cabin.

"What are you doing? Put me down!" I ordered. "I can stand on my own!"

"No."

"What do you mean no'? That's an order!"

"You're injured and it is my sworn duty to make sure you're safe."

I stopped struggling and wrapped my arms around her, but only to make sure that she wouldn't drop me.

"Tsk. Do as you wish."

She carried me inside and sat me on the table before proceeding to rummage through their cabinets.

"Where are the rest of the knights?" I asked.

"They're probably all dead from the ice shards," she answered, while still searching around.

"Why are we back in here? We should go back out there and look for the girl."

"We won't find her in that blizzard," she said while taking out a bottle of alcohol, bandages, and a rag. "Ok, it looks like we have something to work with."

She walked over to me with all the items she found and placed them on the table before stretching out her hand to take mine.

"What are you doing?" I asked, annoyed.

"Cleaning your wounds," she said while pouring alcohol over my arm; it hurt like hell.

"You're too kind." I mocked. "Don't think I would ever show you the same kindness."

"Are you sure about that? You seemed pretty distraught when you almost killed me a moment ago," she shot back before looking down at my torn and blood-stained dress.

"What?" I asked. "Do you want me to take off my dress so you can clean me up?"

She avoided eye contact with me and let out a weak laugh.

"Don't be so bashful," I teased. "It's not like it would be the first time you would see me in such a state."

I snatched the rag from her hand and started to clean the cut on her face.

"I thought you said you wouldn't show me any kindness," she mocked.

"If I just feel like doing something then I'll *do* it. If I want something, then I'll *take* it. And I can never make up my mind. You should know that about me by now."

"I do. And that's what I love about you."

I put a bandage on her cut and gave her a light kiss on the cheek.

"You're an idiot. Love itself creates a web of weakness. Promise me you won't get too tangled in it."

"You know I can't do that."

Ranne gave back the same energy as I did and kissed me. We embraced each other, happy that the other knights were dead and gone, leaving us to ourselves for once. I was enraged that Crystal was gone with the Spirit Caster and I knew my father would give me hell for it. Regardless, I couldn't change any of that at the moment. So why not have just a little bit more fun with my childhood friend?

CHAPTER NINE
CRYSTAL

The storm let up, but it was still dark. Once Silver slowed down, Ana noticed how tired he was and, not too long after, spotted a small cave on the side of a large hill. She pulled the reins, turning Silver into the dark cavity.

As soon as we pulled in, I jumped off Silver and pulled Wren down along with me to check on her leg. My arms trembled from all her shivering, so I sat her down and took my heavy jacket off, giving it to her.

"Here, Wren, put this on," I told her.

She stared off into the distance with a vacant expression filled with tears. She had experienced too much sorrow in too short a time. And only at the young age of seven. I was surprised that she had the will to try and fight off the princess the way she did. Snatching the wand from her must've been that pure instinct to protect that's ingrained into our blood.

After wrapping my jacket around her, I turned my attention to her ankle which had blood all over it. Ana took some items out of a bag hanging from Silver's saddle before saying, "Use this," and tossing a roll of bandages and a bota bag filled with water my way.

"Thank you," I told her before cleaning her leg and my bloodied hands. While I was tending to our wounds, Ana started a small fire with some items in her bag and whatever else she found around the cave. As soon as it was lit, Lumi laid right beside it, exhausted and covered in her own blood.

As I was bandaging us up, Wren finally came to, and asked, "Crystal, are you going to be ok?"

"Of course," I answered. "You're the one we've got to worry about right now, not me."

"Your clothes … they look too light. Aren't you cold?"

I thought about it for a moment and realized that she was right. All I had on were my fur boots, black leggings, and a long-sleeved shirt. The strange part about it was that I actually wasn't cold. The entire time we spent traversing through the blizzard I'd felt warm. I'd say that it was just an adrenaline rush, but even at that point as I stayed motionless and calm, I still felt completely comfortable with the temperature.

"I'll be fine," I told her.

"What are we gonna do, Crystal?" she asked with tears streaming down her face.

I paused for a moment to think until finally saying, "I don't know." I used the end of my sleeve to wipe the tears from her face and continued saying, "But don't worry, Wren, I'll protect you till the end. I'll figure something out. Now lay down and rest. We'll continue on in the morning."

Wren nodded her head and laid down, closing her eyes almost instantly falling asleep from exhaustion. I got up and turned to Ana while asking, "How did you know we were in trouble to begin with?"

"I didn't," she answered. "But I *did* know that you were a liar."

"What?"

"You *lied* to us!" She shouted. "You were planning on handing over the wand, weren't you? Is that why they were there?" she said as she got close to me. "I bet you were planning on giving it to them the whole time!"

"Ana, I didn't have a choice!" I cracked.

"And yet you *chose* to give them the wand!"

"They were going to kill my family!"

"Then why didn't you tell us that?" she fumed.

"Because this was *my* problem. You and Aza have already done so much for me. You even risked your life for me. I didn't want you to do it a second time. I didn't want you to get hurt the way you did."

Ana turned away from me and almost growled out of pure frustration. She walked to the wall of the cave and sat down, leaning against it, seemingly done with the argument. I didn't know if she was done because she understood my case or if it was because she was too angry to think. I couldn't tell from the look on her face; she was covered in blood.

"How's your eye?" I asked.

"It hurts like hell. And I can't open it. Don't even know if I can see out of it," she touched her wound and continued, "That knight. She was so fast. So strong. I wonder if she was even human."

To see Ana in such a state was terrifying to think about. So far Ana has been one of the strongest people I'd ever laid eyes on. Even in combat she seemed second to none. So, to see that this one other woman was able to overwhelm her just shows how powerful their forces are.

I took the rest of the bandages and started to wrap her eye up. She glared at me but eventually her gaze softened before she finally said, "I'm sorry about your parents." Her apology made me freeze. "I wish I could've gotten here sooner. I could've done something—"

"Stop," I could feel my eyes water. "You did everything you could. Besides, their lives weren't your responsibility. Neither are my mistakes. *I* got them killed."

"You weren't the one who swung a blade at them. And you definitely weren't the one to give the order."

She was right. I wasn't the one who gave the order. It was the princess. It was Kira and whatever sick royals who benefited from it.

I got up and turned away to check on Lumi, but Ana stopped me asking, "What are you going to do now?"

I dreaded that question. What *could* I have done? We lost our parents and our home. Going back to the temple would only put everyone there in danger. We were alone. And most likely soon to be wanted.

"I don't know," I finally answered with my back turned. "I'm too angry to think. I want to rip her to shreds, but," my voice started to crack as I tried not to fall apart, "I'm not strong enough."

I turned back to her and saw a blank expressionless look on her face.

"Ana?" I called, but her silence continued. "I'm guessing you're still mad. I'm sorry. I didn't want you to get hurt like this." She didn't move a muscle. "Can you please just say something? Anything?"

"She can't hear you," a voice said from behind.

I immediately turned around to see who it was and found myself face to face with the spirit who guided me before. My grandmother, Eve. I stumbled away.

"You're back?" I asked.

"I never left. I'm always with you as long as you have that Spirit Caster," she answered.

I plopped down on the ground.

"I should've listened to you. I should've fought back from the start," I started to cry. I looked up at her and asked, "What am I going to do?"

"It depends, what is it you *want* to do?"

"I want to kill her!" I cried. "I want to kill the princess and her family for what they did to us! I want to destroy everything they've built!"

"I see. It seems the hatred of our blood lines has survived after all this time. I also want to see them fall, but you can't do it alone."

"But I have no one else except my sister. And she wasn't ready for any of this. *I* wasn't ready for any of this! How could I possibly take any action on my own?"

"You have her," she nodded towards Ana. "And you have an even greater force that rivals that of the royal family."

"Who?"

"Why, the Shēna of course. A lot of them are still alive, just like you. You need to bring them back together. Together you can destroy the royal family."

"How do I find them?"

"I can sense the presence of other Spirit Casters around the continent. The closest one is north of here, in Livádia. I can feel another much farther on Mount Astrapí."

"Do you think they'll actually help me?"

"It might take a little bit of convincing on your part but I'm sure you'll manage."

And just as soon as she appeared, she was gone.

"Crystal, did you hear me?" Ana asked. Her question made me jump. It seemed like time froze once again and I was the only one to witness the sight of the ghostly figure. "I asked what are you going to do?"

I took a deep breath, clenched my fist, and finally said, "I'm going to kill her."

Ana had a look of surprise from my sudden bravado and asked, "How are you going to pull that off?"

I walked up to her while saying, "With you. Please, I need you to help me."

"Last time I helped you I lost an eye," she scoffed.

"So, what are you going to do about it? Nothing? I've seen you fight, Ana. You're a warrior. And warriors don't run with their tails tucked between their legs just from a measly scar."

My words triggered something in her that made her shoot up to her feet before saying, "Don't act like you *know* me."

"I know you well enough to understand that you're not just going to sit around and do nothing right after I've asked you to help me change the world."

There was a moment of tense silence between us before Ana finally broke it. "Do you really think we can beat them on our own?"

"No. But I might be able to find people who can help."

"Who?"

"Don't know yet. But I know where to find them."

"Crystal—"

"Look, I know that I've betrayed your trust before, but I want to make things right. I *need* you to trust me."

Ana rolled her one good eye and begrudgingly thought it over, all the while I didn't take my eyes off of hers.

"I'll sleep on it," she finally answered while getting herself back on the ground. "You'll get your answer in the morning, but right now I'm tired."

A fair answer. And it wasn't a no. With her by my side, I believed we could do it. But now wasn't the time to worry about success. It was time to rest.

I walked over to the fire and sat down next to Lumi who was quietly curled up in a ball, shivering. She was still bleeding. With the amount of blood around her, I doubted that she would make it to see the sunrise, so

I laid my hand on her and gently stroked her fur to put her at ease. Lumi's shivering stopped and a few moments later, her breathing went along with it.

"I'm sorry I couldn't protect you, Lumi. I'm so sorry," I whispered under my breath. I quietly cried next to her for hours until I was too tired to let out any more tears and passed out from the weariness of my sorrow.

CHAPTER TEN
KIRA

"**A**lright," I yawned. "I think we should head home."

We slept in the cabin for the night and were both well rested. It felt ... different. At first, I was disgusted by these living conditions. It was cramped, and the wood was rotting. It was the complete opposite of what life was like inside the castle. Even though this was the case, it still had its charm.

It was an amazing change of pace. Waking up to the smell of burnt firewood put me at ease. And there was no one around to tell me what I needed to do for the day, pampering me and kissing up to me in order to be in my good favor. It was quiet with no one around. Only Ranne and I.

Waking up to see her face next to mine made me feel warm. It felt like a weight off my shoulders with not having to hide our relationship from those around us. It made me wonder if I'd ever have a life like this. I'd gladly give up my title as princess for it.

No.

I couldn't possibly do that. My father wouldn't approve. I'd disgrace my entire ancestry if I were to live a life like this.

Ranne got up and put all her armor back on as I did with my clothes.

"How'd you sleep?" Ranne asked.

"Well," I answered. "You?"

"It could have been better. I'm not very comfortable sleeping in the house of the people we murdered."

"We didn't murder them; it was an execution."

"But I don't exactly understand why. The girl brought the wand back on time."

"Because my father would have done the same. He taught me that all the Shēna that aren't a part of the Royal family and The Five Armaments are dangerous. Their entire race is a threat to the world. Letting them live would lead to dangerous consequences for the Black Continent."

"They didn't seem very dangerous to me."

"Then you're a fool."

I wasn't sure how much I believed in my own words. It was true that my father taught me to think that way, but something inside me didn't like it. Even so I still went and had her family killed. Although I wanted to please my father's wishes, my plans changed when I saw the family. Their threat level was so low that I couldn't imagine a world where they would even *try* to rise against us. I was going to let them go free, but something came over me. At that moment I lost my humanity, and I didn't know how to feel about the sudden change.

I grabbed the Spirit Caster and left the bedroom to go into the living room. Pointing my wand to the center of the room, I spoke these words.

"Please take me away.

Take me throughout the darkness.

Let us travel fast.

Grígoro Taxídi."

A large ball of black flames appeared in front of me, floating in the middle of the room. Ranne walked in after me, with her armor fully equipped.

"Are you ready?" I asked while reaching my hand out to her. She nodded her head and gently held onto my open palm. I walked into the flames, guiding her through them. The flames acted as a doorway to another world. It was completely black with not a spec of light to be seen. I always found this place to be creepy ever since I was a child and I hated going through it. Because of this I'd never explore far into this world.

The air was thick and it was hard to move around. I always felt too hot here in this dark world. I couldn't imagine how Ranne felt while clad in armor.

Only I was able to navigate through there. If I were to let go of Ranne's hand then she would be trapped in the darkness forever. It would have been a hilarious joke but there wasn't much time for that.

Eventually we found the light of day. We jumped out of the ball of flame appearing in the courtyard of the castle that was right in the center of Ebony. Everyone in the area gazed at us in surprise and quickly bowed.

"The princess has returned!" One of the guards yelled. I hated the fact that everywhere I went, my presence was announced. Now there was no avoiding my father. *Might as well get this over with,* I thought to myself.

"Ranne, you're relieved of your duties for now," I told her. "Take a breather. I'm going to meet with The King.

***

I made it in front of the giant throne room doors and the guards pushed them open to allow me through. Once inside, I saw three of the **Five Armaments of War.** This was a group of Shēna who were directly controlled by The King to fight his battles. He used to be a part of the group until he passed the mantle along with the Spirit Caster to me.

"Ah, so our beautiful and amazing princess has finally graced us with her presence!" Morpheus said obnoxiously while taking a bow. He stood up straight while running his hand through his swept back hair, only leaving one long strand to droop down the side of his face. The cloak covering his black uniform was completely white without a speck of dust or dirt. It hurt my eyes just looking at it. It reminded me of the bright snow from Nótio Págo. I hated him more than any other member in the group. There was something in his eyes that felt deceitful and somewhat menacing.

"Morpheus, you're such a kiss up," Arachne complained. She had long red curly hair and was the most defiant of the group. She tore off the legs of her pants, turning them into shorts and did the same to her coat, turning it into a vest, which I thought looked completely unacceptable for someone of her position. But The King still allowed it.

My eyes wandered to the last member in the room, Delta. She was the youngest member of the Five Armaments. Only 13 years old. She was a beautiful young girl with light brown skin, aqua green eyes, and short curly black hair. She was the only one in the room who was silent. I liked that about her, and she quickly became my favorite of the group. She knew her place unlike all the other irritants.

I glanced around the throne room one last time and noticed that we were one member short.

"Where's the old man?" I asked.

My father answered saying, "He's still searching for the Wind Spirit Caster in Livádia. Speaking of which, how did your mission go? Did you find the Ice Spirit Caster?"

I hesitated before answering, fearful of how he might react to my failure but nevertheless, I still answered truthfully.

"I ... wasn't able to retrieve it."

He raised an eyebrow at my answer and asked, "What happened?"

"I-I had it, but it was stolen from me!"

"And why isn't the person who stole it from you dead? Were you and all the guards that I sent with you too incompetent to deal with a simple thief?"

"She wasn't just a simple thief. She was a Shēna."

He glared down at me from his black and golden throne.

"You should have killed them," he scoffed.

"I tried. I killed her parents, but she herself was able to get away."

"Does this thief have a name?"

"Yes. Her name was Crystal Winters."

His annoyed, condescending expression turned into one of fear.

"Did you say 'Winters'?

"Yes, does the name ring a bell?"

He shifted in his seat as if contemplating on how he should answer.

"I want her dead," he demanded. "The Winters's very existence poses a threat to us. You said you killed her parents?"

"Yes," I answered. "The only ones who survived were herself and her younger sister. There was another person with them, but I don't believe that they were related. I didn't feel an ounce of Rēa flowing from her."

"Good. Take the entire group and track her down. I'll call Adam from his mission and tell him to assist you."

"I don't think that will be necessary," Morpheus interjected. "The princess has already tried and failed. Letting her go again wouldn't be wise. I think we should go a different route."

"What?" I growled at him but was immediately silenced by the rising hand of my father.

"What do you suggest instead, Morpheus?" My father was curious about what he had to say.

"I don't believe it's necessary for any of the Five Armaments to go except me. With my Illusion Spirit Caster I believe that I can easily play the role of an ally to her. If I do that I can lead her right into your hands."

My father contemplated the offer and looked at the other members asking, "Do any of you oppose this idea?"

"Of course!" I shouted. "This was my mission! I should be the one leading this operation!"

"Then you should have gotten it done the first time around. You've lost the right to vote on this matter," he said to me in a sour tone, forcing me to bite my tongue. He looked over at Arachne. "What say you?"

"I don't care what he does. Let him go on his own. Just means less work for me," Arachne shrugged.

My father then turned to Delta. She closed her eyes and nonchalantly said, "It means no difference to me whether or not he goes alone. I will do whatever your highness asks of me."

"Then it's decided!" Morpheus yelled with excitement. "Since no one is against it I will go alone," he continued while turning and keeping eye contact with me. I wanted to kill him! It took everything I had to stop myself from taking out my Spirit Caster and ending his meaningless existence.

My father nodded his head. "So be it. You and you alone will lead the girl into our trap."

"Thank you, your majesty," Morpheus said, taking an exaggerated bow. "I won't fail you."

"Yes, that would be in your best interest. This meeting is adjourned."

***

"What the hell was that?" I asked Morpheus as we all exited the throne room.

"Whatever do you mean?" he asked with a smirk.

"Why did you take this mission away from me? And why are you doing it alone?"

"No reason in particular."

"You don't just do things for no reason. There's always a reason! What is it? Do you just like one-upping me? Are you just trying to take all the credit for yourself to gain favor from my father?"

Morpheus let out a sigh and finally answered saying, "I'm doing this simply because I'm curious. I want to see the person that was able to give you so much trouble with my own eyes. And I don't want anyone in the way of that. Does that answer satisfy you?"

All I could do was glare at him. He always tried to undermine me but never admitted it. Making excuses like this only added to the hatred I had for him.

"I'll take your silence as a yes," he continued.

"How do you guys have the energy to argue right now?" Arachne cut in. "It's so early, and none of us have even had breakfast yet."

"You're right," Morpheus agreed. "I'm famished. Let's all go out for breakfast, my treat."

"I'm down," Arachne answered.

I didn't answer.

"Come on Kira, won't you come with?" Morpheus asked.

"I'm not hungry." I said bluntly.

"Fine, be that way." Morpheus turned to Delta and said, "You've been awfully quiet. What about you?"

"Sorry, but I'm busy. There's a lot of stuff that I want to look into back in the library."

"Delta, you're so lame," Arachne laughed. "You're always in the library. You need to loosen up sometimes."

"Well, I believe that it's a great quality to have," Morpheus interjected. "Though I have to say Delta, you still are just a child. You should take a break every once and a while. Have some fun."

Delta let out a weak laugh and said, "You're not the first one to say that. Some kids used to think I was weird for it back when I used to go to school."

"Wow, what a surprise," Arachne joked sarcastically.

"Alright, suit yourselves. Let's go, Arachne." Morpheus finally said before walking around the corner with Arachne close by his side.

"I can't stand that man," I said aloud. "It's like he's got some crazy vendetta against me for reasons that go right over my head."

"Well you're not exactly the most likable person," Delta said plainly, "so it's not a complete mystery on why he would hate you."

"Are any of the Five Armaments likable people?" I argued.

Delta laughed before saying, "I guess not. But I suppose the worst offender is Morpheus. He'll sabotage the livelihoods of others just for some entertainment."

"And for some reason I'm his favorite victim. There has to be a way for me to take back the mission he stole from me."

"I don't understand why you care so much. Before you even went on the quest, you complained about being assigned to it. Now here you are complaining that it's getting taken from you."

"This isn't *just* about it being taken from me. I failed because some newbie who *just* got their wand blindsided me. Do you understand what that does to my reputation as the future queen of this continent?"

"I guess I didn't think of it like that. Well, at least Adam is still a factor."

"What do you mean?"

"When Adam gets back from taking the Wind Spirit Caster, he'll probably be opposed to the fact that Morpheus gets to have all the fun with the ice user. If you get him on your side, then it should be easy to get The King to change his mind about not letting you back on the mission."

She was right. I had completely forgotten about Adam. He was the key that I needed to get exactly what I wanted. And all I needed to do was wait for him to retrieve the Wind Spirit Caster. A task that shouldn't have been too hard for someone as powerful as him.

PART TWO
HOWLING WIND

CHAPTER ELEVEN
ALIZEH

I readied myself in the lush fields with the tall grass tickling my legs and took in the nice gentle breeze as it cooled me off from the hot sun. My father stood behind me at a distance watching me intently. I pulled out the Spirit Caster from my holster, pointed it out to my side and let out a deep breath.

"Pairno Ptisi," I said.

The Spirit Caster activated with a greenish glow as the wind became stronger and circled around me like a tiny tornado. Before I knew it, I was floating in the air. This was the first time that I was actually able to control it! I'd never been able to actually lift myself with consistency using the magic wind of the Spirit Caster! I looked back at my dad with a large smile on my face.

"It looks like you're finally making progress," my father said, looking very proud of my accomplishment. "When I was your age it took me much longer to learn—"

I couldn't hear what else my father had to say because in the middle of his sentence I went flying through the air. It was exhilarating! The wind in my face. The resistance that I felt when I tried to move. It gave me a rush that I had never felt before! The only problem was ... this was all entirely unintentional. I was no longer in control of my flight. Who was I kidding, I was never in control.

Before I could even think, I was up so high that my father looked like an ant from where I was. I was also getting farther and farther away from home. I stopped the spell and the wand stopped glowing right along with it. The wind had completely dispersed. That would have been a positive development if it didn't mean I was hurtling towards certain doom.

There had to be something in my repertoire of spells I could use to slow myself down. I gripped my wand tightly and pointed it below me. Then I thought of something. It wouldn't slow me down but I hoped it would soften my landing. I waited until I was closer to the ground. I had to time it just right.

Once I was close enough to the ground, I shouted ***"Víaii sfýrigma!"***

A powerful gust of wind erupted below me, slowing me down for a single second, creating an explosion of dust. I was grounded. I was alive. To be honest I wasn't sure what the outcome of that gamble would be. The chances of me dying were just as high as me surviving, if not higher.

The dust cleared and I realized that I was in a large crater. The spell was more powerful than I thought. I started to make my way out of the hole, crawling my way up and popping my head out to see where I was. As soon as I got to the edge of the crater I was greeted by a Spirit Caster and a pair of daggers pointed straight at my face by two random girls.

"Stop right there!" the dark skinned one yelled.

I listened and stopped in my tracks. I looked at both the girls. One had pale skin with beautiful long white hair and blue eyes. The other's skin was dark and her hair was twisted in locks. They both looked tired and dirty. Their clothes were torn and they both were shaking as if they were trying their hardest to stay awake. I glanced over and saw a third and much younger girl lying on top of a giant wolf, seemingly passed out.

"Are you a part of the Five Armaments? Why do you have a Spirit Caster?" she yelled in her attempt to interrogate me, but it made her seem like she was more afraid of me than I should have been of her. I got myself out of the crater and dusted off my sundress with my hands.

"Don't move!" the white haired one yelled with her Spirit Caster locked on me.

"I've never seen any Shēna outside of my family before," I said to her. Her entire demeanor changed. She lowered her Spirit Caster slightly along with her guard. "My name's Alizeh," I told her while gently putting my hand on her wand to completely lower it. "What's yours?"

"Crystal," she answered.

I looked to the other one to wait for her answer. Once she saw that Crystal had trusted me, she decided to do the same.

"Ana," she finally said.

"It looks like you guys have been through a lot. Please, come with me."

CHAPTER TWELVE
CRYSTAL

We traveled over the frozen fields on Silver for about a week before reaching Livádia. The lush and beautiful fields made me feel at ease. It was a nice change of pace compared to the harsh and icy conditions of my home, Nótio Págo.

Alizeh was a kind young girl who looked no older than twelve. Even with being so young she still seemed to be a skilled Shēna. It was terrifying to see her fly through the air and make a large explosion of dust in front of us. I thought for sure that she was there to kill me, but I could only sense kindness from her.

"How do you know we can trust her?" Ana whispered into my ear.

"I don't," I whispered back. "But I have a feeling that she can help."

"Great. First I get you, a Shēna who has no idea how to use their powers, and now we're recruiting a child. This plan of yours is starting to unravel before it even begins."

Alizeh looked back at us and asked, "Did one of you say something?"

"No," I quickly answered aloud. "It was nothing."

As we walked, Alizeh fixed her long black curly hair, putting it into a messy bun to get it out of the way of her beautiful sandy brown colored skin. She looked back at us and smiled without saying a word. She had eyes like Jade gemstones, and it looked like they were studying us. Trying to understand our situation. Perhaps she was silent because she didn't want to pry.

We followed the dirt road and cut through a grassy field eventually making it to a small white farmhouse, surrounded by nothing but acres of land and animals.

"This is my home," Alizeh told us.

"It's beautiful," I said back.

"Alizeh!" A voice called. A woman came running from the house over to us. As soon as she got to us, she dropped to her knees and tightly squeezed the young girl. "Alizeh are you ok? I thought something terrible happened to you!"

A man laughed while walking over to us. "I knew she would be resourceful enough to find a safe way down."

"You're much too laid-back Tal! She could've—," she stopped mid-sentence and looked over at us as if she had just noticed we were there. "Who is they?"

"This is Ana, and her dog. I don't know who that kid on the dog is but that's not important," Alizeh answered. "*She's* the important one," she pointed at me, catching me off guard. "This is Crystal and she's a Shēna just like me and Dad!"

The man's eyes widened and as he looked me up and down, examining me for a while until finally asking, "Are you Eve's kid?"

My eyes widened from the sudden accusation, but I still had to shake my head.

"Close. She was my grandmother. You knew her?"

"She was a friend of mine when I was a child. We fought side by side against the Queen of Darkness."

"Who's the 'Queen of Darkness'?"

"It's a long story for another time." He turned his attention to Ana and said, "You look familiar too. Since she's related to Eve, if I had to make a wild guess, I'd have to say that you're closely related to Aza, aren't you?"

"You can tell?" Ana asked, almost shocked.

"Eve and Aza were close friends. It only makes sense for their descendants to stay just as close. Now, come on. It looks like you three have been through the wringer. Let's get you guys cleaned up."

***

I gazed at the mouthwatering meal in front of me. The large steak in the center of the plate with newly grown vegetables sprinkled across the sides looked irresistible. My sister, Ana and I dug in at the dinner table immediately forgetting all our manners.

"So, Ana," Tal said, "how's Aza? Is she safe?"

"Yeah, she's safe," Ana answered. "But worrying about her is pretty much a waste of time if you ask me. She can take care of herself better than most people can."

Tal laughed and said, "Well that's to be expected from a Zubarian. You all age like fine wine and just get stronger as the years go by. And you'll probably end up just like her. I can already see it."

"How so?"

"It's the way you carry yourself. There's a strength to it. Just like your mother."

Ana smiled at the compliment as Tal turned to me and asked, "How's that old witch, Eve?"

"Dead," I answered, too focused on the food to go into any details.

"What? Dead?" He almost choked on his food before asking, "How? Was it in battle?"

"I'm not sure, I never knew her. She died before I was born, and my mother never told me much about her."

"I guess I shouldn't be too shocked. Almost all Shēna have been on the run for years. But Eve, she was powerful. I guess it just goes to show you that none of us are safe anymore."

"Yeah ... none of us."

He was right. None of us were safe. Even people like me. People who had never even known of magic. People like my sister. And people like my parents. None of us were safe because we posed some sort of threat to the royal's way of life.

"Tal," I said, "I detest that thought."

"I do too, but that's just the way things are now."

"How can you say that? How can you accept an existence like that?" I shouted. "They probably killed her. Eve, I mean. And you know who else they killed? My parents. The children of Eve. The children of your friend." Everyone at the table started to shrink into their seats as I spoke. And they remained silent. "Just last week my parents were murdered right in front of my eyes. My sister's clothes are currently stained in their blood! I would do anything to hurt them like how they hurt us! You agree with me, don't you? They need to be stopped."

Tal took a more serious position as he agreed, "Yes, I believe that they do need to be stopped."

"Good, then I need to ask something of you."

"What is it?"

"I need you to help me stop them. I'm looking for other Shēna to help me. I want to get as many as possible to go to war against them."

Tal sighed and said, "Look Crystal. I wish I could help you; I really do. But I have a family of my own that I have to protect. I can't go out to war from such flimsy plans made by a child. It would put my family at risk. And besides, I no longer have a Spirit Caster."

"You don't? Why? What happened to it?"

"I passed it down to my daughter, Alizeh. At the moment, I'm powerless so even if I wanted to go to war, I'd be no help to you."

Alizeh slammed her hands down to the table, pushed herself onto her feet and blurted out, "I can be of help to you!"

"What do you mean?" Tal asked her.

"I can fight. I can help her in her war."

"Absolutely not, young lady!" Her mother ordered. "It's too dangerous for a young girl like yourself."

"But Mom, I'm ready for this! Isn't this the entire reason I learned how to use the Spirit Caster?"

"Alizeh," her father cut in. "The reason I taught you how to use the Spirit Caster was to simply pass it on to you so that the magic wouldn't die with just me. It's my legacy."

"Father. You were a warrior. You fought in wars, against forces of complete evil. *That* is your legacy. I want to carry on that legacy and bring down the people who wronged us!"

Her father stayed silent. It seemed like he was *actually* going to reconsider until her mother cut in.

"This is ridiculous! We are not sending our daughter to war!"

He seemed to have snapped out of his thoughts and nodded his head in agreement.

"Yes. You're right," he nodded before looking at me. "I'm sorry, but we can't help you. You three can stay here for as long as you'd like, but we can't aid you in your battle."

***

"I can't believe they won't let me go!" Alizeh yelled aloud in front of the house, pacing back and forth. "I'm ready for this. This is what I've been training for, right?"

"Well, you *did* almost die earlier today," I added. "Maybe your father is right. Maybe you're not ready for something like this."

She glared back at me and I quickly avoided eye contact with her while looking up at the starry night sky. I continued to rock back and forth on the porch swing, pretending to not notice her death stare. Wren and Ana were tired and decided to call it a night, so it was just Alizeh and myself outside.

"Well, I'm probably more capable at using a Spirit Caster than you!" she yelled.

"That's not saying much. I don't even know how to use this thing."

"Really?" she dropped the attitude. "Have you ever cast any spells with it?"

"Only once. It was in a life-or-death situation. And to be honest, I don't even remember how I did it. It was like the words just ... came to me."

"Come here. Bring the wand."

"Why?"

"Just come."

I got up from the swing and walked down the porch steps to Alizeh while pulling out my Spirit caster. She also pulled her own out, closed her eyes and took a deep breath while holding her wand off to the side. It started to glow with a green tint. The patterns carved into the wand were more visible. They were like wavy squiggly lines. The light seemed to flow in the creases of them and the air around her started flowing and created wind that almost blew me back for a second.

"Can you awaken the spirit caster like this?" Alizeh asked.

Imitating her movements, I closed my eyes, stretched out my Spirit Caster, and took a deep breath trying to concentrate. But there was nothing. It didn't glow or make any reaction at all. Not like how Alizeh's did. It was frustrating but expected.

"Do you remember the first time you used the power of the Spirit Caster?" she asked.

"Vaguely."

"What were you feeling before you used it?"

"I felt cold. And desperate," I answered.

"Desperate? How so?"

"I had no other choice. It was to determine whether me and my sister would live. There was no *feeling*. I abandoned every emotion I had. I didn't do it because I wanted to but because I had to."

"Then let's recreate that lack of feeling. Don't do it just because I'm asking you to. Do it because you have to. Because you won't win without it."

I repeated the process, closed my eyes and slowly let out a deep breath. I let go of everything and just felt the cold. My mind drifted back to that night. Seeing my parents die and saving Wren. I couldn't get Kira's face out of my head. The face of the woman I was going to kill. Suddenly I felt a jolt of energy shoot through my body as if I were struck by lightning.

It felt exhilarating. I felt powerful. It felt like the first time I cast a spell.

I opened my eyes to see that my Spirit Caster was glowing blue, showing the beautiful snowflake patterns carved into it. The grass around my feet was frosted over. Tiny crystals of snow flew around me.

"What is this feeling?" I asked.

"That's the feeling of Rēa being awakened throughout your body," she smiled.

"What's 'Rēa'?"

"Rēa is the dormant energy inside of a Shēna's blood. It's what powers the Spirit Casters and allows us to do feats that seem supernatural to the average human."

"What kind of feats?"

Alizeh grinned at me and jumped up high into the air above my head, landing on the roof of her house.

"W—woah!" I gasped, amazed at the leap. "How can I do that?"

"Just jump," she laughed.

I kneeled down, readying myself for the jump and pushed myself off the ground going higher than I ever thought was possible. I landed right next to her, almost falling on my face but still able to catch myself.

"Wow! I would have never known that anyone could possess this much power," I told her.

"It's all because of the Spirit Caster. Remember, when a Shēna is in close contact with a Spirit Caster, it ignites the Rēa in both the being and the object. One cannot work effectively without the other."

"So it's a symbiotic relationship?"

"Precisely, never lose that wand or you won't be able to tap into that power."

"What else can I do? Can you teach me how to use spells?"

"Well, that'll be difficult since we have two entirely different Spirit Casters," she said as she started to ponder the situation. "Oh, I know! Just ask my dad. I'm sure he'll be happy to help you. He taught me everything I know so he'd be a better teacher anyway. You should ask in the morning though; it's getting pretty late."

The thought of training with the wand piqued my interest. But I couldn't get too excited because at the moment, I was tired. It had been a week since I had a decent night's sleep, and I was looking forward to it.

CHAPTER THIRTEEN
CRYSTAL

*B*oom!

The house shook me awake. Wren wasn't by my side and neither was Ana. I jumped out of bed and rushed out the guest room, coming to a grinding halt once I reached the kitchen.

There was no danger. Wren wasn't missing. She was standing in the kitchen, mixing a bowl of flower while Alizeh's mother was cutting vegetables on the counter.

"Oh, good morning, Crystal," Wren greeted.

"Good morning?" I said back, wondering if the loud sounds and shaking were just a dream.

"Crystal," Alizeh's mother called, "You never mentioned that your sister was an amazing cook."

"Uh," I shook my head, trying to get my composure back, "yeah, our mother taught us. Wren started to learn a little younger than I started, so she knows her way around a kitchen."

"Well, your mother did a wonderful job teaching her. I can't even teach Alizeh how to hold a spatula, much less make an entire meal. She'd rather spend her time either playing with the barn animals or fiddling around with that wand."

Boom!

The house rattled once more.

"Speak of the devil," she shook her head and rolled her eyes.

It started to become clear to me. "Was that—"

"Alizeh?" she answered. "Yeah, it was. She's at it again."

I walked out of the kitchen, passed the living room, and went through the door. I needed to know what she was doing to cause such a commotion. Once I made it outside, all I could see was uneven land. Small craters littered the entire area. But Alizeh was nowhere in sight.

Suddenly, something fell from the sky and crashed right in front of me, causing dirt and dust to fly into the air. It was Alizeh, and she had cuts and bruises all over her body. She stumbled to get herself back onto her feet while yelling, "Did you guys see how fast I went that time?"

The statement left me speechless. Any human who would fall from that height and speed shouldn't be able to stand, much less survive. But Alizeh stood just feet away from me with a smile on her face and a spark in her eyes.

"It doesn't matter how fast you go," her father said as he walked up to us. "The entire point of your training today is to work on your landings."

"But I still landed, didn't I? Why does it matter *how* I land?" Alizeh argued.

"Because constantly using your Rēa to shield yourself from the fall is a waste of your energy. Not to mention the fact that every time you crash land, you mess up a section of our yard!" He told her sternly.

"Alright, alright, I'll slow down next time." Alizeh turned her attention to me and said, "I'm glad you're finally up. You ready to start training?"

"You two are going to train together?" Tal smiled.

"Well, actually," I started, nervous to ask the question, "I was wondering if *you* could help me train."

"You want *me* to train you?"

"If it isn't too much trouble, then yes. I *need* to learn how to use spells like Alizeh."

"I don't think I'm the right teacher for you. If you had a Wind Spirit Caster, then it wouldn't be a problem. I could teach you everything I know. But I don't know much about the Ice Spirit Caster."

That wasn't the answer I wanted to hear. At the moment I was weak. Kira's power was out of this world. I only knew one spell. And all it was good for was running away. If I was planning to take her down, then I needed this.

"Tal, please. With the current power I have, I don't stand a chance against the princess. If you can't help me fight them, please teach me how to fight for myself. Anything you can teach me, no matter how small, will help."

Tal crossed his arms and looked over to Alizeh who smiled back at him, seemingly already knowing his answer.

"Alright," he finally said, "I think I might know a few things to start you off with." He turned around and started to walk off while saying, "Alizeh, work on your landings."

"Got it! ***Paírno Ptísi!***" she said while blasting off into the sky, leaving a cloud of dust behind her.

"Crystal, come with me."

I followed him and he led me to the side of the house. It was there that we passed Ana and Silver. Ana held a spear in hand, took aim at a nearby scarecrow and chucked the spear right at it. Unfortunately, she missed it entirely.

"Damnit!" she shouted.

Ever since she lost her right eye, her aim's been off. The week we spent getting here she couldn't properly hunt and now it seems like she can't properly fight either. I could feel the heat from her rage and frustration, so I decided not to bother her. I'm not the best at consoling people so I just decided to give her space for now. Besides, I'm sure I'm the last person she wants to hear from since the only reason she lost it was because of me.

We walked a few minutes away from the house causing me to ask, "Why'd you take me all the way back here?"

"Two reasons. The first is to get you out of Alizeh's way so she doesn't accidentally kill you while trying to figure out how to land. The second reason is because I don't know how powerful you are. Wouldn't want you accidentally destroying my house."

"Two fair points."

"Well, now that you're out here, tell me. Do you know how to activate the full power of your Spirit Caster?"

I held my wand out in front of me and released its power on command. A look of shock appeared on his face before he formed a smile.

"The amount of Rēa inside you is a lot higher than I thought it would be. I shouldn't have expected anything less from the granddaughter of Eve." The praise made my cheeks change a shade. He continued, "Since you have so much power this actually might work."

"What might work?"

"I don't know how to perform any of these spells, but I've spent a lot of time around your grandmother on the battlefield. Throughout that time, I've seen and heard the names of some of those spells."

"What are the spells?"

"*Ríza Págou, Pagokrýstallos, Págo Toícho,* and *Cheimerinó Fengári.* But let's work on the first one for right now."

"Alright, so how do I do it?"

"It's fairly simple. Just make sure your Spirit Caster is grounded. The spell works by forcing ice to travel on a surface until it reaches its target. Eve used this to trap her opponents."

I crouched down on one knee and stabbed the wand into the ground. "Like this?" I asked.

"Yes. Now all you need to do is say the words *'Ríza Págou.'*

"Ríza Págou?"

"Yes, but with more conviction. Every word that a Shēna speaks holds power. Our voice is the trigger. If you pull it with the intent to destroy or create, then you'll do just those things."

I looked back down at my wand and concentrated. ***"Ríza Págou,"*** my voice echoed, causing ice to inch out of it and freeze the surrounding grass. But it couldn't spread out more than a foot in radius. "It's not doing much."

"That's because you're new to this."

"How do I make more?"

"Hard work, dedication, and most importantly, repetition. I'll leave you to it."

"Where are you going?"

"To check on my daughter. I need to make sure she hasn't killed herself in the middle of her own training."

As he walked off, I looked back at the ground. My grandmother used this spell to trap people, but I couldn't even spread it far enough to trap an insect. It made me realize that I had a long way to go before I was ready to take on Kira. But that fact only made me want to try harder. I promised myself that I would learn this spell before nightfall so there wasn't an ounce of hesitation in my words.

"Ríza Págou!"

***

Night fell too quickly.

"***Pagokrýstallos!***" I shouted, trying to move on to another spell. But just like the other one, it was no use. I could barely produce a semblance of magic.

"Hey, Crystal," I heard Ana say from behind me. I glanced back to see her and Alizeh standing not too far away from me. "Dinner's ready," she continued.

"I'll be there in a minute," I told them before trying yet another spell. "Págo Toícho!"

"You should really take a break," Alizeh urged. "You've been at this all day."

"I can't take a break yet," I argued. "I haven't done a single one of these spells right!"

"It's because you're too flustered," Ana figured.

"And what exactly do you recommend for me to remedy that?" I barked.

"Calm down Crystal, Ana has a point," Alizeh said while raising her arms up to calm me as if I were a raging beast that needed to be tamed. "Your emotions are all over the place. When I first started training with my wand I was frustrated too. But letting my rage take over never helped."

I tried to calm myself and asked, "How did you get over that hurdle?"

"I just have fun with it," Alizeh laughed. "I think about everything that makes me happy and I just go with the flow."

Ana turned to me and asked, "What makes *you* happy?"

I tightened my grip around my Spirit Caster and asked, "What makes *me* happy? My family. *That's* what made me happy. But they're gone. It's just me and Wren now. How is Wren supposed to—," my voice cracked and my eyes watered as they both started to back away from me, "how am *I* supposed to just 'go with the flow' when we've lost everything?"

"Crystal," Alizeh interrupted, "look at your feet."

I did as she said and saw ice slowly spreading around the ground I was standing on.

"Whatever it is you're feeling," Ana said, "no matter how painful it is, keep it locked in your mind. It looks like that's the key to drawing out your power."

I felt so empty inside. Like I could drown in my sorrow, and it could actually kill me. The only other feeling that rivaled it was the intense rage I'd been feeling ever since I fought the princess. To know that I had to feel this way every time I wanted to draw my power sunk me even lower.

"What are you waiting for?" Ana continued. "Are you going to show us the spell you've been working on all day or what?

Her words lit a fire in me. She reminded me that this wasn't just something that I wanted to do but something that I *had* to do. I went back down on my knee and stuck my Spirit Caster in the ground once more before yelling, ***"Ríza págou!"***. The ice quickly spread a few meters out around me and froze the reeds along with Ana and Alizeh's feet.

"I ... I did it," I blurted out.

"I knew you could," Alizeh said as Ana gave me a smirk of approval.

This was my second time performing a spell and I felt just as powerful as I did the first time. It looked like I actually had a chance to pull this off. I might've actually been able to kill Kira.

"But hey, Crystal," Alizeh continued, "my feet are freezing. Could you please release the spell?"

"And can you do it quickly?" Ana added. "I've been waiting to eat for hours."

"I would but," I started to say nervously, "I don't exactly know how."

"Oh, yeah," Alizeh gave a weak laugh. "I guess you wouldn't since this is all new to you."

Ana rolled her eyes and groaned, "This is gonna be a long night."

CHAPTER FOURTEEN
CRYSTAL

I woke up early the next morning to start my training. Alizeh sat on the branch of a nearby tree while Ana and Silver sat under its shade.

"So, what's the next spell?" Alizeh asked.

I stretched out my arm with my Spirit Caster in hand and spoke, ***"Pagokrýstallos."***

My wand started to freeze over as ice protruded from both ends like a long icicle. Once it finished freezing, it took the shape of a long spear-like weapon made completely of ice, with the wand at its base.

"Woah, that's so cool!" Alizeh exclaimed. "Is that like a weapon or something?"

"Looks like it," I answered as I gripped it with both my hands and got into a fighting position. I practiced with it, thrusting a few jabs the same way my father taught me to handle a spear.

"Sloppy," Ana said bluntly.

"What?" I snapped.

"I mean it's pretty standard form if you were trying to kill a bear or something, but if you were to go against a knight with moves like that then it would mean instant death on your part."

"Would you like to show me how it's done, then?" I challenged.

Ana slowly got to her feet and looked around until her eye landed on a gardening hoe leaning against the tree. She picked it up and twirled it around at high speed.

"Wow," Alizeh gasped. "You're so fast."

"I'm just warming up," Ana said with a nonchalant tone. She soon stopped twirling the tool and said, "I think the best teacher is experience."

"You wanna spar?" I asked.

"I wanna see what you're made of."

"What if I hurt you? Or kill you? Our weapons aren't exactly on equal grounds."

"It's fine. You'll need that advantage if you don't want me to kill you."

I knew she wasn't all talk. I'd seen her fight and kill. She was an absolute monster who I could lose to even *with* the advantage.

"What are you waiting for?" She continued. "An invitation? If so, then go ahead. Make the first move. And come at me as if you were trying to kill me or you won't have a chance."

If she really wanted me to show her what I was made of then I wasn't going to disappoint. After gripping both hands on my ice spear, I ran to her at full speed and thrusted my spear towards her face, but she was able to block the attack by using her tool to push mine away. She then stretched her hand over to my chest and effortlessly pushed me back by a few feet until I landed on the ground.

"Remember Crystal, your weapon is only an extension of you just like your arms and legs. In battle, you should utilize every ounce of your body just as you would your weapon."

I immediately got back up and put my whole body into it but, this time, all she did was dodge and block with the tool. I couldn't get a single hit on her no matter how hard I tried.

"Come on Crystal, you'll have to do better than that. Strike faster! Thrust harder! Attack me with the intent to kill! If you don't then you'll never get your revenge!"

Something in her words set me off. The same energy that I felt rush through my body when I said a spell returned to me in that instant, making me stronger, faster and more determined than ever. I sped towards her and put in one final thrust. She tried to block but was too slow. Once my spear made it an inch away from her face, she tilted her head to the side but still wasn't fast enough. The ice scraped right against her right cheek, forcing blood out with it.

I did it! I finally cut her! It was just a scratch, but it was more than she thought I could do. In all honesty, I was probably only able to reach her because of her damaged eye, but surpassing her expectations only angered her.

All I could see in her eye was rage and before I could even react, I was hit with a flurry of blunt attacks all over my body before she sent me flying with a kick to the gut. The attack didn't last longer than five seconds, but my entire body felt as if it was hit by a boulder.

Ana walked up to me and stretched her hand out for me to grab while saying, "Sorry, I don't know what got into me."

I grabbed her hand, and she pulled me back up to my wavering feet.

"Ana, that was insane!" Alizeh shouted as she jumped down from the tree. "My eyes couldn't even keep up with that last attack! Where did you learn to fight like that?"

"Well, my father taught me the basics before he passed."

"He must've been some teacher," I gauged. "You fight as if you've been training for an entire lifetime, yet you're still not much older than I am."

Ana turned around, tossed the tool to the ground and made her way back to Silver while saying, "It's probably because I'm Zubarian."

"What's that?" I asked.

"I heard that they're a race of really powerful warriors," Alizeh answered.

"We *were* a really powerful race of warriors," Ana corrected as she sat back down with Silver. "But just like the Shēna, we were driven to extinction. I've never even met another Zubarian besides my mother and father."

"Really?" Alizeh asked. "There's no one besides you?"

"Well, there was this person I fought recently. The woman that took my eye. She might've been one, but I don't know for sure."

"How did they go extinct?" I asked. "Was it because of the Royal Family?"

"Not entirely. It was actually your race as a whole that drove us to extinction."

Alizeh shared a look with me before asking, "The Shēna did this?"

Ana nodded, saying, "There was a war between us, and you guys came out on top."

"Ana, I'm sorry," I apologized.

"Don't be. All that's in the past now. And besides, you guys are in the same exact situation as me. That means we should be working together to take down the people who've wronged us and I know for a fact that the Royals had the biggest part to play in both of our annihilations. I wanna take them down just as badly as you do, so make sure you master those spells as soon as possible."

I looked at both of them and realized that I wasn't the only one fighting for something. I wasn't the only one who was wronged by the princess's bloodline and no matter what, they needed to be stopped.

"Well it's not just spells," I told her. "I need to learn how to fight."

"And you want me to teach you?"

"Is that going to be a problem?"

"Not for me. It's just going to be painful for you. Getting to my level in such a short time won't be easy."

"I know. So, let's get it over with."

Ana gave me a mischievous grin. She was going to enjoy having a new punching bag to work with, but I was going to show her that I wasn't so easy to break.

CHAPTER FIFTEEN
CRYSTAL

"Crystal," Ana called at dawn with a loud whisper. "Wake up. We need to go."

"What?" I asked, barely awake. "Why?"

"They're here," Ana said while looking out the window.

"Who's here?"

"Who do you think?"

The realization of who it was had me wide awake. I quickly got up to my feet and looked out the window with her. There was a trail of soldiers all clad in black armor beginning to surround the house. Leading them was a tall and massive man. He was bald and had a long, thin gray beard. His brown cloak flapped in the wind, revealing his holster. A holster similar to the one that Alizeh used for her Spirit Caster.

Is he also a Shēna? I thought to myself. It didn't matter. What really mattered was that they found us. I don't know how they did it, but we needed to find a way out. Alizeh and Wren woke up at the same time.

"What's going on guys?" Alizeh asked while wiping the crust out of her eyes.

"Wren, get up, we need to get out of here."

She got up, immediately understanding the situation. I grabbed her arm, pulling her out of the bedroom and into the living room. Alizeh's parents were already both out there. Tal was standing at the door.

"Tal! There's—"

"I know," he interrupted, with full knowledge of what was happening. He walked over to the center of the room, grabbed the carpet and pulled it aside revealing a secret trapdoor. He opened it and said, "Climb down here."

I listened to him and climbed down the ladder that led to a long underground tunnel; once I was down there, Wren came following behind.

"The tunnel leads into the woods not too far from here. Go through there and run far away," he said.

I looked up at Ana, waiting for her to follow behind, but she didn't move.

"What are you waiting for?" I asked.

"Silver's locked in the barn. Can't leave without him."

"What?"

"Once I get him out, I'll catch up with you."

"Ana, that's crazy! The place is surrounded! You won't be able to get him out of here without a fight."

Ana grinned and said, "That's fine. I need the exercise anyway." She then looked at Tal and said, "They're probably after you guys too. I'll hold them off for as long as I can. You guys should make your way out of here."

"No, we're staying. This is still our home and I've survived worse. As long as this house is still standing, we're not going anywhere."

"Damnit," I muttered under my breath. If it hadn't been for my sister, I would have stayed and fought, but she was all I had left. I couldn't have her getting mixed up in this. "You better keep your promise and stay alive."

"That's the plan," Ana smiled. "Now go!"

CHAPTER SIXTEEN
ALIZEH

I jumped out of bed and raced to the door, watching Crystal and Wren go down into the secret tunnel. I wasn't too sure of what was happening, but I knew it was serious. My father shut the trapped door and glanced over at me, giving me an intimidating look.

"Stay in your room and don't come out until I say so," he said in a stern tone.

I nodded my head and went back into my room, closing the door behind me. I heard banging coming from the front door and looked through my keyhole to see what was happening. Ana went to hide while my father opened the door to greet a large muscular man wearing a brown cloak.

"Can I help you?" my father asked.

"My name is Adam Stone," the man said in a deep voice, "and I am a member of the Five Armaments of War. My crew and I are looking for an ancient relic called the Wind Spirit Caster. We have reason to believe that it's in this household."

This was bad. If they were truly only there for the Wind Spirit Caster, then that would mean they had no idea that Crystal was even here. She wasn't in any real danger, but me and my family were.

"Sorry, I can't say I've ever heard of such a thing," my father lied.

"Really?" Adam asked, completely doubting his answer. He looked over to my door and gave my father a quick smirk. I quickly moved my eye from the keyhole, hoping he didn't notice me. "Alright, sorry to bother you then. I'll be taking my leave now."

I heard his footsteps fade away and the door shutting. I slowly opened the door, peeking my head through. My father looked at me with a scowl that didn't seem intended for me.

"Alizeh, get the Spirit Caster," he said in a stern tone.

I ran back into the room and grabbed my holster and Spirit Caster, but a rock came crashing through my window, forcing me to scream from the shock. A soldier jumped through the window and was ready to pounce before Ana slammed through the door to confront them. They charged at each other, but Ana got low and swept her leg under theirs, forcing him to hit the ground. Once he was down, she slammed her foot down on his face, instantly knocking him out.

She looked back at me and said, "Let's go."

We ran out of my room and back into the living room where my parents were, but as soon as we entered, more glass shattered with soldiers following behind. They even managed to break the door down. Four soldiers surrounded us with swords but that didn't stop Ana from going on the offensive.

"Alizeh, stay close," my father ordered, but I already had other plans.

I tightened my grip on the spirit caster and shouted, ***"Grigoros Ánemos!"*** Wind forced me past two of the guards with ease but not before taking the chance to swipe their swords from their grips. "Dad! Ana! Catch!"

I threw the swords over to them and they didn't hesitate to use it to their advantage. With the swords in their possession they cut the soldiers down with ease.

"Good job, kid," Ana grinned.

I couldn't take too much delight in the thanks because, yet again, we were faced with an immediate threat. The floor beneath us started to shake. The walls cracked and dust was raining down.

An earthquake? I thought to myself. It wasn't impossible for there to be one here, but it was extremely rare. And this one felt different. It felt as if I was surrounded by Rēa. This was magic and the entire house was collapsing.

"Come quick!" My father opened the trap door and looked shocked. I ran to it to see nothing but darkness. The hole was deeper. There was no longer any foundation for the house, and it was sinking underground.

I had to think fast. If we were sinking down, then the only way we could go was up. I hadn't mastered the spell yet, but I thought this was the perfect time to practice it. I raised my wand up, activated its Rēa and shouted.

"Paírno Ptísi!"

Wind blew around the entire room, circling around us. It lifted us off the ground and forced us up into the air. The wind was so powerful that it blew a large hole through the second floor and the roof, allowing us to exit into the air without crashing through anything. I looked down at the house to see that it was almost entirely sunken underground and destroyed. My home, my livelihood was completely destroyed by the hands of one man.

I looked down at the man who destroyed everything. Adam, a member of the Five Armaments. I'd remember that name. That was a promise. Our eyes locked. He looked up at me with a sadistic grin on his face that made me sick.

I calmed myself and concentrated on the spell, lowering us to the ground in front of the group of soldiers. Once back on the ground, I stood up straight with my wand still in hand.

"Ha, so you're the Shēna I was sensing? You look like you're the same age as Delta. How do all these children keep getting their hands on such powerful weapons?" Adam laughed.

"Do you think this is funny? Completely destroying my home is a joke to you?" I yelled.

"How else would I have been able to snuff you out? Personally, I think causing a fight inside the house would have been problematic."

I took a couple of steps towards him until I felt a tugging on my arm. I looked back and saw my mother holding me back with tears on her face. "Don't fight," she cried. "Just give him the wand and maybe he'll spare us!"

"I'm sorry Mom, but I can't do that," I told her. "I can't let him get away with this."

I pulled my arm forward and started walking to him again.

"One of you, stop her!" She yelled at my father and Ana.

"Alizeh!" he yelled at me.

"You can't stop me dad!" I yelled back. "I won't let him disrespect your legacy!"

"I wasn't going to stop you," he said, catching me completely off guard. It forced me to stop myself and look back at him to make sure I heard him correctly. "I was just going to tell you to kick his ass."

The thought made me smile. But it wasn't satisfying enough. I wasn't just going to *'kick his ass'*. I was going to *kill* him.

Wind spiraled around me. My entire body felt energized from the boosted Rēa in my blood. I was going to go all out against this man.

I looked back and saw Ana running to the barn for Silver while my parents ran the opposite way to get some distance between us, which was a good call. I wouldn't want to end up hurting them in this battle.

Adam raised his hand and snapped his fingers. The knights surrounding him drew their blades and started to ready themselves for an attack. They didn't pose a big threat so disposing of them would be easy.

"Grígoros Ánemos," I whispered under my breath. A gust of wind blew from behind and pushed me forward, forcing me to run with it. The spell made me go much faster than I normally could on my own. That mixed with the Rēa enhancement made me faster than anyone could react.

I ran past some of the knights entering the center of the group and yelled out the spell, ***"Gale Lance!"***

Air spiraled around my Spirit Caster, creating a drill like construct, made entirely of wind. I thrusted it towards one of the knights; it pierced right through their armor, putting a hole straight through their abdomen. I pulled my arm out and he fell straight to the ground. Wet blood splattered and stained my hand. That was the first time I had ever killed a man. It would have weighed much heavier if I had time for it to sink in, but I was still surrounded. There wasn't much time to think.

The knights started to close in on me but before they could swing their blades, I pointed my wand towards the ground and let out another spell. ***"Víaii sfýrigma!"*** I yelled. A powerful explosion of wind erupted under me, lifting me high up into the air and pushing everyone else back. While in the air, I quickly shouted an incantation.

> ***"Swirl out of control***
> ***Consume my enemies' souls***
> ***Show them destruction,***
> ***Anemostróvilos!"***

The wind spiraled around me, keeping me in the air and quickly becoming more and more powerful until it formed into a large tornado. The knights tried to run away but were sucked into it. Adam himself started to get sucked in but he used a spell before it could happen.

"Pétrinos Toíchos."

A wall of stone protruded from the ground in front of him, stopping him from getting sucked in. I soon realized that I wasn't going to get him with this attack so I released the spell, forcing the knights to go flying in all different directions and rain down from the sky. I finally landed back on the ground and waited for him to make the next move.

His wall crumbled down to pieces as he started to say, "Ha! You're stronger than I anticipated! Looks like I'm actually going to enjoy this."

All the rocks from the broken wall started to levitate around him. I prepared myself for whatever spell he was going to use next. Suddenly, the ground under me started to shake and crack. It lifted into the air, and I went flying right along with it. He did the same with the surrounding area.

Dozens of rocks and giant boulders filled the air. I didn't understand what was happening. He didn't say the name of the spell, yet he seemed to be using one so powerful that I would assume he would have to say a full incantation to use it. Could he have been so skilled that he didn't need to use words? If so, that would make his reaction time much faster than mine.

He pointed his wand at me, and all of the boulders went flying in the same direction. I jumped up and shouted, ***"Paírno Ptísi!"*** allowing me to fly up higher in the air. ***"Grígoros Ánemos!"*** I said to make myself faster than before. I used those two spells in combination to dodge the oncoming attacks. I jumped from boulder to boulder, trying to dodge smaller rocks, making my way closer to Adam.

I jumped onto the side of a boulder and was right over him. There was no longer anything in the way of me getting to him. I used the rock to propel myself in his direction.

"Víaii sfýrigma!" I yelled, forcing the wind in the opposite direction, completely destroying the boulder I used for leverage. The wind shot me through the air at a high speed but before I could make it to him, he used another spell.

"Pétrinos Toíchos!"

Another wall of stone shot up, blocking my way. I used my **"Gale Lance!"** to cut straight through the wall. It broke down and I could see that my spell hit him in his left shoulder. Before I could make another move, the ground beneath me elevated itself, making a pillar and forcing me into the air.

If only that wall didn't get in my way. I would have pierced him right through his chest. But it didn't make any sense. He needed to call out the spell for the wall but not his other attacks. Did that mean his spells that focused primarily on defenses were weaker?

If I had to make a guess, I'd imagine he only trained on offense instead of defense. If his reaction time for his wall was slower than his other attacks, then I would have to take full advantage of that. I had to catch him off guard somehow.

But before I could do *that*, I would need to save myself from this pillar. It was still rising. It was going so fast that I couldn't even stand from the pressure.

I used all my strength to roll off the pillar and as soon as I did, I was sent into a free fall. My best bet was to use '**Gale Lance**' once more. It wrapped around my wand and I swiftly got myself into a position where I could control my fall and aim myself towards him.

As I was falling, the pillar started to crumble into pieces and one of those pieces smashed right into my side. The pain almost made me release my wand, but I held on to it tightly. The rocks flew down to the ground before me and started to form into something monstrous and gigantic. It formed a body with a head and arms like some kind of rock monster.

"Attack Iron Golem!" Adam yelled.

It prepared to swing at me as I got closer. I knew my attack wasn't going to be powerful enough to pierce it. There was no time to create an incantation for a move powerful enough to defeat it. I just had to attack and hope I wouldn't die trying.

As soon as I was about to connect with its attack, it suddenly froze. Ice covered its entire body, completely stopping it. Adam and I glanced over and saw a path of ice leading straight towards Crystal.

She was the last person I expected to see here, but I certainly wasn't complaining. Adam lifted a boulder with his wand and threw it at her. This was just the distraction I needed!

I used my *Gale Lance* to break right through the frozen monster, forcing it to shatter into pieces. Tiny ice crystals flew everywhere like an explosion of snow. Adam couldn't see me until I was just a couple of meters away from him. He quickly tried to use the spell, "***Pétrinos—,***" but before he could finish, I stabbed my Gale Lance straight through his chest.

All the floating boulders came crashing down as he started taking his final breaths. He coughed up blood and stumbled away as I removed the weapon of wind. He started to whisper his final words, but I didn't care to listen and instead turned around to make my way to where I last saw Crystal, hoping that she was still alive.

CHAPTER SEVENTEEN
CRYSTAL

The boulder flew towards me and I just barely evaded it by jumping out of its path. I looked back up and saw ice shatter into millions of pieces, creating a cold mist all around us. Once it cleared, I spotted Alizeh standing over the man.

She won! She actually beat him. I knew that she was skilled, but I didn't think she would be able to beat someone that powerful.

I watched some of the battle beforehand. She was graceful. Every move she made was meaningful and carefully planned out. Every attack was powerful as if she herself was a force of nature.

All of the large stone rocks and boulders fell from the sky, crashing down around us. It must have been from the Shēna's death. His spell no longer had any effect on this world.

Alizeh ran over to me and yelled, "Crystal? Crystal are you alright?"

I picked myself up while dusting off and said, "Yeah I'm fi—"

Before I could tell her, she ran to me and hugged me tightly.

"I'm so glad you're ok! If it weren't for you, I would have died! Thank you!"

"I doubt that. From what I just saw, I think you would've still won without me interfering. I simply just found an opening that I thought would make things easier for you."

Suddenly, she was pulled off me by her mother who was crying.

"Alizeh, please tell me you're alright. Are you hurt anywhere?"

"I'm fine, mom," Alizeh sighed. "Just a few scrapes and bruises I think."

Her father caught up, smiled at me and said, "Thank you for helping our daughter."

"It was nothing," I replied. "Alizeh was the one who did all the work. She can truly hold her own in a fight better than I can."

"It seems so," he said, turning his attention from me to his wife. She looked annoyed from his gaze and went deep into thought.

"Fine!" she finally yelled.

"What is it?" Alizeh asked.

"You can go."

"Go where?"

"Go with Crystal. Go on your little journey to fight the royal family."

Alizeh's eyes brightened with great zeal. "Really?" she asked in disbelief.

"Yes, really. I saw your battle. You're stronger than I thought. I'm not like you and your father. I'm not a Shēna. I can't fully grasp all this magic stuff, but from what I saw, I could tell that you're more powerful than I could have ever imagined. You reminded me of your father when he was young. At that time the world needed him. And now I think the world needs you. I also don't want them to get away with destroying our home. Just promise me you'll come back home safe, ok?"

Alizeh embraced her mother and said, "Thank you mother! I will!"

Seeing her embrace her family made me think of my own. For her to be so powerful that she could do something like that made me feel weak. She had not only the power, but also the will to avenge and protect. If only I had that very will from the beginning of all this. I wondered if I could have saved my family just as she did with her own.

***

By sundown, we were all at the harbor, east of Livádia. We had to cross over the ocean if we wanted to reach our next destination. There was an island not too far off from the Black Continent. Phoenix Island was the name of it and on the island lived a Shēna who possessed a Spirit Caster. At least that's what Ana and Aza had told me. I hoped the stories were true.

I crouched down on one knee to meet Wren's eyes and said, "Wren, promise me you won't cause Alizeh's parents any trouble."

"But I want to come with you," Wren argued.

"Wren, we already went over this. It's too dangerous for you to come. Now, the Greens already have a place they can stay, and I hear that there's a lot of space there to play so you should have lots of fun."

"Fine," she sighed. "But I'll miss you."

"I'll miss you too," I smiled. "But don't worry. I'll be back as soon as possible."

She embraced me, holding on tightly. I held her even tighter. Truthfully, I had no idea when I'd be back for her. For all I knew I could've died before seeing her again. But my will was too strong for that. I promised myself that I would return to her. She was the only thing I had left in this world to cherish.

We both finally let go and went over to the Greens. It seemed like they were all having a heart to heart as well. After a group hug, Tal handed a small pouch to Alizeh.

"This pouch contains seventy-five silver coins. It should be enough for you, Crystal and Ana to make it to Phoenix Island, but I'm not sure if it's enough to bring any of you back. It's all we could find from the wreckage," he said after he dropped it into her hands.

"Thank you, Dad. And don't worry. I'm sure we'll figure something out when we get there."

Ana came walking over with Silver beside her and said to Tal, "Thank you for agreeing to keep an eye on Silver while I'm gone."

"No need to thank me. You two helped save our lives. The things you're asking for are nothing compared to that."

Suddenly we heard the captain shout, "All aboard!" Catching our attention.

"Well, looks like that's us," I told everyone.

"Let's go before they leave!" Alizeh started to run. "Bye mom, bye dad!"

"You three stay safe," Tal told us.

"We'll try," Ana said.

"Until we meet again," I waved.

We ran on board to the back of the ship and waved them off as the ship's anchor was raised and we set sail, not knowing what to expect on this new journey.

PART THREE
BURNING RESOLVE

CHAPTER EIGHTEEN
KIRA

The long dining table stretched across the room, creating a large gap between my father and I. At this point it felt normal. Even without the comically large surface, my father and I were both distant.

A servant walked into the room to take my empty plate and replaced it with another. The new plate was filled with a dozen black truffle macaroons. My favorite dessert.

They weren't always my favorite. When I was younger, I hated them. Tasted too sweet. I only eat them now because they remind me of my mother. They were *her* favorite.

It felt like just yesterday when she laughed with me at this very table. I lost her too soon. She died five years ago in the middle of childbirth.

It's crazy to think that if things went a little differently, then she would have still been here, and I would have had a younger brother or sister by my side to laugh with too. I missed that so much. Just being able to make noise without it feeling tense.

I couldn't bear it anymore. I had to kill the silence somehow. Even if it meant starting small talk with my father, which I knew he surely hated.

"Father," I said after clearing my throat. "How do you feel?"

He looked at me with a dissecting look and said, "Why do you ask?"

"Oh, it's just ... I noticed that you've looked more sick lately. And your coughing fits have gotten worse."

He gave me a scowl and said, "This isn't the time for you to worry about me. You need to be worrying about yourself more. Your skills are lacking. Have you been keeping up with your training?"

"Of course I have," I lied. The truth was that I had been skipping it to spend more time with Ranne.

"Well, you need to work harder. That novice with the Ice Spirit Caster was easily able to escape you."

"I'm sorry father. It won't happen again."

"Yes, that is true. Because that's the last time I'm putting you on a mission like that. You have something much more important that needs your attention anyway."

"And what would that be?"

"Prince Arnold, of course. He's coming tomorrow so make sure you look good for him and be on your best behavior."

"Yes, father," I sighed. I had completely forgotten that he was going to make an appearance. Against all my will I had to put on a smile and act like all was well. All for my father's sake.

***

The next day I sat at the black marble table across from the golden haired prince. His escort was standing by his side while Ranne stood by mine. The boring white room was fitting since it matched the bland personality of the prince.

"So there I was, riding on the waves at the coast of Phoenix Island," Arnold rambled. I wasn't paying too much attention to what he was saying, but I made it look like I was. I stared into his golden eyes, nodding at every other word that came out of his mouth with a smile that I hoped wasn't overly exaggerated.

He was the prince of Phoenix Island and I was his bride to be. A title I wasn't proud of, but a necessary one. Phoenix island wasn't a part of the Black Continent and marrying my way into his family would lead us to the path of owning that piece of said land.

The small island would have never been a goal for us if it weren't for the legends that surrounded it. It is said that there lives a powerful Shēna but none of our knights have been able to step foot on the island to investigate the claims. The outcome could spark a meaningless war. Even if we could easily win, our reward would hinge on the tail of a simple legend.

This way would be far easier for us to seize control. Even if it's the last thing I'd ever want to do. Pleasing my father comes first.

"And afterwards I was saved by Alexia," he gestured towards his escort. She was silent and pleasing to the eye. Traits that I wished Arnold had.

"Wow, you have such an exciting life," I lied.

"Yes, but I'd bet you've probably had all sorts of adventures better than mine. I heard you were just on a mission to find a relic. How did that go?"

I gritted my teeth and almost snapped at him before Ranne placed her hand on my back for a second, out of Arnold's view. It calmed me for a moment. I probably would have killed him for bringing up my failure in Nótio Págo if she didn't.

Before I answered, Delta walked in through the doors. A welcomed interruption, and one I was truly thankful for.

"What is it?" I asked.

"Your father would like a word with you," she answered.

I stood up, turning my attention back to Arnold and said, "I'm sorry to have to leave like this but there are certain matters I have to attend to."

"Go ahead," he sighed. I almost felt bad, but it seemed like there were bigger and better things to worry about. Delta, Ranne and I made our way to the throne room to see what those matters were.

*****

Once in the throne room, my father said, "Kira, I need you to escort the prince back to Phoenix Island."

"What? But he already has an escort." I argued.

"The King and Queen of Phoenix Island have requested for him to have extra protection for his trip back home. Pirates have been spotted in multiple areas on his route back. They see this as a threat to Arnold's safety. Having you be the one to protect him might just strengthen your bond with him."

I knew there was no way for me to get out of this so I just nodded my head and simply said, "Yes, father," in a half-hearted tone.

"You'll need help on this journey if it proves too dangerous."

"I'll take Ranne with me then," I said as I started to make my way out of the room.

"No. She's not capable enough for a task like this. You need another Shēna like yourself to accompany you. Delta, tag along with Kira, would you."

"Yes, your majesty," Delta bowed.

I wasn't angry at that decision. Out of everyone on the Five Armaments, I hated Delta the least. I hoped that with her, the trip would at least be bearable.

CHAPTER NINETEEN
CRYSTAL

Finally getting off the constantly swaying boat felt restoring. If I had learned anything from this trip, it was that I got seasick *way* too easily. I closed my eyes and took a deep breath, appreciating the stillness of the stable dock.

After opening them again, I took in the beautiful sight of the island. Past the dock was a beach with perfectly white sand that seemingly stretched around the entire island while the thick jungle made for an amazing backdrop to the beach. In the distance was a volcano with smoke pouring into the sky.

"Woah, is that volcano active?" Alizeh asked.

"Seems so," Ana answered.

"Wait, isn't that dangerous?"

The bearded captain of the ship overheard us and decided to cut into our conversation.

"Don't worry, that volcano right there is always active. It's been that way for generations. Yet in all that time it's never erupted."

"What, really? Why's that?" Alizeh questioned.

"Some say it's because of an ancient Phoenix that lives inside of it protecting the island from a fiery doom. It's where the island gets its name. But that's just the legend."

An ancient Phoenix? It sounded absurd. But I'd imagine that I'd be saying the same thing about Spirit Casters if I hadn't used one myself. The thought of venturing off to find such a creature intrigued me, but it was far from my current goal.

"Thanks. Nice to know we won't be melting in lava any time soon," I joked before looking back at him and asking, "Do you know how to get to the nearest town from here?"

"Yeah, there's a path that leads straight to it in the center of the beach," he answered, pointing over to his left. "It isn't a far walk from here."

"Thank you," Alizeh gleefully smiled. I nodded my head and we all made our way off the dock. Once on the beach, Alizeh kicked off her sandals and started running through the soft sand.

"Come on Alizeh, we don't have time to be playing around in the sand," I told her.

"But I've never been on a beach like this before! It's so big! And the sand is so white! And the water is so clear!" she shouted in excitement.

Her actions seemed outrageously childish. It was fitting for her age but jarring coming from her. Just yesterday she was a stone-cold killer and now she was just playing, kicking her feet through the sand as if she didn't have a care in the world.

"We've come a long way from Nótio Págo," Ana said. "I've never even seen a beach. Besides in paintings of course. Maybe we should take a moment to enjoy the scenery."

"Ok, fine. After we find the Shēna we're looking for we can go and relax on the beach for a while. Does that sound good to everybody?" I asked.

"Sounds good to me! Let's go!" Alizeh yelled as she started running to the path.

After some time passed, we finally made it to the town. We were in a wide-open plaza with dozens of small shops and buildings surrounding us. The smell of well-seasoned fish filled the air, making my mouth water.

The crowds made the small city seem amazingly lively as most were in a hurry. Others were relaxed, taking their time and some even stayed stationary at a large fountain that spat streams of water high into the air which sat in the center of it all.

"There's so many people here. How are we gonna find him?" Alizeh asked.

"We ask around," I answered.

As I turned to find a person to talk to, a small child ran into me, making me stumble before I caught myself. The small boy fell right on his behind and looked bewildered trying to figure out what had just happened. He looked up to me and immediately apologized.

"I'm sorry miss!"

"Don't worry, it's fine. Do you need some help there?" I asked while stretching out my hand to him. He grabbed it and I pulled him up.

"Thank you," he said as a young girl slowed down behind, seemingly chasing him in a game of tag moments before. They looked quite similar to one another, so I assumed they were siblings. He was going to start running again but before he could, Ana grabbed him by the back of his collar.

"Hey kid, I need to ask you a question," she told him.

"What is it?"

"Do you know of a Shēna with great magical power that lives on this island?"

"'A Shēna'? Do you mean Flint?"

"Perhaps. Tell me about him," she said while squatting down to his level.

Before the boy spoke again, the girl beside him whispered something in his ear. I had no idea what she said but it got him frightened. He took a quick glance at the Spirit Caster on my hip and nervously said, "I'm sorry, I don't know who you're talking about," before running off in the other direction with the girl.

"Wait!" I called, but it was no use. Both of them were out of sight as they ran into the crowd.

"Well, at least we got a name. Flint, right?" Alizeh asked.

"Yeah it was Flint," Ana confirmed. "Though something tells me he doesn't want to be found,"

"Guess that means it will be a while until we can relax," Alizeh sighed. "Alright, let's get moving."

"Yeah," I agreed.

CHAPTER TWENTY
KIRA

The smell of salt filled the air. The sound of seagulls squawking echoed across the sea. I leaned on the edge of the ship embracing the wind as it moved us through the sparkling waters. The swaying of the boat was calming. It almost made me forget why I was there in the first place.

Delta walked up beside me and said, "You seem to be enjoying yourself."

"It's surprising but, yes actually. I like the peace and quiet."

"Kira," Arnold called. "Would you like to join me for a drink?"

I forced a smile out and put as much pep in my voice as possible before looking back at him and answering, "Yeah, in a minute!" I then dropped my facade and looked back at the sea which only held a single boat not too far away from us.

"I'm guessing you're not looking forward to that drink?" She chuckled.

"What are you talking about? Who would be a better drinking buddy than Prince Charming over there?" I joked.

"What about Ranne?"

Hearing her name out loud so suddenly made me pause for a few seconds. In all honesty, it would make me happier to not only drink with her, but to be by her side. The fact that I wanted her so badly at that moment made me feel uneasy.

"It wouldn't make a difference if it were with her. It would be a waste of my time. What made you think of her anyway?" I asked while looking straight into her eyes.

"Well, you two are best friends, aren't you? I've heard you've known each other since you were both kids. And then there's the rumors."

"What rumors?" I asked, scowling down at her.

"You know, the rumor about you and Ranne constantly running off together for some intimate time alone," she teased.

I clawed my nails into the wood and gritted my teeth for just a second before immediately calming myself. It seemed everyone knew what we were up to. That being said, I would still never admit to it.

"Well, only fools would spread such rumors and anyone gullible enough to believe it is an idiot themselves," I argued as I turned around and made my way towards the prince.

"Kira, I'm not judging you. I think you should acknowledge the way you feel and—"

"The way I feel?" I turned back to her and said plainly, "It doesn't matter how I feel. I'm a Princess and one day I will be Queen over all the Black Continent. My feelings will be completely meaningless by then. My father taught me a long time ago that my emotions are irrelevant."

"I don't completely disagree with that way of thinking, but it sounds like a lonely lifestyle to constantly push away those you care about."

"I don't really care about anyone. You, Ranne, the throne. I don't care about any of it. it's all just—"

I trailed off before I finished, realizing that the boat that used to be a distance away was now side by side with our own ship. The men on it had dirt on their faces and their clothes were torn. The windows on their ship opened to reveal cannons that pointed right at us.

I realized exactly what was going on. Those were pirates and we were about to be under attack. I needed to act fast but before I could move an inch, a cannon fired right at the ship, tearing a hole right through it.

The impact forced me down to my hands and knees. I tried to get back up, but before I could, the boards beneath my feet started to crack. The floor immediately gave out under me and I fell right through it, crashing down into the storage room beneath the deck, gaining a few bloody splinters on impact. I noticed the gigantic hole in both walls that were made by the cannon as I struggled to get up. And if it wasn't for that hole, I wouldn't have been able to see Delta getting thrown overboard.

"Delta!" I screamed as I got up and ran over to the gaping hole in the wall. I peered down and couldn't see her anywhere. I would have dove into the water if I hadn't looked up to see pirates swing from their ship and onto the top of ours.

"Damnit!" I shouted as I pulled out my Spirit Caster. How could I have been so stupid? If I hadn't gotten so heated over what Delta had said I would have noticed the ship coming. This wouldn't have been a problem if I didn't let my emotions take over! I hoped that Delta was still alive. Having my last words to her be *'I don't care about you,'* didn't sit well with me.

I ran towards the steps but once I got to them I looked up and saw dozens of pirates rushing down with swords in hand. I aimed my spirit caster at them and let off a spell.

"Désmi Thanátou!"

A thin black beam of dark energy shot from its tip and pierced through them all, like a needle leading thread through fabric. They all came tumbling down the steps like an avalanche. I jumped over them, finally reaching the top of the stairs, pushed through the door and was greeted by the barrel of a flintlock gun just inches away from my face.

"Make a move, and I'll blow your brains out," the woman holding the gun said. I shook away my surprise and immediately grabbed hold of the gun, pointing it away from myself while aiming my wand to her face.

"Désmi—"

Before I could finish the spell, I suddenly felt something sharp pierce through my arm, forcing me to drop the Spirit Caster. I looked at my arm and saw a dagger had been stuck into it. I took a glance at my surroundings and saw a young man juggling daggers from across the ship.

I heard a clicking sound from the woman's gun as she told me, "Don't make me say it again. Next time, I'll pull the trigger."

She stepped on my wand and slid it across the deck. My eyes followed it as it slid off the edge of the boat and into the water. Every part of my being was telling me to jump off the boat and swim after it, but I had to stay put. If I moved, then I would die. But if I didn't move, then I would be losing not only a piece of *me*, but a piece of my heritage forever.

The situation seemed dire until I heard grunts coming from the other side of the ship. There was a fight between dozens of soldiers and just one guard. But calling it a fight might've been a poor choice of words. It was a massacre.

Body after body fell to the floor in a pool of their own blood. And surprisingly, it was only the pirates falling down. The last guard standing was Arnold's escort, Alexia. She held a double-bladed spear in hand and sliced through the pirates like butter.

"Damnit, they must be a Zubarian," the woman who held me at gun-point deduced. "Everyone, take her down!"

Almost every pirate on the ship rushed her in a desperate attempt to stop her but she didn't lose steam. Unfortunately for us, it *did* buy them time.

"Help!" I heard Arnold cry before being knocked out in his own battle. I looked over to see him being carried away by a massively tall and muscular pirate. He was like a damsel in distress taken by the big bad bandits. It was pitiful.

"Thanks for staying put," the woman smiled sinisterly as she lowered her gun, pointing it towards my foot and firing a bullet into it. The intense pressure made me scream and drop to the floor as she ran away laughing, leaping off our boat and back onto hers with what was left of the crew.

Alexia tried to make it to their ship but was held up by the sacrificial meat shields left behind. She couldn't get past them quickly enough, and the boat started to sail away as ours started to slowly but steadily sink.

I couldn't believe what was happening. I failed for a *second* time! Once again, I was too slow to react. What was wrong with me? I was of royal blood. How could I not only lose to some pitiful snow peasants who lived in the middle of nowhere, but now a group of dirty disgusting pirates?

All I could do was cry in pain, wishing I had my Spirit Caster so I could destroy them. Not only had I lost my pride, but now even my wand! If my father were there with me at that moment, he'd call me a disgrace.

In the middle of my thoughts the boat started to sway more fiercely than before. The waves got higher in strange places, twisting and turning in unnatural ways. One could even call them magical. And if so, that would have been the correct analogy because I could feel it. The high potency of Rēa around me.

Only the Water Spirit Caster could have the power to do such a thing. The owner of that wand was Delta. And just from looking at the size and shape of those ferocious waves, I could tell she wasn't happy.

"Tría Epikefalís Fídi Tis Thálassas."

The voice echoed and could be heard from across the entire ocean. Three pillars of water shot up around the pirate's ship and started to twist and turn until they transformed into the monstrous shape of three serpents. It seemed that Delta was going all out.

Trying to ignore the pain in my foot, I dragged myself across the deck and pulled myself up on a piece of the railing that was still standing. Looking over the edge, I saw Delta standing atop the surface of the water as if it were solid ground. She was holding not only her own Spirit Caster, but mine too. I could feel an outrageous amount of Rēa flowing from her. She was going to destroy them.

"Attack!" She ordered.

The three serpents dived down on the pirate's ship, tearing straight through it, which wasn't a good thing. If she destroyed the ship, then there was a chance she could have killed the prince! If that happened, then our entire plan would fail.

"Delta!" I shouted. "Stop! Arnold is on that ship! You might kill them! Just let them go so we can regroup and—"

"No!" she disobeyed.

"What?" I asked, shocked by her outburst.

"I said no! These pirates not only threatened me and the prince's life. But they have drawn blood from the Black Continent's future Queen!"

The statement shocked me even more than her last. The last thing I told her before this was that I didn't care about her at all. Now she wanted to avenge my injuries tenfold.

"Don't worry princess," she continued. "I won't kill the prince, but I still want to send a message to anyone who would even think about hurting you."

"Oh giant behemoth!
Swallow my enemies now!
Sink them to the depths!
Gigantiaía Fálaina!"

The water in the surrounding area started to glow blue and rise next to the pirates. Before I knew it, a gigantic whale came shooting up from the sea and into the air. It was completely transparent as if it too were made completely of water. It made a whistling sound that made its allure even more beautiful.

The whistling and clicking started to drown out from the horrific screams coming from the pirate ship, which reminded me where this situation was headed. An attack that created life in such a beautiful manner was now being used to end the lives of many in the most fearful way possible: death by drowning.

The humongous whale who was at least four times bigger than their ship dived down onto them, sinking them almost instantly. Water exploded into the air, creating a huge wave that smashed into our boat, almost forcing it over. I had to hold on tight to make sure I myself didn't fall into the water.

It seemed the battle was over before it even began. Even so, there was still an extremely pressing matter that needed immediate attention. Arnold was still on that sunken ship.

"Delta!" I yelled.

"I know!" she yelled back, whipping her wand to the side. ***"Dỹtis,"*** she said before diving down straight into the water.

She was out of sight. Even though she couldn't have been gone for more than thirty seconds, it felt as if I were waiting for an eternity. Finally, bubbles started to rise from the water. There was movement underneath the surface and in a few more seconds, Delta came blasting out of the water and into the air with the prince on her back. She landed on the boat and laid him down.

I hastily crawled over to him while asking, "Is he still breathing?"

Delta pointed her wand to his chest and whispered the spell, ***"Roi."***

The spell forced Arnold to spit up the water that filled his lungs, replacing it with air. His loud coughs and gurgles put me at ease. He was going to survive. Delta rose back to her feet and gave me a stern look.

"You're losing too much blood. I'm going to get some bandages," she said as she walked towards the stairs.

"But what about Arnold?" I asked.

"He'll live. But if we don't stop that bleeding then *you won't*, and our mission will be for nothing."

CHAPTER TWENTY-ONE
CRYSTAL

We questioned almost everyone in town about the Shēna for the rest of the day, but our efforts were fruitless. Other than his first name, we gained absolutely no new information on the man we were looking for. Every single person we asked either dodged the question or told us they didn't know anything about him.

We walked through a slim but crowded alleyway with shops spread out on both sides. Some we could walk into while others had serving windows. It was lively and with lots of commotion, it made the perfect shopping district for tourists.

"I can't believe no one knows anything about this *'Flint'* guy!" Alizeh groaned.

"I don't believe it either. They were probably all lying," I told her.

"But why would they all lie to us?"

"If I had to guess, I'd imagine it's because they're trying to protect him from us," Ana suggested. "If he's truly the protector of this island then I'm sure they wouldn't want to give away his position to a bunch of outsiders. We'll have to figure out a way to show people we're not hostile."

"Well, can we figure it out later? I'm super hungry and we haven't eaten anything all day," Alizeh groaned.

"Yeah, I'm pretty hungry too. How many silver coins do we have left?" Ana asked.

She reached into the sewn pocket of her sundress and pulled out the pouch of coins, emptying its contents into the palm of her hand. "Fifteen," she answered.

"I hope that's enough for the three of us. Now, I wonder where we can go to get some food."

Alizeh stopped in place, staring at one of the shops in the alleyway. It looked like it was inside of a large cubby hole from the way it was built into the surrounding buildings, and was set up like a tavern with six chairs in front of a wide countertop where the food was served. Beyond the counter was the kitchen where there were multiple chefs already hard at work.

Without even discussing it with us, Alizeh immediately sat herself down at one of the seats and showed the silver coins to the chef who stood behind the counter. I wanted to stop her but it seemed like I was already too late.

Ana shrugged and chuckled, "Guess that answers my question."

I reluctantly followed and sat down next to her.

"What can we get for this much?" Alizeh asked the man.

He closely expected the coins while continuously looking back at us. He finally gave us a grin and said, "Don't worry. I've got just the thing for you ladies." He then went further into the kitchen and started working his magic.

A few minutes later, he came back with three plates, placing them all in front of us. The dish had a grilled piece of fish with yellow stripes on it and once I dug my fork into it and took a bite, I could taste its sweet flavor all across my tongue. Its slightly tender texture made every bite more enjoyable than the last.

"Wow, this is great!" Alizeh sang.

"Phoenix island has some of the best food in the world," we heard a voice say from behind.

We looked back to see a handsome young man with chestnut skin and smokey brown scruffy hair. He looked at us with intense golden eyes while wearing a long, red trench coat with fur on the lining of the collar. Its sleeves were ripped off ... or maybe they were burned off? I could only assume since the jacket was slightly tattered and blackened on some edges. The jacket was open, revealing his fairly toned physique.

"That's one of the many reasons why everyone comes to visit this place," he continued while taking a seat next to me. "I'm assuming you three are visiting since you don't look like you're from around here. Except maybe you," he nodded past me and over to Ana.

"And what makes *me* look so ordinary?" she asked him with dissecting eyes.

"Who said anything about ordinary? All the women on this island are fairly exotic compared to most of the world."

"Exotic, huh?" she laughed. "Hear that, Crystal? Because I don't share the same beauty standards as the rest of you, he grouped me in my own category like some wild animal."

"He's definitely a charmer." I joked.

"Sorry," the boy apologized. "It wasn't my intention to insult you."

"Well, whatever your intentions are, you've failed horribly at displaying them," Ana said as she looked away, seemingly losing interest. "Your good looks will only get you so far, *boy*."

The boy rolled his eyes and muttered under his breath in almost a chuckle, "Another woman who can't take a compliment. Typical."

Ana quickly stood from her seat and slammed her hands on the counter while saying, "And another man who can't take a hint!"

"That's funny coming from you. Since you three are the ones searching the island for any *hints* you can get your hands on."

I put myself back into the conversation by asking, "What's that supposed to mean?"

"It means you guys have been going all around town asking everyone about Flint, but from what I can tell I bet you girls don't even know what he looks like, much less, where to find him."

I stood in between Ana and the boy and asked, "What do you know about him?"

He didn't answer. He just stood up and started to walk away.

"Hey!" I called. "Where are you going?"

He turned back to me and answered, "I'm taking you to Flint. That's what you wanted, right? I have a feeling he would want to meet you."

I took a couple of steps ready to follow him, but Ana grabbed me by my shoulder forcing me to lean back to her before saying, "I don't think we should trust this guy."

"Me neither, but what other choice do we have?" I turned to Alizeh who had been silent throughout the conversation. She was staring the boy down hard as if she was still trying to figure him out. "Alizeh, what do you think?" I asked.

"I trust him," she answered.

"Really?" Ana questioned.

"There's something about his spirit. It feels familiar somehow."

"His *spirit?* What do you mean by that?" I asked.

"I mean ... I don't know. I'm too hungry to deduce anything right now."

I took a deep sigh and said, "Alright you stay here and eat. I'll go with this guy to see if he can really get us to Flint."

"I'm coming with you," Ana insisted.

"Alright," Alizeh nodded. "You both be safe."

"Are you girls done going over your little game plan?" The boy mocked. "It's a long walk and I'd like to make it to him sometime *today*."

We all broke from our huddle, and I walked straight to him hoping that I wasn't going to regret this.

"Take us to him."

***

We made some distance between us and the town. For some time, we hiked on a trail that led us through a beautiful green bamboo forest. Although the sight was amazing, it didn't outweigh the fact that my feet hurt as if they had turned to stone from the constant hiking.

"Are you ok?" Ana asked as we trailed a small distance behind him.

"Yeah, sorry if I'm holding you guys back," I apologized. "It just feels like we've been walking forever."

"That's because we *have* been walking forever. It's been over an hour, and I still don't see *any* signs of civilization up ahead. Something doesn't feel right."

"Hey," I called out to the boy, "are we almost there yet?"

He stopped and turned around, looking far past us and into the distance.

"You know what?" he said. "This actually might be far enough."

"Far enough for what?" I asked, feeling uneasy about his statement.

He lost his grin and put on a much more humorless look. His eyes had an intensity added to them as he slowly strolled towards us like a lion would its prey. It was clear that his intentions were never to bring us to the Shēna. I took a few steps back, but Ana stood her ground.

"So, you couldn't be trusted after all. What a surprise," Ana said dryly. "If you didn't bring us out here to meet with the Shēna then what is this all for? Are you trying to rob us? Kill us even? Or something worse?"

"I didn't want anyone else to get caught up in this," he answered while reaching his hand into his coat and pulling out the last thing we could have expected. A Spirit Caster. It was blood red and it glowed with a crimson light, showing flame patterns carved into it.

It was then that Ana took a few steps back along with me, finally coming to the realization of who we were dealing with.

"Flint?" she asked.

He answered with a spell, ***"Pyrkagiá!"***

Searing flames erupted from the earth, completely surrounding and trapping us. The heat was intense yet controlled. He truly was the legendary Shēna we'd been looking for.

"I don't like releasing my flames in the city," he continued. "Out here I can go all out without any worries. You two and that other girl shouldn't have come here."

"Wait!" I shouted at Flint. "We didn't come here to fight!"

He placed his pointer and index finger on his wand and swiped the side of it like a match while saying, ***"Seirá Fotiás!"*** A thin stream of fire spat out of the tip of the Spirit Caster and started flailing around like a whip. He waved it up in the air and then swung the flaming whip right in my direction, but I narrowly evaded the attack by tucking and rolling to the side.

Ana ran to him, throwing a punch but he blocked it with his open hand and with his other hand, swiped his flaming whip at her. She ducked and avoided the flames before jumping back in order to prepare for her next attack.

To even the playing field, she pulled out her daggers and went into a defensive position waiting for him to make the next move. But the appearance of these new weapons only stopped Flint in his place.

"You don't have a Spirit Caster?" he asked. "What are you, their bodyguard?"

Ana didn't take too kindly to the patronizing assumption and ran full speed swinging her blades wildly in his direction. He dodged most of her attacks until she landed two bloody slashes across his chest in the form of a cross. For a moment it seemed like he was in too much shock to move so she went for a finishing blow.

Once her blade got close to him he once again whispered the spell, ***"Pyrkagiá."***

The earth beneath Ana's feet started to crack and glow. She instantly jumped back to avoid the fire that spewed out only a moment later with the only casualty being the singed tips of her long locks. Those last two attacks made me realize that if the fight didn't stop then and there, someone was going to end up getting killed. And I couldn't afford for *either* of them to die.

I stuck my Spirit Caster into the dirt and said the spell, ***"Ríza Págou,"*** causing ice to spread all around me and put a stop to the flames that were rising from the earth. Ana and Flint were running straight at each other, but both abruptly stopped against their will. They both looked down to see that they were trapped in my ice.

"What the hell is this?" Flint gawped.

Ana looked at me and yelled, "You seriously need to get that magic of yours under control!"

"You're the one who needs to get yourself under control!" I argued. "Are you seriously trying to kill the one person we've been searching for?"

"He's an asshole," she shrugged.

"He's the reason we're here!"

"And he was obviously a waste of our time!"

"I'm standing right here," Flint interjected.

"I don't care," Ana told him plainly.

I turned to Flint and asked, "Why did you attack us?"

"Did you expect any other welcome?" he answered. "Ranking officers from the Black Continent aren't allowed to step foot on Phoenix Island. That includes the Five Armaments."

"And *there* it is," Ana explained. "This dumbass thinks we work for The King."

"To be fair," I reminded her, "you thought the same about me when we first met."

"Well of course. When you first spotted that wand, you tried *stealing* it. I think I was justified." She turned to Flint and asked, "What made you think we were a part of the Five Armaments?"

"You have Spirit Casters," he answered.

"So do you!" I argued.

"That's because I'm the only legitimate Shēna left! The rest either work for The King, or they're dead."

I relaxed myself and took a long sigh. "No Flint. You're wrong."

He paused for a moment before saying, "Then why'd you come here? Why were you looking for me if you didn't come to kill me?"

"We came all this way because we need your help. We're going to take down The King of the black continent and his Armaments. We need as much help as we can get and we know you're the right man for the job."

He stared at me for a few seconds, completely silent before bursting out into laughter.

"You think you two and that other little girl who's like, what, *Five*? Can go and take on The King and the Five Armaments? That's rich!" He laughed.

"She's twelve," Ana corrected him, "and she's definitely more powerful than *you*."

"Oh, so you guys are *both* jesters," he joked.

I got us back to the topic at hand by telling him, "I think if you help us, we'll have a chance. We already defeated one of them. If you help us we can defeat the rest. I'm pretty sure there are other Shēna out in the world who can—"

"Listen, Snowflake," he mocked while cutting me off. "You don't have a snowball's chance in hell of pulling off something that big. You're too much of a novice. And that one over there isn't even a Shēna."

"For not being a Shēna, I left a few more scratches on you than you were able to put on me," Ana argued.

"And thanks to my spell it doesn't look like you'll be going anywhere for a while so I think I deserve a better title than *Novice*," I added.

He swung his whip at his feet, breaking the ice instantly and as he shook off the shards he claimed, "I let you two win."

"Really now?" Ana asked, seemingly not believing the statement.

"You had no intention to kill me. I could see it in your eyes during our battle. So I put out that same energy," he explained to Ana before swinging his whip at her feet to help her break free.

He tried walking past us but I stopped him by asking, "So what, you're just not going to help us?"

"I have no intention of going to war with The King of the Black Continent," he answered in a much more serious tone than before. "It's a suicide mission that doesn't benefit me in any way and only puts the people of this island in danger. So no, I'm not helping you. Sorry you wasted your time."

CHAPTER TWENTY-TWO
ALIZEH

It had been at least an hour since I took the last bite of my golden striped fish. Crystal and Ana's fish were cold and hard but I'm sure that was the least of their problems. After my belly was full I was finally in a position to use my head. It became clear why that boy's spirit felt so familiar. He was a Shēna. And probably the one we were searching for.

I didn't understand why he was hiding his identity. Maybe he didn't want to draw attention to himself? Or was it something far more nefarious?

Crystal was a pretty smart girl and would probably catch on to his true intentions. And even if she didn't, Ana is the strongest person I know. With her they wouldn't be in any *real* danger, right?

I got tired of waiting. I needed to know if they were alright. I jumped out of my seat and ran in the same direction I last saw them walk in but my journey didn't take me far. Before I knew it, Crystal and Ana were right in front of me forcing me to come to a grinding halt, stopping myself from running into them.

"Crystal, Ana, you're ok!" I blurted out.

"Yeah," Ana reassured me, "we're fine, kid."

"What happened with the Shēna?"

"He's not joining us," Crystal answered.

"What?" I asked, fairly surprised. "Why not?"

We all made our way back to the counter as Crystal answered, "He doesn't think we can pull it off. And he has no interest in fighting The King."

"This whole trip was a waste of our time," Ana scoffed.

I sat next to them feeling just as defeated. "So, what do we do now?"

"We head to Mount Astrapí," Crystal answered.

"Is there another Shēna there?"

"Yeah. At least that's what my grandmother's spirit told me."

"Ok, but how are we gonna get there? That's all the way back on the Black Continent and we have no coins to get ourselves there. It's also getting dark and we have nowhere to stay."

Crystal slammed her face to the counter as if she was giving up on everything.

"Alizeh, I don't know," she sighed.

Our situation was lousy. We still only had three members in our group and we were now stuck on this Island. There had to be a way we could get money.

I looked over at the chef and said, "Excuse me, sir."

He looked back at me and put down a dish he was cleaning. "How can I help you young lady?"

"Is there a way that we can work here for money?" I asked.

Crystal peaked her head up to see his answer.

"Oh, sorry girly, I don't need any help right now. I've already got a full staff."

After hearing that, Crystal put her head back down and went back to her brooding.

"Hey, did you guys say you needed a job?" A voice called from the back of the store. A young man popped his head from behind one of the shelves. "You know, there's a bounty hunting guild that accepts any help it can get."

That seemed to peak Crystal's interests. She looked up quickly waiting for more information.

"Now Oliver, why would you go and give her a crazy idea like that? She's just a little girl," the chef grumbled.

"Hey, when I was that age me and my friends would always find jobs there. Not every job is dangerous. Some jobs have you catching animals or just collecting some random plants."

Crystal had a different aura about her. She seemed to shake off her negative energy and went back to normal. I could see the determination in her eyes as she said, "Oliver, right? Tell us more about this guild."

***

We pushed through the saloon doors walking into what seemed like a bar filled with a bunch of unsavory looking men and women. It was dark inside, lit only by candles and the tiny bit of moon light that shined through the open windows. I stayed close to Crystal and Ana to make sure we didn't get separated in a foul place like this.

We walked through the dimly lit guild hall passing by all sorts of chaotic events. At one table there was an arm-wrestling contest with people cheering and betting coins. A group of disgusting looking men and women who showed too much skin, in my opinion, were all passionately kissing in a booth. In the corner I could see a group of guys stomping and kicking a single man for reasons I couldn't even begin to imagine.

"Crystal, shouldn't we help that guy?" I whispered.

"No," she answered. "Whatever's happening over there is their business. It doesn't involve us."

Ana didn't even bat an eye to the carnage.

The thought of sitting back and watching didn't sit well with me but I listened to Crystal. She was probably right anyway. We had to stay on task and keep a low profile.

We finally made it to the bar and Crystal said to the bartender, "We need a job."

"All job requests are upstairs," she answered as she cleaned a cup without even looking up at us. It seemed like we were just a bother to her. Like she gets a bunch of people like us all the time.

We went up the stairs which led to a large room with yet another crowd of cheering people. The only difference was that this crowd was larger and much more rowdy. I wondered if it was just another arm-wrestling contest, or something more.

I walked over to the crowd and squeezed my way through. What I saw surprised me. It wasn't just another contest of strength. It was an all-out brawl. And the last person I expected to see there was right in the middle of it.

I felt Crystal grab my shoulder and say, "Alizeh, you can't just run off like—"

Her words trailed off as she looked up at the battle. Flint, the Shēna we encountered before, was in the midst of a fast-paced battle. He fought alone against three others.

Flint kicked one of the men in the leg, forcing him to the ground and grabbed onto his hair to knee the man in the face leaving a blood stain on Flint's pants. Another man came from the side and tried to punch him, but Flint grabbed his arm, twisting it and forcing a loud cracking sound that made me flinch and jump back. The last man swung at Flint with his fist and actually connected. But he'd soon regret it because Flint grabbed him by his arm and flung him into a table, completely shattering it into pieces.

Flint let out a loud shout from his victory while everyone cheered him on. He went to a table, grabbed a piece of paper and raised it in the air. It had the drawing of a beautiful bird with flames for wings.

"Does anyone else have a problem with me taking this job?" He shouted. No one dared to challenge him. Everyone in the room stayed silent. "Ok then," he said as he picked his red coat up from off the floor. The crowd dispersed as Crystal and I stayed in the same spot, unwillingly gawking at him as we tried to process what we just witnessed. Ana was the only one of us who had a different look. Hers was one of intrigue.

"He knows how to handle himself in a fight," she muttered allowed. "I guess he really *was* going easy on me."

Once that realization set in, it seemed like there was a silent rage emanating from her. A feeling I could understand. I'm not a fan of being patronized either.

As Flint was putting his coat back on, he glanced at us and did a quick double take. He looked surprised at first but his face quickly went from confusion to pure joy.

"Snowflake!" he looked to Crystal. "Small child!" he said to me. But he paused once he locked eyes with Ana. After advancing over to us, he finally said, "I don't think I got your name yet."

Crystal crossed her arms and said, "You didn't get *any* of our names yet."

It only took a few seconds for Ana to answer but somehow her tense eyes stretched out the moment to feel like hours. But her eyes weren't just filled with hatred. She was analyzing him. "Ana," she finally answered, reaching out her hand to his.

He took her hand and told her, "Flint," never taking his eyes off hers. At least not until Crystal cleared her throat to remind them that they weren't alone. He brought his attention back to Crystal and asked, "What are you still doing here? I thought you guys would have left the island by now."

Crystal hesitantly answered, "We need money."

"Ahh, boat fair, right?"

"Yeah," she sighed.

"Umm, Flint?" I interrupted. "What was that fight all about?"

"Oh, yeah," he said as if he just remembered something. He reached into his jacket pulling out the same drawing of the bird he held up after his fight. "Check this out. It's the bounty for the feathers of the Phoenix that lives inside the volcano. This is what we were fighting over."

I could feel my eyes widen as if they were going to pop out of my head. He was going to see a Phoenix! A creature that I could only see in my dreams. I wanted to see it so badly, but he had already taken the job. The realization made all of the excitement in my body vanish. He must've sensed it because he immediately continued and asked, "Do you wanna join me?"

The energy that had vanished had been ignited again by his words. "Yes!" I blurted out.

"Wait," Crystal cut in saying, "this mission sounds like complete non-sense."

"Like fighting against an entire kingdom?" Flint mocked.

Crystal didn't acknowledge his taunting. "How much does it even pay?"

"1,000 gold coins," he answered with a smile.

The number sounded almost infinite in my mind. *1000 gold coins*. Just one gold coin was worth somewhere around a thousand silver coins! Gold was extremely rare on the Black Continent. I'd never even seen gold. With that much, we'd never need to worry about money again.

Crystal's eyes widened as Flint continued to say, "I'll take half. You three can have the rest."

"So, what you're telling me is that you're willing to fight off a group of thugs to have this job all to yourself, but now you're willing to just give half of that gold away?" Crystal asked, doubting him.

"I feel bad about not helping you guys out on your little suicide mission. And besides, us Shēna gotta stick together. It's more fun that way, wouldn't you agree?"

He started to stroll off and I eagerly followed behind him.

"Wait, I never agreed to—" Crystal started to shout, but I subconsciously tuned her out, getting lost in the thought of finding the legendary beast.

CHAPTER TWENTY-THREE
CRYSTAL

It was dark in the jungle. The only thing lighting the way was a small flame that Flint made from the top of his wand. Even though I could barely see our surroundings, I could still tell we were going in the wrong direction.

"Where exactly are you taking us?" I asked impatiently. "The volcano is on the other side of the island. Are you leading us into another one of your traps?"

"It's late," he responded. "We're going to get some rest back at my place. It's just up ahead."

The thought of being led back to his house in the middle of the night didn't sit well with me. Last time he led us into the woods he attacked us. I couldn't put all my trust in him just yet. I had to keep my guard up just in case he still had some ulterior motive.

He came to a halt and put out the fire from his Spirit Caster before letting out a spell.

"Eídos Skolopákos."

The darkness that had surrounded us was replaced with a soft light. Fire ignited all around us on torches and small candles trapped in jars. More candles were lit leading my eyes over to his house.

It was a treehouse. The steps curled around the tree, spiraling all the way to the top, where it spread into a balcony. The home itself didn't look all that big or glamorous but that somehow made it more charming.

He put away the Spirit Caster and walked up the staircase, leaving Alizeh, Ana and I to slowly follow him while taking in the amazing warm lights around us.

We walked into the house and the space was small with an old black wooden stove in the corner. One of the walls had a massive bookcase with all sorts of old dingy books, which I found strange because I wouldn't take him to be the reading type. His bed was at another wall; right beside it was a ladder that led to the roof.

"You guys can share the bed," he told us. "I'll sleep up top."

"I don't know," Ana said. "The bed looks a little too small for the three of us."

"Well if it doesn't suit you, then you can always sleep up top with me if you want."

The thought made Ana laugh before saying, "Thanks, but no thanks. I think I can make do with the floor."

"Suit yourself," he shrugged while making his way up the ladder before I stopped him.

"Flint," I called. He stopped and looked back at me. "Thank you, for all of this."

He smiled back at me and said, "Don't mention it, snowflake."

I felt like arguing with him over that nickname but I was too tired. It had been a long day filled with interrogations, fighting, and a lot of walking. I was looking forward to finally sleeping in a bed after so long.

Ana took off her large coat that was tied around her waist and threw it to the ground before dropping down onto it like a tiny bed. "Goodnight, guys," she yawned.

"Goodnight, Ana," we both said back, but it seemed like she was already out.

After plopping down onto the bed, I realized how long it had truly been. The last time I had slept in a bed was when it had been my own. Almost two weeks had passed since everything changed. Just before my entire world was destroyed by that twisted woman. I swore to myself that I would kill her and her father.

"Are you ok?" Alizeh asked while getting closer to me. I didn't realize that my eyes were watering before she asked.

I turned over and said, "Yeah, I'm fine. I'm just really tired."

There was a moment of silence, but she didn't pry. She just put her Spirit Caster and holster on the floor and laid next to me, almost instantly falling asleep. After wiping away my tears and closing my eyes I followed suit not too long after.

CHAPTER TWENTY-FOUR
ANA

A strange sound startled me awake—like whispers from above. I looked up to the ceiling realizing that it was coming from where that boy was sleeping. It was still dark as I looked over at Crystal and Alizeh who were both fast asleep. Being a light sleeper made ignoring the sounds impossible, so I decided to go up there to see exactly what was going on myself.

I rose from the floor and went up the ladder, almost tripping because of how dark it was. Once I peaked my head through the opening, I saw that Flint was still asleep, but he was talking and rolling around as if he were awake. I inched myself closer to him to wake him up until he said words that I could actually make out.

"Summer ... Summer no. Please don't go."

I stretched my hand out to him and gently touched his arm. This startled him awake and he firmly grasped my hand while in a cold sweat, looking in all directions as if not yet realizing he was awake. He looked down at my clasped arm and quickly let go of it, using that same hand to run through his hair. His face and demeanor went from a terrified melancholy filled gaze to a cool and confident grin.

"Ana," he said in a calm voice. "What are you doing up here in the middle of the night? You finally decided to take me up on my offer?" he asked as he started to lean in closer to me.

A cute attempt, but I stopped him with my finger before he could get any closer.

"You talk too much in your sleep. I came up to tell you to keep it down."

"Oh, sorry about that," he laughed. "I'll try."

I was too tired to make any small talk so I made my way back to the ladder and started to climb back down. Before my head was completely out of sight I took another glimpse at Flint. His grin was gone as he looked off into the distance. An emptiness could be seen in his eyes. Against my better judgment, I decided to pry.

"Who's Summer?" I asked.

After saying that name, it seemed that for a moment, something snapped in him.

"How the hell do you know that name?" he barked.

"You called to her in your sleep."

His eyes widened and he regained his cool while saying, "Ha, guess I've got a big mouth on me, don't I?"

He laid back down and said nothing else. I thought it would be better if I had just left but I didn't want to leave him as he was. There was obviously something wrong.

I climbed back up and crawled over to him, sitting by his side.

"So, I'm guessing she was someone important to you, right?"

He didn't respond.

"I'm also guessing that she probably isn't around for one reason or another."

He still stayed silent and that was all the confirmation I needed. He lost someone very important to him and he's not done grieving. A feeling I could connect with all too well.

I laid down beside him, sinking into what felt like a soft fluffy moss and looked up into the beautiful bright, starry night sky. It was obvious why he had no problem sleeping on the rooftop. It was like a small secluded paradise.

"There's a lot of that going around," I continued. "Loss, I mean. Crystal just lost her parents a couple of weeks ago. Watched them get killed right in front of her."

Flint looked at me with shocked eyes and said, "I would have never guessed. She seems so ... composed."

"Yeah, she's not one for emotions. Or at least she's not one to show them. She can be a standoffish asshole sometimes but I think that's only because she's really stressed out about this whole situation. So, if she yells at you again, don't take it too personally."

"I'll try to keep that in mind," he told me before finally facing me. "What's your story?" he asked.

"*My* story?"

"Yeah. I'm guessing that whoever you lost is driving you on this crazy mission too, right?"

"No, not really. The person I lost died long before I ever went on this path."

"Who were they to you?"

I paused before answering, opening my mouth, but I couldn't put together the words.

"I'm sorry," he apologized. "I shouldn't have asked."

"No, no, it's fine," I told him. "It's just been a while since I've had to speak about him. It was my father. Happened a long time ago, back when

I was eight. We were out hunting together and I wandered off that day; found this beautiful wolf cub. It was almost larger than me and looked super scary, but it was a peaceful animal. Didn't sense a hint of malice. He was just hungry, so I gave him some food. Once my father found me, he scared the wolf off and scolded me for playing with wild animals."

"Sounds like you were a pretty daring kid."

"No, I wouldn't say that. I've just always found the good in things, ya know? If I saw a person or animal in need and didn't help them then I'd only be wasting my potential in this world. Unfortunately, not everything else has that same outlook. That same day my father and I were attacked by a pack of wolves. My father did everything he could to protect me but that only hindered him. I couldn't protect him the way he did with me and in the end, I watched him get killed."

"I'm sorry that you had to see something like that while being so young. I can't even imagine how you could've survived that all on your own."

"That's the thing. I couldn't do it on my own. You remember that wolf that I was talking about earlier? The one I fed? Well he came back for me and saved me from the rest of them. I guess he thought he had to repay some debt to me. Ever since then he hasn't left my side. At least not until I had to come to this island to try and find you."

"And what a disappointment I turned out to be," he laughed.

I looked back at him and told him, "Currently, you're a rather large one … but you don't have to be."

He avoided eye contact with me for a moment before saying, "Summer told me the same thing."

"Who was she to you?"

"She was my best friend," he answered, taking a long pause. "I loved her more than anything in this world. Her dark skin shined even in moonlight and her long locks were twisted in such a unique way that no one could mimic. Summer was the most beautiful girl on this island. Now that I think about it, she kind of looked a little like you.

"We both grew up in an orphanage together. She and all the rest of the kids who lived there were like family to me. Even now, I love them all as if they were my own flesh and blood.

"None of us really had a calling until some of us decided to join the bounty hunter guild at a young age. It was so much fun scavenging for secret relics in return for coins. And once I inherited the flame Spirit Caster I took on even bigger and better jobs. I could actually fight big targets.

"But I eventually got bored and didn't feel like doing anything anymore. At the same time, there was a gang on the island that wreaked havoc everywhere. People begged me to take the bounty but the reward wasn't enough and I just didn't care because it wasn't like the thugs were affecting *me*.

"I didn't find anyone or anything to be a threat to me at the time. Unfortunately I forgot that I wasn't the only one on this island. The power had gone to my head and I had forgotten about everyone who was close to me. Those worth fighting for.

"Me and Summer argued about it one night. She said I was being too passive with my power and stormed off into the night. I waited too long to go after her.

"When I decided to go and find her, I was already too late. Found her on the floor with some random thug over her taking everything she had. I killed him. Incinerated him to nothing but ash.

"Unfortunately, that wasn't enough. He had already wounded her far beyond help and she died in my arms.

"I don't really remember what happened afterwards. I was just angry and I blacked out. Killed their entire gang, burning every last one of them out of existence.

"Everyone around here calls me a hero for that, but that's not the way I see it. I failed her. I couldn't even keep the person I cared about most in this world safe."

"Flint," I finally said, "that doesn't sound like it's your fault."

"But it is my fault! I'm not like other people. I'm a Shēna. A being that can potentially hold the power of Gods in their hands. With the wave of a wand we create, and with what we create we can use it to destroy. My potential is limitless and yet I sat by and did nothing as Summer was being murdered!"

I put my head down and said, "Yeah, I guess it is kind of your fault." He fixed his gaze on me. I could tell that those words cut deep, but I still pressed on. "But there's not much you can do about that now. Just like how I can't save my father, and Crystal can't save her parents ... you can't save summer. But we're making up for it. Crystal is on her path to get revenge and I'm training to get stronger so that I can help anyone in my path who needs saving. And I know you're not just sitting around and doing nothing either. The people of this island think of you as a hero. That's not a title that's given lightly. You're doing exactly what Summer asked of you."

He turned away from me and let out a weak laugh. "Yeah, I guess you're right."

I grabbed him by his hand and told him, "She'd be proud of the person you've become today." Once I let go, I got back to my feet and said, "You should get some sleep. We've got a big day ahead of us tomorrow."

I started to make my way back to the ladder, but he stopped me by calling my name.

"Ana. Thanks for that. I needed to hear it."

I smiled before descending the ladder and going back to sleep.

CHAPTER TWENTY-FIVE
CRYSTAL

The sword came flying down, painting my mother's blood all over the white snow as if it were a canvas. The second sword turned my father's blood into a storm that rained down on Wren's gown, forever changing its color. My whole world was left flooded until I was left alone drowning in their blood. The worst part of it was that whenever I tried to open my eyes, all I could see was *hers*. Her crimson eyes peered through me like daggers. Her laugh echoed through the flood until I woke up, almost jumping out of bed. With both hands over my mouth, I forced myself not to scream.

My chest tightened from disbelief. I couldn't believe it was real. I couldn't believe that *I* was the one who let it happen.

"I'm sorry," I sobbed. "I'm so sorry."

I'll kill that woman for what she did to you, I thought to myself. *Even if it's the last thing I do.*

My thoughts were interrupted once Ana cheerfully walked through the door while saying, "Hey, Crystal."

As soon as I heard her voice, I quickly attempted to wipe away my tears in vain. Ana's liveliness along with her smile vanished.

"Are you ok?" she asked.

"I'm fine," I told her while getting up to my feet. "I just woke up and my eyes are still adjusting is all. What is it?"

Her eyes became softer before she looked away and said, "I just wanted you to know breakfast is ready." And with that she left me alone to get myself together.

I got out of bed while wiping my face off with the bottom of my shirt and made my way out the door. Once I got outside, I immediately got smacked in the face by the wonderful smell of salmon. Down away from the tree, Flint roasted fish over a fire while Alizeh sat next to him, gobbling down her meal.

Once I came closer to the both of them I heard Alizeh say to Flint, "So just before the rock monster could hit me, Crystal came back out of nowhere and froze it completely! Then I gave him the finishing blow and bam! He was done for!"

Flint laughed and said, "Well if what you're saying is true then that must mean you're a pretty strong Shēna. If so then we've gotta spar sometime, I wanna see your skills in action!"

"Yeah, I wanna see what you can do too. I've heard rumors and the thought of fighting you gives me chills! Let's do it now!"

"Hold on," I interrupted, "we don't have any time for that."

"Yeah, unfortunately Crystal's right," Flint admitted. "We gotta get our hands on those Phoenix feathers for the bounty as soon as possible." He got up from off the log and handed me a skewered fish on a stick. "As soon as you guys are done with breakfast we're heading out."

I nodded my head and took a bite from the fish. It was unlike anything I've ever tasted.

"Did you make this?" I asked.

"Yeah," he answered. "Well, Ana caught the fish while Alizeh collected some of the seasoning so I can't take all the credit. Why? Is there something wrong with it?"

"No, it's perfect. Honestly the best I've ever tasted."

"Well, I already told you, Phoenix Island dwarfs everyone when it comes to our food."

"No, this is even better than what I ate yesterday. Where'd you learn to cook like this?"

Once I asked, it took him a moment to answer, "My mom, I guess."

"Is she still around?"

"No, not exactly."

"I'm sorry to hear that."

"It is what it is," he shrugged before walking past me.

I turned to him and said, "I recently lost my parents too … so if you want to talk about it, I'm here."

He stopped, looked back at me and smiled, "I might take you up on that offer sometime," before going right back on his path, back to the treehouse.

Despite his charm, I could sense an overwhelming heaviness around him. Just like me, he'd been burdened by a lot. And even though at times I found him obnoxious, something in me *was* really hoping he'd take me up on that offer.

***

After we all ate, we took off for the Phoenix. It took some time traversing through the forest and hiking up hills until we finally made it to the slope of the steep volcano. Climbing it seemed too daunting of a task.

"Hey Flint, is there another way around?" I asked. "Like a path we can take up or something?"

"No, not that I know of," he answered. "Climbing is our best bet."

"Well, then we better get going," Ana suggested while stretching. "From the looks of it, we won't get to the top until it's dark."

"I can get us up there," Alizeh claimed.

Flint looked back at her with a confused yet intrigued look and asked, "How?"

Alizeh pulled out her Spirit Caster and looked up with a concentrated glare. The wand started to glow a bright green color and a strong breeze emanated from her. ***"Pairno Ptisi,"*** she said in a deep tone.

The wind surrounding her became more intense. It blew upward, lifting all four of us off the ground. Before we knew it, we were flying through the air.

I hated every moment of it. Having my feet off the ground made me lose all sense of control. Ana's shocked face told me she felt the same, but Flint had opposing views. He was laughing and cheering the entire way up.

We went higher and higher until we finally made it over the top. She released the spell, forcing us to land prematurely on the crater of the volcano. It was too sudden for me so I ended up falling onto the ground while Flint and Ana staggered. Alizeh landed effortlessly in comparison. Flint quickly regained his footing and stretched his hand out towards me. I grabbed it and he helped me up to my feet.

He then turned and said, "Alizeh, that spell was amazing!"

"Thanks," she said back. "It's the newest spell in my arsenal so I still don't have full control over it. I had no idea whether or not I was actually going to be able to carry you three all the way up without dropping any of you."

"Ha, you're kidding, right?" Flint laughed nervously.

Alizeh completely ignored his question and turned, gazing in awe at the giant smoke cloud rising from the vent of the volcano, blacking out the sky above us. There seemed to be a lot of space to walk on the rim of the crater, so we didn't have to worry about falling off the edge or into the volcano as long as we paid good enough attention.

I started to cough and asked, "Isn't it dangerous for us to be this close to the smoke?"

"Not if we act fast," Flint answered.

Alizeh raised her hand, stopping him and said, "There's no need for us to rush. **Katharízo.**"

Once she said the spell, wind blew in every direction. The smoke and ash from the volcano started to blow away from us and all the obnoxious gasses that surrounded the area seemed to vanish.

"Katharízo is a spell that cleanses the air around me. We should be fine as long as I'm using it," Alizeh explained.

"Alizeh, has anyone ever told you how extremely useful you are?" Flint applauded her.

"Not nearly enough."

Flint walked closer to the edge of the crater and looked down into the vent. "Guys, you gotta see this," he said excitedly.

Ana, Alizeh and I followed his lead to look inside the vent. At first, I couldn't comprehend what I was looking at. There was still smoke inside that had yet to clear. The smoke slowly started to disperse and as I concentrated on the depths of the black abyss, I could see glints of red lights in the form of cracks.

"Is that magma?" Ana asked. "This is my first time ever being next to something so hot."

"No, that's not what it is. Look closer."

I peered down the hole, looking closer just as Flint had said to Ana. The smoke almost fully cleared and I could finally see it. It had black charred feathers. Its body was covered in cracks filled with lava. It was a behemoth of a creature.

"Is that it?" Alizeh gasped. "Is that the Phoenix?"

"Yeah," he answered. "And it seems to be sleeping so don't make too much noise."

The sight of the creature was astonishing but the thought of going down there and taking its feathers was terrifying. It looked like it could wake up at any moment. All it would need to do is fly up, chomp down, and eat us all in one gulp. We'd be done for.

"Flint, are you sure this is a good idea?" I asked. "This seems dangerous."

"Yeah, this is definitely a dangerous job for most. That's why the pay is so high. But we're not like most people so this will be a sinch."

He pulled out his Spirit Caster, pointing it down at the Phoenix and said, ***"Travixte."***

One of the feathers was plucked right from the Phoenix and pulled through the air. Flint caught it with his open hand and examined the black feather.

"Okay, I just need to get a few more and then we can get out of here."

"Alright," I said, "just tell me when you're done."

I walked off to the edge of the crater and looked out at the rest of the island. It had lush jungles and small towns scattered across it. The houses looked like white architectural masterpieces, the blue ocean stretched as far as the eye can see, and the breeze coming from Alizeh's spell hit my skin just right to cool me off from the bright sun. It almost made me forget that there was a giant flaming Phoenix of death not too far behind me. But I quickly remembered once I heard the high-pitched shriek that boomed so loudly I was sure the entire island could hear it.

I jumped and looked back at them, hoping that they were just playing a trick on me. I thought that horrifying sound couldn't have been the Phoenix. I didn't want to believe it.

"Guys, what was that?" I asked hesitantly.

They didn't answer. They just stared down the hole in shock.

"What was that?" I repeated myself, this time raising my voice. Suddenly, fire spewed from the hole and up into the sky and before I knew it, the giant Phoenix was floating in the air with flames igniting on the tips of every single one of its feathers. Ash and smoke covered the sky, blocking out the sun. Its eyes were locked on all four of us with a look that I'd seen far too many times from dangerous animals that lived in Nótio Págo. Those were the eyes of an animal with the intention to kill whatever it deemed as a threat.

"Uh-oh," Flint gasped. "We should go."

"No need to tell me twice," said Ana before bolting in my direction. Flint followed but stopped once he looked back. Alizeh was still standing there. I couldn't tell if she was in shock from its ferocity or in awe of its beauty.

He grabbed Alizeh's hand and started running. The Phoenix opened its beak widely and, this time, instead of a shriek, it shot fire from its mouth. The large ball of flames was heading right for Flint and Alizeh.

"Look out!" I warned.

Flint turned around and shouted, ***"Ektrépo!"*** He swung his spirit caster right when the fireball was overhead and bounced it back, hitting the Phoenix right in its chest, forcing it to fall back into the volcano. He looked down at Alizeh and asked, "Can you get us down from here with your spell?"

"Well, um, technically yes, but no."

"What the hell is that supposed to mean?"

"It's one thing to bring you guys up, but trying to bring us down is a whole other thing. I don't have much control over my landings yet."

Suddenly the Phoenix flew right out of its hole again and went high into the sky above the clouds.

"Do you think you scared it off?" Alizeh asked.

I knew that couldn't have been the case. It was just regaining its composure and getting ready for another attack. I quickly pulled out my Spirit Caster and started running in their direction to defend them from whatever attack would come their way. At that same moment, the Phoenix came diving down like a shooting star with its body fully engulfed in flames.

"Págo Toícho!"

Long thick ice crystals emerged from the ground, creating a wall between us and the beast but that didn't stop it from ramming itself into the ice at full speed. Fire exploded around us as the ice wall cracked more and more. I could feel it giving out. The ice started to melt from the extreme heat and it managed to make me feel the same way. It felt as if I was a block of ice tossed into an inferno. Once the flames went around the wall and closer to us I felt like I was going to give in.

Before I could, Alizeh grabbed her Spirit Caster with two hands and yelled, ***"Víaii Sfýrigma!"*** A powerful gust of wind blew the fire and dispersed it around the wide area. It was so powerful that it pushed Ana, Flint and I against the ice wall.

Flint raised his wand and yelled out the spell, ***"Svíno!"*** The spell made the flames and the Phoenix disappear, leaving only small trickles of fire in the air. It was silent. It seemed that we had beaten the monster.

"Flint," Ana said before taking a long pause to try to comprehend what had just happened. "What did you do?"

"I just extinguished the fire. Didn't think the bird would go along with it."

"You are skilled with that Spirit Caster, boy," a voice echoed. The voice sounded disjointed like many people were talking at once, but it was clearly only one entity speaking. It sounded close to how our voices were when we spoke out our spells.

"Who said that?" Alizeh asked, looking around in every direction.

"Tell me boy, what is your name?" The voice asked. *Is this the voice of the Phoenix?* I thought to myself. It kept saying boy, so I guessed it was talking to Flint. I looked over to see him take in a small gulp before answering.

"Flint Zapalac," he hesitated.

"'Zapalac'? Ah now it's starting to make sense. Those golden eyes. That latent power. You're the direct descendent of Ember Zapalac, aren't you?"

"So what if I am?"

"I was just curious. It doesn't actually matter how great your ancestry is. You will all still die for coming here and stealing from me!"

Flames burst around us and quickly rose into the air above creating an explosion of fire.

"Grígoros Ánemos!" Alizeh quickly shouted.

Before I knew it, she was right by my side. She gave Ana, Flint and I a forceful push with wind that sent us all flying back. Before we could even land on the floor, the fire rained down on Alizeh, exploding on impact. We landed and the intense light momentarily blinded me. Once my eyes fully adjusted, the Phoenix's body had transformed into complete fire and its tail was laying over where Alizeh was standing just seconds ago.

She risked her own life to save us. And this thing was just using her like a stepping stool! I swung my wand towards the monster and yelled, *"Cheimerinó Fengári!"*

Ice overflowed from the tip of the Spirit Caster and shot up in the shape of a crescent. The bird screeched and flew up with part of its chest now frozen.

Ana pulled her spear from her back and ran up the ice crescent like a ramp. Once she got to the end, Ana jumped to the Phoenix and with the spear in both hands, jabbed the weapon right into its left eye. The Phoenix created a shout so powerful that it pushed us all back, including Ana, who was sent flying from the wail. She tumbled on the ground before getting a good look at her spear. Half of it was incinerated.

Once it flew up higher, I ran to where it was standing and saw that Alizeh was lying in a small crater with a few small burns on her skin.

"Alizeh!" I cried. I pulled her close to me, checking to see if she was still breathing and to my surprise, she was. It felt like a miracle. I wondered if this was the result of her massive reserves of Rēa.

Before I could finish my thought, a large fire ball came down overhead. Before it could hit us, Flint got in the way and once again used the spell, **"Ektrépo!"** bouncing the attack back at the Phoenix.

"You guys get to safety!" He yelled. "I'll distract it!"

I nodded my head in agreement, picked Alizeh up and ran. I looked back and saw Flint holding off the Phoenix's flames with his own. I made it to the edge where the slope began and thought of ways to get down.

I can't climb down, I thought. *Sliding down might be too rough. Maybe I can create a path down with the ice. Yeah, that's what I'll do. I'll use 'Cheimerinó Fengári' to make a continuous slide and—*

Something stopped my thought process. A voice from beyond. It was my grandmother's voice.

"Crystal, what are you doing?"

"What does it look like? I'm trying not to die!"

"So, you're running again? Just like before?"

Her words slammed into my head, jogging my memory of the night when everything fell apart. The night I ran for my life into that frozen hell.

"Tell me, why did you run away that night?"

"Because it was the only thing I could do! I didn't have the power to fight them off!" I cried.

"So, what you're telling me is that you still don't possess the power to save those closest to you? If you run now, the son of Ember will die. All because you deemed yourself too weak."

"No! I'm not too weak!" I yelled as I looked back at him. He was being overpowered.

A stray flame was going to hit him from above, but Ana tackled him out of the way just barely dodging it herself. They weren't going to win, much less survive on their own. I had to do something!

"I won't let that happen! I won't let them die!"

I laid Alizeh down on the ground and raised my Spirit Caster.

"Good. Then repeat after me."

Her words echoed through my head with such clarity. I immediately understood the power of the new spell I was given. I repeated the words she told me.

"Ice pillars rise up.

Encircle my enemies.

Close them into nothingness."

Giant shards of floating ice were formed above the volcano. They slowly rotated in a circle as if to make sure that nothing would escape. I raised my Spirit Caster to command them.

"Envelop and crush.

Now, take them once and for all.

For eternity."

A white aura surrounded my entire body. I could feel the Rēa making my blood rush. This power was far beyond what I had felt before. With this power, I was going to end this battle once and for all.

The ice shards started to close in on the Phoenix. The shards stretched out longer and thicker than before. The Phoenix stopped its attack on Flint and Ana, finally noticing that I had set up a trap for it. But by that point, it was already too late.

"Chiliádes Chrónia Fylakí Págou!"

The ice pillars swiftly moved to the center, expanding and encasing the Phoenix within its final resting place. A giant floating crystal of ice.

CHAPTER TWENTY-SIX
FLINT

It was a magnificent sight to gaze at. A giant shard of ice floating in the sky. *Did Crystal really possess such power this entire time?* I looked over at her and watched her fall to the ground before running to see if she was ok. She had passed out. That spell must've taken too much of a toll on her body.

"Are they still breathing?" Ana asked as she walked over to us.

"Other than a few scrapes and burns, both of them look like they'll be fine. They'll wake up sooner or later."

"Then let's wait to move them," Ana suggested. "Maybe if she's not under any pressure Alizeh might be able to find a way to fly us down."

Before I could agree, I felt a rumbling beneath my feet.

"An earthquake? Now of all times?" Ana asked.

"No," I answered. "It's much worse."

I looked back and saw a cloud of ash spewing from the crater of the volcano. It was erupting! The legend said that the Phoenix was the one who was stopping the volcano from going off. It seemed like that was true. And we imprisoned the only thing stopping the volcano from laying waste to this island.

I had to get Crystal and Alizeh away, but I didn't know how. Crystal was thin and Alizeh was small. We could carry them easily, but getting down from the volcano wasn't an option.

Before I had enough time to think of another way, the lava had already risen out of the crater. There was no time to move. I had to stand my ground against this unstoppable Force of nature.

"Ana, get behind me!" I ordered before pulling out my Spirit Caster and yelling, ***"Ektrépo!"***

Once the lava came close, it flowed around me. We were surrounded but as long as I was using this spell, it wouldn't touch us. The only problem was that I had no idea how long I could actually keep it up for. In the fight with the Phoenix, I had to use most of my Rēa to fight it off. I had put almost everything I had into that battle. I doubted that I would've even survived if Crystal hadn't put an end to it.

The lava flowed higher as the smoke and ash stretched across the entire island, blackening the sky. Spheres of fire started flying into the air, almost reaching the towns below.

I did this. If I had never taken this stupid job then this wouldn't be happening. Now because of me, Phoenix Island was doomed.

I felt myself getting weaker, dropping to my knees and closing my eyes while saying aloud, "Ana, Crystal, Alizeh, everyone. I'm sorry."

"So, are you going to just let everyone die?"

The voice jolted me back to my senses. I opened my eyes and looked back to Ana to see that she was completely frozen in place. That could only mean one thing.

I looked back in front of me to see a woman standing atop the lava with dark skin, curly hair, and golden eyes just like mine.

"Mother?" I said, surprised to see her here.

"It's been a while, son."

"Yeah. Three years. Why are you here now of all times? I've been calling on you ever since Summer died! Did you come here just to see me in my final moments?"

"'Final moments'? No, on the contrary. I came here to see you be reborn."

"What's that supposed to mean?"

"It means I came to see what your decision would be. Whether or not you would choose to protect everything you hold dear or let it be destroyed just like you did with Summer."

"I didn't *let* her!"

"Oh, but you did. You had the power to stop those thugs. You could have taken care of them with said power! Instead, you decided to waste your greatness and, in turn, you lost the woman you love!"

"Shut up!"

"Now you're still wasting your potential and because of that, everything you cherish will die."

"I don't want that to happen! I don't know what to do!"

"You got yourself into this mess and since you're my son I know you'll get yourself out of it. Claim your power and fix this!"

And just like that, she was gone. Vanished just as fast as she had appeared. Unfortunately, I wasn't ready to snap back to reality. The forest was burning and spreading to the outskirts of town. I could hear cries of fear coming from the distance.

"Flint," Ana coughed. I turned to see her on her knees gasping for air. "I can't … I can't breathe!"

Alizeh had passed out, so her spell had dispersed. There was no longer anything cleansing the air around us. That coupled with the fact that the heat was probably too much for her to handle made for a deadly combination.

"Hold your breath for as long as you can!" I told her. "I'll get you out of here!"

Suddenly the lava around us gushed and popped, splattering in all directions. I redirected most of it, but a few drops still flew into our protective bubble and were going to land right onto Alizeh's face. I wasn't fast enough to stop it, but Ana was. She threw herself over Alizeh and shielded her with Ana's back being the only casualty. The numerous drops of magma burned through her shirt and onto her skin forcing her to claw her fingers into the gravel and growl in pain. But even someone as tough as her couldn't hide the tears that were welling down her face. Her growls turned to whimpers that I couldn't stand for.

"No…" I said aloud. Seeing her in that state, broken and on the ground while only being moments away from death reminded me of the last time I saw Summer. I couldn't let the same thing happen again!

'Claim your power.'

My mother's words rang through my head. Even though they were harsh they still rang true. I needed to be much stronger than I currently was if I wanted to save everyone. If I wanted to save *her*.

I stood back up on my feet, tightened my grip on the wand, and said, "I won't let you die here, Ana. *I will claim what's mine!*"

The lava started to rise into the air and flow into my wand. I could feel an overwhelming force of Rēa boiling through my blood. More than my body could take. But I didn't let go. The Spirit Caster started to suck in everything. The fire, lava, smoke, and ash. It kept going for what felt like an eternity until the volcano was sucked dry.

My body felt like it was on fire. Like I was going to explode at any moment. But my will was too strong to allow that. I held my Spirit Caster tightly and took a deep breath, letting out steam along with it. I was going to make this power mine.

As I forced myself to maintain that power, I could feel the Rēa flowing into the wand. Before my eyes, I saw the Spirit Caster change shape. It glowed red and started to stretch out longer on both ends, turning into a long straight staff.

The center of the staff was still blood red, but the ends were blackened like burnt wood. Cracks on the edge of the wood glowed with an orange hue like embers of a dying fire.

"Flint," Ana asked, seemingly at a loss for words. "What did you just do?"

"I don't know," I answered.

I was in awe. I didn't understand what happened to me at that moment, but I knew I had access to a newfound power. With it things would change. I could now grab greatness by its hand and demand its help to protect everything that I held dear.

CHAPTER TWENTY-SEVEN
CRYSTAL

I woke up to the sight of the starry night sky and quickly sat up to see Flint, Ana and Alizeh sitting at a campfire. For a moment, I thought that we were back at Flint's treehouse, but as soon as I looked up, I realized that wasn't the case. The giant crystal of ice I had created to imprison the Phoenix was right above us. White light from the crescent moon bounced off of the ice like a massive chandelier. A frosty mist emanated off of the ice, adding to its beauty.

Alizeh looked over at me and said, "Hey, Crystal's awake!"

"Welcome back to the land of the living," Flint laughed. "I thought you'd never wake up."

I stood up and walked over to the fire. Flint was holding a long staff in his hands and seemed to be doing something strange with it. He held one of the ends of his staff over Alizeh's burns, and they gradually started to disappear.

"Flint," I started to ask, "what is that staff? How are you doing magic with it?"

"Oh, this thing?" He said as he raised it. "It's my Spirit Caster."

I didn't understand. His Spirit Caster was the same size as me and Alizeh's. Just about a foot long. The thing he was holding was almost the same height as him and its design was different. My skepticism must have been written all over my face because he immediately started to explain himself more after looking at me.

"Yeah, I know. It's a bit different than it was before. I think it evolved or something but I'm not entirely sure. It happened while you and Alizeh were knocked out."

I sat down next to them and looked back up at the sky.

"Seems like I've been out for a while. I'm still exhausted. I feel like I'm going to collapse."

"Well, that makes sense. You used more Rēa than your body could even handle. You need time to recover. We should get back home as soon as possible to get some rest," Flint suggested.

Alizeh stood up and said, "Alright, I think I'm good to go. I'll try and get us down."

"Alizeh, are you sure you're alright?" Ana asked. "It looked like you got hit with a pretty heavy attack earlier."

"Oh, don't worry about me. Rēa makes our bodies more durable compared to the average person."

The statement seemed to be true. Earlier she had taken a point blank attack straight from the flaming tail of the Phoenix and the only thing that came from it were a few burns and a slightly tattered sundress. It made me wonder about the true limits of our bodies.

"So are you guys ready to go?" she asked.

Flint stood up and said, "Yeah."

"Me too," I answered, but as soon as I stood up, I became light headed and could feel my legs giving out. Before I could hit the floor, Ana caught and held me. Normally I would never burden anyone with this, but I didn't mind being held in her arms. For the first time in a while I felt like I could let my guard down in front of these people. In front of my friends. I felt so comfortable. So much so that at that moment, against every fiber of my being, I passed out in her embrace.

CHAPTER TWENTY-EIGHT
KIRA

There was still a lot of pressure in my foot and the bloody bandages only added to the discomfort. Delta and Arnold were at both my sides to help me off the boat. It was degrading being helped by a child and a weakling but after getting shot in the foot I didn't really have much of a choice.

I looked up at the boat and saw it in shambles. The gaping hole in the center of the boat and the splintered wood all over amazed me. If Delta wasn't here to work her magic, we would have sunk straight down to the bottom of the ocean.

A group of soldiers came over to greet us but after taking a look at the ship they realized that something had gone terribly wrong. They rushed over to us, and one man asked, "Prince Arnold, are you harmed?"

"I'm fine," he answered, "but the princess is injured. She needs immediate medical attention."

"Yes, sir!"

The soldiers took me into town. And I was treated by one of the best doctors on the island.

***

I laid in bed while staring at the ceiling, wondering how long I'd be bedridden for. My foot was feeling much better, but I couldn't stand on it yet. The doctors said that I was already making a miraculous recovery. They told me that the average person would be stuck in bed for weeks and wouldn't be able to walk *properly* for months. Luckily for me, I wasn't the *average* person. Being a Shēna had its perks. The Rēa in our blood helped us heal much faster than any normal human.

I heard a knock on the door. The thought of being annoyed by more doctors and soldiers was dreadful. Even worse if the prince came in; I would want to hang myself.

"Come in," I commanded.

Delta alone walked through the doors which made me breathe a sigh of relief. "I thought you were Arnold."

"Don't worry," Delta said. "I told him along with The King and Queen of this island that you needed as much rest as possible and couldn't be bothered with such draining meetings."

"Thank you, Delta, you're a lifesaver."

"How's your foot?"

"Better. I should be able to go by tomorrow."

"Well, that's good to hear. I'll let you have your rest."

She turned around to make her exit out of the room but before she could, I stopped her.

"Delta," I said, making her turn back to me.

"Yes?"

"I'm sorry about what I said to you the other day."

"What do you mean?"

"When I told you I didn't care about you. It was uncalled for. I do appreciate you and to an extent, I care."

Her face changed from her usual stoic expression to one of complete surprise. I never apologize for anything. But the feeling of guilt from my words had weighed heavily for some time now. I'd imagined it was probably the first time she had ever heard me utter the words to anyone other than my father.

"There's no need to apologize, Kira. It's fine, really."

"I don't care if there's a *'need'* to apologize. I just wanted to. Nothing more."

"Of course," she nodded.

"Now, stay with me and keep me company until I'm fully healed. It's boring here by myself."

Delta nodded again, but this time with a happy grin.

"Of course, Kira."

CRYSTAL

I t was morning and I awoke back in Flint's bed which was strange since the last thing I remembered was being on top of the volcano and in Ana's arms. It seemed like I passed out the night before which meant they must've carried me all the way back.

I quickly got out of bed feeling lightheaded as I leaned against the wall until I could come back to my senses. I still wasn't at one hundred percent yet. *Chiliádes Chrónia Fylakí Págou* must have taken too great of a toll on my body and mind.

Once I felt good enough to stand on my own without crashing to the ground, I carefully walked myself outside onto the deck and what I saw took me aback for a brief moment. Flint and Alizeh were having a fierce battle. Flames flickered in every direction. Alizeh swiftly bounced from tree to tree, avoiding all of the fire, and waited to find her opening.

"You can't keep running forever!" Flint yelled at her.

Alizeh stopped on a tree branch, looked down at him and said "Don't worry. I plan on beating you this time."

"Well, come at me then!" Flint yelled, preparing himself for a counter-attack just in case she really meant it.

Alizeh grinned and jumped off the tree, flying down at high speed towards him. I expected some kind of intense clash but instead, Alizeh changed her direction of flight, zooming past Flint, and before I could even realize it, she had landed right in front of me. Her wind almost blew me to the ground while I was in my dazed state.

"Crystal! You're finally awake!" she yelled as she embraced me, squeezing me with all her might.

"How long was I asleep for?" I asked.

"Well, we fought the Phoenix a couple of days ago and you passed out the same night, so like a day and a half I'd guess."

That surprised me. I had fallen asleep for an entire day. Not to mention I had fallen asleep after the battle and had only woken up that night. I had essentially fallen asleep for two entire days. That was something I had to keep in mind. Although *Chiliádes Chrónia Fylakí Págou* was powerful, my body wasn't ready for it. It also took far too long to prepare. I would have to use it very strategically and sparingly for any upcoming battles.

Flint patted me on the shoulder and said "Hey, don't look so grim, Snowflake. I'm glad you're finally up. I wanna show you something."

He walked past me up the stairs and into the house. Alizeh and I followed him back into the treehouse and saw him digging through an old chest. He pulled out a pouch, tossing it at me. The pouch had some weight to it.

"What's this?" I asked.

"Open it up and see for yourself," he answered.

I loosened the strings on the pouch and opened it up. I was speechless after looking at the contents of the bag. Bright gleaming golden coins pervaded throughout the sack. I had never seen that much gold in my life.

"Flint, is this—"

"Your half of the bounty," he interrupted, answering before I could even fully ask. "While you were resting, Ana and I took the feathers back to the guild and claimed the reward. That pouch you're holding has 333 golden coins. Ana already took her portion and is already off shopping around town."

My head raced with ideas of what to spend these coins on. We had more than enough to leave the island and we could bring food with us. We could finally buy some new clothes and even some weapons to fight The King's army. Stealing the Phoenix's feathers was probably the best decision we'd made thus far.

Another thought popped into my mind. A question I had for Flint. "Who wanted the feathers? And what are they going to do with them?"

"Don't know. Some weird old man. Didn't ask what his plans were. I just took the coins and left. Does it matter?"

"No. I guess it doesn't."

"Crystal, can we go shopping too?" Alizeh asked, jumping up and down excitedly.

"Sure, I don't see why not," I answered, already having the idea in mind since we needed supplies for our journey. I looked back up at Flint and asked, "Would you like to join us?"

"Nah, I'll catch up with you two later. I've gotta take care of my own things. You can both have your girl time or whatever."

"Alright, suit yourself. Come on Alizeh."

***

It didn't take long for us to walk through the jungle and reach the town. There were plenty of shops scattered throughout the cramped alleyways, so we decided to go to each and every one of them. I scooped out some golden coins from the pouch and gave a handful to Alizeh.

"Let's split up and get what we both need. We'll meet back here when we're done," I told her.

"Sounds like a plan," she smiled, and then ran off into one of the shops that had pastries sitting at the window.

I told her to get what we *needed* but it seemed like her sweet tooth had taken over. It didn't matter though. With that amount of gold, she could probably buy every sweet pastry in that shop until they were completely sold out and it still wouldn't make that big of a dent in our funds.

I walked and looked around at all the shops until I could find something useful to buy. Then something caught my eye. Within one of the windows stood three mannequins with fine laced dresses and fashionable clothes that would make anyone look like a royal.

I looked down at my own clothes. My shirt was covered in dirt and blood while my tight leggings had rips and tears showing more skin than I was comfortable with. It was time for a wardrobe change. I walked through the door forcing a bell to ring over my head. Wooden mannequins cluttered the shop all over with different varieties of clothing.

"How can I help you, young lady?" A short old woman asked politely from behind the counter.

"Oh, I'm just looking for a new outfit," I responded.

The woman scooted off her chair, grabbed her cane and slowly made her way over to me. She put on her glasses and looked me up and down while circling around me. I felt slightly uncomfortable by her inspecting every inch of me.

She then said, "Follow me," and scurried into the sea of mannequins. I quickly followed but, strangely, it was hard for me to keep up.

As she walked, she took random pieces of clothes from the mannikins and threw them at me. I caught and held the items, making sure not to drop any. She finally stopped and said, "Ok, that should be enough. Now go to the back behind the curtain and try them on. Go on, go!" She shouted excitedly.

I thought this was a pretty unorthodox way to choose clothing, but I still nodded my head and went behind the curtain, completely changing into the outfit she had given me. I opened the curtain showing her the outfit.

"Does this look good?" I asked.

She pulled me over to the long mirrors in the corner of the shop and said, "You tell me."

I had on a black tank top that covered my neck with long black gloves that stretched beyond my elbows making it so that my shoulders were still showing. My pants were white, but my black knee high boots covered a decent portion of it. Finally, she gave me a white fur pelt to wear, but it was too hot on the island, so I just tied it around my waist.

I'd never worn anything so lavish. I'd always worn bland and boring fur coats. If it kept me warm, then that alone was good enough. But ever since I got my hands on this wand, I haven't felt any discomfort from the cold even once. During the entire trip through Nótio Págo I was completely fine while only wearing light clothes. Perhaps it was from the very nature of the Ice Spirit Caster.

I looked at myself in the mirror for a long while before finally saying aloud, "I'll take it."

The old lady nodded her head and said, "Yes, yes, it fits your spirit very well. Come with me."

She led me back to the counter and started doing the math to figure out how much I needed to pay her. Meanwhile, I looked around the shop and saw a knife holster with a strap hanging on the wall. I walked over to it, grabbed it and said, "I want this too."

"Ok, that will be 720 silver coins," she said.

I pulled out a single gold coin and asked, "Will this suffice?"

"Oh, that will be more than enough," she answered while taking the coin from my hand and closely inspecting it. "Hold on while I get your change."

The old lady turned around, opening her safe while getting pieces of silver out. While she was doing so, I began to put the holster under my pelt, completely concealing it. It wasn't just stylish but useful, too.

"You're pretty good at this," I told her. "I could have never picked out an outfit like this."

"Well, that's my job. Someone in my profession needs to understand how to dress a person. I just hope that my work holds up to the great Reshma's standards."

"Who's Reshma?"

"Legends say that she was the greatest seamstress in history. She was so good that one day she was taken by the sister gods to tailor them."

"Those are some high standards," I laughed.

"I want to be the very best at what I do, so I think they are the correct standards," She smiled.

The bell at the door rang. Someone was coming in, but I paid no mind to who it was. That is, until I heard their conversation.

"Delta, stop nagging me," a female voice said.

The voice sounded very familiar, but I couldn't place who it belonged to.

"But Kira, you still haven't fully recovered from your injuries."

'Kira'? That name. That was the name I overheard the night of my parents' death. I turned around to make sure and, to my complete shock, I was right. I was standing in the same room as Kira Black, the Princess of the Black Continent, and the woman who took everything away from me.

CHAPTER THIRTY
CRYSTAL

I couldn't believe it. I stared at her in complete shock without making a move.

"Delta, do you really think I'm so frail that I can't even go shopping for new clothes? I'm royalty. I can't go back to my kingdom with a torn dress. It'll make me look—"

She stopped in the middle of her rant once she noticed me from across the room. Our eyes were locked on each other. All that could be seen in her eyes was an intensely dark hatred.

My body felt like it had completely frozen over. I didn't know what to do. I wasn't ready for this.

Wait.

This was the moment I'd been waiting for. This was what everything was leading up to. *This* encounter. I had been planning to take her on with a powerful group of Shēna by my side, but that was before. Back when I was weaker. Back when I was powerless. This time, things would be different.

The Princess reached to her side for her wand. I regained control of my body, refusing to freeze once again in her presence. The last time I froze, people died. Those closest to me. This time, I would do everything I could to avenge the death of my family!

My instincts told me to fight but something else made me stop. This time it wasn't fear but caution. I looked around. We were still inside. If we fought there, then it would destroy this woman's shop. Or even worse she might get caught up in this and get hurt.

"Kira! Wait! Not here!"

She didn't want to listen to a single word I had to say and didn't hesitate to draw out her wand and say the spell, ***"Skoteiní Sfaíra Sfairón!"*** Dozens of black orbs manifested in front of her and even though I knew nothing of the spell, my first thought was to block it so that the shopkeeper and I wouldn't take damage even though I knew the shop would.

I swiped my Spirit Caster through the air and yelled, *"Toícho Ton Thrafsmáton!"*

What I expected to come from the spell was a wall of ice covered in shards, but instead all I got was a small burst of mist that spewed from my Spirit Caster. My voice flattened and the spell fizzled out. It didn't work at all! The amount of Rēa I felt within my body was at an all-time low. I must have not finished recovering from *Chiliádes Chrónia Fylakí Págou.*

Kira took full advantage of the situation and yelled, "Fire!" causing small bolts of energy to shoot out of each orb like a bullet. The black bullets flew through the shop, destroying mannequins and forcing random pieces of fabric into the air. I immediately turned tail and vaulted across the counter. In the middle of my vault, I was grazed right through the arm by one of the black bullets. I fell over the counter with a sharp pain coming from my left arm. Blood dripped down my arm and to the floor.

I held my arm to stop the blood until I was startled by a large thump. It was the old lady who owned the shop. She had been shot straight through the chest and died before even hitting the floor. Once again, right in front of my eyes, the Princess had taken the life of the innocent. It made me sick to my stomach and my blood boiled.

The bullets stopped and Kira yelled, "Can you believe it? All this time I've been worried that I'd never see your pathetic face again. I thought I'd never get the chance to kill you like I should have done before. But as fate would have it, you're in my grasp once again."

I reached into my holster pulling out the same dagger I used to kill the knights on the day when I first met the princess. I unsheathed it and gripped the handle tightly. I was ready to do everything in my power to end this here and now.

"Why are you so fixated on killing me?" I shouted from behind the counter.

"'Why, you ask? Because every breath you take is an insult to my pride. I failed to do what was expected of me and now my father believes me to be a failure since I let you slip through my fingers."

"So, that's why you murder the innocent? To prove yourself?"

There was a pause from her as if she was actually thinking of an answer for that question, but all she did was change the topic. "Stop stalling. Come out and show yourself. If you surrender now, then I'll make your death—"

Before she could finish her threat, I jumped back over the counter with my dagger in hand. Kira quickly raised her wand and yelled, ***"Skoteiní Volí!"*** That was an attack that I remembered. She used it on me the last time we met. It was my first taste of what magic could feel like; there's still a scar from it. I wasn't going to let myself get hit by it again.

The ball of energy shot from her wand, but I jumped out of its path. It blew one of the mannikins behind me into pieces as I continued my charge.

"Désmi Thanátou!" she yelled, using another spell. A light flashed from it, and I instinctively moved my head from the line of fire. A thin black beam of energy shot out and grazed my cheek. I could tell that it cut me but I couldn't feel the pain. My heart was racing. I pushed forward, going even faster. This was the adrenaline boost I needed to end this.

She was taken by surprise and tried to back away from me, but I was faster. I could tell from the fear in her eyes that she knew that. I was almost within striking distance so I grabbed my dagger with both hands readying myself to thrust her through.

"Fylakí Neroú" the girl next to her said.

Water appeared from thin air and gathered to my position. Before I knew it, I was completely trapped within a floating sphere of water. I wasn't ready for it. I didn't take in enough air before this. I tried desperately to swim out, but I panicked. All I could think about was the last time I almost drowned. The howling of my wolves echoed in my head as I started to black out.

Suddenly, I heard the sound of glass shattering and then the spell was released. The floating sphere of water spilled to the floor with me falling along with it. It was a relief to cough up the water that filled my lungs and regain all my senses. I looked up and saw a broken window with Alizeh pinning the girl who trapped me to the ground.

"Hey Crystal," Alizeh said. "Are these two messin' with ya?"

At that point, Kira pointed her Spirit Caster right against Alizeh's head and said, "If anyone makes a move, I'll kill this kid in an instant!"

"Alizeh!" I yelled. "She's serious! She'll actually do it, so don't move."

"Shut up!" Kira barked at me and then turned her attention back to Alizeh. "I have a few questions for you. I see you have a Spirit Caster in your possession. Where did you get it? Are you actually a Shēna?

Alizeh stayed silent.

"Answer me!" Kira ordered.

"I don't answer to evil and corrupt tyrants like yourself." Alizeh answered.

There was a look of shock on the princesses face that soon turned into a sadistic grin.

"Well, alright," she laughed. "I hope you're fine with those being your final words. Farewell trash."

Suddenly the ground started to shake as if we were in the middle of an earthquake. The floor cracked between Alizeh and the Princess as fire spewed from it. Then the fire went back down into the Earth and the shaking stopped.

"What the hell was that?" Kira asked.

The door swung open, stealing everyone's attention. Flint walked in with his staff in hand and a serious aura about him.

He looked at my face, noticing the cut and said "Crystal, Alizeh. Are you both ok?"

We both nodded our heads.

"Excuse me," Kira said. "Who the hell are you?"

Flint looked up at her while ignoring her question and said, "You must be Kira Black, Princess of the Black Continent." He looked down at the girl who was still being pinned down to the ground by Alizeh. "And you must be Delta. The youngest of the Five Armaments and the wielder of the Water Spirit Caster."

Kira took a moment to examine him and finally said, "And *you* must be the *'legendary'* Shēna who protects this island. So, you really *do* exist."

"I want you off this island." Flint demanded.

"Are you really trying to make demands of *me* right now?" she asked while taking a step towards him, but stopped while grunting in pain. I looked down at her feet and noticed that one of them had a bloody bandage on them. I didn't notice it before, but she was injured. That must've been the reason she barely moved during our fight moments ago.

She looked around and saw that we outnumbered her. Her injury, cou-pled with the fact that her partner was pinned under Alizeh made her chances of winning almost nonexistent and she knew that. The thought made her calm down.

The Princess took a deep breath and continued, "Fine, I'll leave. But I'm taking these criminals with me."

Her sights were set on me as she started to step forward in my direction.

"No. If you lay a finger on her, I'll kill you."

"But she's a fugitive!"

"Of the Black Continent," Flint added. "On Phoenix Island, she's just another innocent commoner. And if you hurt another person on this island then we will declare war on the Black Continent, and I will personally burn your entire kingdom to the ground."

"Why, you little—"

"Kira, we can't afford a war right now," said Delta. "We should listen to him and leave."

There was a look of contemplation and rage in her eyes.

"Fine. Delta, let's get out of here."

"Alizeh, let her go," Flint ordered.

Alizeh did as she was told and let go of Delta. Then Kira let out a spell that made us all put our guard up.

"Please take me away.

Take me throughout the darkness.

Let us travel fast.

Grigoro Taxidi"

A large black orb of flames appeared in the middle of the room. We still didn't know what she intended to do with it, so we still readied ourselves for anything.

"Relax," Kira said. "It's just a portal for us to get back home."

She walked closer to it with Delta walking right behind. But this was all wrong. This isn't how things should've gone.

"Wait!" I yelled. "We can't just let them leave! She's the one we need to kill! We need to end this now!"

"Crystal!" Flint shouted. His eyes burned through my very being. He wasn't his usual casual joking self. He was serious. Like he was ready to kill. His look made me take a step back in fear.

"Ha!" Kira laughed. "Well if you want your chance to kill me so badly then just come back to the Black Continent and face me there. I'll be happy to finish things with you once and for all."

She and Delta then walked through the black flames and disappeared out of sight, the fire vanishing with them.

"Flint!" I shouted. "How could you just let them get away? With all three of us we could have beaten her! That's the point of all of this!"

"Crystal," he said. "You and I don't have the same priorities. My goal is to keep everyone on this island safe. You can still go through with this little suicide plan of yours, but don't drag these innocent people into it. Now, if you'll excuse me, I have to meet with The King of Phoenix Island to get this mess all sorted out."

He then turned around and walked out of the now destroyed shop.

"Crystal, we should get out of here too," Alizeh suggested.

"Yeah," I responded.

She then walked out and I started to follow behind, but I stopped and looked back at the destroyed shop. I could see the legs of the shop owner poking out from behind the counter. She was truly gone. I had no connection to her, but still. She was a kind and innocent woman. This shouldn't have happened. I could've prevented this, but once again, I was too weak to protect those around me.

CHAPTER THIRTY-ONE
KIRA

After a short time of walking through the desert shrouded in darkness, Delta and I finally made it back to the courtyard of the castle. As per usual, everyone scrambled around to bow before me and asked about my journey. This time, I just ignored them. I was too angry to acknowledge the help. Crystal Winters was right in my grasp, and I had to let her go.

The flaming portal disappeared behind us and Delta stood in awe as the fire scattered away. I believed that had been the first time she had gone through 'Grígoro Taxídi' with me.

"Kira, did we just teleport?" Delta asked. "Why didn't you use that to bring us to Phoenix Island?"

"Because I can only use Grígoro Taxídi to bring me to places that I'm overly familiar with. This castle is my home so I'll always be able to come back to it when needed. There aren't many places besides this that I can go to."

"Well, it seems pretty useful."

"Yeah, it is. But it's also pretty draining."

"That makes sense. The more powerful and useful the spell, the more power and energy it requires to pull off." Delta stopped and seemingly got over my spell. She went back to her normal stoic self and asked, "Should we tell your father of our journey and who we found on it?"

"Well, obviously yes. But I'm scared of how he'll react."

"His reaction doesn't matter. What matters right now is the information we have. And the location of three Shēna is some pretty good information on its own."

"You're right. Okay, let's go."

***

A while later, we made it to the throne room and into my father's presence. He looked down at us with a confused look on his face and said, "Kira. Delta. What are you both doing back so soon? You shouldn't have been back here for at least a few more days."

"I'm sorry, Father, but our plans changed."

"How so?"

"Delta and I were unwelcomed on the island."

"How is that possible? You were both invited as guests! This is an outrage! How could The King of that island treat royalty like yourself so poorly?"

"That's the thing, Father. It wasn't The King who banished us. It was a Shēna."

My father stood up from his throne, looking down at us in awe and said, "A Shēna? Do you mean the one that was written off as a myth? So, he's actually real?"

"Yes," Delta answered, "but he seemed different from the average Shēna."

"Different how?"

"His Spirit Caster was longer like a staff. And I sensed an intense amount of Rēa flowing from him."

"He must have had an Evolved Spirit Caster."

Delta and I both looked at each other in joint confusion. I'd never heard of an *'Evolved'* Spirit Caster. I looked back up at him and asked, "What does that mean?"

"It means he's probably stronger than you'll ever be."

The claim that I lacked the power to stand up against him stung. My father had never believed in my skill. He believed that my lack of conviction stopped me from being a powerful Shēna, or even a great ruler like those before me.

"That being said," he continued, "I still believe the four of you will be able to beat him if you work together."

"Pardon me, King," Delta cut in, "but who are you referring to when you say, 'the four' of us?"

"Ah yes, I had forgotten. You both have been gone for the last few days so you must not have heard the news."

"What news?"

"The murder of a member of the Five Armaments."

"What? Who?"

I had the same question. It seemed like an impossibility for a member of the Five Armaments to die. It was shocking news, but it wasn't unwelcomed. I hated the other members so if anything, it would come as a win to me. Especially if it were that twisted snake, Morpheus.

"It was Adam," he answered.

Adam? That seemed impossible. He was the oldest and most experienced out of the five of us. Perhaps his old age and hubris finally caught up to him.

Father continued saying, "Only a single knight survived the attack on his group. He claims that two female Shēna defeated Adam in battle. One with the Wind Spirit Caster and the other with the Ice Spirit Caster."

His words made Delta and I shudder. The Ice Spirit Caster belonged to Crystal Winters. That little brat with her must have had the Wind Spirit Caster. How could those two amateurs have killed Adam, of all people?

Delta gulped before saying, "That's the next piece of information we needed to tell you. I believe we encountered those very two Shēna. They were with the *'evolved'* Shēna."

"And what became of them? Did you kill them?"

Delta and I stayed silent. I wanted to answer, but I was too afraid of what he would do to us if we told him that we let them get away. Regardless of whether or not we answered, our silence was confirmation enough.

"I see," Father continued. "It matters not. This only confirms Morpheus's theory."

"And what theory is that?" I asked.

"The theory that Crystal Winters is gathering powerful Shēna to help her in the coming battle."

"If that's the case, then we should all go back to Phoenix Island and execute the three of them as soon as possible. The fear of an unnecessary war against them is gone because now we know for a *fact* that there's a Spirit Caster on that island."

"No. I will let Morpheus alone handle this task. He has a plan that is certain to work and bring all the fugitives into our possession."

"And you really think he could do it alone?"

"I believe that his chances are better than yours."

Another hard blow. I wanted to fight for this. I wanted to prove that I was good enough and that I was better than Morpheus. But I could probably live my entire life trying to get to that end and he would still find me to be nothing more than a disappointment. So, I just bit my tongue and stayed quiet.

Delta glanced at me and then back at my father, saying, "I think Kira's right."

"What was that?" he asked in an annoyed tone.

"Now is as good a time as ever to strike. The sooner we attack, the less prepared they'll be. Also, if we win, then not only do we get the Spirit Casters, but also Phoenix Island. And with Kira's spell, we can make it out without interfering with Morpheus's plan. He doesn't even need to fight with us. Me, Kira, and Arachne are more than enough for this mission. This is a win-win situation."

My father thought about it for a few seconds, but before he could give his final say he broke the silence in the room by coughing. He covered his mouth, but on his hand, I saw a small drop of blood drip down. My heart almost skipped a beat as I watched the blood fall to the floor, time seeming to slow down.

"Father, are you ok?" I gasped.

A look of frustration was smeared on his face as he said, "Yes, I'm fine. I agree that it would be beneficial for you to attack the island together. I'll call you back when I've decided when you should go. For now, you two are relieved of your duties for the day."

"But father, what about you?"

"I said I'm fine!" he snapped. "You think I'd be so weak as to let a simple cough bring me down?"

"No, but—"

"Then leave at once! I need a moment to rest."

"Yes, my King." Delta said.

"Yes, Father." I said hesitantly. Delta and I then swiftly left the throne room.

CHAPTER THIRTY-TWO
CRYSTAL

"*P*ágo Toícho!" I shouted. Shards of ice rose from the ground but only by a foot. It was much too small. My powers hadn't fully returned but I was determined to try and get them back. So determined to the point where I refused to leave the island until I did. I couldn't get into another fight with Kira in my current state. ***"Págo Toícho!"*** I shouted again. I shouted it a third time. Over and over and over again with the result being no better than the last. After every shout I felt weaker and weaker until I couldn't stand anymore.

I sat in the grass, frustrated with my current state. The ice started to melt away along with all of my resolve. I wished so deeply for strength.

"You look exhausted," I heard Ana say from behind me. I turned my head to see her walking over to my side with a cup in hand. She stretched it out, giving it to me and I saw that it was filled with water; something I desperately needed. I chugged it all down in a few gulps and laid back down into the grass.

Afterwards, I looked back up at her to admire her new attire. She wore a cropped shirt that showed off her impressive abs which would honestly give Flint a run for his money. She also had on some black baggy combat trousers with a bunch of pockets and black boots to go along with them.

"I'm sorry I wasn't there when Kira showed up," Ana apologized.

"Why are you apologizing?" I asked. "I'm the one who was too weak to take her down."

"You were just *tired*," she corrected while taking a seat next to me. "She caught you on a bad day. If you hadn't fought an entire flame monster beforehand, then maybe you could've actually stood a chance."

"But I don't just wanna stand a chance," I clarified. "I want to *win*. I want to *kill* her." I sighed while reaching for my dagger, pulling it out for us both to see. "I was going to use this to kill her. And I was so close. The blade was just inches away from her throat. But I was too slow. If I were just a little faster ... if I were as skilled as you, then I would've killed her."

Ana looked at me for a while before asking, "Then why don't you just do that?"

"Do what?"

"Become as skilled as me?"

I let out a weak laugh while answering, "Because I'm not a Zubarian."

"*So?* You think I got this strong just from being born? I've trained my entire life to get here and I'm still nowhere near my full potential, and neither are you. If you want strength then you've got to work for it. You should know that by now."

I turned to look her in the eye and told her, "You're right. You trained me to use a spear but that's not enough. I want to learn how to do what you do. *Please* teach me."

"Well I guess I *was* in desperate need of a training partner," she smirked. "So what the hell? Why not?" She got back up on her feet and said, "I'll train you but it's gonna be hell. We'll have to work on your strength before I can even show you how to throw a punch."

I stood up to meet her gaze and said, "Alright, what's first?"

***

She truly did put me through hell. Push ups, sit ups, squats, even nonstop sprints around the entire island. We did a variety of workouts to push every muscle in my body to its limits. Going out hunting almost every day in the frozen tundra put its fair share of strain on my body, but never like this. All that meant was that I would gain just as much strength. Or at least that's what Ana kept telling me. And it couldn't have been a lie since after just a few weeks, Alizeh wouldn't stop making such a big deal about my new and slightly toned physique. I even caught Flint staring more than once. The attention was overwhelming but something I could get used to.

It all culminated into finally starting combat training. Ana taught me how to throw a punch, and more importantly, how to take one. With her training, I was faster, stronger, and more agile. I wasn't anywhere close to her level of skill but I was probably formidable against most others.

In the middle of our training, Alizeh shouted, "Come on Ana, let me have a turn! Crystal's been hogging you forever! I want to learn how to fight and get all jacked too!"

Ana laughed and looked back at me, "Crystal, do you mind if I switch partners for a bit?"

"Knock yourselves out," I told them. "I need a break anyways."

I then left them to do as they pleased while making my way back to the treehouse. When I finally made it, I passed Flint who was napping in his hammock most likely out of boredom. I was going to keep walking until something caught my eye. It was glimmering in the shadows. After doing a double take, I saw his Spirit Caster lying on the ground under his hammock. Its allure was powerful.

I changed directions and made my way towards the staff. I made sure not to make any noise once I got closer to pick it up. It was truly a weapon to admire. The Rēa that flowed into me from it was powerful.

"What are you doing?" Flint asked, startling me, causing me to jump and almost drop his Spirit Caster.

"Nothing!" I blurted. "I was just looking at it."

I stretched my arms out to hand it back to him but once he laid just the tips of his fingers on it, I felt something so overwhelming that it made me drop his staff to the ground. It was his Rēa.

He sat up and reached down to his Spirit Caster while asking, "Are you ok?" with a raised brow.

"Yeah, I'm fine," I told him.

He got to his feet and walked past me while saying, "Next time, just ask before you touch my stuff, Snowflake."

"Wait," I turned to him.

He stopped in his tracks and turned his head slightly. "What is it?"

"You never did tell me what happened to your Spirit Caster."

"That's because I don't even know myself."

"You have to have *some* idea."

"Nope, not in the slightest," he shrugged while beginning to take his next step.

I stopped him by grabbing his wrists and said, "The power you obtained when we were on that volcano dwarfs that of what you had previously. I can't make sense of it."

"This is coming from the girl who beat the Phoenix after only just finding a Spirit Caster," he snickered.

The realization made me pause before finally admitting, "Alright, you got me there. But that doesn't matter because it doesn't compare to your power. I need to know what you did because I'm not going to be able to win this fight without it." Flint glared at me for a long while, mulling it over before I continued, "If you won't fight with me, then at least teach me what you know."

Flint finally groaned before saying, "Come on, let's go somewhere with a little more space," and walked in the opposite direction. I couldn't help but smile as I scurried behind him. After a couple of minutes we made it to a large secluded clearing.

"Why are we doing this here?" I asked.

"It's quiet and relaxing," he answered. "Excellent for meditation and reflection."

"Alright then, let's get started. So what do I have to do?"

"I'm not sure. Like I said before, it's hard to explain."

"Well think. What happened to you when your Spirit Caster changed?"

"Well, once you sealed the Phoenix, the volcano started to erupt and was going to lay waste over this entire island. But I couldn't let that happen so I just absorbed all the lava out of the volcano and into my Spirit Caster."

"How'd you pull that off?" I asked, surprised that such a thing could even be done.

"I think it was because of my resolve. I had a burning desire to protect you, Alizeh, Ana and everyone else on this island. I turned my emotional will into physical power."

"So as long as I have a strong enough will then I can gain that power? That sounds simple enough."

I closed my eyes and thought about the princess. I thought about what she did to my parents and what she made my sister endure. What she made *me* endure! I tightened my grip on my Spirit Caster out of pure hatred for that woman. I vowed that I would kill her. That had to be the will I needed to access this power. I reached within myself to draw out that power and with one full motion, released it. At that moment, I felt a huge surge of power coursing through me. But it was only for a moment.

I opened my eyes and saw that I was completely surrounded by large shards of ice. In fact, the entire area was covered in it. The only spot that wasn't covered in ice was where Flint was standing, and the only reason that there wasn't ice there was because fire had already taken its place.

"What ... was that?" Flint asked.

"I don't know, I didn't mean to do this," I told him. "Are you ok?"

"I am. If I hadn't melted your ice before it hit me then I wouldn't have been. The Rēa you just now brought out. It was more powerful than anything I've ever felt. It was only for a moment, but in that *moment* your power surpassed my own."

I looked down at the Spirit Caster and saw that it hadn't gone through any changes whatsoever. And I didn't feel any more powerful than I was a minute ago.

"It didn't work," I told him.

"That shouldn't be the thing you're focused on right now. You should be excited! Not only are you back at full power, but your potential is almost limitless!"

"Potential isn't the same as actual talent, Flint. It was probably just a fluke." The ice around me cracked and started to break down just like my resolve. I walked past him and said, "This is pointless, let's just go back to your place."

"Wait," he stopped me. "There's one more thing we can try."

"What is it?"

"Before my Spirit Caster evolved, I saw my mother."

"What do you mean?"

"Her spirit came to me. She communicated with me through the wand."

"And what did she say?"

"That's not important. I think that you should talk to your past ancestors and ask them if they can help you."

"Alright, seems like it could be worth a try. How do I contact them?"

"Wait, you don't know how?" He asked with a raised brow. "I thought that you've already contacted your grandmother before?"

"You've got it backwards. She's the one that contacted me. I've never tried to do it the other way around."

Flint sighed and plopped to the ground.

"Sit with me."

I did as he said and sat with my legs crossed.

"Lay your Spirit Caster on your lap and meditate with it. Clear your mind until you're only thinking about the person you want to meet."

I listened and closed my eyes. It wasn't too hard for me to completely clear my mind and it probably only took me around 20 seconds to finally see her.

"Hello, Crystal," my grandmother said to me.

"Grandmother Eve!" I blurted, "I didn't think this would actually work!"

"A little faith goes a long way. Now I'm guessing there's a reason you summoned me?"

"Yeah. I have a question for you."

"What is it?"

"How do I undergo the same change that Flint went through with his Spirit Caster?"

"Oh, so you want to know how to gain an Evolved Spirit Caster? You don't need to worry about that yet."

"What do you mean?"

"I mean it's too powerful for you. It's about ten years too early for you to reach *that* level of power."

"But I *need* that power."

"Then get stronger."

After she said that, she was gone, and I was back to reality.

"Any luck?" Flint asked.

"No," I told him bluntly before getting back up and saying, "I'm done here. Let's go find Alizeh and Ana to see how their training is going. Hopefully it's better than my own."

I walked away from the field and he followed close behind. We searched for a while before finally reaching a wide area with no trees. But it looked unnatural. The land was uneven and the trees were all broken down as if there was a large battle.

"Over here," Ana called. As we got closer, I saw that Alizeh was lying right next to her while unconscious.

"What happened?" I asked urgently.

"Relax," Ana answered. "She's just tired."

"I can feel her energy surrounding us," Flint added. "She did a number on this place."

"Are you saying that all this destruction..." I faltered.

"It came from her training," Ana finished.

Flint looked at me and grinned, "Looks like you two are just *full* of surprises."

CHAPTER THIRTY-THREE
FLINT

The training that everyone put themselves through lit a fire in my soul. And I guess I also didn't want to be shown up by a bunch of girls so I trained on my own, pushing my body physically with similar workouts that they were doing. Then afterwards I trained my spirit, trying to relearn what my Spirit Caster could do. Since it had evolved it was like an entirely new weapon with limitless potential.

So much so that just scratching the surface was enough to tire me out. I was sweaty and dirty when night fell and I decided it was time for a bath. And luckily I had just the secluded place to do it.

The moon was shining bright but the bamboo forests was tall so it shaded most of that light. I had to walk through the brush using my staff as a torch, which still didn't spread as much light as I would've hoped.

Eventually I finally made it to the shimmering, steam emitting hot springs. I threw off my shirt and started to undo my pants until something caught my eye. It was long, bright and metallic. When I got closer to it I found out it was a dagger. And clothes were scattered all around it. I wasn't alone.

"Do you need something?" I heard a voice ask from the water. I turned to see Ana submerged from the shoulders down.

"Ana ..." My words trailed not only from being surprised by her appearance but also from the realization that she was completely naked. I couldn't see her body under the water but just knowing made me feel a little more flustered than usual. I didn't want her kicking my ass for seeing something I shouldn't have.

"Spit it out," she demanded in a dry tone.

"I didn't know you were out here," I finally answered while turning away from her, "I figured you had gone for a walk when I didn't see you in the treehouse."

"I did go for a walk. And that walk brought me here."

"Alright then, I guess I'll leave you to it," I submitted before turning back.

"Where are you going?"

"Back home."

"Why?" she asked. "You walked all this way for a reason, didn't you?"

"Just to take a bath but you beat me to it. I'll just come back when you're done."

"There's no need, I don't mind sharing."

The invitation was a shock coming from her. When we first met she literally wanted to kill me, but in this moment it seemed like she was trying to make an advance towards me. That wasn't something I wanted to turn down.

"Are you sure about that?" I asked with a half mischievous smirk.

"Flint, we're both adults here. I'm sure this isn't your first time seeing a naked woman and you're not the first bare man I've seen either. Besides, it's too dark for us to *really* see each other. Especially under the water. So unfortunately for you, a lot of me will have to be left up to your imagination."

A lot of fair points. It seemed like she wanted me to stay. And who was I to deny a woman of what she wanted?

I took the rest of my clothes off and dove into the water on the opposite side from Ana. I wanted to move closer to her but she raised her hand, stopping me from taking even one stroke. It looked like I might've misinterpreted why she wanted me there.

"You can stay right where you are," she told me. "Sit back and get comfortable. There's something we need to talk about."

"What is it?" I asked as I sat my back against the steep bank of the hot spring.

"It's about what Crystal asked of you before. About joining us in our fight. Did you ever think it over?"

So that's what this was about.

"Yeah I thought it over," I told her, "and I gave my answer right then and there."

"You gave *Crystal* an answer. Now *I'm* asking."

Her tone was demanding but not in a whiny or annoying way. It was calm and confident. An overall trait that she exhibited in all facets of her life.

With a little more respect this time I answered, "I'm sorry Ana, but the answer is still no."

"And why's that? You got something better to do?"

"Yes actually. I need to stay here to protect this island from anyone who threatens it."

"You don't see King Cole as a threat? This island is valuable. It has explosive dust, rare ores, even that Spirit Caster of yours. Sooner or later, he *will* come and take everything from you and these people, regardless of the casualties he leaves behind."

"Then I'll wait until that day comes. There's no need to shoot at a sleeping bear."

"You know, Crystal said something similar to me once. Then her parents died."

The statement forced an uncontrollable scowl to form on my face. Crystal lost her parents because of her passiveness. And I lost Summer for the same reason. I'm not being passive. I'm just making the smartest play, but she can't see that.

"What do I truly gain from going with you?" I snapped. "What do *you* even gain? Why are you going on this journey with them when you're not even a Shēna?"

"The Shēna weren't the only race who were wronged by the royal bloodline," she snapped back.

I wondered how Ana could've possibly been affected by them. Most normal humans don't have any problem with how he rules since he isn't an immediate threat to them. The only other race is one that was almost completely eradicated years ago.

Unless...

My lips parted from shock, "You're a Zubarian."

My realization made Ana give me a sly grin, "So you know of my people?"

"I know what you're capable of. My mother wrote about Zubarians in her journals. The potential of your *Warrior's spirit* transcends not just the strength of men but even Shēna."

"That sounds like hyperbole but I'll take the compliment."

"So since you're a Zubarian, it seems like you're implying that you're on this quest for revenge. But I don't buy it. It doesn't fit your style."

"And how exactly would you know what my style is?" she argued.

"Because I'm observant. Now tell me the *real* reason."

Just like the first time we met, she scanned me with her eyes far longer than what I was comfortable with. But this time she gave me a half hearted smile instead of a gloomy scowl. I'd like to think her opinion of me at this point was definitely better than before.

"I wanna get stronger," she finally answered.

"Seriously? You're already stronger than most men."

"You know I haven't reached my full potential. It's just like you said. I have the potential to transcend the strength of man and Shēna alike. This journey has the trials and tribulations my body needs to push its limits."

"That makes sense. And it's a goal I admire."

"But not one you want to imitate?"

"I've got all the strength I need, so it's not something I desire anymore."

"That's a pretty stagnant way of thinking. I wish I could've shown you another way," she sighed before pulling herself out of the water. She was right. It was too dark for me to see anything. At least anything that I *wanted* to see. The moon light reflected off the water that was dripping off her body. She was like a shadow but I could clearly see her edges and curves. The almost hidden definition in every muscle. Her body was perfect and just as she said before, I was left with only my imagination to fill in the blanks.

"It's a shame really," she continued. "If you would've had a different answer I probably would've stayed in a little longer with you. But my moods soured."

"Wait seriously?" I gawked with immediate regret.

"Goodnight, Flint."

She picked up her clothes and daggers before walking into the jungle and out of sight.

I cursed under my breath. Was she serious? It had to be a joke. But If she wasn't then I probably missed out on the best night of my life.

The thought made my throat dry. Well, partially. In all reality it made me wonder if I made the right choice. If staying on the island was the *right* thing to do.

I reached out of the water and grabbed my Spirit Caster, holding on tight. I closed my eyes and took a deep breath.

"Ember," I whispered under my breath.

There was no answer.

"Mom, I need your guidance."

Still nothing. I opened my eyes and let go of the staff. I didn't know why I thought I could rely on that woman for once. I had always been alone. Since the day I was born. I didn't need her nor my nameless father. And I certainly didn't need to be with a group of kids who were in way over their heads. I'll follow my instincts and do what I have to do for the island and pray it won't be my undoing.

DAGGER IN THE SAND

CRYSTAL

On the day that I regained my powers, Ana and I talked it over and decided that there was no longer any need for us to stay on the island. We had been on the island for an entire month and within that time, we've trained, regained most of our strength and gained all the gear we needed to continue our journey. After our final night, as soon as the sun came up, we packed and made our way to the beach to get on the first boat back to the Black Continent.

"Flint, are you sure you don't want to join us in our fight?" I asked him one last time.

"Sorry, but that's not my battle right now. My place is here on the island. Personally I think you guys should just stay here. It would be pretty fun, don't you think?" he suggested.

"If I were here to have fun I might've actually taken you up on that offer. But I have my own goals that need to be taken care of."

"I wish we didn't have to go so soon," Alizeh said. "I still haven't beaten you in a fight yet!"

"Well, if you survive then come back and fight me another time. I'll be here," Flint told her.

She grinned and gave him a nod.

The captain of the ship yelled, "All aboard," letting everyone in the area know it was time for the ship's departure. Alizeh, Ana and I turned around and made our way to the ship.

Then Flint called, "Ana, you're not just going to leave without saying goodbye, are you?"

Ana stopped and turned to tell him, "I didn't think I needed to." She strolled back towards him while saying, "I'm not a fan of goodbyes. They sound too permanent." Once she got close enough, she cupped his chin, turned his face ever so slightly and gave him a light kiss on the cheek. "I'll see you later." And with that, she turned our way, leaving flint speechless.

After a few moments, he finally laughed and said, "I'll be waiting."

Once Ana made it back to us, I rolled my eyes and said, "I don't know what you see in that man."

"In all honesty, me neither," Ana answered. "But I'm sure I'll figure it out sooner or later."

***

Much later, in the middle of the night, Alizeh, Ana and I finally made it back to the Black Continent. More specifically, we were in Livádia. Alizeh's homeland.

We were all too tired to continue any further than that, so we decided to stay the night with our families in hiding. Finally, I was able to see Wren again while Alizeh could see her parents. Just as importantly, Silver would see his master's face again after so long. We greeted them in a barn that belonged to a family friend. That's where they were staying since their house got destroyed.

Silver howled at the sight of Ana and pounced on her, showing all of his pent up affection. She decided to stay outside with him while Alizeh and I went inside.

"Oh, our sweet darling has returned to us!" Alizeh's mother said as they embraced. "I was so worried! I thought you'd never return!"

"So where's the new Shēna?" her father asked. "Did you find them?"

"Yes, but he refused to help us," I answered.

Suddenly, I heard rapid footsteps coming from up above. Wren practically slid down the ladder and ran at full speed in my direction while calling my name.

"Crystal!"

"Wren!"

She jumped into my arms and squeezed me tightly while brushing her nose against mine.

"I'm so glad you're back!" she yelled. "You don't have to leave again, do you?"

"Unfortunately, I do," I answered, forcing her smile to sink into a frown. "But don't worry," I continued. "I'm spending the rest of the night here."

Alizeh's father looked over at me and asked, "What's your next move?"

"We're going to Mount Astrapí. My grandmother's spirit said that there should be a Shēna hiding there."

"Ah yes, Tora."

"You know them?"

"Yeah. She was one of the members in our group when we used to go on our crazy adventures. I think she'd be happy to help you guys out in your battle. But the mountain she lives on is pretty far from here."

"Yeah, I know. We're gonna have to cut right through the Kítrinos Desert to get there."

"The Kitrinos Desert?" Alizeh's mother gasped. "But that part of the Black Continent is a desolate wasteland filled with nothing but thieves! You can't go through there!"

"Especially without the right gear," her father added.

"Don't worry," Alizeh said while opening up her pouch. "We've got enough gold for us to be more than prepared to go out there."

Her parents ogled at the shimmering coins. "How did you get all this?" Her father asked.

"We fought a Phoenix," Alizeh answered.

Her parents had a look of pure confusion on their faces.

"Don't worry," I said. "We'll explain everything in the morning. For now, we should get some rest. We've got a long trip ahead of us."

The very next morning we had all woken up and made our way to some nearby shops to prepare for our trip. We bought black cloaks to absorb our body heat, goggles to protect our eyes from sand, canteens with fruit, some backpacks to hold it all, and two camels for Alizeh and I to ride through the desert. Ana was taking Silver along with us this time. By noon we were fully prepared to leave, so we said goodbye once more to our families and were off.

"Hey, do you think The Kítrinos Desert is really as bad as they say it is?" Alizeh asked as we traveled atop our camels on the dirt path of a forest.

"I don't know," I answered. "I haven't heard much about the place."

"I've heard that it's bigger than what's shown on the maps, and that it's filled with thieves at every corner," Ana explained.

"I hope that's just an exaggeration," I sighed

"Well, I hope it's true!" Alizeh beamed.

Ana and I looked at each other before looking back at her.

"Why's that?" Ana asked.

"I love the excitement. Shēna are supposed to live a life of adventure. My father always used to tell me stories of when he was my age going on adventures with other Shēna like Crystal's grandmother and the lady we're going to see now. I want to be able to have stories just like his."

"That's a very dangerous mindset to have, kid," Ana told her. "Adventures can be fun but equally as dangerous. At any moment, we could all die. When we fought the Phoenix together, I honestly thought we were all done for. Especially when it hit you and you weren't waking up."

"I was fine."

"Only because *we* were there," I added. "If we weren't, you would've *died*. Alizeh, I don't think you understand the consequences of what we're doing. If you died, I would never be able to forgive myself."

"Then just don't let me die and I'll do the same for you guys. I understand the consequences but I don't care. As long as we have each other's backs then we can survive anything."

"How can you put so much trust in us?"

She pondered the question for a few seconds before saying, "Because, you're both like the big sisters I never had. I adore both of you. I've only known you for a little over a month now but ever since you guys entered my life, everything's changed. I've battled and fought beside other Shēna and warriors alike, traveled far off the Black Continent, and not only did I see a Phoenix, but I also fought one! We've known each other for such a small amount of time yet it feels like we've already been through so much together. It's gotten to the point where I now trust you both with my life."

Alizeh's words reached a special place in my heart that no one had ever been able to reach before. If you weren't a part of my family, then I would never have had any feelings towards you. Just pure indifference. But Alizeh truly was different. Ever since the first day we met I felt this warmth that

I've only felt by my own family. Even now I feel it. As if she truly had become a sister to me.

Initially the only other person to get close was Ana. But I didn't feel that way until we started training together, allowing me to fully understand her close and personal fighting style. I'd never felt intimacy quite like that.

I nodded my head and said, "Alright, I promise to keep that trust. Also I'm glad you're both here with me on this adventure. I couldn't have asked for better friends to join me."

Alizeh smiled back at me and said, "Yeah, me too."

Ana simply smirked and chuckled but that was, within itself, fairly telling.

Eventually, we made it to the border that divided Livádia from Kítrinos. The forest that we traveled through came to an abrupt end. There was no sign of life as far as the eye could see and the only thing in sight was a sea of white sand that seemed to have no end.

I looked at Alizeh and asked, "Are you sure you're ready for this?"

She reached into her bag and pulled out a pair of black and gold goggles with green lenses. After tightening them around her face, she then gazed out at the desert with a big grin. "I was born ready. Let's go!

***

The sun was beaming down on me and my body was drenched in sweat. This was the complete opposite of living in Nótio Págo. This was probably the hottest I'd ever felt.

Ever since the Ice Spirit Caster came into my possession, the weather hadn't been a problem for me. In Nótio Págo, I felt completely warm in a snowstorm. But now that I was in the heat, it felt like I was completely melting. Maybe it was the downside of using ice. Heat was an extreme weakness.

"Crystal, it's so hot," Alizeh complained.

"*You're* telling *me*," I snapped back.

"We're running low on water," Ana announced. "How long until we reach the next town?"

I looked down at the ragged piece of paper and said, "If I'm doing the math right for the scaling of this map, then we should get to it by sundown."

"Hmm, I guess that's not that bad," Alizeh sighed.

"Yeah, as long as we keep this pace and stay out of trouble then this trip should go smoothly."

Suddenly, the camel I was riding on made a loud wail and toppled over, making me go down with it into the sand. It took me a second to realize what had happened.

"Crystal, are you ok?" Alizeh asked.

"Yeah," I answered while brushing the sand out of my hair. The camel was still wailing on its side. I quickly crawled over to it and laid my hand on the side of its face, trying to calm it. It was in pain.

Ana's entire demeanor changed before she said, "Crystal, she's bleeding."

I quickly stood up and scanned the situation. There was blood all over its front left leg. I took a closer look and saw that there was something metallic trapped inside its ankle. It was some kind of trap.

What the hell? I wondered who could have set something like this up in the middle of nowhere. I quickly shrugged the thought off. My main priority was setting the camel free as soon as possible.

"Crystal, I have a bad feeling about this. It feels like we're being watched. I don't think that we're alone."

"You're probably just imagining things. Now come down and help me get this thing off her leg."

"No, Crystal, I don't think you get it. I don't just sense the Rēa in other Shēna but I can also sense the life force of other—"

Before she could finish explaining, several men jumped up from under the sand and surrounded us.

"Empty your pockets!" one of the men yelled.

"Give us all of your possessions or we'll kill ya!" another man yelled.

They all had their weapons drawn from swords, daggers, and even battle axes. Me, Ana and Alizeh eyed each other, knowing full well that we weren't going to back down from this challenge. We all simultaneously reached into our cloaks with Alizeh and I whipping out our Spirit Casters while Ana pulled out her daggers.

"Cheimerinó Fengári," I yelled as I swung my wand up. But nothing happened.

"Víaii sfýrigma!" Alizeh yelled, causing a massive explosion of wind to push half of the group back while also forcing a large cloud of sand and dust to shroud the area.

I didn't understand why my spell didn't work. This wasn't like before. The last time this happened I felt completely drained of almost all my Rēa. This time I could feel that I was completely filled with Rēa, but for some reason my spell wasn't working. Was it because of the heat? Was there not enough moisture in the air?

I crouched down and stuck my Spirit Caster into the sand this time, trying a different spell.

"Ríza Págou."

The wand glowed blue but only the smallest bit of ice started to extend into the sand and quickly melted into water. I was right! It *was* the heat.

The rest of the bandits still standing started running in my direction. I couldn't use any spells, but I was still agile enough to evade whatever came my way. One of the men swung his sword at me and I was able to jump out of its path. Unfortunately, that led me further into the cloud of dust where it was hard to see much of anything.

Before I realized it, another bandit was right beside me, ready to strike. He thrusted his dagger towards me, aiming right for my waist. Without thinking, I grabbed his blade before he could reach me. I tried to yank it away but instead ended up snapping it in two.

The man looked at his broken blade in disbelief and then back at me. Before giving him a chance to think any further, I landed a clean hit right in the center of his face, knocking him out completely.

I opened my fist revealing the broken blade to myself. Just like the bandit I was in complete disbelief. Not only did I just break the blade with my bare hands, but it didn't put a scratch on me. This had to be the power of my Rēa. Not only did it enhance my agility, but also my strength and durability to an extremely high degree.

As I was deep in thought, I was suddenly grabbed from behind by a very large man. He tightened his arms around me and lifted me about a foot off the sand as another man came running to us.

"Keep her still!" he yelled before snatching my Spirit Caster right out of my hand. "Let's retreat for now!"

"What do I do about this one?" the man holding me asked.

"We're taking her with us!" he yelled as he started to burrow himself into the sand completely disappearing from sight.

"Alright girly, we're next," the large man said.

I tried to break out of his grip but couldn't. With the wand no longer in my possession, I could no longer feel it's Rēa empowering me. The man jumped in the same spot of sand as the other bandit did and we both started to sink.

"Alizeh! Ana!" I shouted. But it was too late because as soon as I called out to them, I was already buried beneath the sand.

CHAPTER THIRTY-FIVE
ANA

One of the men swung his blade at me from the left while another swung from the right. I spun my body through the air to evade both and before I hit the ground, I kicked one of them down with me. The man who was still standing swung his sword at me again, but I was able to block it with my wrist guard. Before he could think of a counter, I jabbed my fist right into his nose, breaking it and knocking him out instantly.

At that very moment, I heard a howl and quickly scanned the area looking for silver through the sand cloud. I ran until I escaped the dust, but I was too late. Once I got out of the cloud, I saw Lumi tied onto a raft being pulled by two large lizard-like creatures that I had never seen before. They were capturing him!

"Crystal!" I shouted, "They're getting away with Silver!"

"Aeráki!" I heard Alizeh yell. The sand cloud immediately dispersed, and all the rest of the bandits were lying down in the sand. She seemed to have made quick work of them. But I didn't see Crystal anywhere in sight.

"Where's Crystal?" I asked.

Alizeh glanced around. "She was here just a moment ago."

"Damnit!" I growled. My instincts told me that they had to have taken *her* too. "Come on! We're going after them!" I ordered while darting off after the raft. But it was too fast. I had no idea how we would catch up with it on foot until Alizeh said another spell.

"Pairno Ptisi!"

Next thing I knew, Alizeh grabbed onto me from behind and lifted me in the air. We were flying at a decent pace but we needed to go even faster if we were going to catch up to them.

"Alizeh, can't you go any faster?"

"I'll try but you're kinda heavy." She took a deep breath and continued, ***"Grigoros Ánemos!"***

The spell made us go even faster until we were right on their tail. As we got closer, I realized the raft had something mechanical on the back of it. One of the bandits lit a small flame on the object and that's when I knew exactly what we were dealing with.

"Alizeh, watch out!" I shouted. "They have a cannon!"

"A what?"

Before I could repeat myself, it went off, firing straight at us. Alizeh let go, allowing me to evade the incoming danger, but in return, she got hit point blank and was sent flying out of sight. Once I landed in the sand I quickly grabbed onto a loose rope hanging from the raft and was pulled along with it. I held on for dear life and used all my strength to pull myself onto the raft.

As soon as I got on board, I saw a spear heading right for me. I dodged it, quickly got to my feet and tackled the man who threw it. Once I pinned him to the ground, I pulled out my dagger and drove it right into his neck. At the same time, I saw a glimpse of someone coming from my blind side. I jumped out of the way, but my face was still nicked by his weapon, causing me to fall down on the hardwood floor. He held a large ax but he was slow. I would have effortlessly been able to get away without a scratch if it wasn't for this dead eye.

He raised his ax into the air but before he could swing it down, I took aim and tossed my dagger right at him. The blade went right through his eye, killing him instantly. Yet the feeling wasn't satisfying. I was aiming for his neck. My depth perception was still completely scrambled with only one eye.

I looked over to my right and saw Silver pinned down to the floorboards by a large net. I quickly got up, grabbed the dead man's ax and swung it down on the net to free him. Before I could go for a second swipe, I was stopped by an arrow stabbing me right in the shoulder, forcing me to drop the ax and fall to the ground.

A man with a crossbow was across the raft, readying his next attack. He shot the second arrow and aimed it towards my one good eye, but before it could hit, I used my wrist guards to block the attack. He loaded the crossbow with another arrow while coming close to me to make sure he didn't miss next time. Right before he shot off the next arrow, Silver broke out of his bonds in the nick of time.

He wasted no time to maw my attacker. I got back up and looked around. Crystal was nowhere to be seen but even worse, there was no one steering this thing and we were headed right for a large boulder. It would only take us less than ten seconds to collide with the obstruction.

"Silver!" I called while running to the edge of the raft. He soon followed and I hopped right on his back. "Let's go!"

He jumped off the raft and right into the sand, losing his footing on the shifting earth causing us to tumble over, but that wasn't worse than the fate of those on the raft. It crashed right into the boulder forcing wood, materials and even bodies into the air. It would have required a miracle for anyone to have actually survived the crash. And I really needed that miracle because I had a few questions for such an unfortunate soul.

I sat up and looked over at Silver. "Are you alright?" I asked. He got up on all fours and shook all the sand out of his fur before licking me a few times. I'd imagine he was asking me the same question. I scratched his neck and got back up to my feet. "Let's go," I told him while heading to the site of the crash.

After looking around for a bit I only found two bodies. Both being the ones I already killed. I went to one of them and pulled out my dagger from his eye. Albeit gross, these things weren't cheap.

I couldn't find the third man anywhere until I finally heard his voice. "Someone, help," I heard him groan. "Please, someone." I heard his voice coming from a pile of rubble and reached my hand in to pull him up by his collar. He was the same man who shot that arrow into me, but I'd say we were almost even considering all the fresh wounds that Silver gave him for payback.

"Please, spare me," the man begged.

"You shot me with an arrow. And even worse, you shot my friend with a *cannon!*" I shouted while throwing him to the ground and stomping on his hand. From the way he screamed, I guessed that I'd broken his fingers which was a pretty satisfying thought. "You're lucky that I've seen her survive worse," I continued. "But the fact that my other friend isn't anywhere in sight cancels out that luck." I picked him back up so our eyes could meet and glowered at him, "The girl with the white hair. Tell me where she is."

"I don't know," he told me.

I dropped him back to the ground, pulled out my bloodied dagger and said, "Then I don't need you anymore."

"Wait, wait!" he begged. "I'll tell you what you want to know! Just don't kill me!"

I stepped over him and stomped on his other hand, forcing him to cry out even more. That one must've already been broken.

"That's for lying to me."

When I scanned his body, I saw a pouch connected to his belt. As he was still whimpering from my last stomp, I yanked it off him and took a peek inside. It had just what I needed. A roll of bandages.

I took it out and sat down on a nearby rock. "I'm going to bandage up the wound that *you* gave me and while I'm doing that, you're going to tell me everything I need to know. If I'm not satisfied with your answer by the time I'm done then I'll feed you to my dog."

He looked over at Silver who was just sitting there with blood still covering his mouth, waiting for me to give him the order. The man took a big gulp before I continued.

"And just so you know, he hasn't eaten yet today. Since he likes to savor his food, I cant imagine your death would be quick. So tell me, where's my friend?"

CHAPTER THIRTY-SIX
CRYSTAL

After going under the sand, I couldn't see anything. I just sank down, unable to breathe. It made me feel like I was drowning in solid waters.

Eventually it stopped and I could feel myself plop down to the ground, but it was still too dark for me to see anything. I got to my feet but as soon as I did, I could feel someone grabbing me from behind again. I struggled to break free but to no avail.

"Let go of me!" I shouted.

"This girl's a feisty one," the voice said from behind. "What should we do with her? It's not every day we find a woman like this. We should have *fun* with her."

"I swear I'll kill you!" I threatened.

A light within the darkness flickered. Fiery torches ignited and lit the entire area. I was surrounded by dozens of bandits in an underground cavern.

"Yeah, I think you're right, Bedagi," one of the bandits agreed.

"She sure is beautiful," another sang.

"Stay away from me!" I shouted. Never in my life had I felt so much fear. I was defenseless as I was surrounded by a collection of immoral criminals. They all started to get riled up as they came closer to me with a sadistic look in each one of their eyes. I closed my own eyes, not wanting to see whatever horrors they intended to inflict on me. Then one man's voice rose above all the rest.

"Everyone shut the hell up! You're all too damn loud!"

I opened my eyes again and saw all the bandits frozen in fear while not making a sound. Some started to move only to make way for one handsome young man with dark skin and golden eyes. His long black hair was wrapped in a ponytail that hung down to his waist. He was clothed in tattered rags and bandages that looked a lot more damaged than the rest of the men who surrounded me.

He glared at me with seemingly hostile intent and then looked back at the other bandits before asking, "Is this Crystal Winters?"

The question caught me off guard. I didn't know this person and I had no idea how he could have known me. His question scared me, yet at the same time, intrigued me.

"We think so, sir," one of the men answered. "She's a Shēna, and we found her with another woman and a younger girl. We believe the small one was Alizeh Green."

"How do you know about us?" I interrupted.

The young man looked back at me and said, "Because you're wanted criminals."

"What? I'm not a criminal! You must have the wrong—"

Before I could finish, I felt a cold, sharp metal leaning against my neck. The young man had a knife pressed against my throat. With deep hatred in his eyes, he said, "I thought I told everyone to shut the hell up. Stop yelling before I slice your neck open." He leaned in closer to me and continued saying, "I don't think you understand the position you're in. You're currently my slave. If you don't follow my orders, then I swear

I'll tear you apart and let the rest of these guys have what's left. Do you understand?"

I tried to keep my composure, but I could feel myself slipping. My body was trembling, and my eyes started to water. My throat instantly became too dry for me to give him a verbal answer, so I just nodded my head in agreement. Never in my life had another man ever made me feel this intimidated. It was as if I was staring into the eyes of a violent blood thirsty animal.

He took his blade away from my throat and turned to face the rest of the bandits. "If any of you bruise her, or if I catch you doing anything unsightly to her, I'll kill you in an instant. We're going to sell her as a slave, and I don't want to sell her damaged or used. Her value will go down."

"What should we do with her boss?" another bandit asked.

"Tie her up and put her with the rest of our stolen goods."

CHAPTER THIRTY-SEVEN

ALIZEH

I woke up covered in sand. It took me a few moments to remember how I got there. The cannon. The flash of light. It almost killed me. As soon as it hit me, I could feel it. The Rēa that fueled the explosion.

Where did a bunch of bandits get a weapon like that? I thought.

I got back up to my feet while shaking the sand out of my hair and looked around. Ana wasn't anywhere in sight and there weren't any tracks to follow. I needed a better vantage point.

"Pairno Ptisi."

I flew high into the air, pulled off my goggles and looked in every direction; still, there was nothing but sand as far as I could see. As I was floating in the air, I crossed my arms and legs while going into deep thought. The desert was too vast. Trying to find just a couple of people would be like trying to find a needle in a haystack. And there was a good chance that they were both in trouble, so I needed to act sooner than later.

Then a thought hit me. Maybe I didn't need to find *them*, but someone else who might know where they were. Crystal said that the closest town was north from where we were and that we would get there by sundown. If it really was that close, then there was a possibility that someone in that town had information on these bandits. If just one person knew where their base of operation was, then I could easily break their door down, swoop right in, and save them.

Since I didn't need to worry about staying in a group or having to carry someone, that meant that there was nothing to slow me down. I had to move quickly so I put my goggles back on, added the spell *'Grígoros Ánemos'* to boost my speed and I blasted off in the direction of the closest town.

It didn't take long for me to reach my destination. What would've taken half a day on foot only took less than half an hour by flight. This speed was an amazing change of pace that I could get used to. Once I was right over the town, I made my descent, landing right in its center.

It was a decently sized village with small clay houses and damaged structures that looked almost as if they were abandoned. And I didn't see a single person in sight. Some animals like roosters and malnourished dogs roamed around but there weren't any owners. I got closer to one of the houses and poked my head through one with an already busted down door.

"Hello?" I called, announcing my presence to anyone within earshot. But there was no answer. Not a single living soul in the house. The only thing that inhabited the home were piles of sand.

Once I walked back out and looked around one more time I could finally confirm that the village had been completely abandoned. This was definitely a huge setback to my plan. If there was no one in the village then that meant that there was no one who could give me information on those bandits. And if I couldn't get any information then there was no way I could find Crystal and Ana. The situation seemed hopeless.

I went back to the center of the village and sat at the dried-up fountain while trying to think of a new plan, but nothing was coming to me. Well, nothing but one scrawny dog. It could barely stand on all fours and was losing hair on its thin body. He looked too weak to even beg for food.

I dug into my bag and pulled out two large pieces of dried meat and tossed it next to him. That got his tail moving. Once he got hold of it, he strutted away past a few houses and finally turned a corner, out of sight. At least I could help *him*.

I closed my eyes and took a deep breath. The only thing I could feel in the town was the dog's fleeting life force ... and ... wait there was another. I opened my eyes and suddenly, as if appearing from nowhere, I was surrounded by more bandits.

They must have been watching me, waiting for the time when I was most vulnerable. They did a good job this time because I didn't even feel them coming, which was unusual, but I guessed not entirely impossible. Unfortunately for them, I still had my Spirit Caster in hand, so I was ready for anything.

One of them ran towards me with a sword and I punched the air using, **"Mach Grothiá!"**. Strangely enough, it did nothing. No damage whatsoever. He didn't even flinch.

He came within striking distance and slashed his sword at me, just grazing my arm. I jumped up while yelling "Paírno Ptísi," making myself fly high into the air. I looked at my arm to see how bad the damage was but saw that there wasn't the slightest drop of blood.

Did he miss? I thought. No, I could have sworn he connected. I didn't feel pain, but I saw the blade go through my skin. I hadn't the slightest clue what was up with this guy, but he seemed dangerous. I had to use another new technique I learned from my battles with Flint if I wanted to end this quickly.

"Enischyméni Michanikí-" I started to yell but I was interrupted by another voice.

"Pagída Tis Erímou," the voice said.

Suddenly, the sand around the bandits started to rise and swirl around them, sweeping them up into the air and forming into a large sphere. I lowered myself towards the sand sphere to take a closer look and saw that the bandits had been completely buried within the floating sand. This was a Shēna's doing!

"Hope you don't mind me stealing your kill, but it seemed like you needed some help," I heard someone say. I turned around while I was still in the air to see who it was. It was someone I had never met before. Her skin was dark, her eyes brown, and her curly black hair went down to her waist. "Hey there, my name's Mirage. What's yours?"

I quickly flew over to her, releasing my spell to stand before her.

"Are you a Shēna?" I asked.

"That I am."

"That's great! My friends and I are looking for Shēna to help us! Speaking of which, they're actually in big trouble! Do you think you can help me? My name's Alizeh by the way."

Mirage studied me with a look on her face that could only mean she had trouble following my words. Perhaps my excitement got the better of me and forced me to overwhelm her. It wasn't a big problem since it seemed like she started to understand the situation.

"Umm, yeah. Sure, I'll help," she agreed. "What happened to these friends of yours?"

"Their names are Crystal and Ana. Oh, and Ana has a pet dog. His name's Silver. They all got kidnapped by a group of bandits so I came to this village trying to find information on them, but it looks like it's abandoned."

"Yeah, you're right about that. This place was abandoned many years ago due to the constant crimes of the bandits and I'm the only resident left. I've been trying my best to clean this place up so that my people can return one day. But it's hard doing this by myself."

"What do you know about these bandits? Do you know where we can find them? I'll help you take them down if you help me save my friends."

"You're in luck. I know exactly where their base of operation is."

"Alright, let's head there right now. Lead the way!"

"Ha! You sure are a spirited one. Ok, let's go find your friends."

CHAPTER THIRTY-EIGHT
CRYSTAL

I sat down, leaning against the wall with my hands bound together by rope. I was surrounded by piles of gold weapons and other antique treasures. Two bandits stood at the doorway acting as guards so that I couldn't escape. Earlier, I saw the leader of the bandits take my Spirit Caster with him, so it could've been anywhere at this point.

I needed to escape this place, find my friends, and have both of them beat these guys to a bloody pulp until we found my wand. But before any of that, I needed to find a way past these two bandits.

I thought long and hard before finally saying, "Hey, you two should really let me go."

They both laughed. One of them asked, "Now, why would we do that?"

"Because if you don't, then I'll kill you both with my magic in an instant," I warned in a serious tone.

Their demeanors changed, letting me know that they weren't as amused as before by that threat. "*Pfft*, your jokes aren't funny. We know that you don't have your wand with you which means you're powerless."

I let out a wicked laugh and asked, "Do you *actually* believe that? If so, then you know nothing about the Shēna."

One of the men took a step back. It seemed that my bold claims were getting to him. The other smaller man said to him, "Don't let yourself get tricked by this kid. Think about it. If she really still had her power, then she would have used it by now. There would have been no way that we would have been able to capture her for this long."

"Unless that was exactly what I wanted," I added.

"Now I *really* know you're messing with us. Why would you allow yourself to be captured?"

I gave him the most sinister smile I could muster and said, "So I can destroy you all. By trapping me here, all you've done is made it easier for me to accomplish that goal. I'm in the center of your base. I've passed all of your defenses and none of you suspected a thing."

Something changed in the men's eyes. There was complete fear, but they were still suspicious of whether or not I was truly a threat. I needed to give them an extra push.

"So, I'll ask both of you again," I told them as I stood up to my feet, "release me if you don't want me to destroy you!"

The taller man took a few steps towards me, but the shorter man grabbed him by the shoulder, stopping him.

"Don't listen to her! It's a trick!" he yelled.

"You think so?" I challenged as I took a step towards them.

"But what if she's telling the truth? We barely know anything about the Shēna. She might actually kill us!"

"Even so, we'd be in even bigger trouble if Barin finds out. He'd torture us before beating us to death with his bare hands."

"Barin?" I asked as I took a few more steps towards them. "Is that the name of your leader? *He's* the man that I'm going to give a very slow and painful death to? Is that right?"

"Stay back!" the short man yelled.

I inched myself closer to them and said, "I'm going to need an answer."

The men drew their swords, and one shouted, "This is your final warning! Don't move!"

I stopped my slow pace and darted towards them at full speed. There was instant panic from both the men as they raised their swords high, ready to do anything to protect themselves from whatever they believed I had up my sleeve. As I ran towards them, I quickly realized that I had formed a truly stupid plan. If they didn't turn tail and run by the time I'd reach them then I would have to improvise before getting myself killed.

It took but seconds for me to get within striking distance of them and by that time they weren't fleeing. I seemed to have made a mistake, but I had to run with it, hoping I could slip past them. The small man raised his blade high into the air, ready to cut me down with it. I raised my bounded hands up high and once he swung down, his blade cut right through the rope that restricted my arms from moving freely.

As soon as my hands were free, I put all my strength into my arm and swung at his face while trying to envision the power I used from my earlier punch. Then, I forced my fist right in the center of his face, knocking him right down on his back. I didn't knock him out, but it was enough to make him groggy.

I quickly glanced around the room for a weapon I could use to finish him off. It took only a second for me to spot a golden dagger lying next to my feet. I quickly swiped it up from off the floor and as soon as he got back up, I swung at his neck.

Slicing his neck brought back the terrible memory of that night. Or perhaps the feeling. The desperate need to survive and protect. On that night, I cut right through a man's neck just like I was doing now. This was the second time I'd ever killed a man. And in that moment, I felt no remorse.

Blood spilled from his neck. He grabbed it while desperately gasping for air until he toppled down to the ground with his life leaving his eyes. I looked up at the tall man who was shaking with fear as I stood over the dead body.

"You're next," I threatened, hoping it would be enough for him to give up.

He dropped his weapon and turned around, running out of sight. This was my chance to escape. I held up the golden dagger stained with crimson blood. It was the perfect weapon for me. I was well accustomed to using daggers against wild animals and that's exactly what these bandits were. It was the only thing I needed to make my escape.

I made my way through the deep tunnels, taking out everyone in my path. But I didn't use brute force. Without my Spirit Caster, there was no guarantee that I would beat anyone head on. So I had to hunt them the same way I would with any other animal. With stealth.

I had to remember that with every kill. Every slit throat. Every dagger in the back. These bandits were nothing more than monsters and I had to do everything I could to stay above the food chain.

I reached a corner and spotted someone standing outside a door while smoking a pipe. He could've been guarding the way out. If so, I couldn't take the chance of letting this guy be. I had to take him down just like the rest.

I snuck up behind him with my dagger in hand without making a sound. Once he finally turned and spotted me, it was already too late for him to react. I was close enough to take him down, but my plans were foiled by another bandit that I didn't even see coming.

He tackled me, forcing us both through the door, slamming it open while pushing me into the next room. I wasn't ready for the landing. He pinned me down so quickly and with so much force that it caused me to twist my own ankle. I winced in pain, shutting my eyes before opening them again and taking a look around. This wasn't the exit. I was now in a room surrounded by at least a dozen other men. Escape was impossible.

They all came to me and dragged me back up to my feet. But with this twisted ankle, I could barely stand without them.

"Guess who was walking around, taking out all our men one by one?" the bandit who tackled me announced. "Stopped her before she could slit Benny's throat."

How long was he watching me for? For him to gather all that information, he had to have been tailing me all this time without me even noticing. I was careless.

Benny came over to me and, without hesitation, hit me with the back of his hand and choked me with the other, dragging me across the room and slamming me onto a table, pinning me down by my neck. I couldn't breathe and I had no way of escaping from his grasp.

"You bitch!" he seethed. "You tried to kill me while my back was turned? I'd do the same to you if Morpheus didn't want you alive."

Morpheus? That name didn't sound familiar. I was under the impression that *Barin* was his boss. Was there someone else pulling the strings here?

"We can't just lock her back in a room," my first attacker suggested. "There needs to be *real* consequences for what she's done here today."

"Yeah, I think you're right," another bandit chided in. "She needs to be taught a lesson."

"But didn't Barin say not to lay a finger on her?" One in the back argued.

"Barin isn't here right now," Benny barked. "As long as we don't kill her, he won't care."

My first attacker got closer to us and said, "I have a few ideas of what we can do to her."

"I'll let you have her after I ask a few questions," Benny grinned while pulling out a dagger and turning his attention back to me. "Are you right or left-handed?"

I kicked him and flailed my arms wildly trying to do any damage I could. Punching and scratching only made him more angry. I couldn't scream for help or beg for mercy. I couldn't even breathe anymore. I was blacking out and my final thoughts of what they had planned for me rivaled my own death.

Right at that moment, I heard a slam that made the entire room go silent. I rolled my eyes as far as I could to see what it was. Barin, the group's leader, was standing in the doorway with a dead look in his eyes. I couldn't get a read on him. I didn't know if he came here to stop them or help them.

"Barin," Benny asked, "What are you doing here?"

"I smelled blood," Barin answered. "After I followed the trail, it led me right here. What are you doing to the girl?"

"She killed a bunch of our men. We were going to teach her a lesson."

"Get your hands off of her."

"But, sir—"

"I said, get your damn hands off of her!" Barin roared.

The man let go and I could finally breathe again. I collapsed to the floor, not taking a single breath for granted as I gasped it all back in. Barin slowly walked towards me with an angrier look than before.

He crouched down next to me and said, "Let me see your face."

I hadn't even caught my breath yet, so I wanted nothing to do with him. I tried to back away, but he quickly grabbed my arm and pulled me back in.

"Calm down, I'm not going to hurt you."

He cupped my chin and pulled me in even closer to examine my face. His thumb brushed gently across my bottom lip and once he unhanded me, I could see the blood from my busted lip staining his fingers. In that same moment, his eyes became blood red. It startled me. I could've sworn he had golden eyes, but at that moment they were a completely different color. As if they changed a shade to match his rage.

Despite that, he looked fairly calm as he got back up to his feet before heading to the door. But he didn't leave. He just shut it and locked everyone inside before saying aloud, "I thought I said that if any of you bruised her or did *anything* unsightly to her then I'd kill you. Or am I mistaken?"

Everyone in the room stayed silent, not wanting to provoke his silent rage any further, but that only made him angrier.

"Answer me!" he demanded.

Some people muttered the words, "Yes," while others were still too scared and just nodded.

"Then why is she bruised?"

"It's like I said before," Benny finally spoke again, "She needed to be taught a lesson."

Barin pondered the statement before saying, "You know what? You're right about one thing." He slowly made his way closer to Benny as he spoke. "A lesson definitely needs to be taught. So, I'm going to use you all as an example of what happens when you disobey me."

Within the blink of an eye, Benny's head came crashing down right in front of me and it didn't take long for his body to hit the floor behind it. I didn't even see what happened. Barin had just come into striking distance and in a flash was able to draw his sword and decapitate another man before he could even flinch.

Someone tried running to the door, but Barin was quicker. He cut him down with his sword and it didn't take long for panic to spread throughout the entire room. Running didn't do the men any good. Barin killed three more men within seconds, picking them off like loose cattle.

A few men got the bright idea to surround him and attack but that only quickened their death. He cut off one man's arm then another man's leg. They all dropped like flies. He was moving faster than even I could comprehend. Not even *Ana* could move that fast. It was obvious that if they ever fought then she would die just like the rest of these men.

It didn't take long for the room to be flooded with a pool of blood that stained my black robe as I sat in it. Once the last body hit the floor and the screaming stopped, Barin took a deep breath and sheathed his sword. He then made his way over to me.

"Are you ok?" he crouched back down in front of me. His eyes were golden again and this time he seemed more calm. It made me wonder if I imagined the color change. "Answer me, Winters, are you ok?" he got impatient.

"Y-yeah," I stuttered trying to force an answer out so I wouldn't end up like the bodies that surrounded us.

He reached his hand out to me and I reluctantly grabbed it, letting him pull me up to my feet, but my twisted ankle didn't allow me to stay up for long. He immediately picked up on the problem, wrapped his arms around me and picked me right off from the ground. Although I was still too terrified to even object, I wasn't completely opposed to the gesture.

He walked me out of the room without saying a word which forced me to finally ask, "Where are you taking me?"

"I'm keeping you close by my side for a while. Just stay silent and you won't get hurt."

This definitely wasn't the *worst* thing that could've happened. And at this point I needed him. Even though he was the reason I was in this mess, at this very moment he was the only thing keeping my situation from getting any worse, so all I could do was sit back in his arms and go with whatever he had planned for me.

***

After a short walk, he carried and placed me right on the bank of an underground hot spring. The steam hovering above the clear water was quite the sight. And to think this was all underground using a rocky formation as its ceiling. It felt almost man made.

"What are we doing here?" I asked.

"You're filthy," he answered. "I can't have you dripping blood everywhere you go."

"But you're covered in a lot more blood than I am," I pointed out.

He looked down at himself for the first time since he killed his own men and said, "Huh, I guess you're right."

He then proceeded to take his bloody and torn clothes off right in front of me.

"What are you doing?" I asked, a little flustered from his lack of modesty.

"I'm joining you," he said blankly.

"I'm not bathing with you!"

"Fine, then go after me. It doesn't make a difference," he said while throwing off his trousers and exposing himself completely. My instincts told me to look away, but my curiosity got the better of me. His skin was golden all around and his body was fairly lean, yet he still had a good amount of muscle on him. It was my first time seeing a man without any clothes on. I was especially curious since he was rather handsome. Even more than Flint.

The only imperfection he had on his body were his scars. His body was covered in them. But that didn't surprise me. I could tell that this man was a warrior. They were all probably a reminder of his battles. What surprised me were the scars that I saw when he turned around.

He had massive dark welts all stretching across his back like vines. Those weren't battle scars. This man was beaten. No ... he was tortured.

Barin dove into the water and started cleaning the blood off his skin. I wasn't as bloodstained as he was so I only took off my black cloak, gloves and boots to clean them in the water as I sat next to the bank not too far from him.

"Barin," I started to say, "that's your name, right? Why are you helping me all of a sudden? Just an hour ago you had your blade against my neck, threatening to take my life and now you're killing your own men for *my* well-being?"

"Don't be mistaken Crystal. I'm not saving you. My plans to sell you still haven't changed."

"But those guys weren't going to kill me. You could've let them have their fun with me and it wouldn't have changed your plans in the slightest."

"What's your point?"

"I don't know. You just seem a little soft for someone who's into selling humans."

"Hm, maybe I do have a soft spot for you."

Me specifically? The statement caught me off guard.

"What, do you think I'm prettier than the other girls you normally capture?"

"I wouldn't know. You're actually my first ever captive. I never thought I'd actually ever do something like this, but you're special. You're the number one most wanted criminal on the Black Continent so that makes you a great asset. The money I'd get for you would be life changing. But since I don't have many people to compare you to, I can't say that I saved you strictly on your looks. I mean, you do have a beautiful face, but it's your eyes that really made me want to protect you."

"So, you have a thing for blue-eyed girls? Lucky me."

"My mother had blue eyes. And she found herself in plenty of situations like the one you experienced. The only difference is no one came to her rescue."

"I'm sorry to hear that."

He turned to me and said in a stern voice, "Never have sympathy for your oppressors, Crystal. I deserve to die for what I'm going to do to you."

"So you *do* have a conscience!" I mocked. "If you know it's bad then why don't you just let me go so I don't have to kill you later?"

"Because I've already struck a deal with some very powerful people."

"Like the Royal family?"

"Something like that."

I thought about the name I heard from before. *Morpheus.* I wondered what his connection was to it all. But I doubted that Barin would give a straight answer. And it didn't matter anyway. As long as I could find a way out of this, I wouldn't have to deal with any of them.

Once I finished washing my clothes, I looked back up at him and said, "Hey, are you almost done in there? I feel gross from all my travels and I'd like a turn to clean myself too."

"Well, I'm just about done so I'll let you have it."

He finally pulled himself out of the hot spring and once again I could see his entire body, but this time I didn't try to look away. I took it all in and felt a heat in my own body starting to rise. My chest was tight, and my mouth was dry. At first, I thought it was from the steam emanating from the water, but that was just because I didn't want to believe what I *really* felt. I couldn't take my eyes off him.

"I'll be back with something for you to wear so you can take your time and wash the rest of your clothes if you need to," Barin said as he exited the cavern.

Once he was out of sight, I finally took the rest of my clothes off and slowly dipped myself into the steaming water. The heat was comfortable. Perfect for me to relax and think of a way out of this mess.

Barin may have currently been an obstacle in my path of freedom, but he wasn't evil. He had a heart and I had to use that to my advantage. This wasn't normally my style, but I had to manipulate him. I needed to take a page out of Ana's book and pull out the kind of charm and charisma she had to make him let me go. Or at the very least, make him put his guard down.

CHAPTER THIRTY-NINE
ALIZEH

I n order for us to reach the bandit's hideout, Mirage and I left the village and were back in the wide-open plains of the desert. The sun was setting out of the orange-blue sky and the moon was fully out.

"We've been walking for a while," I said to Mirage. "Are you sure you know where we're going?"

"Yes, we aren't too far now," she answered.

"Hey, if you know where they're hiding, then why haven't you gone to take them out yourself?"

Mirage looked away from me and said "W-well that's because ..." her voice started to trail off before she finally looked back at me while saying, "It's because I was too afraid to fight them on my own."

"What? But you're so powerful!"

"You think so?"

"'Think so?' I know so! You took out those bandits with just a single attack from your Spirit Caster. What kind of Spirit Caster is that anyway?"

"Oh, this?" she asked as she raised her Spirit Caster, staring at it longingly. "This is the Sand Spirit Caster."

"Woah, really? I never even knew a Spirit Caster could have such a specific type of element attached to it."

All Spirit Casters had their own element as its power. Elements like ice, fire, and wind were the elements of Crystal, Flint and I. Another element that I knew all too well is earth. That Spirit Caster belonged to Adam Stone. The man I killed for attempting to destroy me and my parents.

His Spirit Caster had so much potential. If I had to guess, that would mean he could manipulate dirt, dust, boulders, mountains and even sand. With a Spirit caster that can manipulate all that, it seemed strange to me that a Spirit Caster could only have said sand as an ability. It seemed almost impractical. I waited for a response from her on the matter but all she did was give me a nervous laugh while saying, "Yeah, I guess mine is just really special."

I wanted to pry more into the topic but before I could, she looked up and said, "Well, this is it."

I looked up to see that we were standing in front of a giant boulder with a wide crack that stretched all the way from the sand to its center.

"Their base is inside a boulder?" I asked, puzzled at the sight.

"Not exactly," she said as she made her way closer to the large crevice. She stuck her head in, then looked back at me and waved her hand in a gesture for me to follow. She then went into the crevice and disappeared into the darkness. I scanned around to make sure no one was watching and followed into the slim opening, looking into the crevice, seeing nothing but darkness.

I took one step through the tight space and immediately lost my footing, finding myself falling and rolling down what felt like a sand hill. I finally came to a stop and it took a few seconds for me to gain my equilibrium back.

As I was on my hands and knees, I looked up to see a bandit running straight towards me. I wasn't ready for combat. I struggled to get back up to my feet only being able to trip and slide atop the sand. As he got closer with his sword, I hastily pulled out my Spirit Caster, too flustered to think of a spell.

He raised his sword in the air to strike me but before he could, a large pillar of sand crashed into him from his side pushing him into a nearby wall and knocking him out. I looked to where the sand was coming from and saw Mirage standing over other bandits who were already passed out.

"Thanks! That was a—"

"Shush!" Mirage yelled louder than I had. "We're in the enemy's territory. We don't want to be too loud."

"Oh, yeah," I realized. "You're right."

I got back up to my feet and brushed all the sand off. Afterwards, I looked around to see that we were in a large spacious cavern that had four tunnels spreading out on all sides. One of the tunnels being the one we entered in and the other three were lit up by torches to show seemingly straight paths.

"Ok, so where to now?" I asked, wondering which tunnel would lead us to Crystal and Ana.

"I don't know," she answered while looking in all directions.

"What? Really?"

"Yes. Really. I only knew the location of their base, but I don't know anything about its layout."

"I guess that makes sense. So that means they can really be anywhere."

"Yes. And since there are multiple paths to take, I'd imagine our best bet would be to split up and search the place individually."

"Really, you think so?"

"Yes. This place could be gigantic for all we know. We can cover more ground if we go on our own."

"Yeah, I guess you're right. Ok then, I'll go that way," I said as I pointed over to the tunnel on my left.

"Then I'll go the opposite way. When we're completely finished searching our areas then we'll meet back in this part of the cavern. If we don't find her then we'll search for her in the last tunnel together."

"Sounds like a plan," I said as I turned to face the tunnel, pulling out my Spirit Caster and murmuring the words, ***"Grígoros Ánemos."***

I took off running at high speeds with the intention of not letting anything get in the way of me finding my friends.

CHAPTER FORTY
CRYSTAL

I opened my eyes and my body felt stiff. I must've fallen asleep because once I pulled myself out of the water my skin was all wrinkly, but at the same time I was well rested. Even my ankle felt better. It wasn't perfect and if I put too much pressure on it then the pain would come back, but at the very least I could walk on my own again. I wasn't sure if it was the hot spring or the Rēa in my blood that healed it so quickly but either way, this was going to help me escape.

I looked down and saw that my clothes had been replaced with something new. It was a short white nightgown. I air dried for a couple of minutes before putting it on and heading through the only exit in the cavern that led right to Barin's room. Avoiding him would've been impossible.

When I walked into the room, I saw my clothes drying on a wooden rack. On the other side of the room I saw Barin shirtless but his back was turned towards me as he sharpened a blade. I could see my Spirit Caster in his back pocket. It was so close yet so far.

I'd seen his reflexes. This man was fast. In order to take it from him I'd have to close the gap considerably. And even then I'd only have a single moment to take him out. I wouldn't get a second chance. Just like the time I hunted the lynx, I would have to be patient before I was able to strike. Even if it took hours or possibly days, I needed to be smart about this if I wanted to make it out alive. And the first step was to make him believe I wasn't a threat.

I leaned against the wall to pretend that my ankle was a lot more injured than it truly was and I got his attention by asking, "Really? Of all the clothes you could have given me, you chose this?"

He looked at me and asked, "What's wrong with it?"

"It's a little too skimpy, don't you think?"

"It's the finest piece of clothing I own," he argued. "Would you rather be wearing one of my rags?"

"Why do you even own clothing like this?" I asked. "Do you make all the girls you bring in here wear this? I don't know what your intentions are but don't think I'll let you have your way with me that easily."

"That gown belonged to my mother," he finally answered.

His answer made me pause for a moment before asking, "What exactly happened to your mother?"

"Does it matter?"

"It seems like it matters to you."

"You shouldn't assume anything about a person you don't know."

I forcibly stumbled over to his bed and sat down to rest my leg.

"I don't have to assume," I told him. "I just know. You and I aren't too different from one another."

"In what regard?"

I looked him up and down, telling him, "You have that cold exterior. That dead look in your eyes. You act tough, but it's just because you don't wanna get too close to anyone ... or rather, you don't know how. I'm still afraid that I'll lose my new friends the same way I lost my parents."

"How'd they die?" he prodded.

"They were killed by the princess and her soldiers. I don't even think she had a real reason for killing them. It's why I'm on this quest to begin with.

I want to kill her for what she did to us. Or at least ... I think I do. I don't really know any more. I haven't really had a chance to just *talk* about it with someone. Their deaths happened so suddenly and I was pushed into this fight just as quickly. I'm sitting here trying to lead a group of experienced fighters when I'm not like any one of them. I'm just a girl who got in way over her head. I'm trying my best but what if in the end I'm not good enough? I figured that all these thoughts would just go away if I ignored them but they haven't. My parents died right in front of my eyes. I don't like complaining about it to anyone because everyone's lost something or someone too, but now that I'm saying it out loud I'm starting to think that maybe my feelings are justified. Maybe I actually *deserve* a chance to talk about it. And maybe talking about it will make that tight feeling in my chest that's been crushing me every night finally go away."

I looked to Barin and he seemed attentive. Like he resonated with every word. So I continued. I told this man everything that'd been eating at me. Everything I'd had to go through up until that point. And at the very end, I couldn't hold back my tears.

Barin moved closer to me and before I could say another word, he tightened his arms around me. It left me speechless. I didn't know he had so much compassion hiding in him.

"I've never really known how to comfort people, but my mother always told me that if I ever see someone else crying then it means they need a hug."

I wiped away my tears and said, "Thank you. Your mother sounds like a very kind-hearted woman."

"She was. Even though she was a slave who was beaten and abused by everyone she came across, she still had so much love in her heart. She tried to teach me how to do the same, but I guess I'm too bitter to follow through. I'm a killer by nature and all I've done with my life is steal to survive."

"Well I've only known you for a few hours, but you seem a lot nicer than you let on."

"That's only because my mother told me to treat every woman I come across with the same kindness and respect she showed me. I've only ever met a handful of women in my life though, since not many of them travel alone through Kítrinos."

Once he said this, everything about him started to click. He was introverted and his people skills weren't as polished as most. I could tell why he had no modesty when it came to showing off his body. He was sheltered just like me. We shared most of those qualities. Perhaps we were even more alike than I had originally thought.

"I wish I met more women like you," he continued. "It's just men out here. Men like my oppressors. Evil men who enjoy inflicting pain on those who can't fight back. I swore I'd kill anyone like them."

"And that's why you saved me from them?" I asked.

"The same thing that those men were going to do to you are the same things that similar men did to my mother and I."

My eyes wandered to his back. I slowly moved my hand towards it, but before I could get too close, he quickly grabbed my wrist as if he were blocking an attack. I looked into his eyes and I didn't see rage. Nor did I see another blank stare. This time I saw fear. I saw the same scared child he used to be far before I ever met him. He looked back into my eyes as I softened my gaze. And with the same energy, he loosened his grip allowing me to explore his body. My fingers passed over every welted scar, each one telling a different story.

"They did all of *this* to you?" I asked.

"They got off on it. A lot of them said that I looked like a girl when I was younger, but I could still take a better beating than any other woman they owned, so I was one of their prized possessions."

Just like he had done for me, I wrapped my arms tight around him, "I'm so sorry. You've suffered so much."

"You've suffered a great deal yourself, Crystal. And you've come such a long way in such a short amount of time since then. You're stronger than most men I know."

I held him even tighter and sniffled, "Thank you for saying that. You're the first person to *really* acknowledge my feelings. I really needed this. I'm probably going to regret what I have to do to you."

"What are you talking about?"

Right at that moment, he knew exactly what I was doing and didn't hesitate to push me off the bed and away from him. He got up and checked his back pocket, but there was obviously nothing there. I had already snatched my wand back during the exchange.

I didn't waste a second getting back up and pointed my wand towards him.

"Pagokrýstallos!" I shouted the spell, but just like earlier that day, nothing came from it. I thought that my powers would return to me at such a crucial time but it looked like I just had to improvise.

Barin gave me no time to think as he ran and forced my back against the wall while holding my arms down against it.

"I wouldn't have expected *you* of all people to take advantage of me at such a low point," he remarked.

"Aren't you the one who told me not to have sympathy for my oppressors?" I pointed out.

I used all my strength to push myself from the wall and to his surprise, it was working. I was overpowering him. Just because I didn't have my spells to defend myself didn't mean I was completely defenseless. I finally got my fingers back around my Spirit Caster and I could feel the Rēa empowering me.

I kneed him in the stomach and punched him in the face, hoping that it would be enough to take him down just like with my last opponent but all it did was make him stumble back with a new busted lip. He wiped his mouth, spotting his own blood and gave me an almost animalistic grin.

"I *really* like this side of you, Crystal!"

He went and threw a punch but I saw it coming and dodged it while throwing my own counter attack right to his side. At the same time as my counter attack, he quickly gave me a light slap to the face before stepping back and saying, "You have the strength but your attacks need more speed."

He didn't seem to be taking me seriously, but in his defense, he was right. He was able to hit me while I was in the middle of a counterattack. My attack didn't deal any damage to him and was slow enough to give him an opening. I needed to be faster.

I threw another punch, putting my whole body into it just like Ana taught me, but this time Barin caught my fist with his own hand.

"Yeah, that's more like it!" he beamed.

I pulled my arm back and threw more punches, but he blocked every single one with a smile on his face as if this were just some game to him.

Soon enough he got a hold of both my wrist, pulled me in close and said, "Come on, be more creative. Don't just come at me head on like that. You're fighting for your life. Do everything in your power to win, no matter how underhanded."

At this point, it just felt like he was training me because everything coming out of his mouth was right. I wasn't putting in every thing I had. I was fighting for my life and I needed to act like it.

I closed my eyes and concentrated all the Rēa I had into a single point. I could still feel it in my veins. There had to be some way I could draw it out.

"What, don't tell me you're giving up already?" he asked with his eyes losing their newfound luster.

I answered by shouting, ***"Pagokrýstallos!"***

Ice came spewing from my wand like a spear as my wand was pointing right towards his face, but even though it only took a second to reach him, he was still able to dodge the attack with only a bloody scratch on his face to show for my efforts.

Once he turned his face back towards me, I saw that his eyes had once again turned red just like they had before when he killed all those men. The next second his fist went flying into my stomach knocking, all the wind out of me, forcing me to drop my wand to the floor and the ice surrounding it to shatter.

He then pushed me back onto the bed and pinned me down. I felt helpless. He was already too strong for me to begin with and on top of that I made him angry. He wasn't going to pull his punches against me anymore.

"You're strong," Barin said as his eyes went back to their normal color. "Really strong. I didn't think you had the power to kill me, but you got so close. I don't know if it's because you're more powerful than I thought or if it's just because you outsmarted me. Now that I think about it, it's probably both. It won't be today, but when the time comes, I'm sure you'll be able to avenge your parents."

His words sent butterflies through my stomach. He praised me the same way my father used to. No one else had ever talked to me like that. It felt like everyone I met looked down on me, but this man ... this man more powerful than most people alive acknowledged my strength.

I couldn't hold myself back anymore, and without thinking, I launched my face against his, giving him a quick kiss and pulling myself back just as quickly. Yet again, there was another new look on Barin's face. He looked taken aback and pulled back even farther than I did.

"Is this your way of trying to lower my guard again?" he questioned.

"No. I think I just really like you."

"I think I really like you, too."

Without saying another word, I pulled him back in and gave him another kiss but this time neither of us pulled back. He embraced me and completely closed the gap between us. I could feel every inch of his body through my thin nightgown and could tell he was excited. I fantasized about what such a strong and assertive man like himself would do to me in a state like that. The anticipation of what my first time was going to be like was killing me.

His hand slowly rustled through my hair and down my neck. It didn't change direction until he got to my waist and before I knew it, he was traveling across my inner thigh and ever so slightly lifting up my gown.

I couldn't hold my mouth to his anymore and let out a gasp from pleasure I hadn't felt before. Even though I stopped kissing him, he wasn't finished with me. He moved his soft lips right down to my neck while beginning to bite and suck in a way that I knew would leave a bruise. That roughness mixed with where his hand was awoke a passion in me that I never knew I had.

I grabbed his hair, tugging it just as hard as he bit me, knowing we both loved every second of the pain. Once I wrapped my legs around him, he knew I was finally ready to take it farther.

Bang bang bang.

The door shook but we didn't pay it any mind until it started banging again.

Bang bang bang.

"Not now!" Barin shouted, but that didn't stop them from banging even harder.

Barin ripped himself away from me while taking all that hot passion with him. I felt empty and the warmth that he produced was gone. The old cold feeling inside crept back throughout my body and it wasn't a feeling I missed.

Barin violently swung open the door and shouted, "I swear if you're wasting my time—"

"We're being attacked!" the man cut him off.

"What? By who?"

"I don't know. But there's large groups of our men down all around the west ends of the tunnels. From the sheer amount of people that are down, I'd assume we're being attacked by an army but so far no one's seen anything."

Barin looked back at me as if we had the same thought. We both knew that it wasn't an army. It was Ana and Alizeh.

Barin put on his jacket while picking up his sword along with my Spirit Caster off of the floor.

"You said you only found them on the west side of the base, right?" Barin asked him.

"Yeah, that's right."

"Good. That means I don't have to worry about this area. Watch the girl while I go deal with them. Make sure she doesn't leave this room. And you better not use any excessive force. I see so much as a bruise on her, and I'll kill you."

"Yes, sir. I understand," the man gulped.

And with that, Barin was gone, closing the door behind him. This made things a lot more convenient. Though I had no idea whether or not it was actually Ana and Alizeh who were truly there to help. For all I knew it could have been anyone threatening these groups of bandits. Either way, it would be stupid for me to wait here and miss my only opportunity to escape. I needed to find a way out before Barin came back.

The only problem with all this was that Barin took my wand with him. I wasn't sure if I could beat this without it. I sized him up and could tell that I definitely had a chance but he had a dagger in his holster. He'd easily kill me if I took him head on so once again, I had to get creative. During a moment of intimacy even someone like Barin let his guard down. This guy should fold even faster.

The man caught me looking him up and down and decided to do the same to me before saying, "Man, Barin's lucky. I can't believe he has a beauty like you all to himself." His tone made my skin crawl but it also gave me the perfect opportunity to put my plan into motion.

"You know it doesn't have to be like that?" I made sure my tone was soft. Even softer than it was with Barin and I continued telling him, "You're a handsome man. I wouldn't be opposed to having a little *fun* with you."

"No way, darlin'," he refused. "I saw the mess that Barin made last time someone put a scratch on you and I'm not trying to be his next victim."

"Then don't leave a scratch," I grinned. "I won't tell him if you treat me right."

He gave me a grin back as I made my way towards him, still eyeing his dagger. His guard was completely down. This was going to be easier than I thought.

Once I got close enough, he grabbed and ran his hands all across me while kissing my neck. This drove me crazy, but not in a good way. He was rough and clumsy with his movements. Nothing like Barin. I was completely repulsed and almost regretted choosing this approach to blindside him, but there was no turning back now.

I touched him back while reaching for his dagger and without him even noticing, I pulled it right out of his holster. No second was wasted as I rammed it right into his stomach, putting a complete stop to this disgusting act.

He fell to the floor quickly and bled out while barely being able to speak from how hard I jabbed him. I almost felt bad for this one. My body count was rising higher and higher in just one day and I still wasn't done. My father always taught me to do anything to survive, and Barin reminded me of that teaching.

I walked over to my hanging clothes and found them all dry. I threw off my gown, put back on all my original gear and made my way to the door. Before I left, I looked back at the nightgown I left on the floor. It was so close to the pooling blood. I went back to it, folded the gown and placed it on Barin's bed, not wanting such a treasure to be ruined. And with that I made my way towards freedom.

CHAPTER FORTY-ONE

ALIZEH

Using Grígoros Ánemos, I sped through the tunnel's many twists and turns. At every corner there was an unsuspecting bandit that I easily took out with *Mach Grothiá*, a spell that released a concentrated gust of wind whenever I threw a punch. I learned it while fighting Flint back on Phoenix island.

Every few minutes, I would see a door on the walls of the tunnel that led to other rooms. Some rooms held weapons while others held food. At one point I entered a room filled with bandits, but they weren't a threat. I took them all out quickly before they could even realize what happened. Unfortunately, there was still no sign of Crystal or Ana.

Within a span of fifteen minutes, I had reached the end of the tunnel. I released my spell and dug my heels in the sand to stop myself from crashing and took a second to catch my breath. Although it was only for a short time, I had used a lot of Rēa in my run.

I looked up at the end of the tunnel to see a large wooden door. I had checked every room in this tunnel except the one in front of me. This had to be it. The place that they were keeping them.

I readied myself for one last charge. This was going to be the final part of my raid. I tightened my fist and swung at the door while yelling, ***"Mach Grothiá!"*** The door flew off its hinges and fell to the floor. I then yelled ***"Grígoros Ánemos!"*** and jumped into the center of the room but as soon as I landed, I saw a golden dagger heading straight towards my face. I tilted my head to dodge, and it ended up grazing my cheek. If I hadn't already been using 'Grígoros Ánemos,' then I would have been a goner.

I looked up ahead to see that the person who threw the blade at me was sitting on the ground, leaning against the wall.

He opened his eyes and started yawning before saying, "It took you forever to get here. Guess I dozed off."

How did he throw the blade at me? I asked myself. It didn't make any sense. This person was half asleep before I came in. I glanced around the room and saw that there was no one else there. No one else could have thrown the dagger besides him.

He got up to his feet and I could fully see his face. He looked young, his skin was almost as dark as Ana's and his hair was long, messy and black. He didn't look anything like any of the other bandits who I came across.

"I'm excited to finally meet you, Alizeh Green. Although you're much shorter than I expected."

Hearing him say my name aloud made me uneasy.

"How do you know who I am?" I asked.

"How could I not? You and Crystal are pretty infamous around the Black Continent."

I immediately put my guard up and yelled, "What did you do with her?"

"If you're worried about her safety, then let me assure you, she's in good hands."

"Tell me where she is!"

"Now, now, don't get so hasty," he said while picking up his sheathed sword leaning against the wall. "If you get too loud then you'll give me a headache."

I had enough of his stalling. I threw my fist in his direction and yelled, **"Mach Grothiá!"** He jumped out of the way of the blast and darted towards me with his sword drawn. I leaped back and used the attack once more to try and maintain distance between us.

"Mach Grothiá!"

The attack didn't reach him. He dodged it effortlessly and without losing momentum. As soon as he got close, he raised his blade in an attempt to slash me but before he could, I stopped myself in my tracks, dug my feet into the sand and used another spell.

"Gale Lance!"

Wind spiraled around my wand, creating a lance. He had too much momentum to stop himself from getting any closer, so I used that to my advantage. I thrusted the lance towards him, and it ran right through his abdomen. He jumped back, staggered as he held his wound.

"Ha! I actually walked right into that one!" he laughed. "I didn't expect you to have such a hands-on type of move set. You're a true warrior."

"Stand down," I ordered, "and tell me where Crystal is."

He laughed at me and said, "Don't count me out yet. You think a little cut like this can kill me? It's gonna take a lot more than cheap tricks to put me down. So please, make sure to use something a bit stronger next time."

He bolted towards me again, this time getting much closer. It surprised me that his wound didn't slow him down in the slightest. I raised my lance up in defense and our weapons clashed. The wind grinding against his sword created sparks that flew around us and stung my hands. For a second, I turned my face away from the sparks because of its brightness but that second was all he needed to turn this battle around in his favor.

Before I turned my head back, I felt a powerful blow hit me right in my stomach. He kicked me so hard that I went flying across the room. I felt the wind fly out of my lungs before I smashed against the wall and slid down to the floor.

"I thought I told you to use something stronger!" he laughed as he ran towards me once more.

The truth was I could've used something more powerful, but the rest of my moves were *too* powerful. They would destroy this entire room and most likely cause the tunnel to collapse. But I was out of options. I either had to take my chances with his sword or a potential cave in. So, I made the choice to use another spell.

It took a couple of seconds for me to get my breath back and by that time he was less than a meter away. Before he could strike, I used the rest of my energy to release the spell.

"Viaii sfýrigma!" I cried out.

An explosion of wind emanated from my body and made him fly back. The wind forced all the fire from the torches to fizzle out and the last thing I saw was sand above my head, falling down until there was nothing but black.

CHAPTER FORTY-TWO
ANA

The first thing I did after my interrogation was retrace my steps in order to find Alizeh, but she was gone. There was a pretty large crater of sand where I thought she would have landed but it was empty and there wasn't a single footprint to track her down. She must've flown off somewhere. And if that was the case then that meant she was alive and kicking. Unfortunately, it also meant that trying to find her would take up too much time. I had to focus all my efforts on finding Crystal first.

I walked through the desert for hours before it finally turned night. Silver walked by my side, only weighed down by the bandit he was carrying on his back. I was beginning to think that this entire journey was all some wild goose chase in an attempt for this bandit to save his own life until I finally saw a giant boulder in the distance.

"Is that the place?" I asked.

"I don't know. I can't see anything," he answered while slumped over Silver's back, unable to move from his broken bones. I grabbed him by his hair and lifted him up, forcing him to groan in pain.

"How about now?"

"Yes," he groaned. "That's it."

"Good," I said as I dropped him back down. "Looks like I don't need you anymore."

I then pushed him off Silver and right into the sand.

"Wait, what are you doing?" he yelled.

"Bringing you too close to the enemy base could become problematic for the mission. If you come along, you'll most likely alert everyone of my presence."

"But you can't just leave me here!" he shouted but I ignored him while lifting myself onto Silver's back. Once Silver started to walk, the bandit continued, "I did everything you asked! Don't leave me here to die!"

I stopped and looked back at the poor soul. Even though he tried to capture Silver and kill me, I still felt the slightest ounce of pity for the man. His death would be slow if I left him there, so I made him a deal.

"If my friends are still alive and well, then I'll come back for you. And if they aren't, then I'll leave you here to share their fate. I think it's only fair." I then leaned into Silver's ear and whispered, "Let's go," triggering him to take off towards the boulder.

It didn't take long for us to reach it. Once I got off, I told Silver to stay so I could take a quick look around. The only noticeable thing about the boulder was a huge crack that formed somewhat of a slim cave at its base. This must've been the way in.

After once more telling Silver to stay, I pulled out my daggers and jumped through, sliding down the sand cave and into an empty open space that was the nexus point for three individual pathways. Crystal could've been anywhere in this base, but my instincts told me to go straight down the center hall, and it was rare for my instincts to be wrong.

I ran through the hall, hoping I wouldn't run into any bandits. Getting caught in the center of the enemy's territory could easily turn into a disastrous situation. I guess the worst-case scenario wasn't too far away because as soon as I turned my first corner I ran into an entire group of bandits. There were probably at least seven of them.

We all stopped for a moment and glared at one another. "Who the hell are you?" the one in the front asked.

I tightened the grip on my daggers and darted through the group, ripping every last one of them to shreds. This wasn't the time to draw out any fights. I simply had to end anyone who got in my way as quickly as possible. I couldn't risk waiting around while Crystal was in trouble.

CHAPTER FORTY-THREE

CRYSTAL

There were bandits at every corner. That meant that at every turn I would have to take another life. A trail of blood followed me throughout the tunnel.

Every time I saw a man I had to move as stealthily as possible. I would grab him from behind and slit his throat. The more I did it, the easier it got. It was like going through the motions of an annoying chore.

It had to be that way. I had to kill every last one of them. I couldn't rely on Ana and Alizeh to be able to find me down here. I was alone and I only had this one chance to escape. I couldn't jeopardize that by being sympathetic to the lives of my captors. Not even Barin.

I made it to a corner and stopped as soon as I heard footsteps, leaned against the wall and waited for them to get close. I waited until just the right moment and jumped out, swinging my blade. They grabbed my wrist and put their own blade against my neck.

She grinned and said, "You're good. I almost didn't hear you coming."

"Ana?" I asked surprised but grateful to see her. "How did you find me?"

"I'll tell you later, but for now I need to get you out of here," she said while running in the opposite direction.

I followed behind and asked, "Where's Alizeh?"

"No idea," she shrugged. "Last time I saw her was when she got shot by a cannon."

"A *cannon*?" I repeated, making sure I heard that right.

"Yeah. She went blasting off out of sight. I went searching but I couldn't find her."

"You're not telling me what I think you're telling me right now, are you?"

"What, that she's dead? Not a chance. I would've found the body. She's out there somewhere. I know it. She *has* to be. We've seen her survive worse," Ana said, as if she were trying to convince herself rather than me.

We made it to a room with three other paths. Two of which were tunnels going to our left and right and the last one seemed to rise up like a hill. Ana started to climb up it so I could only presume that it was the exit.

I followed her lead, clawing onto the gripless sand and pushing my side to the rocky wall beside us until we finally made it out of the caves. Night had already fallen, making me wonder how long I had been stuck in there. Ana didn't hesitate to run to Silver and jump on his back. I was about to follow but something caught my attention. I don't know what. It was just a feeling that made me turn around and look back at the cave.

"What are you waiting for?" Ana asked. "Come on, we've gotta get out of here."

"What if Alizeh's here?"

"What? Why would she be *here*?"

"She could've gotten kidnapped too. Or she might've found this place just like you. I have a feeling that she's here."

"A feeling?"

"I can't explain it. I just ... feel her."

"Look, if Alizeh of all people were here then she would've caused a scene by now. She's not exactly one for subtlety."

She had a point. Luckily, just seconds after her point we both heard the sound of an explosion. We looked back and saw a large cloud of sand and dust fly up into the air far off in the distance. It took me a few seconds to register what I was seeing until I finally made the connection in my head. The only person that could have caused something like that had to have been Alizeh!

For her to make such a ruckus like that could only mean two things. She was either trying to signal us, or she was in the midst of battle. Both possibilities could have been the reality of the situation. Either way, we needed to make our way to that dust cloud and quickly.

I looked back at Ana, and she immediately nodded her head, understanding the situation.

"Get on," she told me. This time I didn't hesitate.

CHAPTER FORTY-FOUR
ALIZEH

I was almost completely buried and crushed under the sand until I used the last of my power for one last desperate spell, ***"Paírno Ptísi"***. With the power of flight, I forced myself out of the sand and only made it a few feet up into the air before falling back down.

I was now outside in a large crater filled with sand from the cave-in I had just created. I couldn't believe that I had to go so far just to defeat one man. All my Rēa was practically gone.

I stood up while dusting myself off and started to make my way out of the crater, but before I could take my second step I fell right back down into the sand. I looked back and saw a hand sticking out of the sand, squeezing my ankle so tight that it felt like it was impossible to escape.

The rest of his body started to rise out of the sand. He seemed completely unharmed physically, but there was an anger in his eyes that told me that I had wounded his pride and he wasn't going to let me get away with it.

I threw my fist and yelled, "Mach Grothiá!" but nothing happened. I used up all my power during my last attack that brought down a small part of their base. I was completely powerless.

He gave me a large grin and continued to claw his way out of the sand as he said, "It looks like you used up the rest of your magic in that last-ditch effort of yours. Luckily for you, my sword is buried under all this sand so that means we can fight with just our bare hands!"

I quickly turned around, got to my feet and ran away as fast as I could. There was no way I was going to beat him in hand-to-hand combat. I couldn't even beat him with my magic!

"What's wrong, Shēna?" he shouted. "Where did your warrior spirit from before go?"

I looked back and saw that he was hot on my trail. I turned and tried to go faster but when I looked back again, he'd caught up to me and was close enough to grab me. I wasn't fast enough to escape him.

He reached his hand out but before he could grab me, something got in between us. To be more exact, it was actually *someone*. They wore a black cloak and had a golden dagger in hand.

They slashed at him with the dagger, forcing him to jump back while holding his arm which was now covered in blood. This was a surprise for sure, and a welcomed one. They removed their hood, causing their long white hair to flow out into the wind. It glistened in the moonlight.

"Crystal?" I called. I didn't expect her to be the one to come to my rescue.

Crystal turned around and said, "Sorry if you've been fighting for a while. We came as fast as we could."

"We?" I asked.

Right at that moment, Ana came sliding down the crater with her daggers in hand.

The bandit looked at Crystal with an annoyed look and asked, "How did you escape?"

Crystal looked back at him and said, "It was pretty simple, actually. Your men are complete idiots."

He let out a laugh and said, "Well, I guess I shouldn't be surprised. You also seem to know how to wield a blade." He took his hand off his wounded arm and stared at the blood. "You're one capable woman. I didn't even see you coming. Let's see if you can keep up that same energy."

He started to make his way towards us and Crystal reacted by raising her dagger. It was very subtle, but I could see her trembling. She was scared. She wasn't using her Spirit Caster which meant they must have taken it. We were in the same boat. We both couldn't use any spells. But Ana stood strong. She raised her daggers and snapped, "Stay behind me!"

The bandit sprinted towards us and dashed to the side, trying to pass up Ana. It looked like Crystal was his target, but Ana wasn't going to let him touch her. She slid her foot out, tripping and causing him to tumble into the sand.

He looked up at her with a disoriented look and asked, "Have you been standing there that whole time?" Ana looked puzzled by the question, so he continued while getting back to his feet. "Sorry, I didn't realize you were here. You don't look like a Shēna so I just assumed you were the weakest and I guess I just failed to acknowledge you."

Not even a second passed before Ana jabbed her dagger towards the bandit's neck. But he was quick to react. He swung his head out of the way and grabbed her wrist. She went to slice him with her other dagger, but he ducked the attack and kicked her straight in the gut with enough force that would bring *me* to my knees. But Ana wasn't so frail. She didn't hesitate to go on the attack again, swinging her blades at him in a frenzy. But he kept up, narrowly avoiding every swing.

"Ok, you've caught my attention," he said before finally going on the offensive. He launched his fist right to the center of her face, hitting dead on before continuing, "Now let's see how long you can hold it."

He threw more punches, one after the other, all hitting the sides of her face with rights and lefts.

Crystal ran towards them, calling him by his name, "Barin, stop it!"

She swung her blade at him but made no contact from his speed and for a quick second, I believe his eyes flashed red before he forced his fist right into her abdomen. The single punch forced her to her knees and took everything out of her. I couldn't even tell if she was still conscious. Before she could fall face first into the sand, Barin grabbed her by the hair, stopping her descent, seemingly not done with her.

"I'm sorry, Crystal," he apologized.

Before he could do anything to her, Ana tackled him into the sand while trying to stab him with her dagger. He grabbed her wrist, stopping her and putting them both into a constant struggle. She started using both hands and all of her strength to bring the dagger down, but Barin was doing the same to stop her except he had a smile on his face.

"Your strength ..." he struggled to say. "Your technique ... that look in your eye ... you're a Zubarian, aren't you?"

Ana looked taken aback by the statement and Barin used that to his advantage. In the moment of her confusion, he kicked her off him.

Ana still barely moved. "How can you tell?" she asked.

"Because you fight just like me," he caught his breath, "except slower."

"So you're a Zubarian too?"

"Yeah," he said while getting back up to his feet. "And now that I know what I'm dealing with, I guess there's no need for me to hold back." Once again, his eyes glowed red. And this time, it wasn't a flash. They stayed that color while his muscles started to grow. Every vein in his body looked like it was ready to pop. There was an energy around him that didn't only frighten me, but Ana too. "I suggest you do the same."

"Wait, what?" Ana got to her feet completely befuddled but there wasn't any time for her to understand the situation. Barin bolted towards her faster than she could react and punched her right in her side. It looked like she was about to fall as her dagger started to slip from her hand, but she widened her stance and tightened her grip before that could happen. She then swung the dagger at him. He only needed one step to evade it before giving her another jab to the face causing an instant bloody nose.

"Come on, why aren't you taking this seriously?" he shouted before hitting her again, causing her to finally drop one of her daggers. "Where's your *warrior spirit*? I'm going to kill you if you don't draw out that power!"

With less strength than before, she used her other dagger to attack him, but he slapped her hand, causing the weapon to go flying, leaving her defenseless. Without hesitation, he went for a barrage of punches leaving more blood on his fist after every hit.

I wanted to move. I wanted to help. I wanted to kill him. But my power was completely drained, and Crystal was already down for the count. I sat there harnessing my rēa, trying to build up any power I could to be of use. But honestly, in our current state we'd only get in the way. So, all I could do was watch the senseless beating and prey that at least a sliver of my power returned to me before he beat her to death.

It didn't take long for her to finally fall into the sand. A look of disappointment was stuck on his face as he scoffed, "Is that really it? Is that really all you had to offer? Do you even know how to draw out your warrior spirit?"

"I-I don't know ... what you're talking about," Ana wheezed.

Barin's eyes lost their red glow and went back to their natural golden color while his muscles finally started to relax. "Pathetic," he spat. "And to think I was actually excited to fight another one of my kind. You're obviously a novice. You've never been in a *real* fight. You've never been on the brink of death with only your Zubarian blood and instincts to guide you." He turned his back towards her and continued, "You're not even worth killing."

He then turned his sights towards me. I was too scared to move and still wasn't ready to fight him again but regardless, he inched his way closer to me. Even though it seemed to be my turn to fight, Ana still didn't back down. She dragged herself to her dagger, clasped onto it and got up to go for another attack. I didn't know what she was thinking. She had nothing left yet she pressed on while his attention was on me.

With the rest of her strength, she ran to stab him, but he sensed her coming. He turned around to kick the dagger out of her hand and into the air. He then turned her around, putting her into a headlock, grabbed the dagger before it could hit the ground and rammed the blade right into her side.

"Ana!" I cried out but her scream was even louder. I couldn't wait anymore. My body wouldn't let me. Out of pure rage, I ran towards them with the intent to kill.

Barin let go of Ana, letting her strained body hit the sand to prepare for me. Once I got close enough, I threw a punch with all my power while yelling, ***"Mach Grothiá!"*** But it did nothing. Not a spec of magic emanated from me. All it took from him was a single backhand to sweep me off my feet.

"What a waste," Barin scoffed. He looked at Crystal who was still reeling from a single punch. Then he looked back at Ana who was bleeding out in the sand. He turned his attention back towards me and asked, "So this is your combined strength? I'm disappointed." He leaned in close to me and grabbed me by my neck, lifting me into the air and choking me in the process. "I'd snap your neck right now if you and Crystal weren't worth more to me alive."

I couldn't believe it. Out of all the challenges we faced. Every Shēna. Every legendary creature. This man alone was the one that took us down.

I was completely at his mercy. And for the first time in my life, I felt more fear than any nightmare could have ever given me.

CHAPTER FORTY-FIVE
ANA

"Let go."

That's what my dad used to always tell me. He said it as we sparred. I was never able to beat him, much less hit him in a fight. It always made me so angry and sometimes I even cried out of frustration.

"I can't do it," I whined while dropping my body to the ground.

"That's because your mind is too tense."

"Of course, it's too tense! I'm fighting *you*! How am I supposed to win?"

"I understand your frustration," he chuckled. "I couldn't understand the concept myself until I was in the heat of battle."

I stopped my whining and shot the top half of my body up like a spring.

"What battle? Who did you fight? What happened? Tell me!" I begged.

"Well, it happened a very long time ago, back when I was in my prime. I fought a powerful Shēna that got the better of me. I would've surely died if I didn't let go."

"But what do you mean by that?" I asked. "How did you *let go*?"

"I was on the ground, waiting for them to deal the finishing blow, but before they could, I saw our ancestors standing above me."

"Our ancestors?" I asked, confused about the meaning.

"Yes. All the warriors who fought before us. Like your grandfather and his father before him. I let them guide me and I felt a newfound power unlike any other."

***

I loved battle. It always came easily to me and I rarely ever lost. But maybe that was the reason I was in this situation. As much as I hated to admit it, this man was right. I'd never been in a *real* battle. I'd never had such a challenge. For someone to back me into a corner ... to the brink of death. This was all new to me.

I rolled onto my back and looked up at the night sky. The stars were beautiful. I'd never appreciated them until now. It was kinda funny. To see so much beauty in something just moments before death.

But something strange started to happen. They started to move. It began slowly. I didn't notice it at first, but they only got faster. Every single one of them swirled in different directions like a swarm of bright fireflies. The only thing that made sense to me was that I must've been hallucinating from all the blood loss.

Soon, the stars started to slowly take the form of people. It was like giants were looking down at me from the sky. Not a single one looked familiar until a cluster of stars formed right above me. This image was much clearer.

"Dad?" I whispered.

It couldn't be. It felt impossible. Unless this was the moment that my father spoke of so long ago. These were my ancestors.

I reached my hand towards the stars and asked, "Please, help me."

I couldn't stop the tears from drenching my face as I begged. I'd done everything I could. I wasn't strong enough. I didn't want to die here without making a difference. Even worse, I didn't want to let Crystal and Alizeh die here either.

There was no answer from the starry figures. They didn't make a move. Barely even a flicker.

"Please?" I shuddered. There was still no answer, and I could feel myself slipping. "I'm sorry, father," I whispered. "I'm so sorry. I failed again, just like on the night I let you get killed. I'm still too weak to help those that need me."

My vision started to blur, so I rested my eyes. It seemed like there was no way to escape this fate. That was until I heard his voice.

"Let go."

I opened my eyes and saw him standing right above me, clear as day. I didn't have the words. I choked before I said anything to him. And I had so much I wanted to speak on.

"Dad, I can't do it," I told him.

He put his hand in mine and said with a smile, "Just trust me. You're stronger than you know. With a heart as big as yours you can break through any obstacle. Even him. Now I need you to try one last time."

I closed my eyes, took a deep breath and let go. All my regret. All my sadness. And most importantly all my weakness. It felt like I was falling. Not to my end nor into despair but something much rawer. I let go of everything until only a few feelings prevailed. My pride, my rage, and my *Warrior's Spirit*.

CHAPTER FORTY-SIX
ALIZEH

I couldn't breathe. His hand wrapped around my neck like a snake. I was scared, but I couldn't blame *him* for all that fear. For some strange reason this felt like only the calm before the storm. Like something even worse was headed our way.

Right at that moment, I looked over Barin's shoulder. I wished I could say this made me happy, but for some reason seeing her made me even more fearful and uneasy than I was before. Her spirit felt different. It felt *wrong*.

Barin could tell something was off from the look on my face and turned back to see Ana standing as if she hadn't taken a fatal blow. She looked different. Her body was somehow even more toned. She was slightly bigger. Had more muscle. But that wasn't even the strangest part. Her one good eye flashed with a crimson glare that somehow overpowered the moon in its radiance. And that aura emanating from her felt wicked. It didn't feel like it was coming from a human. It felt like I was looking into the embodiment of *rage*.

Barin finally let go of my neck, dropping me into the sand so he could turn his attention back to Ana.

"Didn't I just kill you?" he asked. "How are you still standing?"

She didn't answer.

"Well, since you *can* stand, I suggest you run because I promise you, I'm not going easy on you again."

There was still no answer from her, and she didn't move an inch. It was like watching a wolf glaring at its prey, waiting for the right moment to bite.

"Are you brain dead?" he prodded. "I told you to get out of my sight before—"

Ana didn't let him finish his threats. She lunged herself at him like a wild animal, quicker than anyone could react and knocked him down into the sand. I was frozen. Out of the corner of my eye I could see Crystal was at a loss for words too. But the thing that shocked me the most was that Barin was in the same exact situation as us. He didn't move. He didn't speak. He just held onto his left cheek, seemingly trying to figure out what happened to him.

He finally broke the silence with a grin and a vile laugh. "You bastard. You did it. You *actually* did it! You're finally showing your *Warriors Spirit!*"

His muscles started to bulge, and his eyes glowed just like Ana's. Without wasting another second, he moved into attack. Just like before, he went in with an overwhelming flurry of attacks, but this time Ana kept up with him. She blocked every punch and kick and was able to dish out the same attacks right back at him.

Ana wasn't just so much stronger, but she was faster than she was before too. This was turning into an even fight.

Barin ran towards her at full speed and swung his fist against her face. Before, that punch would've easily knocked her down, but she stood her ground and threw another punch of her own. The punch knocked him back and for a moment he seemed dazed. Ana took full advantage and hit him with a barrage of punches. I couldn't tell if it was five punches or ten. It could've been even more. She was moving so fast that I couldn't fully comprehend it, and from the looks of it, it seemed that Barin was almost in the same position. He blocked some of those punches but took the rest right to his face. With every punch more and more blood splattered on the sand and stained Ana's knuckles. She ended the barrage with one final jab right to his nose, causing blood to pour right out, giving her some much-needed payback. Barin took a few steps back while holding his face and screaming in pain.

"Come on, why aren't you taking this seriously?" Ana mocked.

Barin let out a low growl before getting his manic composure back and asked, "Oh, so we're speaking again now, are we?"

"Yeah, sorry about that. For a moment there I really did lose myself. But I'm back now and I'm going to enjoy ending this."

"Is that so?" he mocked.

"Yeah, but before I do, I think I should offer you the same kindness that you offered me."

"Which is?"

"Mercy," she answered, losing any humor to her expression. "Give up now or I *will* kill you."

Barin got back into his fighting stance and asked sarcastically, "Is that a promise?"

"It's very easy to lose myself when I'm in this state," she explained. "If we continue this fight then there's no telling what I'll do to you."

"That's a bold claim coming from someone who just came into that power. Let's see if you can back it up."

He ran to her once again, trying to swing at her, but this time she caught and grabbed his fist with her own hand, pulled him in close, and kneed him right in the stomach before hitting him with an uppercut. He flew into the air and crashed back down into the sand, creating a cloud of dust around him.

Once the dust cleared, Barin looked more relaxed. His body was back to normal, and his eyes were dimming. That strange form he was using before had vanished. She won.

Ana looked down in the sand and kicked something up into her hand. It was her blade. And she was inching closer to Barin with it.

Barin spit some blood out of his mouth before admitting defeat. "Looks like I lost," he laughed.

Ana stood over him with her blade still drenched in her own blood.

"Let me guess. You've *lost yourself* again?" he asked, looking more annoyed than terrified. "Well go ahead. Do what you came to do."

She lifted the blade up, ready to show no mercy, until suddenly, she just let go. The blade dropped to the sand. I was confused until I saw her eye lose its glow and her muscles start to relax. She soon dropped right into the sand, falling completely unconscious.

"Ana?" I called, unable to process what had happened to her.

Barin started laughing uncontrollably at the sight.

"What did you do to her?" I growled.

"Nothing at all," he started to calm down while getting back up to his feet. "She just couldn't take all that power. Especially not with a wound as fatal as hers."

He kicked her over to her back to see the wound, but he was taken aback by the sight. The wound that was once open and pouring blood just a few moments ago was now completely closed. There was nothing left but dried up blood and a scar.

"This girl is special," he continued while picking up her dagger. "That makes her a threat."

He was going to kill her and there was nothing that neither I nor Crystal could do about it. She didn't have her Spirit Caster and I barely had enough Rēa for a single full powered spell, much less enough to actually continue the fight. If this battle was going to continue, then it was going to be a messy one with an uncertain outcome. Fortunately for us, there was one single factor that was missing up until now that would change the outcome of this entire fight.

Small grains of sand started to levitate around us. We all stopped to observe. Crystal and Barin looked puzzled as to what was happening, but I knew exactly what the cause of this was.

More and more sand started to float into the air and swirl around us until they finally started to form into something. Once the sandstorm stopped we could all see three giant floating spikes made completely of sand all pointing at Barin.

"What ... is this?" he asked as he stared up at them in awe.

"Ámmou aichmés," a voice said. We all looked over to where the voice was coming from and could see Mirage standing above us at the rim of the crater. "If you move another inch, I'll skewer you with these spikes in an instant."

He looked at her with wide eyes and Mirage looked right back with a cold glare. It was as if they were communicating with just their eyes alone. Like they knew each other. After a long, suspenseful silence, he finally closed his eyes and let out another hard laugh.

"Alright, I know when I'm beat," he laughed. He reached into his cloak for something and even though he had just admitted defeat, that action put us more on edge. He pulled out the Ice Spirit Caster and tossed it to Crystal's feet. "Getting into another fight with a Shēna isn't worth the trouble. Just take your wand and go. If you all leave now, then I won't kill you."

If any other person would have said that to us, we would have seen it only as a bluff. Some desperate empty threat that was only meant to scare us off. But after fighting this man, I knew that he truly meant it. He would have fought us and still had a chance of killing us all, but he probably couldn't find a good enough reason to actually go through with it because we wouldn't go down without a fight.

I looked at Crystal and said, "We should go."

She nodded her head, picked up her wand and whistled for Silver, who wasn't too far.

"Help me with Ana," Crystal told me.

I nodded my head and helped her onto Silver's saddle.

"Crystal," Barin called quietly. The casualness of him saying her name like they were friends made my spine crawl. "Be careful with the company you keep," he said, not taking his eyes off Mirage.

"What do you mean by that?" she asked.

In my opinion, it felt like he was just trying to waste our time.

"Crystal, we need to go," I interrupted.

She nodded and looked back at him before we turned around and made our way out of the crater.

Later, we were able to get far away from their base and we finally had time to breathe. Crystal regained her composure and turned her attention to Mirage and asked, "Who are you? Why did you help us?"

"My name is Mirage, and I helped you because she asked me to," Mirage answered while gesturing over to me.

Crystal looked back at me with a puzzled look and asked, "So you know her?"

"Yeah," I answered. "I met her earlier today when I was searching for you guys. She said she would help us with our journey!"

"Looks like you've been busy," she smirked.

"Now wait a second," Mirage interrupted, raising her hands in front of us. "I only agreed to help *save* you, not join you. What even is this *'journey'* that you're both on about?"

"I'm gathering strong Shēna like yourself to help fight against The King," Crystal answered.

"And you really think you can accomplish that? You think you can defeat The King and his forces?"

"Yes. I've already decided that I will."

Mirage took a good long look at Crystal and finally said, "Alright, I'll help."

"Really? Just like that?" Crystal gasped.

"That was easy. I thought she was going to say no just like Flint did," I laughed.

"I want the royals dead for what they did to us," Mirage said. "I think teaming up with you will help me realize that aspiration. So, how many Shēna have you allied yourself with thus far?"

"Oh, just me! Ana's here too but I'm not sure if she counts because she's a Zubarian," I cut in.

"So, it's just the three of you?" Mirage asked.

"Yes," Crystal answered hesitantly.

Mirage lowered her head and took a deep sigh. "I guess beggars can't be choosers. What's the plan?"

CHAPTER FORTY-SEVEN
FLINT

I woke up to the feeling of swaying waves grazing against my legs. I was on the beach and had no idea how I got there. Even after looking around at my surroundings, I couldn't piece anything together.

"Did you sleep well?"

I looked over to my side and, suddenly, Ana appeared as if from thin air. Or perhaps I just wasn't paying attention. I was too dazed to fully process it.

"Uh, yeah," I answered. "I'm still a little groggy though."

"Well, wipe the crust out of your eyes, it's about to start," she told me while looking up into the sky.

"What is?"

My question was answered from a burst of color in the sky. It was a stream of fireworks that caught me off guard.

"Aren't they beautiful?" she asked.

"Yeah, but I could've sworn I already showed them to you before you left the island." Then it dawned on me. "Wait, what are you doing back here? Did you give up on your mission already?"

She didn't answer me. She just continued to look at the fireworks.

"Uh, hello," I tried to get her attention. "I asked what you're doing back on the island."

"Shush," she finally answered. "You're gonna miss the best part."

"And that part would be?"

She looked at me with a coy smile before giving a quick yet passionate kiss. Once she was just inches away from my face, she went to my ear and whispered, "This is the part where you get everything you deserve."

Suddenly I heard the sound of another explosion, but this time it wasn't one of color nor was it in the sky. It detonated right next to us causing a flash of light that left me blinded. Once I got my eyesight back the only thing I could see was fire and destruction. The city was laid to waste and the island was in ruins.

"Ana, are you ok?" I shouted while looking back but the only thing left was a burning body.

"Ana!" I cried, crawling over to her but once I got close, I realized that it wasn't her. It was Summer. She laid there in the sand, lifeless just like the last time I saw her. The sight broke me. I wasn't ready to see her again. Not like this.

"You did this," I heard Ana say from behind. I turned to face her and saw that she too was ablaze. But even though her skin was boiling from her flesh, she didn't react. She just stood there looking down at me with disgust.

"Ana," I cried, "I didn't do this!"

"You're telling me that you didn't let Summer die?"

Her accusation left me speechless because she was right. It *was* my fault that she was dead. I just didn't expect Ana to be so blunt about it.

"And you were just going to let me die too, weren't you?" she continued.

"What?" I asked, confused about where she would even get a thought like that from. "No! I would never let you die!"

"Then why didn't you help me on my journey? You could have saved me. You could have saved everyone! But instead, you just let us go alone. Just like you did with Summer."

Before she could go on, a dark beam of energy shot right through her chest from behind and she fell in the sand, taking her last breath. Behind her was Kira and the rest of the Five Armaments. *She* did this. She killed her, but I was no longer able to do anything about it. I just sat there, holding Ana's burnt body as the group laughed over me and all I could do was scream like I never had before.

"Does all this distress you?" another voice asked.

When I looked up to see who it was, everything disappeared. The Five Armaments. The island. Even Ana and Summer were gone. The only thing left was fire and a single person standing in said flames. My mother.

"If so," she continued, "then you're in for a rude awakening. You should have listened to the girl and attacked first because I can feel them. They're already here on the island."

"Who's here?" I asked.

"The enemy. You need to act *now*."

***

I opened my eyes and jumped up in my hammock. It was just a nightmare. I thought those stopped after the first time Ana stayed with me for a night. But this nightmare was different. It felt so real. And I had never seen my mother in my dreams. Unless she was actually there, trying to communicate with me. Was that entire dream her doing? Was she sending me some kind of omen? It was times like these where I wished she was like a normal mother and just talked to me like any other parent would.

While I was in mid thought, I heard another booming sound, just like the explosion in my dream. It was coming from the direction of the nearby town, and it was accompanied by screaming. For a moment I thought I was still dreaming until I slapped myself a couple times. I could feel it. I could also feel the Rēa that was coming from that direction. This was real. The enemy was here.

Once I saw smoke rise up into the sky, I knew I had to act. I leapt off my hammock and grabbed my Spirit Caster before doing a light stretch. Then I knelt down, readying myself to jump and let out a spell.

"Anamnistikí Dónisi."

Fire burst from my feet and the force of the stream propelled me into the air. Anamnistikí Dónisi was a spell that let me fly from area to area rather quickly. I gained this ability after the transformation of my Spirit Caster which I still didn't fully understand.

After a few minutes of using my short burst through the air I finally made it to town. I could see a large commotion right in the center of it confirming my suspicions.

As I got closer, I could see the chaos taking over the town. People were scrambling to get away as knights chased them down. Houses and shops were set ablaze and just like in my dream, *Kira* was in the center of it all. I was so livid that I couldn't even think straight. This time I wasn't going to give her a warning. I was just going to end her right then and there.

"Flóga Dóry!" I shouted. Flames started to erupt from both ends of my staff as I fell from the sky like a shooting star and aimed myself directly at the princess. She spotted me and immediately raised her wand in order to perform a spell of her own.

"Mávri Aspída!" she yelled. A black wall appeared in front of her, but I used my Spirit Caster to ram right into it. The impact made an explosion that completely shattered her wall and sent her flying. She landed right on her back, and I pointed my flaming Spirit Caster right in her face.

"Attacking without warning is unbecoming of you," she sighed.

Her casualness irked me almost as much as her presence on the island. "Why are you here?" I asked her, more angered than ever. "I thought I told you that if you came back here there would be war!"

"I know, and I don't care," she grinned.

"Your lack of caution will be your downfall, princess."

"I could say the exact same thing to you, *'hero'.*"

Suddenly I heard another voice from behind me say, ***"Chéri Tou Poseidóna."***

I looked back and saw a wave of water in the shape of a hand heading straight for me as if it was about to grab me. ***"Anamnistikí Dónisi!"*** I shouted in order to give myself a boost out of its path. The water slammed right into Kira sweeping her away into the air and past a nearby building. My eyes followed where the trail of water came from and saw Delta at the end of it, standing by a water fountain. The attack had to have come from her.

"You missed!" I taunted.

"I wasn't aiming for you," she said. ***"Neró Thólo."***

Once she spoke those words, water rose from the fountain and surrounded her in a dome. I thought about her words. If she wasn't aiming for me then that must've meant her true intentions were to sweep the princess away all along. Her making a shield around herself meant that she needed some defense to prepare for something big. Something so big that it would endanger the princess. If it was something *that* threatening, then I had to stop it before she could pull it off.

I ran in her direction with the ends of my staff still ignited. Once I reached her water dome, I stabbed my Spirit Caster right into it and the water dispersed around us. She then shouted out the spell, ***"Poseidónas!"***

The water around us started to cave in on itself with Delta acting as its center. Before I knew it, we were both completely submerged and surrounded by water. The force of the water was strong, and I was swept in its current. It felt like I was being thrown back until I was pushed out, hitting the ground hard.

I coughed up some water and it took me a few moments to catch my breath. I looked up and saw streams of water moving through the air and rushing right over to Delta. This had to be a part of the spell that she had been planning to use against me. The water circled around Delta and rose high into the air, forming into the shape of a person from its head to its torso. It was like a giant monster with Delta right in its center.

It raised its arm to strike, and it swung at me. Using *Anamnistikí Dónisi* allowed me to dodge the attack just by a hair. While it left itself open, I decided to use my own move against it.

"Bála Pyrkagiás!" I shouted. A large ball of flame appeared at one end of my Spirit Caster. I swung my staff, and the ball of fire went flying at Delta. Unfortunately, as soon as it made impact with the water, it was almost as if nothing happened. It simply fizzled out. Her spell was not only a powerful attack but also the ultimate shield. There was no way I was going to get through it.

Delta took advantage of my shock and forced the monster's arms into me. Its giant hands took hold of me and held tight. I sunk into its grasp and couldn't breathe. I was completely surrounded by water once again and I wasn't going to escape easily. I had to use everything I had left to survive. I tightened my grip on my Spirit Caster to use another new move from it. A spell that I gained from its transformation.

Using the rest of the air I had, I shouted the spell, *"Nova!"*

CHAPTER FORTY-EIGHT
KIRA

I stood atop a small building still trying to ring out some of my clothes since I was soaked from Delta's interference. It was annoying, but it made things easier for us. Her pulling out such a powerful technique right from the start would definitely do some damage to the fire user. Looking at the battle from afar made me wonder if I would even need to step in.

At this point, she had already caught him. No matter how much of a fight he put up, there would be no way he could break free. This fight was as good as ours. Or at least that's what I thought until a bright light shined from the Fire Shēna.

Before I could even tell what I was looking at, a massive explosion was detonated right from the flame user. The water surrounding him and Delta immediately evaporated and the entire island shook as I was pushed back by the force of it all.

The building I was standing on started to collapse. I quickly picked myself back up and ran to the edge with no other choice but to jump. I tightened my grip on my Spirit Caster and activated the Rēa in my blood, hoping it was enough for me to reach the ground unscathed.

My body hit the ground hard but that wasn't the worst of it. Before I even had a chance to stand, debris from the building fell right on top of me. I kept my defense up until the destruction stopped raining down.

Everything was silent and I was covered by darkness. Large pieces of debris from the building weighed me down. If I were a normal person, I would have been crushed and dead long ago, but I was a trained Shēna so lifting the heavy debris was no different than a child lifting a bundle of sticks. I was unscathed, but I wished I could have said the same for my royal garments. They were still damp and now covered in dirt. Even worse, they were torn! If Delta didn't already drown him, then I swore I'd finish the job.

I got up and looked around but could only see dust and smoke slowly starting to clear. The surrounding buildings and shops were toppled down to their foundations. In front of me laid a massive crater where the plaza once sat. In the middle of it stood Delta and the Flame user.

Delta spotted me and said, "Princess, are you alright?"

"I'm fine Delta, just worry about the task at hand!"

"You both talk as if I'm not here," Flint said. "This fight isn't over yet!"

Delta looked him in his eyes and sat in silence for a few moments before finally turning around and saying, "I'm done."

"What?" Flint asked In shock.

"I said I'm done. I used up all of my Rēa already and it seems like you've reached your limit too."

"That's not true! I can still take you both down easily with the power I do—"

Before he could finish his sentence, he fell right down to the floor, knocked out cold.

At that moment, Arachne walked up to us and stood right beside me while taking in the destruction from the battlefield. It seemed that our plan had worked. Arachne was a member of the Five Armaments of war and being a member meant that she was a powerful Shēna. In my opinion,

Arachne has one of the deadliest abilities of all Shēna. That ability being poison.

Our plan was simple. Delta and I would distract Flint while Arachne filled the battlefield with poison. Arachne made sure to give us immunity to it while it would slowly but momentarily paralyze Flint.

"Looks like the poison finally kicked in," Arachne said. "He's a resilient guy. He should've dropped as soon as I released the spell."

Delta looked up at me and asked, "What do we do with him now?"

"Have our knights confiscate his Spirit Caster and we'll take him prisoner. We might be able to sway him to join our side," I answered.

"That's a good call," Arachne agreed, "considering the fact that Adam's dead. Having a guy like this to replace him will put the Five Armaments back at full strength."

I nodded my head in agreement and turned around to let the knights handle the rest, but before I could take another step, a small pouch was thrown in front of me. Black smoke spewed from the pouch and blinded me from my surroundings.

"What is this?" Arachne shouted.

"I can't see anything!" Delta yelled.

The black smoke spread far and fast. I could only see a couple of feet in front of me. I felt completely vulnerable.

And as if from thin air, a man appeared in front of me with a dagger in hand ready to kill. I pulled out my Spirit Caster a moment too late and he ended up slashing down at me and cutting my arm. My body instinctively jumped back, but there wasn't any stable ground to jump to. Behind me was only the unstable slope of the crater. I tripped and rolled down the crater, losing my wand in the process.

I hastily swiped through the mix of dirt and sand to find it but before I could, two more men with swords were at both of my sides, ready with a coordinated attack. I didn't have my Spirit Caster to defend myself and it seemed like this would be my end.

Before they could swoop in for the kill, a sword went flying through the air, hitting one of the men right through his chest. He fell to the ground and before the other man could react, a knight came from behind, grabbing him by the head and snapping his neck. The man's body fell to the ground and it was only then that I could see my literal knight in shining armor's face.

It was Ranne. She stretched her arm out to me and asked, "Are you ok, Princess?"

I grabbed her hand and she pulled me up to my feet. We were now face to face and even though it was a bad time, I was in love with the intimacy.

"I am now," I grinned.

"We're under attack," she said looking away into the smoke as if being able to see the chaos around us.

"I hadn't noticed," I said sarcastically while pulling away from her to look for my wand. I found it on the ground and picked it up, ready to end this. "You should go and protect the others."

"That won't be necessary. I already split up the remaining knights to protect them."

"Good, then make sure they get far away from here and make sure our captive is with them. He's probably the reason why they chose to fight back just now. If that's the case, then we can't let him escape. He's more important to us in our custody and alive."

"Understood!" Ranne said before turning to pull her sword out of her victim's chest. She then ran away into the smoke and out of sight.

I needed a good view of the area, so I spoke the words ***"Skoteinó Stá-dio."*** A black platform appeared under my feet and lifted me high into the air. At that height, I could almost see the entire town. I looked closely and saw that Delta and Arachne had made it away from the crater along with Ranne.

This was my moment to strike. I raised my Spirit Caster in the air and began to say an incantation.

"Come devastation.
Everything must die now.
Take away the light!
Bála Tou Thanátou!"

A black sphere manifested at the tip of my Spirit Caster and started to expand at a fast rate. It was so large that it almost blackened the sky. It was as if an eclipse had appeared over me.

Electricity shot from the sphere, hitting those under me. Even my own knights. I didn't care much for them. They were simply just sacrificial lambs I was using as a distraction to take everyone out in one fell swoop.

Once the sphere was big enough, I decided that it was time to use it. I swiped my Spirit Caster down and the giant black sphere went down with it. As the energy ball came closer to the ground, the smoke started to disperse and the people under it panicked, but it was now too late for anyone to do anything about it.

As soon as it touched the ground it let out a massive explosion, destroying almost everything. The Island shook and every nearby building collapsed. The blast ate up the crater and created an even bigger one taking up the center of the town.

Whoever was attacking us was no threat to us now.

I landed back on the ground and my *Skoteinó Stádio* disappeared from under my feet. Everything around me was gone. All of the buildings and the people. Even my knights were nowhere to be seen. Probably blasted into dust from my attack.

It was probably the only way to do away with our enemies as quickly as possible, but I still felt a lump in my throat after looking at the destruction. A lot of innocent people most likely died by my hand. My *own* men who swore their *own* lives to me suffered the same fate. I looked down at my Spirit Caster and wondered why my first instinct was to destroy everything.

"Princess!" I heard a voice shout in the distance that pulled me away from my thoughts. I looked over to see Ranne, Delta, and Arachne headed my way.

Once they got to me, I asked, "Where's the flame user?"

"Don't know," Ranne answered, "he was gone before I got to Delta."

"That's not the answer I wanted to hear."

"Relax princess," Arachne said as she walked beside me, wrapping her arm around my shoulder in a casual manner that made me sick to my core. "You probably ended him with that huge attack. No one could've survived that."

"Unless he got outside of my range like you three," I argued.

"With my poison in his body, there's no way he could've possibly gotten far."

I paused for a moment to think and finally agreed. "That's a good point."

"See? We did what we had to do so let's get off this stupid island. The sooner that happens the sooner we can get ready to arrest that other Shēna that you hate so much. What was her name again? '*Winter*,' or something like that?"

She knew exactly what to say to get my mind off Flint. I needed a chance to prove myself. I needed Crystal Winters. I used my remaining power to create a portal in front of us.

"Please take me away.

Take me throughout the darkness.

Let us travel fast.
Grigoro Taxid."

The black ball of flames formed in front of us as I said, "Everyone grab onto me. We're leaving now."

It wouldn't be too much longer now. I was finally going to finish what I started.

CHAPTER FORTY-NINE
FLINT

I woke up in bed inside of a room that I was only vaguely familiar with. It looked like a sleeping area on the inside of a ship. My body was weak, but I could still move. I sat up and tried to make my way out of bed causing my foot to brush against my Spirit Caster which was lying on the floor. I grabbed it and tried to stand up, but my body felt too weak to even do *that* on its own, so I used my staff as a walking stick to make my way to the door.

It wasn't locked. Whoever brought me on this ship didn't care if I moved around. I wondered why they would be so lax. If it was the Five Armaments, then I was surely a prisoner. I couldn't imagine that they'd be so careless leaving me unguarded with an obvious exit in sight.

Before I completely passed out, I overheard them talking about some poison. That was probably the reason I felt so exhausted. That, mixed with the fact that I was already low on Rēa, meant I wasn't going to make it far even if I escaped. That could've been the reason for all of this. They could have been so confident that my escape was impossible that there was simply no need to try to stop it. Either way, I had to confirm it.

I pushed open the door and made it into a tight corridor. There was no one there. I made my way through the hall until I got to the last door that led me outside. I was on the deck of a ship sailing under the starry night sky. At the front of the deck were two people staring out into the ocean.

One of them turned their head and caught a glimpse of me. They then fully turned around as the other one did the same.

When I saw their faces, all the anxiety I felt before vanished and was replaced by a feeling of ease and comfort. The two people who were standing in front of me were both familiar faces. The Prince of Phoenix Island; Arnold Phoenix, and his most trusted warrior Alexia, daughter of Titan. I'd known them both personally since I became the hero of the island.

"Arnold, Alexia," I said. "What's happening? Why are we on a boat? Were we able to beat the Five Armaments?"

They both glanced at each other for a second with dread before finally looking back at me.

"Unfortunately, no," Arnold answered. "The Five Armaments were too powerful for us to handle. They laid waste to the capital."

"What? What do you mean 'laid waste'?"

"I mean they destroyed everything. The Princess's power is unlike anything I've ever seen."

"If they destroyed everything then why the hell are we on this boat?" I shouted.

"Because they were all too strong for us to handle. We needed to regroup."

"So what you're telling me is that we're running away? There are probably people dying right now as we speak! Turn this ship around!"

"Flint," Alexia interrupted and lightly laid her hand on my shoulder. "We had to leave. If you would've died, then we would have never had a chance against them. We need you if we're going to win this war."

"Well, I'm here now so let's go back and give them hell."

"No. You're too weak right now."

"Like hell I am!"

After I said that, Alexia proceeded to show me how wrong I truly was. With just a kick she swept me off my feet and pinned me to the ground. The entire exchange took less than two seconds.

"You can't even beat *me* right now. How could you hope to go up against four other Shēna almost as powerful as you are, if not more?"

I didn't say anything. I just sat in silence letting the thought sink in. Even at my most powerful, I still lost. Right now, I couldn't even stand. If I were to go back it would be a suicide mission.

Alexia let go of me and got up to her feet. "We'll wait until you've regained your strength. Once you're at full power we'll go back for a counterattack."

"No," I said bluntly.

"Are you still in denial?" The Prince asked. "You can't beat them in your current condition."

"No," I said again. "That's not what I mean. I'm telling you both that even once I've regained my strength, I won't be able to beat them. Not alone at least."

"I'm guessing that means you've got someone in mind for that role?" Alexia asked.

"Three people, actually. Two Shēna by the names of Crystal Winters and Alizeh Green. And there's a pretty strong Zubarian that travels with them."

"Ah, the two wanted criminals of the Black Continent? Are you sure they would help us?" Arnold asked.

"Yeah, I'm sure of it. They've *also* got a score to settle with the Princess."

"How do we find them?"

"I don't know, but the last I heard they were heading towards the Black Continent. So somewhere around there."

"The Black Continent is a big place. It will be hard to find them without any leads."

"Then I guess we better start asking around."

CHAPTER FIFTY
ALIZEH

I felt a terrifying amount of Rēa one week before we reached our destination. Something about it felt dark and sinister. No matter the cause, I could tell that it led to a massive loss of life. Feeling all those lives simply just *end* gave me shivers.

Crystal noticed my discomfort and asked me what was wrong, but at the time, I couldn't put it into words. I just kept the feeling to myself and hoped that it was exactly just that. A *feeling*.

It didn't take too long for me to shake that feeling once we reached Mount Astrapí. At its base, it was snowy and showed no signs of life. The only structure we could find was a lone staircase made of what looked like rotting wood heading along the steepest part of the mountain that stretched far out of sight, above the clouds of mist.

"I'll meet you guys at the top!" I told them.

"Wait, Alizeh, we don't even know where it leads," Crystal said.

"Well, I don't see any Shēna down here and the only way to go is up. ***Grígoros Ánemos!***"

I then took off with the wind and ran up the steps, leaving Crystal, Ana and Mirage behind. It felt like I was running in circles. The stairs wrapped around the incredibly tall and slender peak like a snake reaching towards the heavens.

After some time, I finally made it to the end. At the top there was a small temple and in front of it was a large space with a stone tiled floor that almost seemed like a courtyard, except nothing surrounded it.

The wind grew heavier and the clouds in the sky became black. Flashes of white light sparked from the clouds with booming thunder following it. A storm was brewing.

It seemed strange. The storm came too suddenly. It was unnatural. Almost as if it had appeared magically. Then I heard the words of an incantation resonate through the air.

"Lightning dragon roar."

I looked over and saw someone with dark brown skin and short, curly white hair as they were looking up into the black sky.

"Strike down on my enemies."

They raised their arm into the air; in their hand was a purple Spirit Caster that glowed a brilliant light.

"Make the perfect storm."

Electricity flew from their body in every direction. I was just a few inches shy of getting hit. Lightning started to rain down from the clouds, hitting the ground around us.

"Fidi Vrontis!"

The lightning swirled around them like a tornado of light until it burst and became something that seemed to be alive. It took the shape of a dragon's head. The beast made of pure lightning lunged itself off the cliff, ramming itself into a far-off mountain and causing a fiery explosion on impact. This magic seemed almost unreal. The only other time I'd ever felt so in awe at the sight of something so magical was when I came face to face with the Phoenix.

They sat down in order to catch their breath and said aloud, "Grandma! I can shoot two in a row now! Should I go for a third?"

They turned their face so I could finally get a good look at them. At first, I thought it was a man, but I couldn't tell from their soft features. They looked as beautiful as Ana, yet they were more handsome than Flint. I didn't know what they were, but either way, their face took my breath away and they didn't look much older than I was.

When they looked back, their face appeared excited and then purely confused once they caught sight of me. They immediately got back to their feet, tightening their fist around their Spirit Caster, causing electricity to wrap around their slim body. It looked like they were ready to attack.

"Who are you and what do you want?" they asked.

"Oh, I uh—" I blurted out, too flustered to think, "My name's Alizeh Green. I'm looking for a Shēna by the name of Tora."

"Alizeh Green?" I heard a voice say from behind. I turned around to see the front door of the temple opening and right behind it was an old lady who looked fairly similar to the Shēna who had just performed a spell before me. "You wouldn't be related to Tal Green, would you?"

"Oh, yeah! He's my father."

"That little runt had a kid? It seems a lot of time has passed since I've been on this rock."

"Wait, if you knew my father then that must mean you're Tora."

"Indeed I am. So tell me, darling, what brings you all the way to these mountains? Livádia is a long way from here."

"Well, it's actually a pretty long story."

"Don't worry, we've got all the time in the world. Come inside and I'll make us some tea."

***

After going inside and sitting down with Tora, I told her about everything that happened to me since I met Crystal and Ana. I told her of our battles against the Five Armaments and our meeting with Flint and the Phoenix he helped us fight. Even of the bandits and how we were saved by Mirage. The entire time she listened with a large grin.

Just as I was about to finish, the door came swinging open. It was the Shēna from before who had the power over lightning, and following behind them was Crystal, Ana and Mirage.

"Grandmother, you have more visitors. They say they came here with the girl."

"More visitors?" Tora asked. She looked at me and said, "Are these the three people you were telling me about before?"

I simply nodded my head and smiled. Crystal walked into the room to introduce herself.

"Hello, my name is Crystal Winters. I'm a Shēna who's here to—"
Before she could finish, Tora cut her off.

"You're the spitting image of Eve. Tell me, is she your mother?"

Crystal looked taken back by this and said, "Oh, no. She was my grand-mother."

"Grandmother? Man, time really has passed!" Tora laughed. "I guess that means now is as good a time as any to battle The King. It would be a shame if I died before seeing him fall."

I jumped up out of my seat almost spilling my tea and said, "Does this mean you'll help us fight him?"

"No. Unfortunately my days of using the Spirit Caster are long gone. I'm too old to fight."

"So we came all this way for nothing?" I said, lowering myself back down to my seat.

"Oh, don't worry, young one. You haven't come here for nothing." She looked over to the short haired Shēna and said, "Rai, you will go with these kind ladies to end things."

"Wait, me?" Rai blurted. "Are you sure I'm ready for that?"

"You've been training for this your entire life. You're more than ready." She turned back to me and said, "Oh where are my manners. I haven't even introduced you yet. This young person right here is my grandchild, Rai."

"Oh, so this adorable young man is going to be joining us?" Ana smirked while nudging me. "This will be an exciting change of pace; don't you think Alizeh?"

"Um, Ana," I whispered a little too loudly, flustered at what she was insinuating. "I'm pretty sure they're a girl."

This made Rai chuckle to themselves and say aloud, "Call me whatever you want. It doesn't really matter to me."

Their answer threw me for a loop. Why would they leave it up to us? How could they not care? It was confusing, but I found it endearing. I wanted to ask more questions until Crystal finally cut in.

"Rai's orientation isn't the thing we should be focusing on," Crystal told us before turning to Rai. "The real question we should be asking is if you're mentally prepared for something like this. This mission is going to be dangerous, and I don't want to force you to do it if it's not something you're willing to do on your own."

Rai answered, saying, "It's just like my grandmother said. I've been preparing for this my whole life. It all just feels a bit sudden is all. But besides that, I'm ready to fight. I can even prove my strength to you right now if that will convince you."

"Don't worry," I told them. "There's no need for you to prove yourself." I looked back at Crystal and said, "Rai's strong. I can tell. I haven't seen much from them but from the small amount that I've already witnessed,

I'd have to say that they're probably either the second or third strongest Shēna that I've ever met."

Crystal smiled and said, "Alright Rai, welcome to the team."

Rai smiled at me, and it sent butterflies through my stomach. I didn't understand why. It was just a smile. A beautiful one at that. But a smile, nonetheless.

Those were feelings that I had to sort out later because in that same moment, I felt goosebumps across my entire body. There was an eerie aura in the room as if we were being watched. At the same time, Rai's smile vanished, and they quickly turned their attention to the door.

"Does anyone else feel that?" Rai asked.

"Yeah," I answered while jumping up out of my seat.

Everyone else in the room seemed to be unaware of the sensation, but Rai and I both knew that we weren't alone. After sensing so much Rēa we both knew not to wait around and bolted through the door with our Spirit Casters drawn. But once we were out in the middle of the courtyard, we saw nothing. Not a single person. The only thing out there was Silver. And even he was uneasy. He growled while strutting in circles as if he was trying to find an invisible enemy.

Crystal and Ana came running out behind us.

"Guys, what is it?" Crystal asked. "Are we under attack?"

"I don't know," I answered. "I feel a lot of Rēa out here, but I don't see anything." I turned around to look at Crystal and lowered my guard. "We should go. I've got a bad feeling about this."

Ana went to Silver and tried to calm him down, but he didn't even look at her. He just passed her while sniffing around and howling every so often.

"I've never seen him like this," Ana told us. "You might be right."

"Hey, is anyone else seeing that?" Rai asked.

I looked away from Silver and back at Rai. They were staring at something not too far from us. I couldn't make it out at first. It looked like a light. No. It wasn't just a light but a crack. It was just floating there in midair as if the sky was broken. The crack got bigger and bigger, extending all around us until finally, reality shattered like glass. We all had swords at our throats with armored warriors surrounding us on all sides.

"You're all under arrest! Drop your wands and weapons immediately."

No one moved an inch or said a word. This was all too sudden and none of this made any sense. It didn't feel real. One second, we were alone and the next second, we were surrounded by a legion of knights.

I glanced around and saw that it wasn't just knights. There were Shēna too. I couldn't see their Spirit Casters. They were probably hidden under their cloaks. But I could sense the overwhelming amount of Rēa coming from them. There were three of them, all female.

Only one man stood out from the rest of them. His jet-black armor shined and his mantle moved with the wind as he slowly circled around us. There weren't any doubts in my mind. This man was definitely The King of the Black Continent, Cole Black.

"So, these are the Shēna who have been evading us all of this time? *These* are the ones that have given you so much trouble?" he scoffed while turning to the Shēna with the black cloak. "They're just a bunch of children."

Before he could insult us any further, he started to have a coughing fit. And it wasn't like any old cough. There was a wheeze to it. I found it strange. He didn't seem like he was in any condition to confront us. But I guessed he had to make an exception.

"How'd you find us?" Rai asked The King with a serious look. "I thought your people pulled out of these mountains years ago?"

Once The King caught his breath, he simply just looked at them and smiled. He then gestured towards the temple and right at that moment, the door swung open with Rai's grandmother falling down as if pushed through them. Behind her stood Mirage with a mischievous grin.

"Grandma!" Rai shouted with a look that could kill. They took a step in her direction, but that just caused more blades to be pushed back towards them.

"Mirage!" I fumed, enraged at what all of this meant. "Did you lead them here?"

She answered by saying, "My name isn't Mirage."

Her body then started to change. Small particles of light dispersed from their body like an explosion of stardust. Their physique and face changed from feminine to masculine in seconds. Their long, luscious hair started to fall from their head and blew away in the wind until it was all gone, leaving only their short, slicked back hair. Their skin turned from dark to pale in an instant.

"My real name is Morpheus Morningstar and I am a member of the Five Armaments," he said with a considerably deeper voice.

At that moment everything clicked. In his possession he wielded the Illusion Spirit Caster. That's how they were able to sneak up on us. He made it seem like they weren't even there. His ability wasn't just the key to defeating us. It was the key to *betraying* us!

"So," I said, "this entire time you've been lying to us? You stuck your neck out and saved us just to betray us?"

"Saved you?" Morpheus asked. "Oh, do you mean from those savage desert bandits? I paid them to kidnap you and Crystal so I could swoop in and 'rescue' you later. It was all so I could gain your trust, and it worked perfectly."

I couldn't believe it. This was all my fault. I was too trusting of a stranger I knew nothing about and led the enemy right to us. I suspected that something was off about them, but I never would've guessed that *this* was their true intentions. Without thinking I put Crystal and Ana in danger. And Rai and their grandmother.

Seeing this man find so much enjoyment in toying with me enraged me to no end and I refused to let him get away with it! Apparently, everyone around me knew that fact. Because without even realizing it my Rēa skyrocketed from my killer intent and at that same moment, everyone reacted, friend and foe alike. Every Shēna pulled out their Spirit Caster in preparation for what I would do. But I didn't let a single person take one step towards me before shouting, ***"Víaii sfýrigma!"***

I was going to tear this man apart.

CHAPTER FIFTY-ONE
CRYSTAL

A large explosion of wind blew everyone, including me, away from Alizeh. I almost flew off the edge of the cliff, but I was able to use my Spirit Caster as an anchor, sticking it into the ground to stop me from going any farther. Knights flew past me, completely falling off the cliff and to their doom.

I looked back up and saw Alizeh and Rai speeding over to Morpheus while Ana and Silver quickly got to work, disarming any knights still standing. My immediate instinct told me to help so I got up and started heading in that direction until a black bolt of energy shot past me like a bullet stopping me in my tracks. I looked to see where it came from and saw the princess pointing her wand right in my direction.

"You're mine!" she yelled as she lowered her wand and ran towards me. Seeing her here made things more convenient for me. I'd been wanting to get my hands on her for what felt like a lifetime. Getting ambushed like this just saved me the trouble of finding her.

I raised my wand up in anticipation of what was to come. As soon as she came close, she yelled ***"Psalídi Thanátou!"*** She slashed her wand through the air and at its tip came a burst of dark energy. I jumped out of its path as it sped past me in the shape of a black crescent, cutting everything and everyone in its way.

If I hadn't moved in time I would've been cut right in half. Kira wasn't messing around this time. That meant I wouldn't be either.

"Pagokrýstallos!" I yelled. Ice instantly formed around my Spirit Caster, making a spear as I thrusted it, aiming right at her gut. She lunged away but right before she could I cut right through her black cloak.

I missed, I thought to myself until I looked down at my ice spear. It was covered in blood. I looked back at Kira as she held her side. The color red now stained what was once her all black cloak. *I hit her! I actually hit her!* I was getting faster, stronger, and more agile. Beating her alone with my own strength was turning into an actual reality.

Apparently the excitement that I felt inside showed on my face because the princess looked absolutely livid after looking into my eyes.

"All you did was graze me! Don't think for one second that this will give you any sort of leverage against me!" she yelled before raising her wand back at me and screaming *"Skoteiní Sfaíra Sfairón!"*

Black spheres appeared all around her and shot out black bolts of energy. This was the same spell she had used against me back on Phoenix Island. It almost killed me back then but that was when I was helpless. Things were different now.

I raised my wand and yelled, *"Págo Toícho!"* An ice wall immediately rose from the ground, protecting me from the incoming bullets. But I knew it wouldn't last long so I stabbed my wand into the ground and whispered, *"Ríza Págou."* Trails of ice flowed from my Spirit Caster, slowly but steadily making its way towards Kira.

As soon as it reached her, the bullets stopped. She must've been in too much shock from not being able to move. It crept from her feet and slowly up her legs.

"Damnit! What is this?" she shouted. I decided to use the chance to make my move. I released my ice wall and ran at full speed to attack. The

Rēa in my body made me faster than humanly possible and before she could even look up at me I already had her.

I gripped my wand and yelled, *"cheimerinó—"*

Before I could finish my spell, I fell right to the ground and dropped my Spirit Caster. It rolled a few feet away and I was barely able to move. Just then, a woman with red hair and a green cloak stepped between me and my wand.

"Don't even try it," she said. "You've been poisoned so you won't be able to move for a while. If you struggle, you might put too much strain on your body."

I looked over to see where Alizeh, Ana and Rai were but to my shock it seemed that they were in the same position as I. Face down on the floor and unable to move. I couldn't even call out to them. I felt my mind drifting away, but I tried to stay conscious. If I lost here, then everything would be over. Everything I worked for would be shattered in this moment.

"Don't lay a finger on her, Arachne!" Kira yelled. "She's *my* prey!"

"Oh, don't worry your majesty. I wouldn't dare. Besides, getting my own hands dirty isn't really my style."

I could feel my arms twitch and with that I tried to force myself up, only able to get a few inches off the ground.

Arachne looked down at me and said, "Wow, you're a resilient one! How the hell are you still able to move?"

Right at that moment I heard footsteps making their way over to me. I looked up and saw that it was none other than The King himself looking down at me.

"This game has gotten tiresome. It's time to put an end to it."

He raised his boot and slammed it right down on my temple. All I saw was black. I had felt the full brutality of what the royals fully stood for. Crushing their enemies until there was nothing left.

***

I woke up sore all over, pushing myself off the hard stone floor to look up at the mossy, blood-stained walls. It was hard for me to keep my balance and I had no clue why. I had no idea where I was or why I was there. The last thing I remembered was getting to the top of the mountain and meeting Tora and Rai.

"You finally up?" a voice said from behind. I turned to see Rai standing on the other end of the room while staring out of a set of prison bars. "Took you long enough," they said.

"Where are we?" I asked.

"What does it look like? We're in a prison." Rai scoffed.

It was at that moment that my memories came flooding in. I remembered exactly what happened. We were ambushed and we all went into battle. I fought Kira and I almost beat her! My revenge was so close. It was right in reach, but in the end I still failed.

I reached inside my coat to look for my Spirit Caster, but nothing was there.

"Don't bother," Rai said. "You think they would just leave us in here with the only thing that could break us out?"

I glanced around the cell and asked, "Where's Alizeh and Ana?"

"How should I know? I'm stuck here with you."

"Hey, could you lose the attitude? We're both in the same boat here and I think the best way to work through this is if we do it together."

"*'Together'*? You want *me* to work with *you*? You're the reason we're in this mess!"

"*Me?*"

"Yes, *you!* It's because of your carelessness that we got captured! Me and my grandmother were fine right before you led the enemy to our doorstep!"

"I-I'm sorry ... I didn't think it would've gotten to this point."

Rai fully turned around and stepped towards me, looking even more upset from my response than before. But before they could speak, loud echoing sounds of footsteps came from outside of the cell. Soon there was a small group of knights standing on the other side of the bars. One of them pulled out a key and opened up the cell.

"The King demands an audience with the both of you."

CHAPTER FIFTY-TWO
ALIZEH

"**L**et us out of here!" I yelled while shaking the bars as hard as I could in an attempt to break them. At the moment it was impossible. It might've been possible with the use of Rēa, but without my Spirit Caster it was only a fantasy. That didn't stop me from trying though.

"Alizeh, it's no use," Tora said. "Don't waste your energy."

"But we can't just sit here and do nothing!" I shouted. "I need to find Crystal and Ana to make sure they're alright!"

"And I need to find Rai, but now isn't the time for that."

"Then when *is* the time?"

"We'll know when it comes to us."

"That doesn't make any sense!"

"It may not make sense, but it's always worked for me."

I decided to ignore her words and continued to try to open the bars. The thought of waiting around and doing nothing while my friends were in trouble made my stomach turn. I had to get out of this cage!

"You seem to have so much determination for someone so young," Tora said. "Tell me, Alizeh, what drives you? What even made you want to come on this adventure? I doubt that it's really all just for one person that you barely know."

I loosened my grip on the bars from exhaustion and answered, saying, "I love the excitement and thrill of it all. I've heard stories from my dad about what you and the other Shēna did. All of the adventures you went on, the power you all gained, and the evil you've vanquished. You even beat the Queen of darkness who gained the power of a god."

I turned around to finally face her and continued. "You're asking what drives me? Well, it's simple. The reason I decided to come on this adventure was *for* the adventure. And the people I have to thank for giving me this chance are probably in harm's way, so keeping them alive is the only way to repay them."

Tora added, "But I'm sure your father has also told you about the Shēna who've lost their lives on said adventures, hasn't he?"

There was a long pause before I answered. "Yes. Yes, he has."

"And even knowing this, you still want to fight? Even with the lingering chance of death?"

"I won't die."

"How can you be so sure?"

"Because I can't. I won't allow it. Not until I've seen everything that this adventure has to offer. I'm going to see this through all the way till the very end."

Tora hung her head down and chuckled before saying, "I was just like you when I was young. So let me be the first one to tell you that you should be careful about this goal of yours, because it may very well come true."

"What exactly do you mean by that?" I asked. But before she could answer, the gate behind me opened. I looked back to see a group of knights with one of them holding handcuffs for me.

"Alizeh Green, The King demands an audience with you."

CHAPTER FIFTY-THREE
CRYSTAL

I walked through the gigantic golden halls of the castle with Rai by my side. Knights surrounded us as we were escorted to The King. Seemingly their presence wasn't enough since they had us restrained in heavy shackles that were tightened so much to the point where I could barely feel my hands.

After some time passed on our walk through the almost never-ending hallway, we finally made it to a pair of giant black doors. It was decorated with gold lines that connected together to make a castle surrounded by clouds as if the structure sat in the heavens. It must have represented how The King saw his kingdom—above the rest of the world.

Two knights went to the doors and opened them from each side. The doors opened slowly and in that moment, I started to understand the gravity of our situation. There wasn't going to be an easy way out of this. We were truly going to be judged by the devil himself.

The King sat on his golden throne looking down at Alizeh and Ana. I didn't expect to see them here. They were also going to be judged with us, but at least I could take solace from the fact that for the time being they were still alive. Alizeh turned her head to see me and had a look of relief on her face telling me that she had the same thoughts.

At the bottom of the steps to the throne stood four of the Five Armaments, including Kira, who didn't look pleased to see me. Beside them was a legion of knights with their swords drawn, ready to fight if any of us fell out of line.

"Crystal Winters. Rai Leoht," The King spoke, "come and bow before me."

A request that I was in no position to deny. I walked towards him and stopped once I got to where Alizeh and Ana were, then dropped down to my knees as Rai did the same. I looked up at him with a scowl as I tried to think of a way out of this.

"Now then," The King started to say, "since you're all gathered here, we can finally decide your fates." He turned to Ana and continued, "Before I speak with the Shēna, I'd like you to introduce yourself. What is your name?"

Ana decided to stand despite having significantly more chains wrapped around her body compared to the rest of us and proclaimed, "I am Ana, daughter of Xander. And I am a proud warrior of the Zubarian race."

"Ah, so you're a *Zubarian*. It all makes sense now," The King acknowledged. "I saw you fight off a good number of my soldiers before being subdued. You're a very skilled fighter. Morpheus has seen even more of what you're capable of so when he suggested taking extra precautions with your shackles, I could only assume it was *more* than necessary."

"Oh, I'm flattered, but don't you think this is a little overkill? I mean, I can barely breathe with all these chains wrapped around me. Can't you just take off a couple?"

The King ignored Ana's sly request and looked to Kira, asking, "This is the same woman that took out your soldiers on your trip to Nótio Págo, is it not?"

"Yes, father," Kira answered. "She's dangerous. Definitely more dangerous than most of our soldiers. But she didn't seem like much of a challenge to Ranne."

"Ranne," The King ordered, "step forward."

Ranne stepped forward just as The King instructed, allowing me to get a good look at her. This was the same knight who helped Kira invade my home. The same woman who pointed their blade towards my sister's throat. But more importantly, this is the same human that took away Ana's right eye.

"Yes, my lord," Ranne obeyed.

"Tell me, Ranne," The King commanded, "what did you think of your battle with Ana? Does she rival you in strength? I'd like an honest answer."

"Ana is strong," Ranne answered, "but she is also inexperienced. When we fought, I saw a lot of promise, but I doubt she could ever actually beat me."

"You're wrong," Ana interrupted.

"Excuse me?" Ranne questioned.

"You're wrong about me," Ana explained. "You may have beaten me once before, but I've changed since our last battle. I'm much stronger now and I *know* I can beat you."

Ranne stayed silent. She gave off an air of indifference as if she didn't care what Ana had to say about the situation. But something in her eyes told me she was at least curious of Ana's power.

"You seem confident in your abilities," The King said to Ana. "I like that. How would you like to serve under me?"

"What?" Ana asked in a dry tone.

"You would have a similar position to Ranne and—"

"I don't care what the job is!" Ana interrupted. "How could you ever expect me to serve under you after what your family did?"

"And what exactly has my family done to you? My vendetta is with the Shēna alone. If anything, we share a common enemy. The reason for why you would even want to help them in their war against my kingdom eludes me. Especially since their ancestors are the ones that drove your race to extinction."

"Don't play stupid and shift the blame on them. You know damn well that it was *your* ancestors that started the war between us. Before your family was even in power, they convinced the rest of the Shēna to destroy us just because they saw us as a potential threat. You manipulated both sides just for the sake of conflict. And somehow after all that you still have brainwashed Zubarians fighting for you." Ana turned towards Ranne and continued, "You're a Zubarian, aren't you? How could you of all people fight for him? *Kill* for him even ... after what he did to our entire race."

Ranne avoided Ana's eye, looking fairly conflicted on how to respond. Her lips moved to try and give an answer, but The King cut her off before she could.

"Whether or not any of what you're saying is true is irrelevant. I personally had nothing to do with the tragedy of your race and frankly I don't care for your situation. If you're not going to join me then get back on your knees and accept your punishment."

Ana glared at him for a few moments and instead of obeying his order, actively defied them by walking straight towards him. She didn't make it far since his soldiers were quick to put her back in her place. They kicked her in the back of her legs and pointed their swords towards her, bringing her to her knees.

"Good," The King grinned. "Now, for the Shēna. I want to know which one of you murdered the member of the Five Armaments who went by the name of Adam Stone?"

"'Adam'? Who the hell is that?" I asked. That name didn't sound familiar.

"I know that name," Alizeh answered. "It was the name of the Shēna who tried to kill my family. The old man with the power over earth. He's the one you're talking about, right?"

"That would be the one," The King nodded.

"It was me. I killed him. But it wasn't murder. It was self-defense. He attacked me and my family first without any warning or reason!"

"Your reasoning for killing him matters not. The law on my continent is that if you harm a member of the Five Armaments, you will be put to death. It's as simple as that. But for you, there's an ultimatum. You don't need to die if you agree to one condition."

"And what condition would that be?"

"I want you to join the Five Armaments."

Alizeh took a long moment to ponder the thought. It seemed that she was actually considering it before finally saying, "No. I hate every last one of you."

"So, you choose death?" The King asked one final time.

"I'm sorry, but I don't wanna associate myself with a bunch of evil and corrupt tyrants. And that's exactly what every single one of you are."

Kira seemed to take offense to that. Her face went from enraged to sorrowful. I couldn't tell if she was insulted or ashamed, and the fact that I couldn't tell got to me.

The King continued to speak again. "An unwise choice. It's unfortunate that you have the mind and body of a child. You could have become a great and powerful Shēna."

He turned his attention to me and said, "Crystal Winters. I've recently gained news that the great Phoenix on Phoenix Island has been imprisoned in a giant block of ice. Tell me, were you the one who pulled such a task off?"

"Yes," I answered.

"That's an impressive feat. I've heard that you've also been able to evade death from my daughter. And from what I saw yesterday, it seems like you would have killed her if there wasn't any interference. She may not be the most powerful Shēna out there, but she is still *my* daughter. She can't be taken down so easily."

I glanced over at Kira and as soon as we made eye contact, she immediately looked the other way. Probably out of shame, which put a smile on my face.

"So I will give you the same ultimatum," The King continued. "Join the Five Armaments or die."

Unlike Alizeh, I didn't need time to think about my answer.

"Hell no."

"So you would also rather choose death?"

"I'd never work with you! It's because of you and your daughter that my parents are dead! It's because of you that my life was ruined and I swear that just because I'm bound by chains doesn't mean that the situation is any different! I'm going to *kill you* and get revenge no matter what!"

"You're going to get revenge? And what about *my* revenge? Does your revenge cancel out mine?"

"What the hell are you talking about?"

"What am I talking about? I'm talking about how I've been wronged by your past generations as well."

"What do you mean?"

"You still don't understand? I'm referring to the death of my mother. She was murdered by a group of wicked Shēna. Three of those Shēna were Tora Leoght, Tal Green, and Eve Winters."

The words surprised me.

"Your mother was a tyrant!" Alizeh yelled. "My father did what he had to!"

"She was a great ruler who was betrayed by those closest to her. I was younger than you are now when I watched them kill her." Alizeh just scowled at him. His eyes started to move towards me as he said, "I'm sure that some people in this room could relate to watching the ones you care about most die right in front of your eyes and wanting to raise hell because of it."

His life seemed to have paralleled mine in some way. After watching my parents die, I wanted to kill him. But he probably wanted the same for Eve. It made me wonder if anyone was truly right in this situation. Who were the good guys? I thought about it and realized that there were no good people in this situation. This was a cycle of hatred that was never going to end. As soon as a person decided that they are willing to kill. That was the point where they became the villain. Everyone in this situation... including me... was considered evil.

The King continued, "In my eyes you all have too much power and cannot be left unsupervised with it. And since you refuse to be compliant then you must be eliminated. The only reason Tora isn't in this room is because it was already decided that she would die."

"No!" Rai shouted while getting back on their feet. "You can't do that!"

The knights around us started to close in and pointed their blades right at Rai.

"Everyone stand down," The King said while raising his hand. He lowered it back down and grinned at Rai. "I like that spirit. That *selflessness*. Alright, I will give you another ultimatum, different from the one I gave your comrades. I will let you choose who dies. You, or your grandmother?

"What?" Rai asked in disbelief from the choices given to them.

"It's simple. I was going to execute your grandmother but now I'm giving you a choice to die for her sins. If you do that then she will survive, but if you don't … well I think it's self-explanatory. What is your choice?"

"No," Rai panicked, "You can't do this! You can't make me choose between those options!"

"Would you rather the decision be left up to me?"

"To hell with that! I'd never let *any* man decide my fate. And I won't let you give me any of your stupid ultimatums! *I'll* make a deal with you that will benefit the both of us. But I'll do it on *my* terms."

Rai's sudden demand had the three of us slack jawed. It seemed as if they were oblivious to the situation that we were all in. The others may have hurled insults and I may have thrown some threats, which now that I think about it, may be worse, but none of us ever even thought it was a possibility to make demands.

"And what exactly do you have to offer me, boy?"

Rai's eyes flared.

"Don't call me that," they warned in a sharp tone.

"Oh," The King paused, "so you're a girl?"

"I'm neither to you. You haven't gained my respect so call me by my goddamn name."

"Really now?" The King narrowed his sights on them.

"Like I said before … my terms," Rai reminded him, mimicking his deadly glare.

The silence between both of them was loud. Everyone waited on some lashing or beating. I thought there would be some consequence to this. But there wasn't.

The King burst out laughing before saying, "Okay Rai, you've gained an iota of my respect. What are your terms?"

I couldn't believe that worked.

"You're going to let me live, you're going to let my grandmother live, and you're going to let these three live."

"And what do I get in return?"

"My services. If you let us all live, then I'll join the Five Armaments."

Although Rai was trying to save our lives, it still almost felt like a betrayal. They were trying to join the enemy. A group of people that wanted us dead. And a group that we most likely would have to kill if we wanted to get to The King.

"Do you really think your services are required?" asked The King. "I doubt you're powerful enough to fill the power vacuum that Adam left behind."

"Do you want to test that theory? If you free me now, then I'll show you my strength. Come on, this isn't an opportunity that you can just pass up. You need another member, and I'm the right person for the job. Killing me would be a waste," Rai argued.

The King leaned back in his throne pondering on the thought until he finally gave an answer.

"You might not be wrong. Alright I'll give you my final offer. If you join us and pledge your undying allegiance to me then I'll let you *and* your grandmother live."

"What about them?" Rai asked, looking at us.

"What *about* them? I told you that you're all too dangerous to be left alive. You should be grateful that I'm letting *you* live."

"But—"

"I'm done bartering child!" his voice halted Rai's. "Give me your answer now. If the next words that come out of your mouth isn't a *yes*, then I'll assume it's a no."

Rai looked back at us but couldn't look any of us in the eye. Regardless of what they would say, we'd all still die. It was obvious what their answer was.

"Alright you bastard," Rai said while looking back at The King. "You win. I'll join you."

"A wise choice," he grinned. "Then it's decided. Crystal Winters, Alizeh Green, and Ana; Daughter of Xander, will be executed within a week's time. Rai, you'll live … for now."

CHAPTER FIFTY-FOUR

KIRA

"Kira, are you ok?" Ranne asked as she followed behind me.

"I'm fine," I answered bluntly while picking up the pace. I didn't feel like talking to her, or anyone else for that matter.

"Are you sure? You looked pretty upset back in the throne room."

"Don't I always look upset?"

"Well, yes, but I could feel that something was off."

"There was an entire trial going on right in front of us and all you could think about was me? You're so sweet," I mocked.

"It's my job to be concerned."

"No, it's your job to simply be my sword and shield. You're simply just a tool to me and for you, I'm just another job! Don't get it twisted."

"What the hell is your problem?" Ranne snapped. It caught me off guard. She had never yelled at me, nor had she ever shown any hostility towards me for our entire lives. She continued, "You've changed so much. When we were younger, you were one of the nicest people I've ever met and for some reason you're not that person anymore. You're not the same person I fell in love with."

"Well, things change," I snapped back. "And we're not children anymore."

"This has nothing to do with age. It was when you got that damn Spirit Caster ..." she trailed off as she looked down at my left hip, where my Spirit

Caster was hanging. "That's what changed you. All of that power's gone to your head. You should get rid of it."

"What?"

"You should get rid of it. The wand, the power, the royal title. It's what you always wanted to do. It's what you wanted before you got the wand."

I took a second to think about what she was saying. "But I can't stop now. I'm more powerful than I've ever been. If I stop now, then my father will never see me as a worthy successor."

"Haven't you ever wondered if there was anything more to life than trying to impress your father?"

"Like what? *You*? Are *you* supposed to be my knight in shining armor ready to give me *meaning*?" I scoffed. "You keep bringing up our childhood as if any of that matters. As if we've always been great friends who've had each other's backs. But here's a reality check for you. We aren't friends. To even call us lovers feels like a stretch. You're just a weapon to me. And I don't care for you beyond that."

Ranne looked taken back by my words. I didn't understand why. I'd always told her this, but this time it seemed like she was finally starting to understand.

She didn't say another word. She simply just turned around and left. The silence left me with an uneasy feeling in my gut. She'd never acted this way towards me. She'd always been there for me no matter how badly I treated her. And that made me wonder. Why *did* I treat her like that? I wasn't always like this. It was never my intention to hurt her, and yet I did. Was she right? Had I really changed into something unrecognizable? I turned to the wrong side of justice. I was truly the *'evil corrupt tyrant'* that the child said I was. And I didn't understand why I even cared! None of my thoughts made any sense; I needed to figure this out.

***

I sat on the floor in my bedroom with my Spirit Caster resting on my lap. I was going to do something that I hadn't done in years. I was going to commune with the royals of the past. The ones who lived before my time. I needed answers.

I closed my eyes and meditated. Trying to get back into the rhythm of it. The process almost felt foreign, but I eventually started to let myself slip. Once I opened my eyes again, everything was gone. The only thing I could see was black. It was like being in an endless void.

Finally, something came into view. Or rather someone. The first thing I could see was their red eyes. Slowly everything came into focus, from her black hair to her royal dress.

"Kira," She called. "It's been too long."

"Yes it has, Grandmother," I responded. "If my memory serves right then it's been seven years."

"And look at you now. You're no longer the young child I taught before. You've grown into such a beautiful young woman."

"It seems so," I said, lacking any spirit. I wasn't so sure if me growing up was for the best if I truly was different from what I used to be.

"What bothers you, Kira?"

"I wanted to ask you something."

"Alright, ask me anything."

"I was wondering about this Spirit Caster ... does it have any side effects?"

"'Side effects'? Well, if you put out more power than you can handle then it could be fatal—"

"No! I know that. It's just ... I've felt different."

"Different how?"

"Emotionally, psychologically. My personality. It's all different. I'm not the person I used to be. It feels like ... it feels like ..."

"You're losing yourself?"

"Yes! That! Exactly that!"

Her eyes softened, like she was trying to understand me. No. It was like she already understood. "I once felt like that too," she said. "And I believe the cause was from that very same Spirit Caster that's lying on your lap right now."

"How? Why? I don't understand what makes this thing affect me the way it does."

"I don't understand it either. But either way, its power is something sinister. It's different from other Spirit Casters. Whoever possesses it changes into their worst possible self. I wish I would've realized that before it was too late for me."

"What do you mean by that?"

She gave me a halfhearted smile and said, "Kira, let me tell you the story of how I died."

CHAPTER FIFTY-FIVE
CRYSTAL

I sat in the farthest corner of the cell away from Rai. I guessed it would be more fitting to say that they sat furthest away from me. There was a tense silence between us that was caused by a number of things. First off, they had officially joined the people I swore to kill. And they were leaving us to die ... but obviously not by their own volition. Before we went into the throne room Rai told me this was all my fault. I dragged them into making such a difficult decision. I dragged Alizeh and Ana to their imminent demise. It was all because I let my selfishness take control. All of my rage and vengeance led everyone to this point and I never stopped to consider how it would affect anyone else.

But something that bugged me even further was the hatred that was out of my control. The vengeance that started far before my time. The murder of The King's mother.

I didn't understand why my grandmother killed a former Queen. Was the Queen just as evil or was my grandmother a criminal that made the royal family the way they are now? I wished that I could find out the truth. Luckily, unbeknownst to me, I was about to get it.

"Crystal, you look distressed," I heard someone say. I looked up and saw my grandmother standing right in front of me. "What's wrong?" she asked.

"'What's wrong'?" I repeated. I stood up and shouted, "What's wrong is that everything I've worked for is crumbling down. Because of *my* actions everyone is going to die! And what's worse is that all of this stemmed from you! You killed The King's mother, so he did the same to me!"

"I had no choice but to kill her."

"Why? Tell me what happened."

I glanced over at Rai, remembering that I wasn't the only one in the room. I would have thought that they'd be interested in the commotion that was happening just a few feet away from them, but their attention wasn't on me. It didn't seem to be on anything. They didn't move an inch. It seemed like, once again, time was frozen in the presence of my grandmother.

My grandmother then said, "Kali Black was the Queen of this kingdom when King Cole was just a boy. She was a good friend of mine, but her actions were sometimes questionable."

"Questionable how?" I asked.

"She craved power. She wanted to expand her reach over the entire world. She declared countless wars for years while claiming territory making the Black Continent what it is today. Over time, her concern for the people of her own kingdom became nonexistent. She used them for her wars, tearing families apart and turning children into soldiers. She eventually became known as the Queen of Darkness. Me and the rest of the Six Mágisses could no longer stand by and watch. We had to intervene.

"The *'Six Mágisses'*? What's that?"

"It's what we called ourselves," she smiled. "It's the same group that Alizeh's father and Rai's grandmother were a part of. We all went to talk things out but she refused to even do *that*. She lashed out at us and we had to defend ourselves. She went completely insane and used an overwhelming amount of power against us. But in the end, we came out victorious and she unfortunately died from the encounter."

"What made her go so crazy? What could have possibly driven a person that mad?"

"It was her Spirit Caster. Its dark properties changes the wielder."

"So it wasn't her fault? She was being manipulated by her own weapon."

"That is correct. I sometimes wish I could have helped her out of that dark abyss. I should have tried harder to pull her into the light."

I stood there thinking about her story and her regrets. If the wand truly manipulated its wielder, then that meant that Kira was also being manipulated. If that was the case, then was she truly evil? She killed my parents, but was that *really* her choice?

"Why didn't you tell me this in the beginning?" I asked.

"Would you have listened? In that moment when Kira killed your parents you were at the lowest point of your entire life. Debatably, you still are. All you saw was rage and all you wanted was revenge. Would hearing this story in the beginning have stopped you?"

"No, I guess not."

"Then are you satisfied with my answer?"

"Yeah. Thank you for putting things into perspective for me."

"If you are satisfied then why do you still look so grim?"

"Because the answer came too late. Even with this information, it doesn't change the fact that we're all going to die in a week's time."

"I'm sure you'll be fine."

"How can you be so sure?"

"Because there's still one more *cinder* of hope left that you haven't even acknowledged."

And just like that, she was gone. Time resumed, and I found myself sitting in my original position in the corner. The only difference was that I could feel that her words left an uncontrollable grin on my face.

CHAPTER FIFTY-SIX
KIRA

"I caused so much death and destruction. I betrayed those closest to me, forcing them to seek me out and kill me just so the madness could end. The worst part was that I didn't know just how bad my actions were until it was too late. The moment I died was the first time I saw the light. So tell me, Kira. After hearing this, what will you choose to do?" My grandmother asked.

"What do you mean? I'll do what I've always done," I answered. "I'll use this wand to keep getting stronger."

"Even after hearing of my failure?"

"The reason you failed was because you were too weak."

She laughed at this and said, "So it seems that you're making the same mistake as I did. I hope you know that it will lead to your ruin."

I didn't care for whatever else she had to say. I closed my eyes and opened them back up to find myself back in my room with my grandmother out of sight. I had no intention of being like her. I was going to become better. At least that's what I hoped.

PART FIVE
BEFORE THE STORM

CHAPTER FIFTY-SEVEN
RAI

"Rai Leoht, we're moving you."

They opened the barred door and forced my hands behind my back, slamming the large shackles around them once again.

I looked back at Crystal and felt like I should've said something to her, but I couldn't find the words. On the one hand I was still angry at her for dragging us into this mess but on the other hand I felt guilty over the fact that I couldn't save her.

The guards pulled me out before I could make up my mind. They held on tight and dragged me through the castle halls until we finally stopped at a set of doors that weren't as big as the throne room's, but just as lavish.

The soldiers opened the doors and guided me in.

It was a decently sized room with large windows that showed the city scape. There were couches scattered in a semicircle and a large round table in the center of them.

It looked like a lounge that could have been used for meetings or special events. I had never been in one before and never thought I'd be in such a luxurious place. Unfortunately, I couldn't enjoy my time there because the guards didn't leave. They just stood there, watching me. I guess at that point I was still a prisoner.

I walked over to one of the couches and sat down making myself comfortable since I didn't know how long I would be held there. The guards glared at me, but I glared back, never taking my eyes off of them. They couldn't hold that same energy. It was hilarious seeing them act tough when in reality they were terrified of me. Of what I could do.

The humorous tension in the room was shattered once the door behind the guards swung open. Morpheus walked through with a large warm smile that made me want to punch him right in his face. This was the same man who betrayed Crystal and hurt my grandmother. It was because of *him* that I had to degrade myself by joining his cause.

The red headed girl walked in behind him.

"It's okay," Morpheus said to the guards, "You can wait outside."

Both the soldiers nodded and walked out the room with the woman closing the door behind them. I wondered why they were here. *Maybe to kill me?* I thought. If so, then I wasn't going down without at least *trying* to bash in his skull with the metal vase beside me.

My blood lust must have been tangible because he raised his hands in surrender right after the thought.

"Wow, talk about a look that can kill," he laughed. "Don't worry I'm not here to cause any trouble."

"Then what *do* you want?" I asked, not changing my killer expression.

"Just to talk," he sat on the other side of the same couch. The red headed woman sat on the other couch seemingly uninterested in whatever business Morpheus had with me.

"I don't think we have anything to talk about," I told him plainly.

"Come on, don't be like that," he grinned. "We're teammates now. And teammates should cooperate with each other. *Especially* when they have the same goals."

I could feel the tense face I gave him loosen. "What do you mean by that?" I asked, already knowing that there wasn't a single possibility that our interests aligned. But I was still curious about what *his* goals were.

Our conversation was cut short when another Armament walked through the door. It was the girl who was even younger than me. But she was the only one who shared my dark complexion.

"Ahh the backbone of the team," Morpheus greeted her before looking back at me. "This is Delta." He looked back at her and asked, "Have you come to greet our new friend?"

Delta looked at me for a brief moment but quickly turned her attention back to Morpheus.

"The King wants us all in the courtyard. Including Rai."

"For what?" I asked.

"Isn't it obvious?" Morpheus answered for her. "Your initiation."

***

I was in the center of the courtyard surrounded by the other Armaments and The King himself. If I didn't know any better I'd assume that they had me out there for an execution. If I had my Spirit Caster I definitely wouldn't make it easy for them. I might've be able to take down a couple before my end.

King Cole walked up to me and pulled my Spirit Caster out of his cloak. It's almost as if he had read my mind because he held it out towards me. Goading me into enacting my fantasy.

"Go on," he told me. "Take it."

I was hesitant since I didn't understand his play, but I still grabbed it. Energy rushed through me. It wasn't mine. It was his.

It gave me shivers and wrapped around me, making it feel like I was going to drown in it. Everything about it was sinister and overwhelmed me with a kind of fear that I had only felt in nightmares. And there was still much more of it. His rēa felt endless.

I needed this to end. I tugged on the wand but he didn't let go. He glared into my eyes and gave me an uneasy grin. He was enjoying this. He wanted me to know exactly what he was capable of. Then finally, he let go.

It was over. It only lasted a few seconds and I doubt that anyone else even saw the situation the same way that I did. But regardless it was still one of the most terrifying few seconds of my life. He showed me his full power and crushed any hope I had of beating him alone.

"I want you to give me a demonstration of your power," he told me after he knew I got my bearings back. "Raise your Rēa as high as you possibly can. Pretend as if your life depends on it."

Which it did.

I shook off the fear and did as he said, closing my eyes and concentrating. My power rose not just in a spiritual sense but also in a physical sense. Electricity surrounded my body along with it.

"That better not be it," The King said flatly.

Not even close.

I raised it higher and higher while giving out a shout to push myself to my limit. The sky darkened and thunder could be heard booming above us. This was close to my peak.

"Is this good enough for you?" I asked.

"It certainly is impressive," King Cole nodded before turning his attention to the rest of the Armaments. "Now I want you all to do the same thing. Go up as high as you can."

Every member looked taken off guard for a moment, but they didn't hesitate to obey his order. Unlike me they didn't have to shout to hype themselves up; they were silent as their Rēa surrounded their bodies in a variety of colors that all fused together like a fluctuating rainbow. Their combined auras shot into the sky like a geyser.

This gave me a good look at their power. Morpheus and the red headed woman were close in power to me. If it came down to a real fight I could probably take them both down as long as I could get around his illusions and her poisons. It was the other two that I'd have a problem with.

Delta was strong. Too strong. Her power dwarfed my own. And it wasn't crazy to assume that she was probably the strongest of the four of them. It was no wonder why someone so young would be allowed into the highest-ranking group of knights in The Kingdom. She was an absolute prodigy.

And then there was The Princess. Her power wasn't as impressive but there was something off about it. She wasn't giving it her all. I could tell. And yet it reminded me too much of her father's. Feeling her Rēa was like looking into an abyss. I could only imagine how dangerous she would be if she ever decided to show us the bottom.

"That's enough," he told the Armaments before turning to me. "I want you to know what you're up against if you ever get the idea to run away or fight any of them." He turned back to them. "And until further notice, if any of you feel threatened by Rai then feel free to put them in their place by any means you deem necessary. Though I hope it doesn't have to come to that."

"It won't," Morpheus reassured him. "I'm sure once Rai gets comfortable around us, they'll come to be quite fond of the situation. They just need to spend a little time around each of us."

"That doesn't sound like a terrible idea," The King agreed. "Show Rai around the castle and if you have time, show them the rest of Ebony. I want *all* of you to be present on this tour until sunset. That's an order."

Everyone groaned like siblings being forced to hug it out after a fight. This group wasn't as professional as I'd imagined before meeting them. The only one who looked happy was Morpheus.

He bowed and said, "Of Course my liege. I know just the place to help us all bond." He turned to the rest of us and said, "Everyone, follow me."

I followed this group for an entire day seeing how they interact and treat each other coming to the conclusion that I hated every single last one of them and there was no way that I'd be staying here for much longer. I was either going to escape with my grandmother or die trying. *Really* hoping for the former though.

CHAPTER FIFTY-EIGHT
RAI

I awoke to the sound of rapid knocking at my door. It wasn't aggressive. It actually felt as if they were making a long melody. But it went on long enough for me to want it to end sooner rather than later.

I slid out of the royal bed that was big enough to fit two families and dragged the earthly silk sheets off to cover my bare body. I opened the door to stop the constant banging and unsurprisingly enough, it was Morpheus on the other side to greet me. He was holding a small chest in both hands.

"You're a late riser," he teased.

"I didn't get much sleep," I told him blankly.

"I get it. It's hard to adjust to a new environment."

"Yeah. Especially when that 'new environment' is a glorified, cushy jail cell."

"All of us were prisoners at one point or another," he admitted before walking right past me and into my room. "You'll adjust."

"I never said you could come in," I growled. "I'm not even dressed!"

"Then I caught you at the perfect time," he told me while placing the chest on my bed.

"What is that?" I asked.

"Your new uniform. Put it on and meet us in the throne room in thirty minutes."

And with that he made his swift exit while closing the door behind him. I looked back at the chest and threw off the silk sheet before examining it. Once I popped it open, I was surprised to see something so luxurious.

I threw everything on and posed myself in the mirror. I had on a fitted leather-like jacket with brass buttons and a high collar. The jacket had structured shoulders which made me look broader and more *manish* than I really was.

The bottom half was the complete opposite. I was wearing a buckle pleated skirt made from the same leather-like fabric as the jacket. Under that was fitted leggings that showed off the muscle on my legs.

Even though the top and bottom half were completely different. The large blue sash that wrapped around my waist somehow made the transition between the two seem so much smoother than it should've. The whole look gave an hourglass shape to my body. And the black gloves and boots made me look professional.

All in all, I liked it. It had both a masculine and feminine feel to it, refusing to conform to one or the other. It's like it was made for me.

Once it was time, I walked through the door where guards were already waiting for me. It wouldn't surprise me if they had been there the whole night. They walked with me to the throne room and opened the doors for me to get through. At first I thought they were simply just escorting me as a prisoner, but the more pampering that went on made me feel as if I was actually getting the royal treatment.

The other four Armaments turned to see me as they were already standing in front of The King for the meeting.

"You've come just in time, Rai," King Cole looked at me with relaxed eyes. "That uniform suits you."

"You like it?" Morpheus asked The King as if he were the one receiving the compliment. "I put together that outfit with the goal of trying to make something that just screams *Rai*." He turned to me. "What do you think of it?"

"I don't hate it," I shrugged.

"I'll take the compliment."

"Are we done with the side conversations?" The King asked with bored eyes. Morpheus turned back to him and stood tall. I did the same and that was all the confirmation he needed. "Good," he continued, "now let's get down to business. Lately there have been rumors of an uprising against me."

"Is that really news?" Arachne asked as if her time had been wasted. "People will always talk but it's not like they're a threat to us, much less *you*."

"I wouldn't normally disagree with that outlook, but this time the circumstances are different. Normally we have to deal with average citizens starting an uprising but this time, it's a Shēna."

"Another one?" Kira questioned while tightening her fist. Her eyes seemed more an intense than usual. If she was trying to keep her cool, she was failing.

"No," The King answered. "Not another one. The same one you failed to capture before."

"The flame user ... he's still alive?" Delta asked aloud. Not to a specific person but more as if her own personal thoughts had manifested into reality.

This put everyone on the same page. Everyone but me. I was completely lost on who they were all talking about. And I was a little nervous to ask when everyone looked so tense.

"Where was he last spotted?" asked Kira.

"Kardiá. I want all of you to track him down immediately," The King ordered, but Kira was already a step ahead of him as she rushed to the door, pushing past me to leave. Everyone else followed suit even though we weren't dismissed. I guess Kira's leadership overpowered King Cole's even if it was just for a moment. And he didn't seem to mind that. He only had one thing to say to us as we exited. "This time, make *sure* he's dead."

***

We rode out on horses, traveling until the sun went down. I could tell we were getting close to Kardiá, the heart of Livádia. But at this point I doubted that our target would be there.

"So," I finally broke the silence, "How are we going to find this Shēna without any leads? Do we even know what he looks like?"

"He's a young man with dark skin," Delta answered. "Not as dark as you or me, but pretty dark. His hair is brown and curly. A little longer than yours. And his eyes are golden. He goes by the name Flint. We fought him before but failed to capture him."

"That must mean he's pretty strong."

"No, it was a miracle that he was able to slip out of our grasp," The Princess corrected me. "He couldn't even take three of us on, and back then we weren't even *trying* to kill him. Luckily this time we don't need to take him back alive, so as long as the five of us work together then he can't beat or evade us."

It didn't take much longer for us to reach our destination, a large village that was hugged by the surrounding forest's embrace and cooled off by its towering canopies.

Once we strolled through the village, Morpheus said, "He's definitely here."

"Do you feel him?" Kira asked eagerly.

"No but look around us. There are so many unnerved faces. They don't want us here. I can feel their terror. Their dread. No one's surprised by our arrival. They know exactly why we're here."

"Good." Kira said. "Let's all spread out and ask around. I don't care what methods you use. Just figure out what you can and let's meet back here afterwards."

"What about Rai?" Delta reminded everyone to my detriment. "Are we just going to let them go out on their own?"

Kira looked like she was going to give an order, but Morpheus spoke before her.

"Rai will come with me. I'll make sure they don't stray too far."

Kira had a hint of doubt on her brows but went along with it anyway.

"Fine, go ahead," she told him.

And with that, everyone dispersed. Even Arachne went on her own, leaving Morpheus and I to ourselves as we walked through the village. This conversation was long overdue.

"You seem to be taking a liking to me," I teased dryly.

"Don't flatter yourself," he said, somehow even more dry than I was. "You're much too young for me."

"Then why have you been keeping such a close eye on me?"

"Because it's my job."

"Bullshit," I rolled my eyes. "Everyone else was tasked with the same exact job but not a single one of them gives a shit about me. Hell, none of you even give a shit about each other! So what's *your* angle?"

"You're an observant one," he chuckled. "I like that."

His grin was soft. Easy on the eyes. If I were a few shades lighter it would've made me blush.

"The reason I've been keeping an eye on you," he continued, "Is because of your association with Miss Winters."

"What does Crystal have to do with this?"

"She's a special one. She has the potential to completely topple the power dynamic of this reality ... maybe even the next."

"What exactly do you mean by that?"

"Oh, don't trouble yourself with the thought. At this current point in time, it's probably beyond your level of comprehension. But ironically enough you're just as important a piece in this game as the rest of them."

I ignored the condescending statement and asked, "How's that?"

"Isn't it obvious? You're the only one on her side that's still on the board. What you do next decides how this game progresses."

I stopped in place at the new revelation from his words, "You make it sound as if you *want* Crystal to win this little game of yours."

"In the grand scheme of things, it doesn't matter if she wins or loses. If she dies by the end of this week then it won't affect *my* plans in the slightest. But I do think it'd be pretty boring if The King got his way so easily."

His plan seems to be much bigger than me. It was bigger than all of us. But with how cryptic he was being, I doubted that I'd be able to get a straight answer out of him about it. So I asked him a different question.

"How exactly do you expect me to change anything in my current position? If I desert the team, The King will kill my grandmother before I ever even have the chance to face him.

"Not unless you died in battle," he clarified. "If that were to happen, then you would have given your life for hers."

"Are you telling me to *kill* myself?"

Morpheus rolled his eyes at my assumption and corrected me. "I'm telling you to make everyone *believe* you killed yourself. And if you need a little help with that then just know that I'm pretty good at making people believe in what I want them to.

"You're risking a lot for my sake, so I have to ask, who's side are you on anyway? *Ours* ... or *theirs*?"

"I'm on the winning side darling. *My* side."

He took a good look around and I did along with him. The other Armaments were out of sight. With this knowledge he turned around and trailed off into a different direction.

"Don't try to run off immediately. I'll have no choice but to catch you in order to keep my status. And I won't be able to stop the others from killing you themselves. So *think* before you try anything. And above all else, make sure you make a spectacle of it."

"What do you want me to do until then?" I asked.

"Your job," he laughed. "What else?"

"My job?" I asked myself. "Oh yeah." I was just like him now, wasn't I? An Armament. I guess it didn't hurt to spend the time I had at least looking like I was taking this seriously.

I closed my eyes and focused. There were five other high energy individuals in the area. Obviously, the rest of the team. But one of them were much lower than the rest. Like they were suppressing their own energy. Looked like no one else on this team was that good at sensing Rēa. If they were then they'd already know exactly where to find our wanted man.

I walked straight to the source, an abandoned house that had boarded up doors and windows. It seemed out of place. There were no other houses like this in the village. Seemed more like a choice made to overt attention from it. But I could see through its disguise.

I drew my wand from my hip and jumped all the way to the second story window. It was the only one that wasn't boarded up. And it was already broken so it wasn't hard to get into.

The inside was dark but other than that it was fine. Not too much dust, still fully furnished and structurally sound. Or so I thought. After a few steps through the room the floor crumbled beneath me forcing me to crash through the first floor and down into the cellar. The fall wasn't enough to kill me, but *holy shit* did I not want to get back up today. But my problems were just beginning there.

When I opened my eyes, I was greeted by what looked like the dying embers of a lit torch right in my face. It was being held by a tall boy with amber skin and golden eyes.

"Call for help and I'll burn your face off," he threatened.

"Wow, that's morbid," I said aloud to his dismay.

"Do you think I'm *joking*? I'll turn you to dust before you can even blink!" he shouted, forcing flames to erupt so close to my face to the point where I genuinely questioned whether or not I still had eyebrows. He wasn't joking about burning my face off.

"No, no, I believe you. I just have a bad habit of making horrible jokes in tense situations. Especially situations that escalate as quickly as this," I laughed with a little bit of a crack in my voice.

"How many of the Armaments are here?"

"All of them, unfortunately."

"Damnit," he cursed to himself only half taking his attention from me.

"Even if you kill me now, you won't be able to beat the other four alone. If you're lucky you might be able to take down two, *if that* ... but in the end you'll die trying."

"Is this your way of saying I should turn myself in?"

"I just think we should sit here for a moment to examine your options."

"And what exactly are my *'options'*?"

"Option number one; you try and kill me now but I'm not going down without a fight. The others notice and once you're outnumbered it's over. Option two: You try and run but I'll of course alert the others, we catch you and you die."

"What's option number three?"

I grinned at him and grabbed his staff moving it away from my face. There wasn't any resistance because he now understood that he had no leverage on me. Regardless of what he'd do, he'd die. He *needed* option three to be something good.

I got up to my feet, never letting my mischievous grin go and finally answered him.

"Option three, is us working together to escape."

"What?" he asked, dropping his whole tuff guy act. "What the hell do *you* have to escape from?"

"I'm a prisoner to The King. He's *forcing* me to do this job. Probably forces the rest of them too. Unlike them I don't plan on spending another second under his thumb."

"How do I know that I can even trust you?"

"Well, I think the fact that I haven't tried shooting a lightning bolt through your chest at any point during this conversation should be pretty telling."

He looked down at my Spirit Caster as if just realizing it had been in my hand this entire time. He knew I wasn't bluffing. And with that he finally lowered his Spirit Caster.

"Thank you," I nodded, happy that all that hostility was gone.

"Okay so what's your plan?" he asked. "What do you need me to do for us to walk free?"

"Well, your job's pretty simple actually," I chuckled. "I just need you to kill me."

CHAPTER FIFTY-NINE
ARACHNE

I sat at the bar hoping to get a bit of a break from everyone and every-thing else. The journey here was too long for anyone to actually expect me to waste my time searching for someone that we probably weren't going to find even *if* I helped.

The bartender poured the fine wine and put the glass in front of me. I swirled it around and gulped it down quicker than he could turn and a walk away.

"That's actually pretty good," I told him while tossing him a gold coin. "Leave the bottle."

The look on his cute little face was priceless. That bottle wasn't worth a tenth of that coin but what can I say? I'm a pretty generous tipper when it comes to quality wine. They don't make stuff this good back in Ebony.

"Are you seriously not even going to *attempt* to find Flint? I heard Morpheus say from behind. He sat down next to me waiting for an answer.

Only after I wiped my mouth from my last swig did I answer him saying, "What for? I'm sure someone else more dedicated to the cause will end up finding him long before I do."

I went to take another sip from the bottle but he grabbed it from me before I could and poured some into my old glass for himself.

"One day you'll regret that laid back mindset," he warned.

I doubted that. This job was beneath us. And I know he obviously didn't care for it either.

I looked around the bar and didn't see Rai anywhere in sight.

"Where's your pet?" I asked.

"Out for a walk," he answered casually while taking small sips of my wine.

"Didn't you *volunteer* to watch over them? You know they're going to run away the first chance they get, right?"

"I'm counting on that."

Boom!

The ground shook forcing my bottle to topple over. I stood up looking at the door knocking down my chair behind me. Morpheus didn't move. He didn't even *flinch*.

"That was quick," he smirked.

"What was that?" I asked.

"My *pet* I presume."

He finally got up and we both swiftly made our way out of the Tavern. Smoke clouded the sky and one house was consumed by a mountain of fire. And emerging from the flames was none other than Flint. And right beside him was Morpheus's pet, Rai. They both looked dead at us and started running in the opposite direction.

"Hey!" I shouted with the intent on stopping them, but Morpheus placed his arm in front of me, forcing me to pause.

"Let them go," he told me. "You *never* saw them."

I didn't understand why and wanted to ask but Kira and Delta arrived before I could.

"What happened?" Delta asked.

"We have to put that fire out!" Morpheus shouted seemingly almost exasperated even though just a moment ago he didn't seem to care. "Rai was in there before it exploded!"

"What?" Kira hissed. "How could you let them out of your sight?"

"Kira!" Delta shouted over her. "Our priority should be to put out this fire before it spreads to the rest of this town!"

With a low grunt Kira submitted and snapped her fingers to alert the knights around us. "Smother this fire! Now!" she ordered.

"Arachne and I will go to the other side of the fire to see if we can find any signs of life," Morpheus said while running to the other side. I followed after him until we were out of sight.

That's when I finally asked Morpheus, "What are you up to?"

"I'm just having a little fun," he smirked. "Believe me, this'll make things *much* more interesting."

Right at that moment we saw a low-ranking soldier run to us with an important message.

"Lord Morningstar, Lady Isley! I spotted the prisoner and the wanted fugitive running in that direction!"

"Who else saw this?" Morpheus asked.

The soldier looked a little perplexed at the question. I didn't blame him. The question shouldn't have mattered. Our priority should've just been to catch them.

"I was alone when I spotted them," he answered, "but I don't believe I was mistaken on who I saw."

"Who else did you tell?"

Another perplexing question that seemed to only waste time.

"Just you two, sir."

That made Morpheus grin. It wasn't a normal smile. But a smile I've seen before on him. It only showed in his face whenever he gained the satisfaction of victory.

"Excellent work soldier. Now show me one more time. What direction did they go in?"

The soldier turned around and pointed in the opposite direction. Turning his back on Morpheus was his fatal mistake. A mistake that not even I was ready for.

Morpheus pulled out his dagger, grabbed the young man from behind and slit his throat. The man struggled and tried to call for help but Morpheus covered his mouth and held him still while blood sprayed all over his hands. It didn't take long for the soldier to go limp and once he did, Morpheus through his lifeless body into the fire to burn.

"Morpheus," I said with hesitation, "I don't understand."

"We need to make Rai's death look real," he explained while taking out his Spirit Caster. The body he threw in the fire morphed into that of Rai before my very eyes. He was using his illusions.

"No," I told him, while trying to regain my cool. "I don't understand why you're going to such lengths to save some stupid kid."

"I'm not saving anyone. I'm just giving them a fighting chance."

"But why?"

"Because a win for Crystal and her allies is a loss for The King."

It was all starting to make sense now. He didn't care about the safety of Rai or the success of Crystal or about anyone else for that matter. All he wanted to do was see our pig of a King squirm.

"You do realize if that kid shows their face again then people will probably point the finger at you since you're the only one who could pull something like this off, right? What will you do then?"

"Do you really have to ask?" he came in close as he spoke, leaving only a few inches in between us. "I'll kill anyone who doesn't look the other way. I don't care if it's Delta, Kira or The King himself. Eventually they'll all fall the same."

His words made my body tingle. His determination. His will. Nothing would stop him from getting what he wanted, and I loved that about him.

Before he could step away, I pulled him in even closer and kissed him making sure to not let go until I was satisfied.

"You're more dangerous than even my deadliest poison," I breathed into him.

"Oh, my dear Arachne," he took a breath. "You've only seen the least of what I'm capable of."

PART SIX
THE MOST IMPORTANT BATTLE OF MY LIFE

CHAPTER SIXTY
CRYSTAL

I sat in dark silence for what felt like the longest week of my life. After seven days passed, the guards finally came to take Alizeh, Ana and I to our final resting places. We went through the dimly lit halls and out a doorway leading outside. It had been so long since I had last seen sunlight. When the light hit my eyes, it felt as if it was blinding me.

Once my vision adjusted, I realized that we were in the courtyard of the castle. Legions of knights and servants of the land surrounded us, including four of the Five Armaments, and The King himself. But oddly enough I couldn't find their newest member, Rai anywhere. It made me curious whether or not The King held up his part of the bargain. The only other reason I could think of for why Rai wouldn't attend would have been through their own volition. Either out of respect or shame. Either way I didn't harbor any resentment towards them. In the end Rai was just protecting the one person closest to them and if I was given the same ultimatum two months ago then I would've made the same choice.

Although Rai was missing, there was still enough Armaments to make sure we stayed in our place. We were surrounded on all sides by a small army. With so many people here, it seemed like there was no chance of escaping.

They took the three of us onto a wooden platform with three giant stakes protruding out and stretching upward. They then tied us up to them before walking off the platform and leaving us there. The King then spoke.

"Crystal Winters, Alizeh Green. For your crimes of illegally possessing unregistered Spirit Casters and the murder of Adam Stone, you will both be sentenced to death by fire. Ana, daughter of Xander, for aiding and abetting the Shēna, you will share the same fate. Do any of you have any last words?" No one answered and he continued. "If you all have nothing to say then we will proceed immediately."

He then raised his hand in the air and snapped his fingers. Behind him, knights began to light their torches.

"Alizeh," I whispered, "you haven't come up with any plans to get us out of here, have you?"

"Yeah," she answered.

"Really?" Ana questioned. "Mind sharing it with the rest of us?"

"My plan is to wait for an opening."

"Alizeh, I think it's too late for that," I doubted.

"No, not yet. It's not too late until we're dead. So I'm gonna keep looking for it until then. That's what Rai's grandmother told me to do at least."

Ana chuckled and said "It seems like good advice. Alright, let's look for that opening."

Her words were sarcastic but not in a patronizing way. It seemed like she was trying to lighten the mood and that attempt put a smile on my face.

Once their torches were ignited they threw them at the platform, forcing it to quickly catch fire. The flames circled around us, slowly closing in with blistering heat. But I had felt worse heat from my battle against Flint. His flames were dangerous yet so brilliant that they created their own kind of beauty. And the Phoenix's flames were at least ten times more intense. I had endured so much on this journey that these flames almost felt meaningless. It was too anticlimactic of a death for me. And that feeling helped me to take solace in this tragedy.

We were all in too high spirits for an execution. I wanted to hold onto that feeling so I closed my eyes and waited for the flames to consume me.

But once I had closed my eyes, something incredible happened. I heard the booming sound of a massive crash. I opened my eyes to see fire and lightning not too far from us shooting into the air. Knights went flying back and all that was left was a massive gaping hole and smoke. An explosion had just occurred in front of us.

And as soon as the fire and static from the explosion faded out, the flames around us disappeared with it. Our demise no longer seemed imminent and my gloom was replaced with that *cinder* of hope. I stared hard into the smoke left from the explosion and smiled once I realized what I was looking at. Flint, The Flame Hero of Phoenix Island. Right behind him was the last person I'd expected to see helping us. It was *Rai*. Seemed like I was too quick to judge them.

Flint started running towards us while Rai started to shoot lightning all around the courtyard to draw attention but they weren't alone in their assault. Climbing out of the hole was a crowd of people with weapons ready to fight. They scattered out along the courtyard attacking everyone in their path. The chaos added to the smoke, making it too difficult for me to truly comprehend what was happening.

My eyes went back to Flint who ran into knights but easily beat them in seconds using only his staff. He finally made it to the platform, jumping on it and greeting us.

"Hey guys, how's the suicide mission going?"

"We've got everything under control," Alizeh answered.

"Really? So I guess you won't be needing these?" he said while pulling out two daggers from the inside of his jacket. He swiped down, instantly cutting Ana's binds and setting her free. "I believe these belong to you."

"My daggers?" Ana asked. "Man, you've been busy."

The Four Armaments all started to make their way over to us while easily killing everyone who got in their way. Rai was the only one strong enough to slow them down but they couldn't beat them alone. This was bad. We still didn't have our Spirit Casters so we wouldn't be much help to the both of them when it came to fighting them head on.

Flint turned to Ana and placed the daggers in her hands. "I'll handle them while you get these two free," he told her before going back into battle.

Ana quickly got to work on getting me free. Once I was unbounded, she quickly did the same for Alizeh.

"Looks like Tora was right," Alizeh said. "All we needed to do was wait for the right opportunity and bam! Instant escape!"

"It's a little too soon to celebrate," I told her. "We're not out of this yet."

We all jumped off the charred platform and onto the battlefield, making our way to Flint and Rai who were in a losing battle against the Four Armaments. Rai glanced over at me, reached into their pocket, and pulled out a Spirit Caster. *My* Spirit Caster.

"Crystal! Catch!" Rai yelled as they chucked it in my direction. It seemed like the wrong choice because as soon as it left their hands the entirety of the Four Armaments all began their attacks to take them both down. I knew it was up to me to save them and I had to act quickly.

I jumped up into the air and caught the Spirit Caster. Not a moment later I thrusted my wand and shouted, ***"Págo Toícho!"***

Rēa rushed through my body and ice quickly came spewing from my direction, cutting in between my two allies and the Four Armaments, withstanding their attacks. It rose into the air creating a massive wall that expanded across the courtyard, separating them from us. It was at that point that I fully realized how much I had missed magic.

Once I got close to the both of them I asked if they were okay. Rai said, "Yeah, thanks for the save," while Flint briefly nodded his head. He quickly turned his attention to Alizeh, reached into his jacket and pulled out another Spirit Caster, passing it to her while saying, "Alizeh, I need you to fly us over that wall. We're getting out of here."

"Alright, sounds like a good plan," Ana nodded. "I'll catch up with you guys later."

"Wait, where are you going?"

"To find Silver."

"Ana, your pet can wait! We need to get out of here!"

"That *pet* is my best friend and I'm *not* leaving him behind!"

"Ana ..." Flint couldn't find the right words to convince her.

"Give it up, Flint," Alizeh cut in. "Just the other day Crystal got kidnapped while I got hit by a cannon and the only thing she could think about was Silver. She won't be able to focus without him so let her go."

Rai finally spoke and told Ana, "I'm coming with you. I need to find my grandmother."

"No, you're leaving with them," Ana ordered.

"What? No, I need to save her!" Rai argued. "Its why I came back here in the first place!"

"Rai, look. You see all these people here? They're fighting for *you*. They're fighting so that all of you can live another day and return the favor."

Rai looked at her with an intense rage, but they didn't say anything. Rai knew that she was right. There wasn't much time for a rebuttal anyway.

From the other side of the ice came a loud booming sound forcing it to crack.

"Guys!" I shouted. "I can't hold them off for much longer. We have to make a move *now*."

Ana nodded and ran off into the chaos.

Alizeh released her Rēa and said, "Nobody move or speak. I'm not used to flying with this many people so I need to concentrate."

She then closed her eyes and took a deep breath.

"Paírno Ptísi."

Heavy winds started circling around us and lifted us into the air. Before we knew it, we were already far beyond the wall and high over the city that surrounded the castle. If she kept it up then it would have been smooth sailing. Unfortunately, we weren't that lucky. I looked behind us at the castle and saw a large black ball of energy hurdling right for us.

"Alizeh!" I shouted to warn her.

She looked back and fear shot across her face, but it was short lived. From pure instinct, she turned and shouted, **"Víaii Sfýrigma!"** which forced a powerful wind to make impact with the attack before it could reach us; it exploded. The force from the explosion pushed us back and broke Alizeh's concentration until she lost her hold on us. We all went flying in different directions out of each other's sight. The worst part of it was that without Alizeh, we were all at a free fall and had no way to slow ourselves down.

CHAPTER SIXTY-ONE
RAI

I fell towards the earth at a high speed and had to find a way out of this quickly. I needed metal. Any kind would do. I glanced around and caught sight of a large clock tower not too far away, pointed my Spirit Caster toward it, and shouted, ***"Magnítis!"***

Electricity shot out of it and attached itself to the long hand of the clock. I yanked the Spirit Caster and the large hand was ripped off the clock, flying towards me as if I was a powerful magnet.

As soon as it got close I grabbed onto it, pulled myself up and got my footing on top of it. I flew with the clock hand through the air as if I was surfing on water. Having control over electricity also gave me control over the electromagnetic spectrum. So I could use my power to control any metal I wanted.

I lowered myself deeper into the city and found myself above a canal while standing on the metal pole thinking about what I should do next. I had no idea what became of the others. For all I knew they could have all died from the explosion, or the fall. Was it worth seeking them out? I could've just left right then and there, but my grandmother was still in the castle.

I wanted to take her with me but if I went back now I would have to fight against four other Shēna with no chance of winning. I needed the others to fight them. I *needed* the others to be alive.

My mind was made up. I was going to scour the city until I found the others so that we could beat these Armament assholes together. Unfortunately, my mind was made up too late because I had already been found.

"I'm glad you're alive." I heard someone say from behind me. I turned to see Delta standing on top of the water as if it was solid ground with her Spirit Caster in hand.

"Is that sarcasm?" I asked.

"I get asked that a lot. But no. I'm serious. I'm glad you're not dead. Unfortunately, I'm going to have to take you in."

"You don't have to do this, Delta. I don't know you all that well but even a fool can tell that you're not like the rest of them."

"That doesn't matter. I've got a job to do and I'm going to fulfill it. Now stand down, Rai. This is your last warning."

I sighed and took off in the other direction, following the route of the canal. Fighting her wouldn't be easy. Her Rēa was tremendous. Way larger than anyone else on her team. And besides, I didn't feel like taking orders from another kid who looked even younger than I was. And at the speed I was going, there was no way she would be able to keep up with me while I was hovering on the long minute hand. But she didn't have to keep up. I knew now that she only had to stop me.

As I was fleeing, a large column of water shot up from the canal like a geyser hitting me from underneath, knocking me straight off the piece of metal and right into the water. I immediately swam back up while the metal clock hand continued to sink down. My head emerged from the water and I took a deep breath. As soon as I did, I felt something tug at my leg and before I knew it, I was being dragged back down to the bottom of the canal.

I looked down and saw Delta right below me. She swiftly swam up to me and swung her fist against my face. The punch was powerful. I tried to hit back but being underwater slowed me down. She hit me again. *And again. And again.* She was too quick. It was as if she was fighting me on land. The water didn't seem to hinder her movements at all.

I was losing air and probably only had enough breath to shout out one spell. And then that would be it. If I used a spell to shock her while I was underwater with her, then I would probably end up shocking myself.

In that moment, I caught a glimpse of the clock hand that was still sinking down to the bottom of the canal. That was my ticket out of this! I pointed my spirit caster to it and with my remaining breath, I uttered, *"Magnitis,"* and yanked my arm back.

Delta paid no attention to my efforts and continued to beat me, probably believing it to be a failure. But she soon realized that this was a mistake, because as soon as I pulled my arm back the clock hand pulled itself towards me at a high speed and she was the only thing in its way.

It slammed into the back of her head, knocking her right out. I then grabbed it and forced it to pull me back up to the surface. My head stuck out of the water and I could finally breathe again. It was a relief. I had honestly thought I was going to drown down there.

I readied myself to get back on the metal clock hand so I could fly out, but something stopped me. The thought of Delta. She was young. Too young to be fighting in wars. Too young to die. And I left her down there to drown. It was a thought I couldn't ignore. I took a deep breath and dove back down into the water, grabbing Delta and pulling her back out of the water and onto land.

She didn't move. She was unconscious and it didn't look like she was breathing. I put my head on her chest to see if I could hear a heartbeat.

Ba-dum ... Ba-dum.

It was faint but still there. She was dying and I had to act quickly. I looked at my Spirit Caster to think of a spell I could use. I thought of something that my grandmother once told me when she first taught me how to use it.

To wield electricity is to wield energy. With it you can give enough energy to save a life.

I always wondered if she meant that literally or figuratively. I hoped it was the former. I put the tip of my wand to her chest and said, ***"Apoplixia"***.

A light electrical pulse shot right into her chest and a second later, she started showing signs of life. Water splattered from her mouth and she began coughing. I had saved her. But it probably wasn't a good idea to wait around for a thank you. We were still enemies and there was no telling what she would do once she woke up.

I quickly looked around the area, scanning the houses and buildings that surrounded the canal. There was a narrow alleyway close by that seemed like a perfect escape root. I got back on my feet and ran as fast as I could towards it. Traveling around the city on foot to look for the others was a lot more inconspicuous than flying on a clock.

CHAPTER SIXTY-TWO
FLINT

The impact of the explosion threw me straight towards the earth. Luckily this wasn't my first free fall. I turned my body, stretched my arm out and pointed it downwards before shouting, ***"Anamnistikí Dónisi!"***

A sharp stream of fire shot from my hand and then from my feet, slowing down my fall, stopping me in midair just a few feet from the ground. I released the spell and landed right in the middle of a cobblestone street surrounded by tall houses.

I made it down safely but I didn't know what became of everyone else. If they were hurt then I had to help them. I looked in every direction, wondering to myself where I should go to try and find them.

There were dozens of people out in the street looking in awe of what they had just seen. Some pointed at me while others whispered. The words "Shēna" and "criminal" were thrown around, but I didn't care to give them much of my attention.

Everyone looked up and an aura of fear could be felt throughout the entire street, causing everyone to run back into their homes. I looked up with them and caught a glimpse of something in the air. One of the Four Armaments was standing on a floating black platform. She jumped off and landed close to me.

"Oh, lucky me," she said, "looks like I got the cute one."

If the circumstances were different then I would've been flattered and reciprocated the same energy, but she was the enemy and she was in my way. I gripped my staff and fire erupted from it.

"Woah, woah, woah," she said as she put her hands up. "I don't wanna fight you. I just wanna talk. My name's Arachne Isley."

I smothered my fire into a light ember. I didn't know what game she was trying to play but if there was a chance that I could end this fast and without a fight then I was going to take it.

"Flint Zapalac," I said back.

"Oh, I know who you are. I was there at the siege of Phoenix Island."

"I don't remember you."

"That's because you passed out before I could introduce myself."

Now that greetings were out of the way I decided to get down to the main question. "What do you want?"

"What do *I* want? I could be asking you the same question. What is all this? Is this your way of getting revenge for your fallen island? If it is then it's disgraceful. All you get in the end is a bunch of other weak Shēna. And what's up with that ragtag army you brought with you? They barely look like they could spar against a group of children, much less go to war with our army."

"They're foreigners from Phoenix Island who were scattered around this continent. And they're still loyal to us."

"They're fighting a losing battle."

"They know."

"Then why fight at all?"

"Because they can't stand by as their homeland gets ravaged by you and your people. Today is the beginning of a new—"

I couldn't finish my sentence because in the middle of it I fell right to my knees. My body felt numb and I was going to collapse, just like during the siege of Phoenix Island.

"Oh good, the poison is setting in," she said excitedly.

"Poison? When did you—"

"As soon as I landed. I spread my poison through the air, using a spell called *'Chimikós Pólemos'*. It's the same spell I used on you back on Phoenix Island."

I let out a weak laugh, "Ha, so you're the one who took me down?"

"Yup, and unfortunately for you I'm going to do it a second time. Luckily it didn't have to take as long as before. But I'm guessing that the adrenaline in your blood probably held it off for as long as it did last time. Since you're calm now, the process has become a lot smoother. I thought I'd be sitting here forever having to ramble on about hopeless nonsense that doesn't matter. But now all I have to do is sit here and wait for you to kick the bucket. Hopefully *that* doesn't take too long. I have a million better things I could be doing right now."

I could feel myself slipping. It was a poison that was in the air. I could've tried to hold my breath but what would've been the point? If she was there then the poison would stay. I couldn't move so there was no way to attack her. At that moment, everything felt hopeless until a voice from above said, "If you've got better things to do then why don't you just kill him now?"

I looked up and saw Alizeh sitting on top of a nearby house. Man was I happy to see her. If she hadn't shown up I would have been a goner for sure.

"What was that?" Arachne asked Alizeh, seeming very irritated by the wild-card that had just shown her face.

Alizeh answered, "I'm asking why you don't kill him with your hands. Why wait for the poison to kick in if you're so impatient?"

Arachne was slightly taken aback by the question but soon let out a grin and said, "No one's ever asked me that before. Well, you see kid, it's quite simple. I don't like getting my hands dirty."

"That sounds pretty lazy to me."

"What?" Arachne asked, looking almost offended.

"I was raised on a farm so I've had to get my hands dirty all my life. I can't understand why you wouldn't want to do something so simple. And the thought of it disgusts me."

"You seem to be misunderstanding me. It isn't that I'm lazy. There are people in this world who were made for that. People in this world who have the job of cleaning and disposing of trash like yourself. I on the other hand was made for so much more."

"And what exactly is '*so much more*'? Does that mean you get to terrorize the weak while being an underling to a pitiful pig who calls himself a king?"

"Oh, please. Give it a year or two. Within that time I'll take the throne away from the royals with extreme prejudice. Then you'll truly see what I mean by '*so much more*'.

Alizeh stood up and uttered the spell, ***"Katharizo"***. She then jumped off the roof and stood in between me and Arachne.

"Flint, are you ok?" Alizeh asked.

"Yeah, I'm fine," I lied. "How long have you been watching us?"

"The entire time."

"And you're choosing *now* to show your face?"

"While I was imprisoned, Rai's grandmother helped me with a new realization. Every time I rush into a battle I end up being extremely unprepared. I don't wanna do that anymore. I won't rush into things. I'll wait and observe so I can be as prepared as possible."

"And are you prepared for this battle?"

"That depends on how fast you can get up."

She then darted towards Arachne, jumped into the air and yelled, ***"Gale Lance!"*** causing a spiral of wind to envelop her hand. She dove down, attempting to attack Arachne with the move but Arachne was fast enough to jump out of her reach.

"Oxý!" Arachne shouted while swiping her Spirit Caster through the air. A green ooze spewed from the tip of the wand and it was going to spill all over Alizeh.

Alizeh acted quickly and shouted, ***"Víaii Sfýrigma!"***

A heavy burst of wind forced the goo back, making it splatter all over the ground. As soon as it hit the ground it started to melt the stone, forcing smoke into the air.

"Woah!" Alizeh yelled. "That's so cool! If that would have hit me, I would've been a goner!"

"If you think it's so cool then stay still so you can get a closer look!" Arachne laughed as she pointed her wand at Alizeh. ***"Bála Oxéos!"***

A green ball appeared at the tip of the wand, but Alizeh was fast enough to dodge it so instead of it hitting her head-on, it hit a house, burning a hole right through it.

"Grígoros Ánemos," Alizeh said under her breath. She then sprinted towards Arachne much faster than before with a more determined look on her face. I could tell she was planning to end this, and I believed Arachne knew that too.

Arachne continued firing blast after blast but Alizeh jumped over, ducked, and dodged every single one with such speed and agility that even *I* couldn't keep up with her. Eventually, Alizeh finally got close enough to land a solid hit right to Arachne's face, knocking her right off her feet.

I was filled with so much excitement that I pushed myself up onto my knees and cheered her on. But then I realized something. I was on my knees! I could move again. It didn't make any sense. Arachne was still there so the spell should have kept affecting me. That was what I thought until I remembered what Alizeh said.

'That depends on how fast you can get up.'

She obviously knew that this would happen. Her spell from before. She used one before her battle even started. '*Katharízo*'. She once used that spell to purify the air when we were on top of that volcano on Phoenix Island. She must have used it to clear out the poison while they battled! She truly was using her brain for once. Now I could finally find my opening.

I looked back over at the fight and saw fear in Arachne's eyes. She knew she wasn't going to win this battle. She jumped up and shouted, ***"Dilitiriódis Kissós!"***

Long vines with large thorns shot out from not only the ground but the houses as well. They all stretched towards each other, tangling and interweaving with one another until a giant wall separating Alizeh from Arachne was formed. She was trying to escape.

Unfortunately for her, she trapped herself on the side that I was already on. I got back up and fire erupted from my staff. This time I wasn't going to hesitate.

She turned and began to run in my direction until she realized that I was back on my feet. She came to a screeching halt as the fire flared from one end of my staff. I swung it in her direction while yelling, ***"Bála Pyrkagiás!"***

A gigantic ball of fire almost enveloped the entire street, making it so that there was nowhere for Arachne to run. The attack hit her straight on and she was swept along with it burning right through her vines. Alizeh jumped high into the air to avoid the blast and watched as Arachne was sent flying with the fire into a far-off building.

As far as I knew, Arachne was dead. I didn't check to see. I couldn't even if I wanted to. Because of all the Rēa I put out added with the fact that my body hadn't fully recovered from the poison, I fell face down to the ground unable to take another step.

CHAPTER SIXTY-THREE
ANA

I ran into battle with the sole purpose of finding Silver, but I had no idea how I was going to pull that off. The courtyard alone was massive and riddled with chaos so much so that I couldn't begin to imagine scouring the entire castle aimlessly for him. I needed a lead.

Soldiers and rebels battled all around me so I chose the closest person to be my opponent. While he was in the midst of battle, I came from behind and grabbed him by his shoulder, yanked him to the ground and pinned his chest beneath my boot.

"Where's my wolf?" I asked.

"What?" he shuddered.

"Where the hell is my dog?" I barked.

I guess my shouting attracted some unneeded attention because it didn't take long for me to get surrounded by a dozen soldiers. It didn't look like they were taking prisoners this time. Taking all of them alone would be difficult. Luckily this time I wasn't the only warrior on the battlefield. A woman came from behind one of the soldiers and knocked them out with one swing from the back of her spear. I'm glad Flint could find good help.

Once the soldier hit the ground, the chaos began and they all swarmed us. I disabled every one that got close. But what was more impressive was that the woman who came to my aid was holding her own just as well, if not better, than I was. With her by my side it didn't take longer than thirty seconds to beat everyone in our path.

Once every soldier close to us was down I was finally able to get a good look at her. Even while she was standing still it was hard to see her face through that curly mane of hair until she turned towards me. Her eyes were golden and her skin was darker than my own.

"What's your name?" I asked.

"Alexia," she answered, "and I am a proud warrior of Phoenix island. You don't look familiar. Who are you?"

"Ana, daughter of Xander."

"That sounds like a title that only a Zubarian could hold. So you're the one that Flint told me about. The one who travels with the Shēna?"

"He talks about me to his friends?" I confirmed with a sly grin.

"He spoke highly of your strength. I'm glad to see he wasn't exaggerating. But I'm confused as to why he didn't take you with him."

"He tried to but I can't leave just yet. I still need to find my wolf."

"Your wolf?" she questioned.

"Yeah, I'm pretty sure he was captured with the rest of us."

"I think I've seen him."

"Wait, really?" I almost doubted.

"Yeah. There's an entire room filled with exotic animals right next to the armory where we found the Spirit Casters and in it we saw a giant white wolf caged in its center."

"That's him! You have to take me there!"

Before she could give me an answer, her attention was drawn to the other side of the battlefield. I looked in the same direction and one person wearing extravagant golden armor caught my eye. He was outmanned in his fight against The King's soldiers so the odds weren't in his favor.

"That mission will have to wait," she told me with her eyes fixated on them. "I can't let him die."

She then took off towards him and since she was my only key to finding Silver, I followed close behind her. She attacked every soldier in her path and whichever ones she didn't finish off, I took care of myself. And after an attack from her, it didn't take much for me to knock them out.

Of the two men that were fighting the golden armored warrior, Alexia pushed away one and I took care of the other. They both didn't see us coming so taking them out was child's play.

Alexia looked at the golden warrior and asked, "Are you harmed, Prince?"

His face had a few cuts and bruises but I couldn't spot any fatal wounds.

"Thanks to you, I'll survive," he answered before switching his attention to me. "I'm just as grateful to you too. But you don't look familiar."

"This is the woman Flint was telling us about," Alexia explained.

"This is Ana?" he asked, seemingly already having knowledge of me. He turned to me and said, we need to get you out of here."

"No, I can't leave yet," I told him.

"Why not?"

"You remember that giant wolf we saw next to the armory?" Alexia cut in. "It's hers."

"And I can't leave without him."

"I'll take her to the wolf," Alexia told him, "then I'll come right back."

"No," the Prince decided. "We need you here. *I'll* take her."

"If that's an order, then alright. Just make sure to be careful."

He nodded his head, turned to me and said, "Let's go."

CHAPTER SIXTY-FOUR
CRYSTAL

I got back to my feet and stood atop the frozen ground, looking up at my creation. A giant slanted wall of ice supported by only the two buildings at its sides. I was surprised that I could make a structure so large without feeling completely drained. I could feel that I still had lots of Rēa left. It seemed like my stamina had gone up from my last few battles.

Just then, I heard the sound of clapping behind me. I turned around to see Morpheus Morningstar slowly applauding and looking up at the ice structure. I stumbled away from him in shock of his sudden appearance.

"Wonderful!" he shouted. "Truly magnificent. You're becoming quite the prodigy. And how long have you had that wand for? Only about two months, right?"

I didn't care to start a dialogue with the likes of a traitor, so I thrusted my Spirit Caster towards him and shouted, ***"Pagokrýstallos!"*** A long ice spear formed around it as it extended right through Morpheus's chest.

"Your movements are quick," he said calmly before disappearing out of sight. I didn't understand what I just saw. He was there one moment and gone the next. It didn't make any sense. The next thing I knew, he was walking towards me from a different direction.

"How are you—"

"Alive? Still standing?" he interrupted. "I'd imagine that was the gist of your question, right? Well, the answer is simple. It's because you didn't hit me."

"What? But my ice ... it went right through you."

"Tsk, tsk. Did you forget already? I am the possessor of the Illusion Spirit Caster."

While he was answering me I decided to use that chance for another attack. I went to stab him again but the spear just passed right through him, and he was gone once again.

"Idiot," I heard him say behind me. I quickly turned around to see that he had a dagger in his hand and before I could react, he ran it right through me. But I didn't feel anything. And just as quickly as he stabbed me, he had disappeared once again. This was getting annoying. Every time I saw him it was just an illusion. Coming to this realization forced me to lower my guard but as soon as I did, I could feel a stabbing pain right in my hip. I looked down and saw a wound with blood dripping from it. Then as if from nowhere, Morpheus appeared right in front of me with his dagger sticking into me.

"Do you get it now? With this power, reality is whatever I want it to be. You're going to die here Crystal. But don't worry. I won't make any of the cuts too deep. We wouldn't want this to end so quickly now, would we? Because I hate when reality gets boring."

"You bastard!" I yelled as I swung my spear towards him. But I was too slow. He jumped back, pulling his blade from me, leaving my body in intense pain. He then disappeared once again and appeared in front of me with another attack that I attempted to parry. But it was another failure. He just ended up slashing at me on the other side. He repeated the move over and over and over again. More and more my blood was drawn. I couldn't get a single hit on him. All I could feel was the stabbing pain of steel slicing my flesh. This was a battle I couldn't win. At least not on my own.

"From the left."

I heard a voice. It sounded like the Spirit of my grandmother. If this was her guiding me then I wasn't going to hesitate for even a second to take that guidance.

I slashed my spear upwards to the left. There was some resistance and the attacks stopped for the moment. I looked at the tip of my ice spear and saw something that gave me a glimmer of hope. It was blood. I had hit him! I still couldn't see him, but I had hit him!

"To your right!"

I slashed to my right and could feel my spear clashing with his blade. I was able to block him! With my grandmother's guidance I could win this!

"In Front of you."

"Shield your neck."

"Dodge!"

All orders that I followed. And each one led me closer to victory. Suddenly, Morpheus finally showed himself in front of me and I went on the offensive, ready to attack.

"Behind you!"

But I could see him in front of me. No. I couldn't fall for that again. I had to put my faith in her words. I could see Morpheus coming at me from the front, but I thrusted my spear to the back.

At that moment, the Morpheus that was in front of me disappeared and a new one appeared behind me. This time I had truly hit him. My spear stabbed right through his hip. I didn't want to waste my chance to end this so I pushed all my weight onto him, forcing him down to the ground. This was the *real* Morpheus.

I pulled my bloody spear from his hip and was ready for one final attack. I thrusted it towards his chest but before I could, something stopped me.

"Get out of the way!"

I stopped myself and immediately jumped back. Once I did, I saw a black ball of energy shoot right past me and hit Morpheus head on, exploding on impact. The force of the explosion pushed me back and forced dust into the air.

I quickly got up to my feet and glanced around to try and figure out what had just happened. It didn't take long for the dust to clear. Amongst the settling dust, I could finally see who threw the attack. The person I had been wanting to kill since the death of my parents. The person who turned me and my sister's life right on its head.

"Kira," I called. "You've finally caught up to me."

"Well, did you really think I would just let you run away?" Kira laughed. "You can never escape me. Your death has always been inevitable."

"I wasn't running. I just didn't feel like settling things there. I'm actually really glad you're here now. Now we can finally finish what you started."

"The feeling's mutual," Kira grinned.

I looked over at where Morpheus was once laying and saw that he was gone. Kira noticed this and said, "Don't worry about him, his body's probably been completely disintegrated. That attack was meant to atomize the both of you."

"And you're fine with that? Killing your own partner?"

"Fine with it? I'm elated! He was a thorn in my side and he had it coming for years. And now I'm gonna do the same to you."

Her disregard for life sickened me. How come every time we crossed paths someone had to die? First my parents, then an innocent woman, and now her own ally? How evil could one person be? I had made up my mind. I didn't care how much the wand blackened her heart. She was too dangerous to be left alive. And if I had to be the one to put her down, then so be it.

CHAPTER SIXTY-FIVE
ALIZEH

After the battle with Arachne, Flint and I decided to head to the newly formed ice monument. There was no doubt in our mind that Crystal landed there. On our way to Crystal we found Rai, who had the same exact idea as us. They were just as exhausted as we were. That meant that the only way we had a chance of making it out of this alive was if the four of us were together.

After some time passed we finally made it to the ice wall and saw Crystal confronting Kira.

"Crystal!" I called "We're here to help!"

"Alizeh? Guys! You're alright!" Crystal gasped with a large smile on her face. Kira looked at us with a furious glare. With us showing up here, it was now a four on one battle!

We were all weak though. Flint could barely stand on his own two feet. Our previous fights all took a toll on us, but Kira didn't know that so that gave us an advantage. If we played our cards right, then we could beat her once and for all.

"I'm happy to see you all," Crystal said, "but I'll have to ask you not to interfere."

Her request took us all aback.

"What do you mean?" I asked. "You don't want us to help?"

"That's correct." Crystal answered.

"Crystal," Rai said, "you can't beat her alone!"

Crystal didn't respond. She only started to slowly make her way closer to Kira.

"Crystal!" Flint shouted as he fell to his knees, no longer able to stand on his own from the toxin. "What the hell are you doing? We need to regroup and recover so we can beat her together! Isn't that why you formed this group? So we could help you?"

Crystal stopped walking and turned to Flint. "Did you all take care of the last members of the Five Armaments?"

Flint looked confused before answering. "Yeah, we did."

"Then you've helped me. I wouldn't have been able to make it to this point without the three of you. Just let me have this one battle. Please?"

"Like hell we—"

I waved my hand in front of Flint in order to silence him before he could finish.

"It's ok. We'll stay out of it," I agreed.

Crystal smiled and said, "Thank you," before turning back around to face the princess.

"Why are *you* of all people letting her do this?" Flint asked furiously. "Isn't she your best friend? Why would you let her do something so dangerous and stupid?"

"It's *because* she's my best friend that I'm letting her do something so dangerous and stupid," I answered. Flint and Rai both looked at me with a confused look. "I'll explain to you guys later. Now let's move out of the way. We'll only serve as a distraction for Crystal if we stay too close."

They reluctantly agreed and we made our way to a farther place to watch the battle from. They didn't understand how much Crystal needed this. In every single battle we'd been in she'd never been able to truly prove herself. Someone either had to jump in to save her and if it wasn't that, then her own battle was cut short.

The princess had personally hurt Crystal more than she had to any of us. Crystal *needed* to be the one to defeat her. This was the perfect way to prove herself. I could always see the potential inside of her but this time we could all actually see what she was really made of.

I stopped myself for a second and called her name.

"Crystal!"

She answered, "You don't have to worry about me. Just go! I can handle this."

"I wasn't worried. I was just gonna tell you to make sure you kick her ass for us!"

I turned around and made my way off the battlefield.

CHAPTER SIXTY-SIX
KIRA

"So you're going to kick my ass, is that right?" I laughed. It was a hilarious sentiment. To think that she would actually be a threat to me.

"That's the plan," Crystal answered flatly. There was a dull but determined look in her eyes which pissed me off. It was like she was analyzing me. Like she was actually trying to think of a way to beat me! As if there was an actual possibility!

I tightened my grip on my Spirit Caster and let the dark Rēa flow through my veins. I was going to go all out against her so that by the end of this she would know that she never had a chance against royalty like myself!

"Well, come at me then!"

Crystal started to run towards me while yelling, ***"Pagokrýstallos!"*** An ice spear formed around her spirit caster just like in our last battle. This time I wasn't even going to let her graze me.

"Psalídi Thanátou!" I shouted as I swiped my wand causing a dark energy wave to go flying towards her. She jumped over it and shouted, ***"To Pagáki Ekteínetai!",*** forcing the icicle to extend and stretch over to me at a high speed. Lucky for me, I was able to step over to the side, missing it just by a hair.

Crystal broke off her spirit caster from the long spear and continued her pursuit. I stuck my wand out and shouted, ***"Skoteiní Volí",*** shooting blast after blast. But she had become so agile just like her young friend. She was dodging every single attack I dished out, all the while, making her way to me. She got so close that she could've used her spear to end me right then and there, but I wasn't going to give her the chance!

Right before she could thrust her spear in my direction, I shouted, ***"Mávri Aspída!"***

A black shield manifested between us, completely stopping her attack. I swiftly tapped my wand against it and it went flying away from me while simultaneously pushing Crystal with it.

I then uttered the word, **"Syntriví"**, causing the shield to expand and wrap around Crystal like a bubble. It started to shrink with no intention of stopping. I was going to crush her.

But suddenly shards of ice ripped through it and expanded causing the black bubble to tear apart and silently explode. She had broken free and she was inside the ice. It was like she trapped herself within a small jagged dome.

She didn't just use it to break free but to also put something in between us. I assumed she must have been overwhelmed and stalling for time. The thought of that angered me because the only thing she accomplished was delaying the inevitable.

"Skoteiní Sfaíra Sfairón!"

Hundreds of dark energy bolts appeared in front of me and shot towards her like a barrage of arrows. They bombarded her ice wall, slowly but steadily chipping away at it. I was almost there. I just needed a couple more seconds and she would be mine.

But just as I got to the last layer of ice, a white explosion of frost and snow flew all over the battlefield. The bitter cold brought back the sour memories of the last time I was in Nótio Págo, and the first time I met Crystal.

This move. It was the first move she had ever used against me. And the same one she used to escape me. The fact that she would even think to use such a cheap spell against me was an insult within itself.

I was going to make my way towards her to close the gap but I couldn't. My feet were frozen to the ground. She had used this move against me in our last fight! And I had been caught in it again! I didn't understand how I could have been so naive. Unable to see that the blizzard she made was just to distract me from *this*. So she could trap me. But if she was trapping me then that meant there was something even bigger coming for me.

I looked back up and saw a glint of light before feeling a stabbing pain in my chest. I looked down and saw that I had been run through. *To pagáki ekteínetai.* That was the move she used to end it. With the blizzard circling around me, combined with the speed of the spear made it so that I couldn't see it coming.

I coughed up blood. I could feel the warm liquid running from my chest, staining the white snow. It reminded me of the day I had Crystal's parents killed. Their blood splattered across the snow just like mine. Was this in fact punishment for that? Was I truly in the wrong? Did I deserve this? Maybe.

It could've been from a lot of things. My arrogance. My poisoned brain. Or maybe even the fact that I was a failure. That's what my father would think. That I failed.

I didn't even want any of this. The crown, the magic, the power. I just wanted him to acknowledge me as his daughter. And now I couldn't even do *that*.

The insides of my body felt cold. It started to freeze over from my open wound. I couldn't believe that this was the end of me.

No.

This couldn't be it. I needed him to acknowledge me! I needed him to love me and treat me like the daughter he's always wanted. I *would* become that person! I would kill Crystal to obtain that. I'd destroy everyone and everything to obtain that!

But unfortunately, it didn't seem like that would happen. Because a moment after that thought, everything went dark, and I lost myself. The only words that stayed in my mind after everything had vanished were ...

*I **will** kill her!*

CHAPTER SIXTY-SEVEN
CRYSTAL

The battle was over. Everything that I had fought so hard for. All of my efforts finally bore fruit.

I walked through the thin, crunchy blanket of snow before reaching her frozen corpse. Her body didn't fall to the ground. It just stood there like a statue. A terrifying one, at that. The expression of rage and pain stained her face along with her blood and tears.

It made me sick to my stomach. I killed her. And she deserved it. But why did I feel so terrible about the act? In my most triumphant moment, all I could feel was sorrow. She was sick. I could have saved her, but I didn't. And killing her didn't fill the hole that she left behind.

Mid thought, I felt something sinister rush through my spine. It wasn't something physical but spiritual. It felt like Kira but much worse. Something terrible was about to happen and I had no idea what.

The sound of ice breaking caught my attention, causing me to stare hard at Kira. The ice on her body was cracking. She was breaking out!

But it didn't make any sense. She was dead. I stabbed her right through the heart. How strong of a will did this woman have?

Dark energy boiled from her body and before I could even think of a way to stop her, a grand force broke the ice and pushed me back along with all the snow around us.

A black aura swarmed her body as she screamed, ***"I will kill you!"***

Her voice was different. Whenever a Shēna let out a spell, their voice changed. It got deeper and there was an echo to it. But at that moment, Kira's voice sounded distorted. As if she was possessed.

The black aura cleared the area and I could finally see her clearly. She looked almost unrecognizable. Her skin became deathly pale and her veins turned a dark purple, making her face look like a cracked porcelain doll. The whites of her eyes became jet black which only intensified the glow of her crimson pupils. Her hair turned snow white just like mine, but it was much longer. It hung down to her knees now.

"What is this?" I asked myself hesitantly. She stared vacantly into the sky. As if she had no idea where she was. I decided to try and get her attention. "What is that form?" I asked.

She didn't answer. She didn't even look at me. I tightened my grip on my spirit caster and this time I shouted, "Answer me! What happened to you? Are you even the same person I was fighting? What are you?"

Kira finally regained focus and peered at me before screeching at the top of her lungs like a wild animal. No, it sounded more like a demon.

She leaned forward and opened her mouth wide, revealing sharp fangs. A ball of energy started to form right at the opening of her mouth and she shot it right in my direction. I dodged it by a hair and instead of hitting me, it hit the giant ice structure that I had made before and detonated on impact.

A massive explosion spewed into the sky while ice and smoke flew at me, obscuring my vision. Before I knew it, Kira was right in front of me and about to throw a punch. I quickly put my arms up to block my face and used Rēa to make my defenses strong. Once she threw her punch I was sent flying across the battlefield. After I hit the ground, my left arm felt like it was shattered! I couldn't move it. Not even an inch.

Kira's new power terrified me. It wasn't just her appearance that changed. Her speed was blinding and her strength was boosted to new heights. With a single punch she was able to break my arm. And the amount of Rēa that she was outputting made it hard for me to breathe. She had destroyed my ice wall with such ease and swiftness. This was a level of power that I didn't even think existed.

I looked back at the explosion and saw three more energy blasts shooting from the smoke. The energy scattered in different directions, stretching across the city. Once they made contact with their targets it created massive explosions, destroying different parts of Ebony. Every attack was indiscriminate. She went completely berserk.

She was probably killing hundreds, if not thousands, of innocent people. It looked like she couldn't be reasoned with and she couldn't be overpowered. I had no idea how I was going to pull this off, but she needed to be stopped.

CHAPTER SIXTY-EIGHT
ANA

I followed close behind the armored warrior as he ran through the large halls. It seemed like all the guards were in the courtyard because we met almost zero resistance inside the castle. At least if you didn't count the defenseless servants who didn't dare stand in our way. I took the moment of silence to try and understand my situation a bit more.

"That girl from before," I started to say, "Alexia, I think her name was. She called you a prince. What exactly are you the prince of?"

"Oh, where are my manners? I haven't properly introduced myself to you yet, have I? My name is Arnold Phoenix and I'm the noble son of Phoenix Island."

"Wait, *you're* the prince of *Phoenix Island*? I thought your people wanted to avoid a war against the Black Continent."

"Well, that was the plan until they attacked us first. They caused so much destruction. Kira killed so many people. And to think that I was actually fond of her before. Our parents wanted us to get married so that there would be peace between our two nations, but that can't happen anymore. She needs to be stopped. We need to kill her for what she's done!"

"I'm sorry but I'm not letting that happen," we heard a familiar voice from up ahead say. Ranne stepped forth from around the corner, blocking our path. It made me freeze, but Arnold didn't hesitate to attack with his sword in hand. He didn't know how dangerous she was. Not like I did.

"Wait!" I shouted, "You can't take her!"

But I was too late. Ranne unsheathed her sword, blocked his attack and parried in an instant. For a brief moment, her eyes sparked red and she cut right through his armor, leaving a trail of blood on her sword before using all her strength to kick him back over to me. Her kick left a dent in his armor that might've even broken a rib or two.

"Don't worry," she assured him. "That cut shouldn't be deep enough to kill you, but you *will* bleed out if you move. If you don't surrender yourselves now, then I'll be forced to kill you."

I couldn't move my body out of sheer fear. This was the first person to ever beat me in battle. She was stronger and faster than I ever was. And this was the same woman who took my right eye. I couldn't beat her before. But I wasn't the same fighter anymore.

I pulled out my daggers to get ready to face her, but Arnold stopped me by saying, "No, wait. You're at a disadvantage with those blades."

"I don't have any other options."

Arnold reached for his blade and this time I had to stop him.

"Arnold, stop. You can't fight anymore or you'll bleed out. Just sit there and let me take care of this."

"I know I can't fight. That's why I'm giving this to you." He stretched his golden sword out towards me. "This sword is made from Chrysó-Pyk, one of the strongest metals in the world. It's been in my family for generations, so it'll be the perfect tool to take down a monster like her."

I wasn't too skilled with the way of the sword but I knew it was a better weapon to use in this situation, so I grabbed it and said, "Thank you."

"Are you sure about this?" Ranne asked. "Crystal won't be here to save you like last time."

"I thought I already told you," I said as I ran to her and clashed my sword against hers, "I'm different now and this time, I'm not going to lose!"

To her surprise, I activated my *Warriors Spirit* and was able to push her back. And I didn't let up. I swung my sword like a mad man and she could barely keep up. Our swords continued to clash but this time, I was the one who overpowered her. That was short lived because as soon as it seemed like I was going to win this, her eyes flashed red and she was able to push me back, putting some distance in between us.

"So, you've learned to bring out your *warrior spirit*? I'm impressed. You really *are* different now. Looks like I'll actually have to try against you!"

She ran towards me at full speed, faster than I could react. I put my blade up but didn't know how to defend myself from the oncoming attack. Using her sword, she pushed mine out of the way to get ready for a more fatal blow. She raised her blade and swung it through my left shoulder blade all the way to my bottom right rib.

The pain in my chest was intense but I couldn't stop. I had to fight. I swiped my blade towards her, hoping she would be open from her last attack, but she evaded with ease and performed a counterattack, slicing me in the side. The pain was overwhelming this time and she took full advantage of that.

"You're wide open!" she roared.

Her sword was fast. I could barely see when she hit me but I sure as hell felt it. Death by a thousand cuts was a good way to describe the attack. My body was covered in blood and gashes. Even so, she still stepped away from me as if there was a way I could counter. But I had nothing left. I could barely stand because even my legs had deep cuts on them from her barrage of slices. I felt weaker too. I wasn't sure if I'd even be able to finish this battle.

Ranne relaxed herself and asked, "What's wrong? That glow in your eyes has vanished. Has your warrior spirit left you already?"

Ranne was still so much stronger than me. She was even stronger than Barin at his peak strength, and I couldn't even finish the fight with him when he was injured. Fighting Ranne and winning felt like trying to push a mountain with my bare hands.

As I tried to wrap my head around her, I saw a glint of light from out of the large wall-sized window of the hall. It was a fiery explosion with smoke emanating from it all the way in the distance. It was probably Flint. I had almost forgotten that I wasn't the only one fighting. Everyone had to fight their own battle. Even Crystal was probably fighting for her life down there. And not just for her life. She was fighting to change the world. I wanted to see how she was going to do it. I wanted to see Flint again. I never said goodbye to my mother. There was too much I still wanted to see. I couldn't die here yet. Not until I knew for a fact that I had made a difference.

"Alright, I think it's time to end this little game, don't you think?" Ranne finally said before running towards me to deal the finishing blow.

I closed my eye. I needed that same primal mindset that I had against Barin. I needed to let go. With one deep breath, I felt it.

My body moved on its own and with my eye still closed, I caught her blade with my bare hand. The blade sliced my hand but stopped before it could reach my chest. While I had her right where I wanted her, I finally opened my one good eye and jabbed my sword towards her face, but she was too fast.

Ranne jumped back away from me and I could see blood pouring down her face from a gash I made over her left eyebrow.

"Damnit," I panted, "I missed."

"No," she grinned while pointing to her wound. "You got me right here. You almost took off my head."

"Well, I was aiming for your eye."

"*Ha!* Looking for a bit of payback, I see. I had almost forgotten about what I did to your other eye. No wonder you're resorting to such foolish tactics. You're basically blind."

"It's ironic that you're calling *me* blind since you're the one with the blind sense of justice."

Ranne looked a little more serious and started circling around me when she asked, "What are you talking about?"

"I'm talking about how you, a proud Zubarian, bends over backwards for a man that hates you," I laughed. "Ya know, you never answered my question."

Ranne stopped and asked, "What question?"

"The one I asked you back in the throne room. Why do you serve him after what he did to us? He practically wiped us out and you seem to worship him for it."

Just like before, she took a long pause before saying anything, but this time she actually answered me.

"I didn't know," she finally said.

"What?" I shuddered.

"I didn't know what his ancestors did to us. Not until you told me at least."

"How could you not know?" I raged.

"I never had parents. Or a family for that matter. I was a slave working in the Kítrinos mines for as far back as I can remember. *That* is my history and the only thing I've ever known. I've never known anyone else like me. Until I met you."

I dropped my golden blade to the ground which startled her.

"What are you doing?" she asked.

"I'm not fighting you anymore."

"Why?"

"There's no reason to. He tricked you. You don't have to fight for him anymore."

"I don't fight for him," she explained as she pointed her blade towards me. "I fight for Kira."

"But she's to blame just as much for what happened to us."

"No, you're wrong. Kira *saved* me. She's the one who got me out of captivity and I owe her my life for that. If she wants you and your friends dead, then killing you is the least I can do for her. So pick up that blade and fight because I'm not stopping until one of us is dead."

"I already told you; I'm done."

"Have it your way."

She took a step towards me but stopped as soon as we both saw a flash of light from the window. We both looked towards it and it was so bright that it almost blinded me. Once the light dimmed all that could be seen was a massive explosion that stretched towards the sky.

"What is that?" Ranne asked with a fearful look that I never imagined would have come from her.

Only a couple of seconds passed after the explosion detonated, causing the windows to shatter from the force of it, creating a loud boom that pushed us both back. I was dazed. That mixed with the fact that I was bleeding out made it difficult for me to get back up.

Ranne got up quicker than I did and ran to the window before freezing at what she saw. Once I got up I could see the city and it was in shambles. Not all of it was destroyed, but tens of dozens of buildings collapsed while fires spread across Ebony. And the only thing that could be heard was screaming. Hundreds, if not thousands, of people crying in unison.

"What did this?" I shuddered.

Ranne looked at me as if she had just looked into the eyes of a monster and said, "We need to get to Kira, right now."

"What? Why?"

"Because if she isn't stopped right now, then she's going to kill us all."

CHAPTER SIXTY-NINE
ALIZEH

The three of us watched while atop a nearby building, horrified by what we were witnessing.

"What the hell is that thing?" Rai asked.

"I don't know, but I've never felt anything like it," I answered. The Rēa that Kira was putting out made me shiver. It felt terrifying. Just looking at her made my soul feel like it was being torn apart.

"I think I read about this a long time ago," Flint said.

"What do you mean?" I asked.

"One of the only things my mother left behind was this Spirit Caster that I'm holding and a mountain of books that documented her adventures. She once fought something like this. It was an ability that only those who possessed the Dark Spirit Caster could obtain."

"So that thing is just one of her spells?" Rai asked.

"In a way," Flint answered. "It's more of a transformation. Another stage in the Dark Spirit Caster's evolution."

"I've changed my mind," I told them. "We need to help her. She won't survive against that thing alone."

"Agreed," Flint nodded. "Let's get down there and—"

Before Flint could fully finish, a black ball of energy shot from the battlefield and hit right in the middle of the building we were standing on. It detonated, making a large explosion that forced the building to collapse in on itself.

"Alizeh, fly us out of here!" Flint demanded.

"Yeah," I nodded. ***"Pairno—"***

I started to say the spell but before I could complete it, the floor beneath Flint caved in and he fell right through.

"Flint!" I shouted as I tried to run to where he fell, but right behind me was Rai, suffering the same fate. They were both out of sight and before I could even think of my next move, I felt the ground beneath my feet crack and fall as I plummeted down into nothing but dust and darkness along with my friends.

CHAPTER SEVENTY
CRYSTAL

There was nothing I could do to stop the havoc she was wreaking. She wasn't even after me anymore. She was just shooting at everything she could see.

She lifted her hand up and a black sphere appeared in it. But the Rēa flowing from it was much more powerful than her other blasts. She was putting all her energy into one attack. And if she shot it off, it might have enough power to completely eradicate the city.

The only thing that could possibly stop her now was my ultimate move, *Chiliádes Chrónia Fylakí Págou.* The same move I used on the Phoenix to imprison it. I didn't think I had enough energy to pull it off. At this point, it could've even been detrimental to my body to use all that power, but I had to try.

I lifted my Spirit Caster up and began to speak the chant but before I could finish someone put their hand on my wand and gently pushed it down. I looked over and saw that it was a knight. But not just any knight. This was the same knight that was with Kira. The same one who put her sword against my sister's neck and took away Ana's right eye. Ranne, I believed her name was. I didn't even see her approach me.

"Are you really trying to stop me right now?" I shouted at her. "The *Princess* that you've sworn to protect is about to destroy us all! Including you!"

She didn't look at me. She just stared at Kira with a serious look before finally saying, "I know. But that look on your face told me that you were going to destroy her." She finally looked at me and continued saying, "And even though at the moment she doesn't care about you or this city, or even me ... I still care about her. She's not herself right now and I want to fix that. So please, let me try and talk her down before you do anything too drastic."

I was conflicted on whether or not I should leave it in her hands until someone called out to me.

"Crystal!" I looked back and saw Ana wounded on top of Silver. "Let her try."

"You trust her?" I asked.

Ana nodded her head. She was the last person I'd expect to trust Ranne after what she did to her, but I guessed she'd learned to forgive and forget. I turned back to Ranne. The look of determination and sadness in her eyes pierced through my heart. I could tell that she cared deeply for Kira. And maybe there was a chance that Kira cared about Ranne, too. And if that was a possibility then that meant there was a chance that she could fix her. If it was going to be anyone, it had to be Ranne.

I simply nodded my head in approval and stepped back to give her a shot at Kira. She started to walk towards her and before she got too far, I told her, "Good luck!" Because I knew that if anyone needed it at that moment, it was her.

CHAPTER SEVENTY-ONE
KIRA

I wasn't in control. My body was moving but not of my own volition. It was attacking, but that wasn't my intention. I couldn't speak. The only thing I could do was watch as I was destroying everything. My own kingdom. My own people. Everything was going to end by my hands. And I wanted absolutely nothing to do with it! With no way to stop it, all I could do was scream. But when I did, it only sounded like the shrieks of a monster.

Then I saw something. My vision was blurry so I couldn't completely make it out. It looked like a person.

"Kira."

The voice sounded familiar but too far away to truly make out.

"Kira, can you hear me?"

That voice. It was Ranne! I wanted to scream "Yes!" I wanted to tell her I could hear her, but the only thing that came out were growls.

"Man, that wand really did a number on you. Why don't you give it to me? Let me help you."

My arm swung at her, punching her right in the chest. I watched as her body slammed into the ground.

Ranne!

I wanted to shout. Her armor plate was shattered, and she looked like she just got the wind knocked out of her. But she was breathing and that was all that mattered.

She struggled to get back up.

"Damn," she coughed. "If I wasn't wearing armor I definitely would've died. Guess there's no need for this now, is there?"

She then struggled to rip off the upper part of her armor and threw it to the ground. She held her chest tightly as if I had broken a rib, but still pressed on.

"Why are you doing this Kira? Is this all because of the wand? Or is it something deeper?"

I then felt my arm twitching. I was going to hit her again! But she wouldn't survive another hit like that.

Run!

My words didn't reach her. I couldn't stop my fist from rising; I was going to kill her!

"If I had to guess, I'd imagine that all of this fury and hatred is coming from how you feel about your father."

My fist stopped in place. For a moment, it felt like I was in control.

"Kira, you don't need his approval. He's never treated you like a loving parent would. All you've ever done in your life is try to make him happy and you're distressed over the fact that you think you're never enough. But you've always been enough." She started to close the gap between us but I didn't want her to.

"Stop! Don't get any closer!" I shouted. Then I realized I had shouted! I spoke and she could hear me. But I still didn't feel in control. ***"I don't want to hurt you,"*** I started to cry. Shedding tears from what I had become.

"Don't worry. I'm not afraid of you. I love you. Always have. Ever since we were kids. All I've ever wanted to do was protect you," She grabbed my hand and pulled me in close and held me tight. "Let me protect you this one last time."

At that moment, all I could do was hold her even tighter and cry on her shoulder. I could feel my body changing. My skin cracked and the new pale skin started to peel off, revealing my normal skin underneath. My new white hair started shedding, leaving only black hair behind.

With Ranne I felt safe. I thought about my entire life and at that moment, I realized she was the only human besides my own mother who ever truly cared about me, and I had always treated her like trash.

"I'm sorry, Ranne," I cried, "I'm so sorry."

"It's okay," she said with a small smile. "Don't apologize, Kira. And don't cry either. It's unbecoming for a royal like yourself."

And for the first time in a long time, I couldn't help but laugh in her arms.

CHAPTER SEVENTY-TWO
CRYSTAL

Ranne did it! She actually managed to get through to the Princess! But all she did was manage to fix the immediate problem. She may have managed to bring the normal Kira back to us, but the normal Kira *wasn't* a good person. She was still the same person that killed too many innocent people, including my parents.

I made my way over to them and she was still crying in Ranne's arms. I couldn't wait for them to be done because the question that I had for her was far more important.

"I'm sorry to interrupt whatever this is but I need to ask you something, Kira. What are you going to do?"

"What do you mean?" Kira asked as she wiped away her tears.

"What are you going to do right now, at this moment? Will you attack me or give up? Imprison me or let me go?"

Kira let go of Ranne and took a few steps towards me. Her eyes were still flooding.

"I don't want to fight you anymore," Kira sobbed as she dropped her Spirit Caster to the ground. "I don't want to hurt anyone anymore."

"And why is that? You had no problems with doing it before. What's different now? Why shouldn't I kill you right now for the lives you've taken away from me and everyone else you've hurt?"

"I can't justify what I've done. I've hurt people. I've hurt you. Killing me right now in my most defenseless state would be justice. And the only reason I can admit that is because for the first time in years, my head finally feels clear again. Like the poison inside of me has been cured. And because of that I finally feel remorse for what I've done. So strike me down if that will satisfy you. And I know that this probably means nothing to you, but if you do kill me here then I want my final words to be an apology. I'm sorry for what I've done and I accept any retribution taken towards me."

I raised my Spirit caster, pointing it towards Kira and said, ***"Pagokrýstallos."*** The ice spear formed around it and the tip was right at her chest. "So just to clarify, you're giving me permission to kill you?"

Ranne grabbed onto her sword and yelled, "I do not consent to this!"

Kira looked over at Ranne and said, "Your consent isn't a factor. This is my call."

"Oh, please," another voice chided in. We all looked over and saw The King before us. He continued saying, "We all know that you've never truly had any power in this situation. Whether you live or die is up to me."

No one spoke. We were all shocked to see him on the battlefield. I had no idea what he would do. Was he there to defend his daughter? To fight and kill me? Did he even have the power to do so? These were all questions I asked myself because in reality, I knew nothing about The King. I wasn't even sure if he had a Spirit Caster of his own. The ambiguity of it all forced me to stay silent and frozen along with Kira and Ranne.

"Kira," The King continued, "have you truly given up? Is this really what you've been reduced to? Pick up your Spirit Caster and fight!"

"No," Kira answered.

"What was that?"

"I said no! I'm tired of listening to a human who doesn't even care about me. All I am is just some tool for you. You treat me more like a weapon instead of what I truly am, your daughter! And I'm done with that!"

"Kira, is this really how you feel?"

"Yes."

"Then I have no need for you. You're a disgrace of a child and I wish you the best in hell." He then looked over at me and said, "Do it. You came all this way to kill her, right? Then end her right now for being such disgraceful scum."

His words triggered something in me. "*'Scum'*? I repeated. "Yeah, she's scum alright. Probably the worst there is in this world. But someone who doesn't even care about their own daughter, their own flesh and blood...they're even worse than scum!"

"Is that so?"

"Yeah, and I don't even care about killing her anymore," I said as I removed the ice spear away from Kira's chest. "I'm gonna kill you instead since you're the center of all that scum."

The King gave me a grin and said, "That's exactly the answer I expected from you." He then stretched his hand out and the Dark Spirit Caster flung itself through the air and into his grasp. As he gripped it, black flames erupted from the ends of it and the wand itself started to extend from both ends. It was a staff now, just like Flint's. "Crystal Winters. Let me show you the full power of an *Evolved Spirit Caster*."

And with a nonchalant swing, everyone was blown back. Rubble included. The ice around my Spirit Caster shattered, forcing me to drop it. The force of his swing had so much power behind it. The worst part about it was that it wasn't even a spell. Just him releasing his power.

As soon as I hit the ground, I immediately stretched my arm out to pick my wand back up but it was nowhere in sight. It had blown away with the rest of the debris and now I was completely defenseless.

The King pointed his staff towards me and, without saying a word, a dark energy blast shot from its tip. Before it could hit me I felt something grab me and push me out of the way. The blast went flying into the distance and created a massive explosion. If I would have been hit by that, there wouldn't be anything left of me.

I looked up at the person who saved me and it was none other than Alizeh. I had told her to stay out of this battle but at that moment, I was *so* thankful she intervened.

"Crystal, are you alright?" Alizeh asked while grabbing my left arm. I yelped in pain and she had immediately realized her mistake. "Your arm, it's broken isn't it?" I nodded my head as I struggled to get myself back up. "Well, I'm sorry to tell you this but at the moment we need you. Can you fight?"

"Yeah, but I can't find my wand," I answered.

"Well, look for it, we'll cover you until you find it. Now go!"

I then ran in the opposite direction with the intention to find my wand as soon as possible so I could help in this final battle.

CHAPTER SEVENTY-THREE

ALIZEH

"Trying to run now, are we?" The King said as he pointed his Spirit Caster towards me and Crystal with the intent on firing another attack at us.

Flint stood on a large hill of rubble and shouted, ***"Bála Pyrkagiás!"***

He swung his Spirit Caster, causing a fireball to shoot from the staff and it was headed straight for The King. When it came close enough The King noticed it and used *his* Spirit Caster to knock it right back to where it came from, hitting Flint point blank and exploding on impact.

"Flint!" I shouted. Normally, if he were hit by his own attack like that I wouldn't even flinch. He would've been fine. But in his current state it was questionable whether or not he could even survive an attack like that.

"That attack was pitiful," The King said. "The amount of Rēa infused in it was almost nonexistent. It's a miracle that he was still standing with such low levels of energy."

Rai sped up to him from the other side and grabbed him from behind. "That attack wasn't meant to kill you. Just distract you."

"Unhand me!"

"But this attack? *This* is meant to kill you! ***Astrapí!***"

Suddenly, they were both consumed by a flash of light followed by the sound of thunder exploding. It only took a second for the lightning to strike and leave. It was an epic second. But something told me that this wasn't over.

Rai jumped back to wait for the smoke to clear to see if they had done any damage. But before we could even see The King, a sudden dark energy beam shot from the smoke and was headed right for Rai.

"Víma Flas," they said quickly. Electricity surrounded their body and they swiftly moved out of the way of the attack. It reminded me of my own spell, *Grígoros Ánemos.*

The attack didn't miss them entirely. Once Rai stopped, I could see blood dripping from their side. It grazed them. But that wasn't the end of it because the thin beam didn't just go in a straight line. It turned around like a serpent and went in for another attack.

Rai jumped out of the way again but the beam followed them wherever they went. Rai ran away in zig zags, jumping up and down and bouncing off of any wall in the area that was still standing, but it still continued its pursuit.

The smoke finally cleared as The King said, "You do not seem to understand my abilities. I'm far stronger and more experienced than my daughter ever was. Don't underestimate me."

I couldn't stand by anymore. I leaped into action with my speed boosting spell still activated and shouted, ***"Gale Lance!"***

Right before I could hit him with the attack, an almost transparent black bubble surrounded him, acting as a shield. He put up the ultimate defense but in exchange he had to give up his attack which meant that Rai was safe for the moment and free to prepare another attack against The King. I just had to give them the chance to pull it off.

"Mach Grothiá!"

I punched at his shield without pause or hesitation. Although each punch was explosive with a booming sound echoing across the area, they didn't make a dent. And every punch was draining my Rēa. Even so, I didn't let up.

Then something miraculous happened. Something that would give us our only edge in this battle. He coughed. Blood came spitting out of his mouth. And when I punched his shield again, I cracked it.

Every time I had seen The King, he had been coughing. I assumed he was sick but not to this extent. He wasn't just sick. He was dying. And we were pushing him closer and closer to that end. Even if he was stronger than us, he had to run out of steam sometime and that sometime was now.

He got his composure together and as soon as he noticed the crack in his shield, he pushed his hand forward and the shield forced me back. But it didn't stop there. It wrapped itself around me, inclosing *me* in the bubble this time. He was going to crush me just like Kira tried to crush Crystal.

"Viaii Sfÿrigma!" I shouted, but it was no use. I had used almost the rest of my Rēa in my last barrage against him. Trying to use a powerful move to break out was useless. I could feel the black sphere caving in on itself as it slowly started to crush me and there was nothing I could do about it. It felt like I was in the giant grasp of death's grip until suddenly the shocking sound of thunder brought me back to reality.

Lightning bolts shot down from the sky. It didn't hit The King but he flinched as if it had. He looked behind himself and was so distracted at where it was hitting that he unintentionally released me from the bubble, causing me to fall right to the ground. I was free.

I looked up and saw the magnificent sight of Rai's ultimate spell. The blue lightning formed itself into the face of a dragon. Rai's Rēa rose to outrageously high levels. This spell was powerful enough to end The King, but there was no way it was fast enough. He could easily dodge it since he could see it coming. But I wasn't the only one who knew that.

Flint ran from behind and didn't stop until he reached The King. This was a shock for me. I didn't even know how he was standing but somehow, at that moment, he thought he was ready to face The King?

Flint grabbed The King from behind and put him into a full nelson. He wasn't fighting The King. He was stopping him from dodging.

"*You?*" King Cole questioned. "How are you still alive?" he shouted.

"Rai!" Flint yelled. "Hit him with everything you've got!"

"Gladly!" Rai grinned.

If they let off that attack then Flint would surely take just as much damage as The King, if not more from his current state. But he knew that. He was making the sacrifice play. And at this point, it was the most important play, so I wasn't going to stop him.

Rai shouted, ***"Fidi Vrontis!"*** And the dragon stretched its way toward us at high speed. I jumped out of its path as the dragon ate everything in its wake. The King and Flint were enveloped in an explosion of light that almost blinded me. Although it was destructive, it also had a certain beauty to it that almost made me forget that we were fighting for our lives.

CHAPTER SEVENTY-FIVE

CRYSTAL

"Come on, where is it!" I shouted while shifting through the rubble of a nearby building with my one good arm. This was the most important battle of my life and I was missing it.

Boom!

Rai's lightning startled me, making me jump and intensifying the pain in my arm. I felt so weak. With this broken arm I would've been lucky to even harness half the power I had when I fought Kira. Even if I found my wand, how much help could I possibly be? At this point it just made more sense to give up. And I hated that this was the reality. So much so that I couldn't stop my tears from pouring onto the gravel below me.

"Crystal," I heard a voice call from behind me. I looked over my shoulder and saw Ana still sitting on top of Silver, probably resting after everything she'd gone through today. Her blood was staining Silver's beautiful white fur. "Give Silver your hand."

"What?" I asked while wiping away my tears. "Why?"

"You're looking for your Spirit Caster, right? Give him your hand so he can help you. Hurry, we can't waste any more time."

I didn't quite understand but I lifted my hand towards Silver anyway and let him vigorously sniff my hand and arm until Ana finally gave him a command.

"Find it."

Silver quickly raised his head in the air and continued sniffing before bringing his head closer to the ground. He walked a few meters away from me and stopped. He then started digging through the rubble. I had no idea Silver could track down lost items like that. I immediately came to his aid and started to dig alongside him until its faint glow started to show. We found it still intact.

"Good boy, Silver!" Ana said as she rubbed the side of his neck.

I slowly reached for the wand but hesitated after hearing Alizeh's sonic punches boom through the battlefield.

"What are you waiting for?" Ana rushed. "Grab the damn thing!"

"Why?" I trailed off. "What's the point?"

"What are you talking about?"

"If you would just take a good look at me, then you'd understand. I can't fight in the condition I'm in. I couldn't even kill Kira before with most of my strength. How am I supposed to help them kill her *father*? I'd just get in the way." As I spoke, the sky darkened with clouds that spewed lightning down around us. Another one of Rai's attacks that was probably too much to properly control.

"Crystal, you can't be serious right now. After everything we've been through, *now* is the time you want to give up?"

I gestured towards the storm Rai created and yelled, "Look at what they're all capable of! They've been training for years to get to this level of power while I only *just* got this wand."

"And look at how far *you've* come in such a short time," she pointed out. "You've saved my life; you helped take down one of the Five Armaments ...hell you even defeated a Phoenix in battle. That's something that shouldn't even be possible! Not even Flint could have done that." She hopped off Silver and stumbled over to me with what little strength she had. "You're strong, Crystal, and you deserve to be here. None of us would have ever made it this far without your determination to seek revenge. It's almost inspiring."

Ana's words almost brought tears to my eyes. I never took a moment to look at everything I'd accomplished to get to this point. And I did deserve to be here. She was right about all of that. But there was one thing she was wrong about.

A massive explosion detonated from behind that made the earth shake and forced Ana to continue. "Crystal, if you want your revenge then it needs to happen right now or we're all going to die."

I took a short moment to think about my answer and said, "No. I don't want revenge."

"Are you serious right now?" she groaned.

"Yeah, I'm serious. Revenge isn't going to fix anything. It hasn't for generations. It just creates a cycle of hatred." I finally picked up my Spirit Caster and continued telling her, "It's just like you told me when we first met: 'If you wait until it's too late to start caring, then you'll live to regret it.' And I regret not being proactive. If I had listened to you, then my family would still be alive today. I'm not going to let that bastard take away my new family. I'm not going to kill him, but I'm not gonna let him hurt anyone else either. From this day forward, I'm not fighting for revenge. I'm fighting to protect the people I love."

I gathered all the remaining Rēa in my body, hoping it would be enough, but something strange happened. My Rēa started building more power than I thought I had left. More power than I ever thought I had to begin with.

"Crystal ... what are you doing?" Ana asked while looking down at my Spirit Caster. It was glowing brighter than it ever had before. The brilliant light stretched from the wand and onto my body. My wand was changing in a way that I'd only seen two others do before. I had finally found the power I was looking for. I was finally *evolving*.

ALIZEH

It only took a few seconds for my vision to come back to me and as soon as it did, I laid my eyes on a huge crater that was taking up the center of the battlefield. I looked over at Rai and saw them on their knees while panting. They must've put everything they had in that attack. But was it enough?

I quickly got up and ran to the edge of the crater. Flint and The King were both lying right in the center of it, motionless. I prayed that Flint was still alive and ran in, almost tripping and falling, but I was able to keep myself up despite my low stamina levels.

"Flint!" I cried. Once I got to him, I saw him face down in the dirt. I pushed him onto his back and threw my ear to his chest.

Ba-bump.

There was a pulse! It was faint, but it meant that he was still alive. He must've used up the last of his Rēa to shield himself from the attack. But if he was able to live, albeit just by the skin of his teeth, then what of The King?

I looked over to The King. He was still breathing but he looked to be in the same state as Flint.

"Did I do it?" I heard Rai shout from a distance. "Is he dead?"

"No! But he's down for the count! We won!" I shouted back.

Rai slowly made their way back to me, barely even able to stand, and asked, "How's Flint? I don't feel a spec of Rēa from him. Don't tell me he actually got himself killed."

"He's alive, somehow. And it's a good thing too. Ana would've killed me if I had let him die. I'm pretty sure they're in love with each other or something. Crystal probably would've been pretty mad too."

"Where the hell is Crystal anyway?"

"I don't know. She went off to look for her wand but I haven't seen her since. Her arm *was* broken, and she seemed pretty tired from her battle with Kira so maybe she's resting somewhere."

"Tired my ass! There's a lot of that going around right now. Luckily we didn't need her to beat this guy."

"You should cut her some slack," I sighed. "You don't know what she went through to get us to this point. She's a lot more capable than she lets on."

After I said that, I was going to tell them what I thought our next move should be but before I could, I heard a nearby voice echo a single word that sent terror through my very core.

"Anástasi."

Suddenly, a huge burst of black Rēa erupted from The King's body. *Anástasi.* That was the same transformation that Kira went into!

He slowly started to stand up and his body started to morph. I couldn't believe what I was seeing. He could still stand after an attack like that and still had enough energy to pull off such a terrifying transformation.

His skin turned pale, his hair turned white and his irises black. He looked just like Kira did when she transformed with the only difference being that he started to grow a horn on the right side of his head.

"I commend you," he spoke with an altered voice. ***"With your combined might you were able to push me this far. To think that the***

three of you at only half strength would force me to use all of my power. You're all magnificent. It's a shame I must kill you. I would've gladly used you all as replacements for the Five Armements."

Every word he said drove us more and more into despair. Rai and I had almost zero Rēa left to fight him, Flint was completely incapacitated, and I had no idea where Crystal was. And the worst part of it all was that The King held the power to destroy us with just a few gestures, if he so desired.

I looked at Rai and they looked back at me. We both understood our situation, but I could see a glint in their eyes that told me they weren't done fighting. They weren't going to give up and neither was I. We held on tight to our Spirit Casters even though we didn't have enough energy to pull off one single spell between us. But it didn't matter. We weren't going to die on our knees!

At the same time, we both lunged ourselves at him, but he halted us with a single word.

"Stop."

An outrageous amount of Rēa flowed from his body. The overwhelming force made us fall to the ground. It felt as if gravity had been multiplied by ten. No matter how hard we tried, we couldn't get back up to our feet.

"There is no longer any need for you to fight. You've already lost."

He started to levitate and float in the air. He went high up and looked down on us like a god would look down at the earth. He then raised his hand in the air and a small black orb with tons of power manifested into it.

"Dammit! We never stood a chance against him!" Rai cried.

"We can't die here!" I shouted. "We have to get up!"

"Take solace, children. You should be happy to know that it took a god like myself to kill you."

I tried to get back up until I felt something wet drop on my head. I looked up and saw snowflakes in the air. The King stopped his attack and looked around.

"What is this?" he asked.

I looked farther up to see what he was talking about. He wasn't distracted by the snow. He was distracted by several floating ice pillars in the air circling around him.

"Is this ice?"

At that moment I felt another powerful source of Rēa coming from somewhere else. I used what little strength I had left to turn around and saw Crystal at the edge of the crater raising something in the air. It wasn't like her normal Spirit Caster. It looked entirely different. It was as long as a staff but it wasn't like her spear. It was glowing with a light blue aura. It was like Flint's Spirit Caster. It was also like The King's. It was as if it had evolved.

"Crystal Winter. Do you truly believe you can beat me alone when all of your allies together couldn't?"

She didn't respond. She just kept muttering an incantation to herself. Whatever spell she was trying to perform was big.

"You're a foolish child."

The King once again raised his hand up in the air and created the black orb to destroy us.

"Now die!"

At the same time, Crystal shouted out the spell, *"Chiliádes Chrónia Fylakí Págou!"*

The ice pillars started to spin faster and closed in on The King. He tried to throw the attack, but his arm froze. And the rest of his body started to freeze with it.

"No ... This can't be! I am a god amongst men! It isn't possible for a low-level spell like this to bind me!"

"Cole Black, King of the Black Continent," Crystal spoke, "You take amusement in others' despair. You treat life like it's a disposable commodity, even when it comes to your own daughter. You unfairly judge those who break nonsensical laws that you made for your own personal gain. And now it's time for you to be judged for your sins. I sentence you to 1,000 years of imprisonment. Hopefully within that time you'll be able to learn what *true* justice really means."

"You insolent child! I will destroy you all!"

But his threat was empty. Crystal slammed one end of her Spirit Caster down to the ground and a second later, the ice closed in and completely trapped him in a beautiful floating ice prison in the sky.

CHAPTER SEVENTY-SIX
CRYSTAL

I did it. I was able to pull off the spell. It was the same exact spell I had used against the Phoenix to imprison it. And as far as I was aware, it was still trapped there, so I thought The King wouldn't be a problem to us for a long time.

I went down into the crater to see how everyone was doing. "Are you guys ok?" I asked.

"Yeah, thanks to you," Alizeh smiled.

"You came through for us when it really counted. I didn't know that you possessed so much power," Rai said.

I looked over at Flint and I guessed Alizeh saw how worried I was because before I could even say anything, she had already answered, "He's alive. He's just knocked out. We're probably going to have to carry him out of here, though."

"Alright," I said. "We should get going right now. Knights could come swarming this place any minute."

As Rai helped me get him up, Alizeh picked up his Spirit Caster and asked, "So what happened to your Spirit Caster? It looks just like Flint's."

"I believe it turned into an Evolved Spirit Caster," I answered.

"You managed to evolve it? How?" Alizeh asked excitedly.

"Well back on Phoenix Island, Flint told me that he made his Spirit Caster Evolve because of his will to protect. I finally adopted that same will once I saw that you guys were in danger. After that it, just evolved on its own."

"Woah, what does it feel like to have that much power?"

"Let's save the questions for later," I told her. But right when I said that, I heard the sound of something shattering. I looked up and saw that it was the ice prison. It was cracking!

"Crystal, what's happening?" Alizeh asked in fear.

"Is that normal?" Rai asked.

"No," I answered. "It's not."

The ice continued to break until it shattered into thousands of tiny pieces. The only thing left was The King. He somehow survived. And he was strong enough to break through it! A feat that not even the Phoenix could accomplish. This man was a bigger threat than I could have *ever* anticipated.

He glared down at us like a wrathful god. Once he started to float back down to the ground, his form started to shed off, just as Kira's did when she came back to her senses.

"Did you really think that you could defeat me with a thin sheet of ice?" The King asked angrily with his voice turning back to normal. "You should all just give up now. I'm no longer amused with this game."

"Don't bluff," I said calmly. "That form you had before is gone. That must mean that you no longer have the power to sustain it. This battle has made you weak while I've only gotten stronger." The King stayed silent, which only confirmed my theory. I let go of Flint and said, "You two, stay behind me. I'm the only one with the power to—"

Before I could finish, the ends of my Spirit Caster suddenly shattered, reverting back to its original form, and with it I felt all of my new power drop like a stone.

"What is this?" I asked aloud, completely shocked by the state of my Spirit Caster. "What's happening?" I shouted.

The King laughed and said, "You're too inexperienced, *child*! You put out more power than your body could even handle. Your evolution was just a fluke and without it, you can't hope to beat me!"

He raised his Spirit Caster and pointed it towards us while charging up a powerful blast to end us all. This felt unreal. We all fought so hard. We went through so much and our best wasn't enough. This wasn't justice! But I guessed this was the cost that we had to pay for fighting against this kind of darkness.

The King had a demented smile on his face as he yelled, "Die!"

But then something that none of us could have possibly foreseen happened. His Spirit Caster broke in two. All of us were shocked, but not more than The King himself.

"What ... what's happening?" The King shouted. He started to cough up blood and gasped for air.

Alizeh said, "It looks like you're suffering the same fate that Crystal did but to a larger degree." He then fell to his knees as his Spirit Caster continued to break apart into black dust. "You're sick, aren't you? If that's the case, then it means that your body is weak. Too weak to handle the power you've been outputting. Crystal pushed you to your limits and that only worsened your condition."

"No ... I can't die ... I won't ..."

Those were his final words before he fell. After everything. All the fighting. The pain and despair. After all of our perseverance. We had won the battle and The King was dead.

CHAPTER SEVENTY-SEVEN
KIRA

I stood at the edge of the crater as I watched my father die. Even though I resented him, and he had always hated me, it still felt like a piece of me died along with him. But maybe that wasn't such a bad thing. This must have been how Crystal felt when I had taken away her parents. No. Their bond was stronger. I had not suffered nearly enough to have my guilt dissipate. But the irony of having Crystal take him away from me did take a blow to my pride, that was for sure.

Crystal and her friends came out of the crater bloody and beaten. When they all spotted me in their path, they glared with intense anger; everyone except Crystal. She didn't look happy either, but there was a certain look in her eyes that stared right into my soul. As if once again she was trying to understand me.

They all walked right up to me so that Crystal could say, "I wanted to ask you again. What are you going to do now? Is your answer the same as before?"

"Yes," I answered, "it's the same as before. I don't want to fight you anymore. And since my father is dead that means I'm the current ruler. And I've decided to let you all free with that power. You can go and I will not send anyone after you."

Crystal nodded and with the rest of her group, started to make their way past me. I stopped her and asked, "What will *you* do?"

"What?" she asked.

"Do you still hold a vendetta against me? Do you still plan on impaling me with your ice?"

"To answer your first question, yes. I still hate you more than anything in this world. And for your second question, I don't know. I'm tired. I don't feel like it right now. But there's no telling how I'll feel tomorrow."

"That's quite ominous," I replied before hearing metal clanging against the ground in the distance. "You should all leave immediately. I can hear my soldiers coming and at the moment it's uncertain whether or not I'll be able to stop them from killing you all after they see what you've done here."

After saying this, they all made their way out of sight.

"Kira," Ranne said. "Are you really just going to let them go after a threat like that? They're dangerous."

"It doesn't matter," I told her. "We have bigger things to worry about."

"Like what?"

"Like the revival of our kingdom. At the moment, Ebony is in ruins and people are dying. I'm going to assign all available soldiers to search and rescue. And then we will rebuild. And we will make this city better than it has ever been."

Ranne broke out into laughter as if to make fun of my words.

"Is there something funny about what I just said?" I asked with an attitude.

"No," she laughed. She then grabbed me and pulled me in for a kiss that forced butterflies into my stomach. I embraced it, and I wasn't embarrassed. For the first time, I didn't care if anyone saw what truly made me happy. "I just really missed this," she continued. "I missed the old you."

"Don't be mistaken, Ranne. Just because I'm not the same as I was a moment ago doesn't mean I'm reverting back to my old self. I'm turning into someone new. And for that to happen there's a long path of redemption ahead of me that I must stay on. For the first time in years I want to step away from the darkness of my heart and into the light of the world."

For a brief moment, I was in high spirits for the future, until something from my past came back to haunt me.

"Kira ..." I heard him groan.

I looked down at the crater and saw my father, still alive and trying to drag himself out of his new grave with little success.

"What should we do about him?" Ranne asked.

I closed my eyes and took a deep breath before answering, "Follow me."

We walked down the massive crater until we finally reached the old man, still clinging to life from sheer will. It seemed like that was the only positive trait I inherited from him.

He looked up at me with a relieved expression on his face and panted, "Daughter ... good ... you're here. I need you to—"

"You told her to kill me," I cut him off.

"What?"

"You told Crystal to *kill* me!" I screamed. "You called me scum and you didn't even care if she went through with it! You *wanted* her to kill me!" I couldn't hold myself together anymore and fell to my knees, sobbing. "Why? After everything I did for you ... the people I've killed in your name ... the unspeakable evil I put out into this world for you. Why did you still hate me?"

He took a moment to reflect before answering. Like for the first time he truly wanted to tell me how he felt inside. Perhaps he too was cured of the poison that was the Dark Spirit Caster.

"Kira," he finally said, "I don't *hate* you. I just never knew how to love you. Especially after what happened to your mother. Your face was a daily reminder of what I lost."

"Of what *we* lost! You weren't the only one suffering from that fact. I *live* with this face. I see her every morning and every night when I look in the mirror. *Her blood* runs through *my veins*. So don't you dare even pretend for one moment that her death affected you more than it did me."

Once again, he took a moment to ponder. For once, I thought my words were finally able to get through to him.

"I suppose I never stopped to consider how this all affected you. I never really cared about too many people besides myself, so I guess that means I was never cut out to be a father. In hindsight, your mother's death was a blessing."

"What do you mean?"

"I mean it was a good thing she died before bringing another one of my failures into this world."

What? *Failure*? Is that what he still thought of me? He was the one that failed *me!* And even in the end, he couldn't acknowledge that. He couldn't acknowledge *me*. My head was spinning with rage. I thought that after the Spirit Caster was destroyed then maybe, just maybe, there was something worth saving within my father. But now I knew that even without it, there wasn't a single redeeming bone in his body.

Ranne put her hand on my shoulder, instantly calming me down and bringing me back to the current situation. She must have felt me spiraling. She was always good at reading me and helping me get through my feelings. And I needed to take her advice. I was done seeking his approval.

I finally got up from my knees and wiped the tears off my face to regain my composure.

"Ranne," I said dryly, "for my first decree as Queen of the Dark Continent, I order you to execute this man."

"W-wait," my father begged.

Ranne walked to him while drawing her sword and said, "As you wish, my Queen."

"Wait!" my father shouted. "You can't do this! Think about what you're doing! I'm your father!"

"You aren't my father," I told him as I turned my back towards him. "All you are to me is *disgraceful scum.*"

"Kira, don't you dare turn your back on me! Don't you—"

His words trailed off. I didn't know if she impaled him through the heart or sliced off his head. I didn't look back. It still hurt just as much as if I had watched. But it needed to happen. Not only to my father, but also to me. My family was answering for its sins. Perhaps this is what Crystal kept going on about. This was true justice running its course.

CHAPTER SEVENTY-EIGHT
ARACHNE

"Arachne. Wake up."

I awoke to him calling my name. I was lying in the middle of what was once someone's home, but now it was just a charred wreckage. The fire user must have sent me flying through here with his last attack.

I looked up and saw Morpheus standing above me. "Arachne. Are you okay?" he asked.

The left side of my face stung. I touched it and it hurt even more. It was burned and it was probably going to leave a scar.

"The King is dead."

His words made me shoot up from the floor and ask, "That means it worked right? The *cancer* I put in him?"

"Yes."

"So now you can use your illusion to take over, right? Have you already done it?"

"No, it's not that simple."

"What do you mean?"

"The King went to fight the criminals by himself. They pushed him so hard that the poison you put in him was accelerated. He died in front of the Princess instead of in his sleep like we originally planned."

"Dammit! So what now?"

"Do not fret. The appearance of Crystal Winters changes everything."

"How so?"

He raised his hand to show me one of his prized possessions. A *Phoenix feather*. One of the same feathers that he posted a bounty for on Phoenix Island. He told me before that Crystal and her allies had collected them, and sold them to us without even realizing it. Those feathers were powerful relics in the right hands and were the key to us gaining more power than anyone on this world could ever comprehend. But he was saving them for *phase two* of our plan. It looked like Morpheus was finally ready to enact it.

Morpheus answered me by saying, "At this very moment, multiple pieces have been placed on the board that weren't there prior. If we use these pieces wisely, then we can both obtain power beyond the title of kings. Maybe even beyond that of gods. But in order to do that, we mustn't hesitate with our plan. We must take immediate action and be swift."

CHAPTER SEVENTY-NINE

CRYSTAL

It took us the rest of the day to reach the nearest inn on foot. Ana, Alizeh, Rai, and I had all our money confiscated once we were arrested but luckily Flint still had some gold in his pockets. He hadn't woken up yet, but we were sure he wouldn't mind us using his money to get us all a room for the night.

We all stayed in one room with two separate twin beds in it and gently put Flint in one of them since he was still unconscious. Ana and I let the kids have the other bed while we slept on the floor; although Alizeh did blush from the suggestion, she didn't argue.

As soon as the sun rose, we rose with it to talk about our next move.

"Well, we beat the King and toppled his empire," Alizeh said. "Now what?"

"I'm going back," Rai decided.

"Wait, what? You're going back to Ebony? But we were just there, remember? In that crazy battle to the death with The King? Are you just looking for another fight?"

"You don't have to remind me, Alizeh, I was there. And no, a fight is the last thing I want."

"Then why *are* you going?" I asked.

"It's your grandmother, isn't it?" Ana guessed. "I'm sorry I couldn't get her out like I promised."

"Don't worry," Rai said to her. "You had your own thing you were trying to protect, and our situation was time sensitive. I would've done the same."

"Wait!" Alizeh cried out. "How could I have forgotten about Tora? We need to go back now!"

"No, we're too weak. We need to wait until our Rēa is back up to do that," said Rai.

"But Rai," I said, "I don't think we actually need to fight. I know this sounds crazy but I think the Princess has actually changed. I really don't think she wants to fight us again. And yesterday, she just let us go. Maybe if we just asked then she would let your grandmother go too."

Rai thought for a few seconds before saying, "Alright, I'll just go by myself then."

"Are you sure you don't need us?"

"Yeah, I'm sure. Didn't you three have something else to do anyway?"

"Well, I promised my sister that I would get back to her as soon as possible and Alizeh's parents are probably worried sick about her."

"I didn't even tell my mother where I was going so I *know* she must be pretty worried," Ana said.

"Wait, wait, wait. You've been gone for almost two months and Aza has no idea where you are?"

"I didn't even tell her I was leaving. I was in too much of a rush to say anything. Besides, I left to stop you from doing something stupid with that wand. I didn't expect to fight in a war afterwards. But I do need to get back so she at least knows I'm still alive. I just don't want to leave Flint here in his current condition."

"It's fine," Rai cut in. "I'll stay with him until he wakes up."

"But that might take a while," Alizeh said. "One time Crystal got knocked out like that in battle and she didn't wake up for a few days. And his condition is even worse. If I weren't able to hear his heartbeat, I would have assumed that he was as good as dead. I can't imagine the long-term effects of this or even how long it'll take for him to wake up."

"I don't mind," Rai insisted. "I need to lay low for a while anyway until I gain my energy back. Might as well have his company while I'm waiting."

The thought of leaving before being able to say goodbye to Flint was disappointing but seeing my sister was more important, so I agreed. I could tell Ana was even more disappointed, but she stayed silent.

"Aww, this is so sad," Alizeh sighed.

"What is it?" Rai asked. "Aren't you happy that you finally get to go home and see your family?"

"Yeah, I am but ... I really like you guys. I don't know when or if I'll ever get to see you and Flint again."

"Oh," that was all Rai could say at that moment. A look of sadness slowly started to overcome them.

"Wait," I said. "How about we all meet back here in one month's time?"

"And do what?"

"We should all go to the beach," Alizeh blurted out.

I had totally forgotten about that. I told her I would take her back on Phoenix Island but so much happened to the point where the promise escaped me. The thought made me laugh and that made Rai and Ana laugh right along with me.

"I'd like that," they answered.

"Alright, then it's decided!" Alizeh proclaimed. "In one month, we'll all come back here and go to the beach."

Rai laughed again and said, "Okay, I'll make sure to tell Flint."

CHAPTER EIGHTY
ARACHNE

A few days passed after I finally made it to Livádia, hoping that Morpheus's information was right. I didn't want my time to be wasted. It was a dark and misty night. Perfect for me to make my move. I didn't want anyone to see me or what I was about to do.

I walked up to the large red barn and banged on the door. After a few moments, it slid open and I was greeted by a small young girl who at first was excited, but soon became frightened at the sight of me. It must have been from the scar. It looked like she was my first target.

I crouched down and looked her in her eyes before saying, "Hi, I'm a friend of Crystal. You wouldn't happen to be Wren, would you?"

She hesitantly nodded her head and asked, "Where is Crystal? Is my sister, ok?"

"Oh, so she hasn't come back here yet?"

Wren shook her head which filled me with relief.

"That's good to hear. I made it back here before her. This is all going to be a lot easier then."

"What is?" she asked as she took a few steps back.

I heard a groggy voice from inside the barn asked, "Wren, who is that at the door?"

That was most likely my second target, Tal Green. Both of the pieces that I needed were ripe for the taking. I walked into the house, closing the door behind me so that there would be no interruptions. And with just two words, Morpheus and I were one step closer to Godhood.

"*Chimikós Pólemos.*"

ACKNOWLEDGMENTS

There aren't too many people that I need to thank for the making of this book but those that I *do* mention were instrumental to its creation. First off is you, Jo. You read all my horrible first stories and hyped me up with each and every chapter, inspiring me to think that I was good enough to actually put my work out there one day.

Then there's my mom who constantly asked me for years about when I was finally going to publish this book, adding on to my determination to publish this book. And my dad who I inherited said determination from, always making sure I applied myself with whatever I wanted to do with my life.

And to my first editor Monica M for helping me flesh out this story a bit more. Along with my second pair of editors Xyana and Leilani who really helped me craft my vision. And finally, Helena Nikulina for creating such amazing cover art for this book to look professional. Thank you all.